FALLEN ANGELS

FALLEN ANGELS

Larry Niven
Jerry Pournelle
Michael Flynn

PAN BOOKS

First published 1991 by Baen Publishing Enterprises, New York

First published in Great Britain 1993 by Pan Books
This edition published 1994 by Pan Books
an imprint of Macmillan General Books
Cavaye Place London SW10 9PG
and Basingstoke

Associated companies throughout the world

ISBN 0 330 33599 5

3 5 7 9 8 6 4

A CIP catalogue record for this book is available from
the British Library

Printed and bound in Great Britain by
Cox & Wyman Ltd, Reading, Berkshire

For Science Fiction Fandom

CHAPTER ONE

"Aspiring to Be Gods . . ."

High over the northern hemisphere the scoopship's hull began to sing. The cabin was a sounding box for vibrations far below the threshold of hearing. Alex MacLeod could feel his bones singing in sympathy.

Piranha was kissing high atmosphere.

Planet Earth was shrouded in pearl white. There was no break anywhere. There were mountain ranges of fluff, looming cliffs, vast plains that stretched to a far distant convex horizon, a cloud cover that looked firm enough to walk on. An illusion; a geography of vapors as insubstantial as the dreams of youth. If he were to set foot upon them . . . The clouds did not float in free fall, as was proper, but in an acceleration frame that could hurl the scoopship headlong into an enormous ball of rock and iron and smash it like any dream.

Falling, they called it.

Alex felt the melancholy stealing over him again. Nostalgia? For that germ-infested ball of mud? Not possible. He could barely remember Earth. Snapshots from childhood; a chaotic montage of memories. He had fallen

1

down the cellar steps once in a childhood home he scarcely recalled. Tumbling, arms flailing, head thumping hard against the concrete floor. He hadn't been hurt; not really. He'd been too small to mass up enough kinetic energy. But he recalled the terror vividly. Now he was a lot bigger, and he would fall a lot farther.

His parents had once taken him atop the Sears Tower and another time to the edge of the Mesa Verde cliffs; and each time he had thought what an awful long way down it was. Then, they had taken him so far up that down ceased to mean anything at all.

Alex stared out of *Piranha*'s windscreen at the cloud deck, trying to conjure that feeling of height; trying to feel that the clouds were *down* and he was *up*. But it had all been too many years ago, in another world. All he could see was distance. Living in the habitats did that to you. It stole height from your senses and left you only with distance.

He glanced covertly at Gordon Tanner in the copilot's seat. If you were born in the habitats, you never knew height at all. There were no memories to steal. Was Gordon luckier than he, or not?

The ship sang. He was beginning to hear it now.

And Alex MacLeod was back behind a stick, where God had meant him to be, flying a spaceship again. Melancholy was plain ingratitude! He had plotted and schemed his way into this assignment. He had pestered Mary and pestered Mary until she had relented and bumped his name to the top of the list just to be rid of him. He had won.

Of course, there was a cost. Victories are always bittersweet. Sweet because ... He touched the stick and felt nothing. They were still in vacuum ... thicker vacuum, that was heating up. If there wasn't enough air to give bite to the control surfaces, a pilot must call it vacuum.

How could you explain the sweetness to someone who had never conned a ship? You couldn't. He relaxed in the acceleration chair, feeling the tingling in his hands and feet. The itching anticipation. Oh, to be useful again, even if for a moment.

But bitter because ... That part he did not want to think about. Just enjoy the moment; become one with it. If this was to be his last trip, he would enjoy it while he could. If everything went A-OK, he'd be back upstairs in a few hours, playing the hero for the minute or so that people would care. A real hero, not a retired hero. Then back in the day-care center wiping snotty noses. It would be years before another dip trip was needed. He'd never be on the list again.

Which meant that Alex MacLeod, pilot and engineer, wasn't needed any longer. So what do you do with a pilot when pilots aren't needed? What do the habitats do with a man who can't work outside, because one more episode of explosive decompression will bring on a fatal stroke?

Day care. Snotty noses. Work at learning to be a teacher, a job he didn't much like.

Look on the bright side, Alex, my boy. Maybe you won't make it back at all.

Sure, he could always go out the way Mish Lykonov had in *Moon Rat*, auguring in to *Mare Tranquilitatis*. They'd have a ceremony—and they'd miss the ship more than him. Even Mary. Maybe especially Mary, since she'd got him the mission.

He straightened in his seat and touched the controls again. Maybe just a touch of resistance ...

"Chto delayet? Alex!"

Something had prodded Gordon awake. Alex glanced to the right. "What is it?"

"I'm getting a reading on the air temperature gauge."

"Right. There's enough air outside now to *have* a temperature."

Gordon nodded, still unbelieving.

Gordon had read the book. Come to that, Gordon read a lot of books, but books don't mean much. No one ever learned anything out of a book, anyway. This was why they always teamed a newbie with an old pro. Hands-on learning. The problem with on-the-job training for *this* job was that there was not a hell of a lot of room for trial and error.

Alex moved the stick gently, and felt the ship respond. *Not vacuum anymore!* He banked and brought them up level, feeling the air rushing past just outside the skin. His eyes danced across the gauges. Here. There. Not reading them. Just a glance to see if something was wrong, or if something had changed since the last glance. Dynamic air temperature. Stagnation air temperature. The Mach number needle sprang to life, leaped from zero to absurdity, then hunted across the dial. A grin stretched itself across his face. No blues now. He hadn't forgotten at all; not a damned thing.

"What is funny?" Gordon demanded.

"Old war-horse heard the trumpet again. Now it's your turn. Take the stick." Fun was fun, but it was time for the kid to wrap his hands around the real thing. There was only so much you could do in a simulator. "There. Feel it?"

"Uh . . ." Gordon pulled back slightly on the copilot's stick. He looked uncertain.

He hadn't felt anything. "Take over," Alex growled. "You're flying the ship now. Can't you tell?"

"Well . . ." Another tentative move at the controls. *Piranha* wobbled. "Hey! Yeah!"

"Good. Look, it's hard to describe, but the ship will tell you how she's doing if you really listen. I don't mean you should forget the gauges. Keep scanning them; they're your eyes and ears. But you've got to listen with your hands and feet and ass, too. Make the ship an extension of your entire body. Do you feel it? That rush? That's air moving past us at five miles per second. Newton's not flying us anymore. You are."

Gordon flashed a nervous grin, like he'd just discovered sex.

"What's our flight path?" Alex asked.

"Uh . . ." A quick glance at the map rollout. "Greenland upcoming."

"Good. Hate to be over Norway."

"Why?"

Why. Didn't the kid listen to the downside news broadcasts? *Gordon, this is your planet! Don't you care?* No, he probably didn't. It was his grandparents' planet.

"There's war in Norway. If we flew over, somebody would cruise a missile at us sure as moonquakes, and we'd never even know which side did it."

The new tiling was wonderful. In the old days, the ship's skin would be glowing; but now ... Four thousand degrees and no visible sign at all. Still, they'd be glowing like a madman's dream on an IR screen, new tiles or no, and that was all the Downers would need to vector in on.

"Which side?" Gordon mused. "What are the sides?"

Alex laughed. "That's one of the reasons we can't be sure. When it started, it was what was left of NATO defending the Baltics." Non-nuclear, but it just went on and on and on. Alex didn't really care who won any more than Gordon did. "After a while, the Scandinavians and the Russians took a nervous look over their shoulders at the glaciers, and East versus West became North versus South."

"Silly bastards. Nye kulturni."

"Da." It didn't surprise him anymore. All the younger Floaters spoke Russian as automatically as English. Russlish? Ever since *Peace* and *Freedom* had pooled their resources, everyone was supposed to learn each other's language; but Alex hadn't gotten past "Ya tebye lyublyu." Hello was "zdravstvuitye." Alex thought there was something masochistic about speaking a language that strung so many consonants together. "Be fair, Gordon. If you had ice growing a mile thick in your backyard, wouldn't you want to move south?"

Gordon mulled it. "Why south?"

He couldn't help the grin. "Never mind. Let me take her again. Hang on, while I kill some velocity. Watch what I do and follow me." He stroked the stick gently.

Here we go, baby. You'll love this. Drop the scoop face-on to the wind. Open wide. That's right. Spread your tail, just for a moment ... Alex realized that his lips were moving and clamped them shut. The younger ones didn't understand when he talked to the ship. Gordon was having enough trouble *feeling* the ship. "Okay," he said finally, "that's done. Take over, again."

Gordon did, more smoothly than before. Alex watched him from the corner of his eye while pretending to study the instruments. *Piranha* was a sweet little ship. Alex had flown her once, years before, and considered her the best of the three remaining scoopers. Maybe that was just Final Trip nostalgia. Maybe he would have felt the same about whichever ship he flew on his last dip; but he would shed a special tear for *Piranha* when they retired her. The scoopers were twenty-two years old already and, while there was not much wear and tear parked in a vacuum, screaming through the Earth's atmosphere like a white hot banshee did tend to age the gals a bit. *Jaws* was already retired. Here was Gordon at nineteen, just getting started; and the ships at twenty-two were ready to pack it in. Life was funny.

Alex ran a hand lightly across the instrument panel. Scoopships were pretty in an ugly sort of way: lifting bodies with gaping scoops that made them look like early jet airplanes. They could not land—no landing gear—but they didn't dip into the atmosphere deeply enough for that to matter. But they were the hottest ships around.

Piranha skimmed above the glare-white earth as hot as any meteor, but never too hot at any point. Humming, vibrating, functional.

Gordon was functional, too. Alert, but not tense; holding her nose just right while flame-hot air piled through the scoop and bled into the holding tank. The velocity dropped below optimum on the dial and Gordon bled some of the air into the scramjet and added hydrogen until the velocity rose again. He did it casually, as if he did this sort of thing every day. Alex nodded to himself. The kid had it. He just needed it coaxed out of him.

"Alex?" Gordon said suddenly. "Why not Greenland?"

"Hmm?"

"Why isn't anyone in Greenland shooting missiles?"

Alex grinned. That was good. Gordon was flying a scoopship on a dip trip, sucking air at five miles per, and trying to make casual conversation. *That's right, Gordo.*

You can't do this sort of thing all tensed up; you've got to be relaxed.

"Nobody there but Eskimos," he explained. "An Ice Age doesn't bother them any. Hell, they probably think they've all died and gone to Inuit Heaven."

"Eskimos I do not know. Gogol once wrote good story that speaks of Laplanders but I did not understand—" The sky had turned from black to navy blue. Wouldn't want to get any lower. Gordon glanced out the windscreen and said, "Shouldn't we be seeing land by now?"

Alex shook his head, realized Gordon wasn't looking at him and answered. "No, the cloud-deck off the pole . . ." He stopped. The white below them wasn't the cloud-shroud any more. They must have gone past the southern edge or hit a hole in it. White on white. Cloud or ice. If you didn't actually *look* you might not notice. "Damn, damn. The ice is still growing."

Gordon didn't say anything. Alex watched him a moment longer then turned his attention to the gauges. Gordon was nineteen. There had *always* been an Ice Age, so it did not surprise him that the glaciers had crept farther south. Alex *thought* he remembered a different world—green, not white—before his parents brought him upstairs. He wasn't sure how much of it was genuine childhood memories and how much was movies or photographs in books. The habitats had a fair number of books on tape, brought up when they still got along with the Downers.

The green hills of earth, he thought. Now the glaciers— not rivers of ice, but vast oceans of ice—were spreading south at tens of miles a year. Hundreds of miles in some places. In the dictionary, "glacial" meant slow; but Ice Ages came on fast. Ten thousand years ago the glaciers had covered England and most of Europe in less than a century. They'd known that since the sixties . . . though no one had ever seen fit to revise his schoolbooks. But what did that matter? To a school kid a century was forever anyway.

As for Gordon . . . He glanced again at his copilot. Well, what the world is like in our lifetimes is what it should be like forever. As it was in the beginning, is now, and ever shall be. It was funny to think of groundside environmentalists desperately struggling against Nature, trying to preserve forever the temporary conditions and mayfly species of a brief interglacial. Alex looked again through the cockpit windscreen and sighed.

"We could have stopped it," he said abruptly.

"Eh?" Gordon gave him a puzzled glance.

"The Ice Age. Big orbiting solar mirrors. More microwave power stations. Sunlight is free. We could have beamed down enough power to stop the ice. Look what one little SUNSAT has done for Winnipeg."

Gordon studied the frozen planet outside. He shook his head. "Ya nye ponimál," he admitted. "I faked the examiners, but I never did get it. The what-did-they-call-it, polar ice cap? It stayed put for thousands of years. Then, of a sudden it reaches out like vast white amoeba."

All of a sudden, Alex's earphones warbled. He touched a hand to his ear. "*Piranha* here."

"Alex!" It was Mary Hopkins's voice. She was sitting mission control for this dip. Alex wondered if he should be flattered. . . . And if Lonny was there with her. "We've got a bogey rising," said Mary. "Looks like he's vectoring in on you."

So, they don't shoot missiles out of Greenland? Find another line of work, Alex-boy; you'll never make it as a soothsayer. "Roger, Big Momma." He spun to Gordon. "Taking over," he barked. "Close the scoop. Seal her up. Countermeasures!"

"Da!" He said something else, too rapid to follow.

"English, damn your eyes!"

"Oh. Yeah. Roger. Scoops closed."

Piranha felt better. Under control. "Close your faceplate." Alex pulled his own shut and sealed it.

"Alex, I have something." Gordon's voice sounded tinny over the radio, or maybe a wee bit stressed. "Aft and to the left and below," he said.

Seven o'clock low.

"Constant bearing and closing."

"Drop flares." That wouldn't do any good. *Piranha*

was the hottest thing in the sky right now. But like the
lady said while spooning chicken soup to the dead man,
it couldn't hurt. "How are they seeing us?"

"K-band."

"Jam it."

"Am."

He sure enough was. Alex grunted. At least Gordo had
read *that* book. Alex squinted at his radar. There was the
bogey, sure enough. Small. Constant bearing and closing.
"Hang on." He peeled off to starboard and watched the
heat gauge rise. *Piranha* didn't have wings for a near
miss to tear off. Just small, fat fins and a big, broad, flat
belly to be melted, evaporated or pierced. Alex bit his
lip. Don't think about that. Concentrate on what you can
do.

The sharp turn pushed him against the corner of his
seat. Alex relaxed to the extra weight and prayed that his
Earth-born bones would remember how to take it. De-
cades of falling had turned him soft. The acceleration felt
like a ton of sand covering him. He felt the blood start in
his sinuses. But he could take it. He could take it because he had to.

Gordon sat gripping the arms of the copilot's seat. His
cheeks sagged. His head bowed. Gordon had been born
in free fall and thrust was new to him. He looked frightened. It must feel like he'd taken sick.

The turn seemed to go on forever. Alex watched the
bogey on the scope. Each sweep of the arm brought the
blip closer to the center. Closer. He pulled harder against
the stick. The next blip was left of center. Then it arced
away. Alex knew that was an illusion. The missile had
gone straight; *Piranha* had banked.

"You lost it!" Gordon shouted. He turned and looked
at Alex with a grin that nearly split his face in two.

Alex smiled back. "Scared?"

"Hell, no."

"Yeah. Me, too. Anyone flying at Mach 26 while a heat-
seeking cruise missile tries to fly up his ass is entitled to
be scared." He toggled the radio. It was Management

Decision time. "Big Momma, we have lost the bogey. Do you have instructions?"

There was a pause; short, but significant. "We need that nitrogen," said Mary's voice.

Alex waited for her to finish, then realized that she had. *We need that nitrogen.* That was all she was going to say, leaving the ball in his octant.

Of *course* we need the nitrogen, he thought. Recycling wasn't perfect. Gas molecules outgassed right through the walls of the stations. Every now and then someone had to take the bucket to the well and get some more. The question was when. When someone with an itchy finger was sitting in a missile farm somewhere below?

He could pack it home and be the goat; his last trip a failure. Delta vee thrown away for no gain. Or he could fly heroically into the jaws of death and suck air. Either way, it was going to be his decision.

He sensed Lonny Hopkins's spidery hand behind things. If Mary was performing plausible deniability on his bones, it must be because her husband was floating right behind her at the comm console, one hand gentle on her shoulder, while she downlinked to the stud who had . . .

Jesus, but some people had long memories.

Well, Mary was a free citizen, wasn't she? If the wife of the station commander wants a little extracurricular, it's her choice. She had never pushed him away; not until that last night together. We're hanging on up here by our fingernails, she had said then. We've got to all pull together; stand behind the station commander.

Right.

Nobody could stand behind Lonny Hopkins because he never turned his back on anyone. With good reason. *Maybe he's right. He is good at the goddam job, and maybe our position is so precarious that there's no room for democratic debate. That doesn't mean I have to like it.*

And it's decision time.

"Understood, Big Momma. We'll get your air." *Take that, Commander Lonny Hopkins.* He clicked off and

turned to Gordon. "Open the scoops, but bleed half of it
to the scramjets."

"Alex . . ." Gordon frowned and bit his lip.

"They say they need the air."

"Yeah-da." Gordon's fingers flipped toggled switches
back up.

Alex felt the drag as the big scoop doors opened again.
The doors had just completed their cycle when Gordon
began shouting. "Ekho! Ekho priblizháyetsya!"

"English!"

Something exploded aft of the cabin and Alex felt his
suit pop out. His ears tried to pop, and Alex MacLeod
whined deep in his throat.

He'd forgotten, but his nerves remembered. It wasn't
falling he feared, it was air tearing through his throat,
daggers in his ears, pressure trying to rip his chest apart.
Five times his suit had leaked air while they worked to
save *Freedom Station*. He wore the scars in ruptured
veins and arteries, everywhere on his body, as if Lonny
Hopkins had given him to a mad tattoo artist. There
were more scars in his lungs and in his sinus cavities. A
sixth exposure to vacuum would have his brains spewing
through his nose. Alex couldn't come out to play; they
had to keep him in the day-care center.

His fists clenched on the controls in a rigor mortis
grip. He heard his own whine of terror, and Gordon's
shout, and felt *Piranha* falling off hard to port. And his
suit was holding, holding.

He fought the stick hard when he tried to steady her.
Had he recovered too late? "Hold fast, baby," he said
through clenched teeth. "Hold fast." Hold Fast was the
ancient motto of the MacLeod. Alex wished fleetingly
that he had the Fairy Flag that Clan MacLeod unfurled
only in the gravest peril. *Piranha* vibrated and shuddered. Something snapped with the sound of piano wire.
"Come on, baby. Steady down."

Incredibly, she did. "Good girl," he muttered, then
tongued the uplink on his suit radio. "Big Momma, Big
Momma. We've been hit." There was nothing for it now
but use up all the air they'd scooped, and anything else,

to light off the jets. Get back in orbit; out of the Well.
When you're in orbit, you're halfway to anywhere! Get in
orbit and pickup would be easy. He toggled the switches.

The rocket wouldn't light. The rocket wouldn't light.
Air speed was dropping steadily. The rocket wouldn't
light. He suppressed the knot of panic that twisted itself
in his gut. Time enough afterward, if there was an afterward. The scramjet alone was not enough to reach orbit
again. It wouldn't be long before *Piranha* would be
moving too slowly to keep the jet lit. She would become
a glider.

And not a terribly good glider.

Alex swallowed. It looked awfully cold down below.
And the rocket wouldn't light.

"Mayday," he said. "Mayday. *Piranha* has a problem."
A part of his mind was detached, admiring the cool way
he reacted after that one moment of terror.

"This is Big Momma. What is your status?"

Well, I'm just fine, Mary; and how are you? "We're
going in, Mary. Tell my family. It's all in my file directory. Access code word is *dunvegan*." He glanced over at
Gordon, but the teenager just shook his head. His face
was white through the plexiglas face shield. "And the
Tanner family, too." Gordon didn't have any children
yet. He was the child. Damned near unwanted child at
that: a stilyagi, a JayDee on parole. *Some parole!* "Watch
where we land and get the message out. Tightbeam."

The phones hissed for long seconds. "Sure, Alex. We
have friends on Earth. Maybe not many, but ... We'll
tell them. They'll take care of you. Can you—can you get
her down?"

"I may not be good for anything else, but, by God, you
paint stripes on a brick and I can fly her."

"Then that's two things you do well."

He felt warmth spreading outward from his belly. Was
Lonny still there? Would he understand that message?
Alex almost hoped he could. Mary said something else,
but he was too busy with the ship to hear her. Airspeed
had dropped to near Mach 2, and he tilted her nose
down to keep the scramjet lit and tried to turn south.

Ice. Ice all around and the cloud deck closing in again. *Piranha* was shaped like the bastard daughter of an airplane and a cement mixer. The slower she flew, the more she acted like a cement mixer.

Not on the ice, baby. Not on the ice. Hang in there. . . .

"Do you really fly that well?" Gordon asked tightly.

"I landed on Earth once before, Gordon. Who else do you know who can say that?" *Tom Corbett, Space Cadet. That's me. Disguised as a washed-up day-care gopher, he is in reality Alex MacLeod, Hot Pilot. Lord, just let me get us down in one piece.*

Fifteen miles up and the air was thick. Mach 3.5. The clouds below were puffy with turbulence. *Piranha* was diving into a storm. He wondered whether North Dakota was flat or mountainous.

Maybe an ice landing would be all right. Ice was smooth, wasn't it? Or was that only true in free fall? *Piranha* was hot from friction. She'd melt her own runway across the glacier.

Sure, but step outside afterward. Your eyeballs will freeze so cold they'll shatter when you blink. . . .

The clouds closed in and he was flying by radar. Dropping. Dropping. Lose velocity in the turns. Mach 2.5 and falling.

Gordon couldn't lift his head against the acceleration. "At least we'll have life support," he said suddenly. "Life support for four billion people, my teacher told me. And it doesn't get really cold, right? Cold enough to freeze water, but not carbon dioxide."

Alex grunted. Cold enough to freeze water. *Gordo, what is the human body made of?* Another turn. "Right," he said. Gordon wasn't a distraction. He was just a voice. The last thing Alex wanted during his last moments was dead silence. There would be enough of that afterward.

Think positive, Alex-boy. You'll live through the landing, so you can freeze to death on the ice.

Piranha shuddered as she dropped below Mach 1. The missile must have left some holes, creating turbulence in the airstream. Then the scramjet quit and she was diving at the ground. Ice crystals impacting on the skin created a rustling sound. When radar read a thousand feet up, Alex lifted the nose and waited.

Piranha didn't have wheels.

Friends on Earth, Mary had said. He wondered who she had meant. Earth's four billion hated the *Peace* and *Freedom* space stations with a passion. A dozen nations had declared war when the nitrogen dipping started; but they had no space capabilities, so it never meant anything but noise. Now *Piranha* was diving into their hands.

Two hundred feet up and slowing. He dropped the nose, trading altitude for speed, and pretended that the scoopship had wheels. Wind battered the ship. She yawed and Alex fought with the stick. Once the ship dipped suddenly and Alex fought a moment of pure panic. *Don't lose it now! Don't lose it now!* The ground looked smooth on the radar. Gordon's hands were on the dash, his elbows locked. *It won't be too cold, Gordo. Not cold enough to freeze carbon dioxide.*

It was the second best landing he had ever made. Second by a long, long margin. *Piranha* hit the ice and skipped like a schoolgirl; hit and skipped again. There was probably a third or fourth skip, too; but Alex never knew.

☆   ☆   ☆

Soren Haroldsson had watched the flame from his steading. He was wrapped in his fur parka, heavy boots, mittens like bowling balls, but still he shivered. His breath was frosty steam in the evening air. He always took a turn around the house before they battened down for the night, checking the gate, the wolf-traps, making sure none of the animals had been accidentally left outside.

It came just at dusk, a fiery stream low across the sky still large and burning as it touched the ice and sent up clouds of steam. Not a shooting star. Not a sky stone like he'd heard of. It had come in too shallow, too controlled. A ship of some sort.

Ah, surely it was Angels.

He shook his swaddled fist at the sky. "Be damned, you air thieves! We've got you now. Heh!" His breath froze on his graying blond mustache and beard. Tomorrow he would saddle up Ozzie and ride into Casselton to notify the authorities. They were probably hunting the Angels already; but only a fool went riding at night, and Ozzie, at least, was no fool.

Inside, bundled in the warmth of family and livestock, he told Lisbet what he had seen and guessed. Haughty, technomaniac Angels down on the Great Ice. Poetic justice, he said. Poetic, she replied and, smiling, quoted from memory:

> *"In pride, in reas'ning pride, our error lies;*
> *All quit their sphere and rush into the skies!*
> *Aspiring to be Gods if Angels fell,*
> *Aspiring to be Angels men rebel."*

CHAPTER TWO

"One Moment in Childhood . . . "

The phone warbled and Sherrine Hartley pulled a pillow over her head, even though she knew it would do no good. She'd been allocated a phone precisely because they might want to call her in the middle of the night. Neither rain nor sleet nor snow nor cold of night shall keep the programmers from being rousted out of bed to untangle every little glitch in operations. Didn't anyone know how to run programs anymore?

The phone warbled.

It was warm in bed, buried beneath the down comforter. The thermostat was turned down to 55, as the law required, and the last thing she wanted was to get out into the chilly air. Her arm snaked out from beneath the comforter, groped for the phone set and pulled it under the covers with her. The plastic was cold, but she was bundled in flannel and felt it only in her hands.

"Dr. Hartley here." She winced. It was like holding an ice cube to her ear.

"Sherrine?"

Not the University, after all. That really ticked her off.

16

The 'danes who signed her paycheck bought the right to wake her up, sometimes and for some things; but ex-boyfriends did not. "Bob," she said, "do you know what time it is?"

"Certainly. Two-forty-three. Plus or minus three sigma."

She sighed. Never ask a physicist a question like that. "What do you want, Bob? And why can't it wait until morning?"

"I need you, Sherrine. Now."

"What? Look, Bob, that's all over." And why couldn't some men ever believe that?

"I'll be there in five minutes."

"Bob!" But she was talking into a dead phone.

She thought about staying put under the comforter. It wouldn't help. Bob Needleton was persistent. He was quite capable of standing on her doorstep all night, banging on the door until she opened. Sometimes that sort of persistence was invaluable. In the lab, for instance. Other times it was just a pain in the ass.

Damn him. She was wearing heavy flannel socks, and she kept a pair of wooly slippers under the sheets with her. She played contortionist for a while finding them and putting them on. Then she slipped out of bed, leaving the covers carefully in place so the bed would stay warm. A heavy housecoat hung over the back of the chair next to the bed. She snuggled into it and shivered her way to the bathroom.

When she flipped the switch on the bulb glowed at about quarter-strength. Sometimes a brownout could be convenient. Real light would have blinded her just then. She brushed her teeth to get the nighttime fuzzies out. The water in the basin wasn't quite frozen, but it shocked her teeth when she rinsed. She spat out into the commode, because there was no sense in wasting the rest of the water in the sink.

"Conservation will see us through," the posters said. *And when there's nothing left to conserve?* She ran a comb through her hair. It needed brushing, but she was too cold.

"So what does Bob Needleton see in you," she asked

her reflection, "that he's coming out in the dead of night?" The beanpole in the mirror did not answer. Big nose. Big mouth. Not quite pretty. She could explain why Jake left; but not why Bob wouldn't.

She opened the door on the first knock and stood out of the way. The wind was whipping the ground snow in swirling circles. Some of it blew in the door as Bob entered. She slammed the door behind him. The snow on the floor decided to wait a while before melting. "Okay. You're here," she snapped. "There's no fire and no place to sit. The bed's the only warm place and you know it. I didn't know you were this hard up. And, by the way, I don't have any company, thanks for asking." If Bob couldn't figure out from that speech that she was pissed, he'd never win the prize as Mr. Perception.

"I am that hard up," he said, moving closer. "Let's get it on."

"Say what?" Bob had never been one for subtle technique, but this was pushing it. She tried to step back but his hands gripped her arms. They were cold as ice, even through the housecoat. "Bob!" He pulled her to him and buried his face in her hair.

"It's not what you think," he whispered. "We don't have time for this, worse luck."

"Bob!"

"No, just bear with me. Let's go to your bedroom. I don't want you to freeze."

He led her to the back of the house and she slid under the covers without inviting him in. He lay on top, still wearing his thick leather coat. Whatever he had in mind, she realized, it wasn't sex. Not with her housecoat, the comforter and his greatcoat playing chaperone.

He kissed her hard and was whispering hoarsely in her ear before she had a chance to react. "Angels down. A scoopship. It crashed."

"Angels?" Was he crazy?

He kissed her neck. "Not so loud. I don't think the 'danes are listening, but why take chances? Angels. Spacemen. *Peace* and *Freedom*."

She'd been away too long. She'd never heard space-men called *Angels*. And— "Crashed?" She kept it to a whisper. "Where?"

"Just over the border in North Dakota. Near Mapleton."

"Great Ghu, Bob. That's on the Ice!"

He whispered, "Yeah. But they're not too far in."

"How do you know about it?"

He snuggled closer and kissed her on the neck again. Maybe sex made a great cover for his visit, but she didn't think he had to lay it on so thick. "We know."

"We?"

"The Worldcon's in Minneapolis-St. Paul this year—"

The World Science Fiction Convention. "I got the invitation, but I didn't dare go. If anyone saw me—"

"—And it was just getting started when the call came down from *Freedom*. Sherrine, they couldn't have picked a better time or place to crash their scoopship. That's why I came to you. Your grandparents live near the crash site."

She wondered if there was a good time for crashing scoopships. "So?"

"We're going to rescue them."

"We? Who's we?"

"The Con Committee, some of the fans—"

"But why tell me, Bob? I'm fafiated. It's been years since I've dared associate with fen."

Too many years, she thought. She had discovered science fiction in childhood, at her neighborhood branch library. She still remembered that first book: *Star Man's Son*, by Andre Norton. Fors had been persecuted be-cause he was different; but he nurtured a secret, a mutant power. Just the sort of hero to appeal to an ugly-duckling little girl who would not act like other little girls.

SF had opened a whole new world to her. A galaxy, a universe of new worlds. While the other little girls had played with Barbie dolls, Sherrine played with Lummox and Poddy and Arkady and Susan Calvin. While they went to the malls, she went to Trantor and the Witch World. While they wondered what Look was In, she wondered about resource depletion and nuclear war and genetic engineering. Escape literature, they called it. She missed it terribly.

"There is always one moment in childhood," Graham Greene had written in *The Power and the Glory*, "when the door opens and lets the future in." For some people, that door never closed. She thought that Peter Pan had had the right idea all along.

"Why tell *you?* Sherrine, we want you with us. Your grandparents live near the crash site. They've got all sorts of gear we can borrow for the rescue."

"Me?" A tiny trickle of electric current ran up her spine. But . . . *Nah.* "Bob, I don't dare. If my bosses thought I was associating with fen, I'd lose my job."

He grinned. "Yeah. Me, too." And she saw that he had never considered that she might not go.

'Tis a Proud and Lonely Thing to Be a Fan, they used to say, laughing. It had become a *very* lonely thing. The Establishment had always been hard on science fiction. The government-funded Arts Councils would pass out tax money to write obscure poetry for "little" magazines, but not to write speculative fiction. "Sci-fi isn't literature." *That* wasn't censorship.

Perversely, people went on buying science fiction without grants. Writers even got rich without government funding. *They couldn't kill us that way!*

Then the Luddites and the Greens had come to power. She had watched science fiction books slowly disappear from the library shelves, beginning with the children's departments. (That wasn't censorship either. Libraries couldn't buy *every* book, now could they? So they bought "realistic" children's books funded by the National Endowment for the Arts, books about death and divorce, and really important things like being overweight or fitting in with the right school crowd.)

Then came paper shortages, and paper allocations. The science fiction sections in the chain stores grew smaller. ("You can't expect us to stock books that aren't selling." And they can't sell if you don't stock them.)

Fantasy wasn't hurt so bad. Fantasy was about wizards

and elves, and being kind to the Earth, and harmony with nature, all things the Greens loved. But science fiction was about science.

Science fiction wasn't exactly outlawed. There was still Freedom of Speech; still a Bill of Rights, even if it wasn't taught much in the schools—even if most kids graduated unable to read well enough to understand it. But a person could get into a lot of unofficial trouble for reading SF or for associating with known fen. She could lose her job, say. Not through government persecution—of course not—but because of "reduction in work force" or "poor job performance" or "uncooperative attitude" or "politically incorrect" or a hundred other phrases. And if the neighbors shunned her, and tradesmen wouldn't deal with her, and stores wouldn't give her credit, who could blame them? Science fiction involved science; and science was a conspiracy to pollute the environment, "to bring back technology."

Damn right! she thought savagely. We do conspire to bring back technology. Some of us are crazy enough to think that there are alternatives to freezing in the dark. *And some of us are even crazy enough to try to rescue marooned spacemen before they freeze, or disappear into protective custody.*

Which could be dangerous. The government might declare you mentally ill, and help you.

She shuddered at that thought. She pushed and rolled Bob aside. She sat up and pulled the comforter up tight around herself. "Do you know what it was that attracted me to science fiction?"

He raised himself on one elbow, blinked at her change of subject, and looked quickly around the room, as if suspecting bugs. "No, what?"

"Not Fandom. I was reading the true quill long before I knew about Fandom and cons and such. No, it was the feeling of hope."

"Hope?"

"Even in the most depressing dystopia, there's still the notion that the future is something we build. It doesn't just happen. You can't predict the future, but you can invent it. Build it. That is a hopeful idea, even when the building collapses."

Bob was silent for a moment. Then he nodded. "Yeah. Nobody's building the future anymore. 'We live in an Age of Limited Choices.'" He quoted the government line without cracking a smile. "Hell, you don't *take* choices off a list. You *make* choices and *add* them to the list. Speaking of which, have you made your choice?"

That electric tickle . . . "Are they even alive?"

"So far. I understand it was some kind of miracle that they landed at all. They're unconscious, but not hurt bad. They're hooked up to some sort of magical medical widgets and the Angels overhead are monitoring. But if we don't get them out soon, they'll freeze to death."

She bit her lip. "And you think we can reach them in time?"

Bob shrugged.

"You want me to risk my life on the Ice, defy the government and probably lose my job in a crazy, amateur effort to rescue two spacemen who might easily be dead by the time we reach them."

He scratched his beard. "Is that quixotic, or what?"

"Quixotic. Give me four minutes."

She found five more fen waiting outside by Bob's van. Three she knew from an earlier life. She smiled and waved and they nodded warily.

That griped her, but she could see their point of view. She had been out of Fandom for a long time and they weren't quite sure about her.

Bob's van had less than half a tank of alcohol, so they topped it with the fuel from her car. She rolled her eyes up watching them. Typical fanac, she thought. Six people trying to work a syphon at the same time. Finally Thor took over the whole thing and Sherrine retired gratefully to the van with the rest and shivered while she waited.

Thor was outside, but he wasn't shivering. Sherrine watched him through the window. He was built like the god whose name he used, and nothing about him had changed since she had known him except for the beard.

Even with the last drop of alky sucked from the car's tank, the van had less than a full tank. Thor climbed into the van and slid the door closed. He still had the syphon. Sherrine poked her nose out of her coat.

"Keeping the syphon?"

His grin was lopsided and too wide. Siphoning alcohol ... He held the rubber hose up like an Appalachian snake handler. "We can't make it to Mapleton and back on one tank. Might not be too smart to gas up at a public station. 'Specially after we collect Rafe and Gabe."

"Who?"

"The Angels."

"Oh. You know their names?"

"Those are code names." That was Mike Glider, grinning on her right. "Gotta have code names on a clandestine operation."

"Sure you do; there are standards to keep up."

She shook her head. Mike knew everything there was to know and had opinions on the rest. He'd been a county agricultural agent since quitting the IRS; but that was just cover for his true identity as Oral Historian of Fandom. He was "tall and round and three hundred pound," in his own words. If they froze on the Ice, he'd freeze last.

Bob started the van and Sherrine felt that electric thrill surging deep and strong. Real spacemen. Oh, God, to talk to them! Space stations. Moon base. Angels down; fans to the rescue!

She looked around at her companions. "Thor, you look like a Mormon patriarch."

"The beard's for warmth. I shave the mustache off so snot won't freeze in it. Ever wonder why Eskimos don't grow more hair? Evolution in action."

"Hunh. No." Fans were a wellspring of minutiae, a peculiar mix of the trivial and the practical. Try asking about Inuit tonsorial practices in a group of mundanes! She tried to banish snot-encrusted mustaches from her thoughts.

"Welcome back, Sherrine." Bruce Hyde was riding shotgun. He twisted around in his seat to look at her. "We heard you'd gafiated."

"Fafiated." She looked him straight in the eye, daring him to disagree. She hadn't *gotten away from it all;* she'd been *forced away from it all.* She resented Bruce's probing. "The jobs I wanted I couldn't get if I were a known fan. My thesis advisor kept dropping subtle hints about getting down to earth and being realistic. So Jake and I went mundane."

Bruce was overweight, but not in Mike's league; and his bulk was more muscle than fat. He was stronger than he looked. His black beard was wild and bushy, wildly unlike Thor's silken, Nordic god look. "How is Jake these days?" he asked.

She dropped her eyes. "I wouldn't know."

Bob put in his two cents. "Jake left her for a New Cookie five years ago."

Thanks, Bob. You could hand out flyers! "Jake really did gafiate," she explained. "I became a 'dane because I had to; but he really wanted to. He kept making digs about 'sci-fi' and 'Buck Rogers stuff.' Trying to yank my chain. So . . ." A shrug. "We drifted apart." And in the end they couldn't even talk about it. The teasing turned into arguments; the arguments into fights. Eventually she had to watch what she said around him because she couldn't be sure that he wouldn't denounce her for fannishness to the University. And wasn't that a hell of a basis for a marriage?

Besides, that was certainly a better explanation for why he left than the one she saw in the mirror every morning.

"That's okay," said Bruce. "We couldn't have used him anyway."

She pulled her parka hood tighter around her face. That was like Bruce, to evaluate everything, even her personal life, in terms of its utility to the current fanac. "You never did like Jake, did you?"

He shook his head. "That's not right. But he had his chance, and he went mundane."

"So did I."

Bruce wasn't embarrassed at all. "Like you said, it was different with him."

She let it drop and looked at the two strange faces. "Hi. I'm Sherrine Hartley."

"I know." The man sitting to her left was massively built and had a shaggy mane of white hair circling his face. He looked like an elderly lion, or an Old Testament patriarch. "Will Waxman, from L.A. Bob told us we were stopping to pick you up." He dropped his hand onto the shoulder of the man next to him. "And this is Steve Mews. He's a Mean Dude."

Steve was sitting lotus position on the floor of the van. He was five-nine, black, and about the most perfect physical specimen she had ever seen. A moment ago he'd been perfectly still, completely relaxed; but his name turned him on like a switch.

He grinned up at her, a wide white grin in a dark face. "Will exaggerates, as usual. I haven't maimed anyone in years." He reached up a heavily mittened hand that engulfed hers. A strong grip, but not overpowering. She had the feeling that, had he wanted to, he could have crushed the bones in her hand.

The van walls were insulated with blankets and comforters. Sherrine settled back into one. She loved car heaters. They were like blowtorches for warming up. The alcohol they burned would have been burned anyway, to move the car. In ten minutes she was warm and could stop huddling.

"I've been fafiated for years," she said by way of conversation, "but I keep hearing about the conventions. Weird ways. Cryptic notes in electronic bulletin boards, things like that. I think you guys really love playing undercover."

Mike grinned. "The word do get around."

"How's Worldcon?"

"It's Minicon. That's a pun. Minne-sota; but also 'mini-' because there's only fifty-four in attendance."

"Forty-eight," she corrected him. "You guys are here."

Mike couldn't just be clever; he had to know that you knew he was clever. A grin and a raised forefinger: "Wrong! This is a special Con Committee meeting, so we are still officially in attendance. In fact, counting you, there are now fifty-five."

"Anyhow," said Thor, "the Cruzcon was smaller. Only twelve people showed up in 2008. We camped out in pup tents on the lawn of the old Heinlein estate. So, if any con deserves the title Minicon—"

"Oh, sure, if you want to be numerical about it. But 'mini-' wouldn't pun with 'Santa Cruz'...."

Sherrine laughed. They were heading for the Dakota Glacier with less than a full tank of alcohol to rescue two downed spacemen from the clutches of the government. All of them but Thor were putting their mundane jobs on the line. And ... and they were arguing about what to name the convention! She had forgotten what it was like to be among fans. Her gut relaxed like a fist un-clenching after many years.

"Who showed up?" she asked. "At the con. Anybody I knew?"

Thor cocked his head. "It's been a while since you've been around. Let's see. You know Chuck Umber. He's there; but he's not in on this. Too much risk he might let something slip into his fanzine. You know Tom Degler and Crazy Eddie. Wade Curtis is supposed to show. There are even rumors that Cordwainer Bird is in town."

"Real pros?"

"Yeah, I know. They try to keep a low Pro-file." He grinned and nudged Mike with his elbow. "Ever since Archcon in '06. Somebody on the Con Committee forgot to tell the Pro Guest of Honor that it was cancelled. You know Nat Reynolds, he showed up anyway and said the hell with it, let's have a party, and the police nabbed him. So the professionals have been staying clear of cons."

"Now, there," said Mike, "is the real Minicon. It was cancelled. You can't have less than zero attendance." Sherrine guessed he had forgotten which side of the argument he was on.

Thor shook his head. "I think there were twenty or so at the party in his hotel room—"

"That was a con party, not the con itself—"

"—before the cops busted us."

"Minicon is still going," Bruce said, breaking in. "It has to be going. The last thing we need is for the cops to find a broken convention and wonder where we all went."

"Hmm, yes." It was starting to hit her. She'd never been underground before. Now ... One hint and her job was gone. A couple of slips and she'd be a wanted woman. "Thor, you've been hiding out for a while—"

"Eight years." He sounded proud.

"What's it like?"

A shrug. "Not too bad, if you have friends. And if the 'danes aren't hunting you too hard. There are folks in the midwest, farm country, who are only too glad for a hand with the chores; room and board and no questions asked. You try not to spend too much time in one place, though."

"No," she said. "I suppose not."

Bob glanced over his shoulder. "Having second thoughts?" he asked, turning back to his driving.

"Sure. And third and fourth." She took her mittens off and rubbed her hands together. "So. What are the plans once we get there?"

They all looked at her. "Plans?" said Mike in a simulated Mexican accent. "We don' need no stinking plans."

Sherrine snorted. *Fans.*

They sailed west on I-94, headed for the Dakota Glacier. Bob drove carefully, trading speed for certainty. On clear sections of the highway, he floored it; where roadside clutter and shrubbery provided cover for police cars, he slowed to a respectable sixty. After a while, the chatter died down and everyone settled into their own thoughts. Sherrine tried to imagine what they would need for a short trip onto the Ice. Her grandparents kept a lot of equipment in their barn.

Thor carried an Irish tin whistle because, as he put it, you never knew when you might need one. After a few miles had passed and the talk had died down, he pulled it from his pocket and began playing. His fingers fluttered through a few traditional tunes: jigs and reels and such; then he started in on some serious filking. Sherrine joined in the singing. Thor played "The Friggin' Falcon," "Banned from Argo," and the classic "Carmen Miranda's Ghost Is Haunting Space Station Three."

Just past St. Joseph, Sherrine stopped singing and stared north through the van's side window. One by one the others dropped out, their voices dying in mid-chorus, until Mike was singing alone.

"'I wrote *Dying Inside* and you snubbed it! *Son of Man*'s out of print totally! You'll be sorry you didn't buy *Nightwings*! No more damn science fiction for me!'"

Mike trailed off. Following their gaze, he twisted and looked over his shoulder. "Great Ghu!" he said.

"Yeah," Sherrine said quietly.

The northern horizon glowed a pale, phosphorescent white, as if an artist had drawn a chalk line across a blackboard.

Steve hopped to the other side of the van and peered through the window. "I didn't know it was this far south," he said.

Mike peered out. "The Ice Line runs northwest from Milwaukee to Regina. It doesn't come as close to the big cities because of the waste heat."

The California fans had never seen the Ice. They stared in respectful silence.

Sherrine spoke up. "You can't live in the Twin Cities without feeling the weight of the Great Ice somewhere over the horizon, flowing toward you like crystal lava."

"Three years ago," said Bob, "you couldn't see it from the highway."

"And last year," she added, "you could only see it in midwinter." The Ice ebbed and flowed with the seasons, like tides on a hard, white ocean. But some of the snow that fell each winter failed to melt the next summer. The weight in the center of the pack forced the edges to flow outward, and the Line moved a few more miles toward civilization. She began to shiver uncontrollably, even though she was wearing a thick down coat and the car heater was running full blast.

Thor noticed and smiled. He blew a few plaintive notes on his whistle; then declaimed:

"Some say the world will end in fire,
Some say in ice.
From what I've tasted of desire
I hold with those who favor fire."

Everyone chuckled. "That's from 'Fire and Ice,'" Thor
said. "By Robert Frost."

"Frost," said Mike. "That's appropriate."

Will Waxman grunted. "Finish the stanza," he said.

Thor stopped smiling and looked out the side window
at the shimmering horizon. After a while, he continued
in a voice so soft she had to strain to hear him.

"But if it had to perish twice,
I think I know enough of hate
To say that for destruction ice
Is also great
And would suffice."

The farther west they drove, the closer the Ice came
to the highway. What had begun as a distant white smear
on the horizon crawled closer and closer. She knew that
the movement was an illusion, that the Ice was not
actually moving toward them. It was only that the highway and the Ice Line were converging. Still, it was
creepy to watch that slow, implacable approach. Mike
started singing "The White Cliffs of Dover," but no one
joined in, and he soon fell silent.

CHAPTER THREE

"The Ice Was Here, the Ice Was There, the Ice Was All Around . . ."

Bob noticed the lights of a General Mills gasohol station shining like a baby's smile just off the highway. A barely legible sign proclaimed the town of Brandon. He turned onto the exit ramp and drove into town. Twenty-four-hour gas stations were on the endangered species list. The van was down to a quarter tank and he didn't want to pass up the opportunity.

The snow on the state road was a foot deep and unplowed. The van with its oversized tires was an ice breaker on a frozen sea. The snow made eerie crackling sounds in the night as the van drove through it.

Brandon was deserted. Everything in town was dark, except the few streetlights. The moon reflecting off the crusted snow cast a dim, pearly light over the blank houses. There was not so much as a porch light on. Sherrine didn't suppose that Brandon had ever been very lively at four-thirty in the morning, but this felt different. Not just sleepy, but empty.

Bob pulled into the General Mills station and honked the horn, but no one responded. After a minute or so,

Thor said the hell with it and climbed outside. His boots broke through the crust and he sank into the snow to his knees. He waded through the snow to the row of pumps. "Premium okay?" he asked. He unhooked the hose and flipped the switch. "Power's still on." When he squeezed the pump handle nothing happened.

"Mechanism's frozen," he called out. He unscrewed the gas cap and stuck the nozzle in. Then he stood there squeezing and releasing, squeezing and releasing until the gasohol began to flow into the tank. Mike gave a huzzah and he and Bruce slapped each other's hand.

"Sherrine," Bob said, "there's a two-gallon jerry can back there somewhere. Pass it up, would you? We might as well get as much gas as we can."

She rummaged around under the greasy blanket and tool kit and came up with a sturdy, red plastic container. She passed it up and Bob rolled down the window and gave it to Thor.

Thor climbed back inside a few minutes later. He handed the gas can to Steve, who stowed it in the back.

"Shouldn't we pay for the alcohol?" she asked.

"Pay who?" said Thor, clapping his hands together. "This town is dead. Everyone's gone. The Ice chased 'em out."

"There's still power," she pointed out.

"Yeah." He pulled his gloves off with his teeth and stuffed his hands under his armpits. "Ghu, but that pump handle was cold! I wonder how close the Edge is to town?"

Bruce turned around in his seat. "I think we should see if there are anymore gas cans inside the station. We should fill them up, too. We mightn't get another chance like this."

That was Bruce; a take-charge kind of guy, although she noticed that he didn't leap out into the snow himself. Thor gave him a disgusted look. Why think of it after he had gotten back into the van? Thor didn't volunteer, either; he had done his stint.

Steve shrugged and untwisted himself from his lotus position. Like Thor, he opened the sliding van door only wide enough to squeeze through. There was plenty of residual heat inside the van from the heater and from their bodies, and no need to waste it.

She watched him try the door to the station. It was open. Steve hesitated and glanced back at the van. Then he shrugged and disappeared inside. A few minutes later he emerged juggling five more gas cans, which he filled at the pump that Thor had unfrozen.

When everyone was back inside and the cans strapped in place, Bob started the engine and pulled back out onto the state road. Steve held his hands palm out over the car heater vent. "Thor was right," he said. "The town is abandoned. The gas station was stripped. All of the tools and most of the stock is gone." Steve bounced as he talked, rocking on the balls of his feet. "I found a couple of packing crates that had broken open. Empty; contents salvaged. When folks left here, they left in good order. No panic. No looting. I'll bet there's not a U-Haul or rental truck left in town."

"Good." Will Waxman crossed his arms over his chest and settled back against the quilted wall of the van. "That's the way it should be. A fighting retreat, not a rout. I'll bet the station owner left the lights and pumps running on purpose. For travellers like us."

Sherrine didn't say anything. She stared out the back window as the night swallowed the town. It was only Labor Day and already there was a foot of snow on the ground. By midwinter Brandon would be half-buried. By next winter it would be gone; and the shared memories that had given it life would be gone with it. No more bake sales. No more Harvest Queens or church socials. In a generation, its very name would be forgotten. As gone as if it had never been, more forgotten than Lake Woebegon. . . .

"They took all their stuff with them," Steve continued. "But they didn't bother to lock things up or turn things off."

Bob shifted the van into high and pulled off the ramp

onto the interstate. "They knew they'd never be back," he said.

The Edge was a faerieland sculpted by winds and summer meltings and the inexorable, constant pressure of the Great Ice behind it. For miles it ran along parallel to the highway, as abrupt and high as the Great Wall of China, glowing faintly with trapped moonlight. Then it would recede once more into the night. Sherrine saw great ice slides, where the vertical wall had buckled and collapsed to strew giant white boulders onto the desiccating prairie lands ahead. Landbergs, they were called. Those that were big enough would survive the summer and grow back into the glacier come winter, as if the Ice were a living organism casting its seeds abroad.

At Evansville, the Edge loomed close by the Interstate and she could see the caverns and crevasses that made up the wall of ice. A playground of the imagination. There were castles with battlements of crenels and merlons; cathedrals of buttresses and spires. Wormholes bored by fantastic creatures. Faerie pillars of gleaming crystal standing isolated like sentinels on the prairie, yards in front of the tidal wave of ice. In other places, the Edge was a gradual sloping ramp leading up to the frozen plateau above.

Steve and Will were entranced by the sight; and even Sherrine and the other hardened Northerners gazed in awe. It was one thing to live near the Ice, to see it in pictures and photographs. It was another thing to look upon it in all its cold and terrible beauty.

"I never thought it would be like this," said Steve. "I expected—I don't know. A solid wall. A slab of ice a mile thick sliding south. The boulder fields I can understand; but why does it slope upwards like a ramp in places?"

"The Edge is only two, three hundred feet high," Mike told him. "But it gets thicker toward the northeast. It's easily a mile thick over Ontario. Ice melts under pressure. There's actually a thin film of pressurized water underneath the ice. Acts like a lubricant. The bottom layers of the ice are less rigid than the upper layers; so they crack and slide along sheer planes. The top layers usually raft on the bottom layers; but if there's rotten snow in between, the weight of the top layers can extrude the bottom layers like toothpaste." He grinned.

Sherrine listened to the byplay. Mike so loved playing the expert; but she supposed most of what he said was nearly enough true to rely on. Rotten snow. The Eskimos had dozens of different words for snow and ice to describe its many different phases and properties. *We'll have to learn them all by and by.*

Just past the Fergus Falls exit, Bob grunted and hit the brakes. The van fishtailed and slewed across the road. There was a confusion of arms and legs and a great deal of shouting as Sherrine and everyone else tumbled around in the back. When the van had stopped, she untangled herself and gave Mike a dirty look. He spread his hands.

"Hey, I just grabbed something to keep from bouncing around."

She gave him another look to suggest he should be careful of what he grabbed in the future. "Bob, what happened?" she called.

"Take a look at this, you guys." Bob reached under the dash and flipped the switch for his outside floodlights. Sherrine crowded forward with the others and stared through the windshield. She sucked in her breath, and even Mike was uncharacteristically silent.

A great half-completed arch of ice was poised over the westbound lanes, like a tremendous wave frozen in the moment of breaking. "Shit," said Steve. It sounded like a prayer.

"Sometimes," said Mike, finding his voice at last, "the upper layers slide out *over* the bottom layers."

Bob kept the engine running, but he opened the cab and stepped outside. Sherrine followed. She pulled her parka hood closed as tightly as she could and stood in the glare of the van's floods. The others huddled around her. Beneath the hum of the engine the silence of the night was broken by muted sounds. The ice snapped; it creaked

like an ancient door. A subsonic groan surrounded them,
wrenched at their teeth. " 'The ice was here, the ice was
there, the ice was all around—' "

"Onk?" Mike asked.

Bob said, "The Ancient Mariner. Do you think the
road to Fargo is still open?"

"Looks bad," Mike said.

"What do you think?" asked Bruce, scowling at this
latest obstacle to his plans. "Can we make it through?
How far does it go?"

Bob whirled on him. "How far? All the way to Regina!
How the hell should I know? The people at AAA told me
the road was open, but their last report was a week old."

A week old! Sherrine looked up at the star-studded
night sky. The last weather satellite had reentered years
ago. She remembered sneaking outside her parents' house
in the middle of the night, bundled up against the chill
(oh, to be that *warm* again!) and watching for the spark
that marked its fall. The newsreaders played it up: the
final remnant of discredited Big Technology was no more.
The fact that all low orbits decayed from atmospheric
friction and that all such satellites were temporary was
somehow supposed to prove the folly of "spending money
in outer space." Better to spend the money here on
Earth relocating the people of Newfoundland, made homeless by "an unusually severe winter."

She remembered feeling as if the world had lost an
eye. Time was, a celestial pickup truck could have climbed
skyward on a pillar of fire and put the satellite back
where it belonged. No longer.

Bruce scowled and pulled at his beard. "Do you want
to take a chance driving under that, Bob? It looks strong
enough."

Drive underneath several tons of unsupported ice?
She thought only Crazy Eddie came up with notions like
that.

And Bob was shaking his head. "Too chancy."

As if to punctuate his remarks, the ice moaned and the
sound of far-off thunder rolled in their ears. A cloud of
ice crystals as fine as mist billowed toward them out of

the darkness. Somewhere farther down the road a part of
the frozen wave had broken off.

She was starting to feel the cold. She gazed longingly
at the van. The others stood around, shuffling their feet
and looking at each other. She waited a moment longer.
This has gone on long enough. "The eastbound lanes are
clear," she pointed out.

Bruce looked shocked. "You want us to turn back?"

She rolled her eyes up. "For Ghu's sake, no!" It took
them a moment longer to catch on, then Will began
chuckling.

"For a gang of taboo-shattering imagineers," he said,
"we sure do let the Accepted Customs of our tribe
blinker us. Drive on the left side of the road? What a
revolutionary notion!"

They drove more cautiously headed west in the eastbound lanes. Bob put the floodlights on blinker so oncoming traffic would notice. Not that he expected much
oncoming traffic at six in the morning in rural Minnesota, not along the edge of the glacier, but it never hurt
to be careful. A few miles farther on, Steve pointed
silently out the side window at the westbound lanes and
they saw where the ice had collapsed across the roadway,
blocking it completely with landbergs. Bob and Bruce
exchanged glances and Bob hunched his shoulders over
the steering wheel. Sherrine's fingernails dug into her
palms. Two Angels had been down on the Ice now for
four and a half hours.

Past Elizabeth, the glacier had flowed entirely across
the road, and the Army Corps of Engineers had blasted
and dug a channel right through it.

Fargo Gap. Sherrine's heart beat slightly faster. A
name of romance and bravery and determination. Fargo
Gap. Minneapolis's last link to the ice-free West. Arc
lights staged around the worksite made the area almost
as bright as daylight. Portable generators chugged and
men and women with picks and airhammers fought the
encroaching ice. They didn't look heroic; they only looked
tired. But wasn't that how heroes always looked? She saw

a cadre wearing Army Corps of Engineer uniforms, but most of the workers were civilians, with only a brassard on the left arm to show that they had been drafted into the corvée.

A state trooper stopped them well short of the work area. He walked toward the van and Bob rolled down the window and waited. The trooper wore sunglasses even though it was dark. For the glare of the arc lights, she supposed. Or for the macho look. He pulled a pad of traffic tickets from under his parka.

"Where do you think you're going," he said without preamble.

"Fargo, officer." Bob could be very sincere and submissive when he wanted to be. "Our friends here from California have never seen the Ice, so we drove them up here from Minneapolis."

Sherrine thought it was a pretty good story for having been made up on the spot; but the trooper just shook his head. "Ice tourists. Now I've heard everything." His face, what they could see of it, showed what he thought of Californians who drove to the Ice for kicks. "You're driving on the wrong side of the highway," he said. She wondered if he thought they didn't know that, and saw Mike bite his tongue to keep from making a smartass remark.

Bob explained about the ice wave that had broken over the westbound lanes and the trooper lowered his pad. "Ah, shit," he said without feeling. He turned and called over his shoulder. "Captain!"

A short, stocky man in an Engineer uniform broke away from a small knot of people and trotted over. His name tag read Scithers, and he was wearing a headset with a throat mike. The trooper had Bob repeat the story. The captain listened carefully and nodded. Then he keyed his mike and barked orders. Within minutes, a tank outfitted with a plow and carrying a work gang on its skirts had rumbled east. A conscripted civilian pickup truck followed, pulling a portable generator and work lights. Scithers watched them out of sight. Then he sighed. "We've kept the Gap open all summer," he said to no one in particular, "but this winter will kill the road for good."

The trooper didn't respond. He laid a hand on the door of the van. "You might as well turn around," he said. "We're going to be evacuating Fargo in the next couple weeks anyway."

Sherrine felt her stomach go into free fall. *We can't turn around. We can't!* The Angels were depending on them. But they couldn't tell the trooper that.

"Oh, let them through, trooper," said Scithers. "What the hell's the point of keeping the Gap clear if we don't let people through?"

The trooper shrugged. "Suit yourself. But stay on the right side of the road from here on. There's two-way traffic. And try not to freeze to death." Sherrine couldn't tell if his request was sincere or pro forma.

Mike, of course, couldn't leave well enough alone. "We heard that a spaceship crashed on the Ice earlier tonight. Do you know where that was?" She wanted to kick him, but he was out of reach. The trooper adjusted his sunglasses and Scithers, who had been turning away, stopped to listen.

"Where did you hear that?" the trooper asked.

Since Mike couldn't exactly mention a tightbeam downlink from *Freedom*, he was at a temporary loss for words. And while normally Sherrine might have enjoyed that, she didn't think a long, strained silence would be too smart. So she spoke up. "My grandparents live near Fargo," she said. "They saw a fireball go down on the Ice and called me and told me about it. As long as these guys were coming this way to sightsee, I thought I'd tag along and see if I could pick up some souvenirs."

The trooper rubbed a heavily gloved hand across his chin, and she wondered why he didn't wear a beard like most men did these days. Dress policy? "Yeah, we heard about it, too, at the barracks. Goddam Angels. A couple of planes from Ellsworth flew over a few hours back; though I don't know what they hoped to see at night. IR, maybe. Come daylight the glacier'll be crawling with helicopters and search parties. No rush. Those Angels will be froze dead by then."

"Froze," she repeated.

"And serves them right, too."

She noticed Mike's jaw twitch an instant before he spoke. "Why?"

Mike, she thought, don't let your mouth talk us into trouble. So far, they were just a van load of jerks out joyriding. If the trooper began to suspect that they were "Angel-loving technophiliacs," they would be in serious shit.

"Why?" The trooper waved his arm at the glacier. "Because they started this, asshole! They did it to us. Stealing our air until the Protective Blanket was too thin to keep us warm."

Captain Scithers nodded. "Damn right," he said. "All that air they took, hundreds of tons—" His voice was serious.

Sherrine nodded her head as if she agreed. So did Steve and Will. Thor said nothing, but he twisted his finger in his right ear as if to unplug it. She prayed to Ghu that Mike would take the hint and keep quiet.

Bob decided not to trust in Ghu. He put the van in gear. "We better get going," he said over his shoulder, "if we're going to reach your grandparents' house in time for breakfast. Thanks for your help, officer." He gave a wave that was half-salute.

The trooper turned away, but Captain Scithers lingered. He leaned an elbow on the frame so Bob couldn't roll the window up. "Thought you might be interested," he said. "The Red River is pretty much frozen solid north of Perley. Bad news for Winnipeg, but I heard you could drive a truck across without falling through." He straightened and nodded to them. "Good luck," he said.

Bob rolled the window up and pulled through the break in the median into the westbound lanes. Mike frowned and looked out the rear window, where the engineer captain was deep in conversation with his lieutenants. "Why the hell should we care about Winnipeg and the Red River of the North?"

"The Corps has been fighting a losing battle trying to keep I-94 and I-29 open," Bruce responded. "He probably hasn't thought about anything else but ice conditions for the last five years."

Thor ran his fingers through his beard. "Must be one hell of a dinner conversationalist."

"I don't know," said Bob. "Some of the strange stories I've heard about conditions on the Ice, he must have some weird tales to tell."

And with that they entered Fargo Gap, the ice on both sides of the highway rearing straight and high as canyon walls and sparkling with the reflections of the work lights behind them.

CHAPTER FOUR

Eliza Crossing the Ice

He woke up hard, tried to move, and thought better of it. Memories flowed back slowly.

Consciousness was a mixed blessing, thought Alex MacLeod. It meant that he was alive; but it also meant that he hurt. His left arm throbbed with a dull ache. To draw breath took immense, frightening effort, and his rib cage burned every time he succeeded.

Groggily, he took inventory. He figured that if a bodily part hurt, he still had it. By that criterion he had at least come down in one piece.

He tried to lift his head to see how Gordon was doing.

He couldn't move. Paralyzed? A moment of panic washed over him as he imagined himself lying here slowly freezing to death, unable to do anything but wait. But, of course, it was only gravity. When he realized that, he laughed out loud, which was a mistake, because his ribs hurt worse than ever.

What difference did it make why he was unable to move? Helpless was helpless.

He tried the suit radio. "Gordon?"

Static for answer. Gordon must be dead or unconscious. In either case, there was nothing he could do for him. Come to that, there wasn't much he could do for himself. He tongued the uplink on his radio.

"Big Momma? *Piranha* here."

Hiss and crackle. Maybe the radio was broken. He tried again. "Big Momma, do you read me?"

Mary's voice came through the noise. "Alex? Is that you?"

Who did she think it was? . . . Churlish. "Big Momma, this is MacLeod. I am conscious. I do not appear to be seriously injured except that I cannot move. This must be due to gravity. Tanner does not respond, I say again, Gordon does not respond. Can you give me a reading on Gordon?"

"Roger your situation report, MacLeod. Alex, I'm glad to hear your voice. Stand by one for report on Tanner."

Alex waited while she scanned the medical monitors. Medi-probes were a pain in the ass—literally—but they had their uses. He wondered if Mary had been standing by in Mission Control the whole time he was unconscious, and whether it had been from duty or something else. *That's right, Alex. Build yourself a few fantasies. You've got nothing else to do.*

"Tanner is all right, I say again, no serious injuries," she said. "He's all right, Alex. Unconscious, but his vital signs look good. I can't tell you about broken bones or such. Your readouts are okay, too. That was one hell of a landing, Alex. The book says you can't land a scoopship."

"The book's not far wrong. Where are we, Mary?"

"On what our contacts call the Ice. Not the Great Ice, but the vanguard glaciers. You're only a few hundred meters from the Edge. If the ship hadn't stopped, you'd have gone over a ninety meter ice cliff. Do you want your latitude and longitude?"

"Sure, but I don't see how that will help."

"Sorry. We're feeding the Navstar data to your rescue party, so—Oh, I forgot, you don't know."

"Rescue party?" He started to sit up, but gravity and

his ribs kept him flat. He stifled a groan. "You mean you're coming to get us?"

"No," said Mary. "You know better than that." He heard the chill embarrassment in her voice. Some things weren't talked about. There was an etiquette to being marooned.

So much for fantasy, Alex thought. They say Love Conquers All; but it doesn't conquer the fuel-to-thrust ratio or the law of diminishing returns. *Peace* and *Freedom* were barely hanging on. There was nothing that could be spared; least of all the rocket fuel needed to land and take off again, even if there had been a ship capable of doing it. "I understand." He tried to keep the bitterness out of his voice. It wasn't her fault he was here.

It was not that they wouldn't come that bothered him. They wouldn't come to get him if he were Lonny Hopkins himself. But Station Chief Hopkins would never have been on a dip trip in the first place. You don't send indispensable personnel on potentially one-way missions. Dippers were folks the station could afford to lose. Good at what they did, but not particularly useful at anything else. Janitors, gophers, day-care fathers, stilyagi like Gordon. *A brotherhood of mediocrity,* he thought. The habitats would still function without him. Even the variety of the gene pool, small as it was, was unthreatened. Gordon and he had already made their deposits at the sperm bank.

"Then who *is* coming to get us?" he asked.

"I told you we have friends on Earth. There's a team heading for you right now. They have an illegal Navstar link, so they know your precise bearing. The government search parties are still wandering around on the Ice thirty kilometers to the northwest. They don't have you located, yet. From what we can overhear of their radio traffic, they got a bum steer from a local peasant who couldn't estimate distances properly. But it won't be long before they expand their search pattern. With any kind of luck, we'll get you out of there before they reach your position."

Alex grunted. Not with *any* kind of luck, he thought. It

had to be good luck, currently in short supply. "How long before this rescue party arrives?"

"Make it half an hour. They got a late start onto the Ice. It took them a while to find enough bedsheets. Watch for them to the south of you. The team leader is code-named Robert."

Code name? Alex snorted. "Roger. I'll let you know when they arrive."

He saw no point in asking which way was south. He couldn't move, and all he could see through the windshield was a white wall of ice. They would get here when they got here. Staring southward would not make them come faster.

He closed his eyes. Maybe if he slept, he could forget how much he hurt. And how cold the cabin was growing. The space suit's heater ran on batteries. A half hour wouldn't exhaust them; but he wasn't sure how long he would need them. He decided to keep the heater on low. Just warm enough to remind him how chilly it was.

Lying there, he had the oddest sensation that *Piranha* was accelerating, hard; but that her engines were located under the deck rather than aft. It was gravity, of course. Gravity was acceleration; and his body interpreted it as movement because one kind of acceleration felt like any other.

He reminded himself that Downers would say "up," not "forward." Crazy planet. Still, he remembered what gravity had been like. He would get used to it again. It would just take a little time.

His eyes jerked open. *Bedsheets?*

The second time, he was wakened by the muted sound of motors outside the hull. Alex listened carefully, holding his breath. Yes, definitely motors. He tongued the radio. "Big Momma?"

"I'm here, Alex." Her voice came faintly through the spitting and crackle. There was definitely something wrong with the radio. He prayed that the comm would not fail.

"I hear noises outside. Friendlies or government?"

"It's the rescue party. I think they just spotted you. Look, Alex, one thing."

"What?"

"Your rescuers. They may seem, well, a little strange at first. Just bear with them. They're good folks. Considering how things stand on Earth these days, they're risking a lot to help you."

And beggars can't be choosers. He hadn't known the space dwellers had any friends on Earth; let alone strange ones. "Roger. Out."

He waited and listened uneasily to the sounds of feet moving around atop the scoopship. Strange. What had Mary meant by that? Sure, Downers were a different breed. Yet, how strange could they possibly be? People were people, right?

A face appeared upside down in the windshield and stared at him. Alex blinked. Someone atop the scoopship had leaned over the cockpit and looked in. A hand appeared by the face. It waved.

Alex raised his right hand as much as he could and wiggled his fingers. *Greetings, Earthling. Take me to your leader.*

The face turned away and he heard a faint voice shouting, "Told you so. They're half-buried in the ice!" It turned back and waved again. It was an effort to return the gesture, and after a moment Alex lay back and waited for them to open the hatch. There was more banging and stomping over his head. Strange, Mary had said. So far they didn't seem strange. No stranger than anyone who could move about freely in this horrible gravity.

Scoopship cabins were built for two people and Alex marveled that so many more had managed to crowd inside. It seemed as if they all wanted to talk at once. They asked questions about the ship, about the habitats and Luna City, about space travel. About everything. Finally, an older man with bushy white hair and beard hollered and drove them out.

"Let me apologize for my friends," he said as he crouched by Alex's side. "They're a little excited at the idea of meeting you."

"Me?" Alex was surprised. "Why should that excite anyone?"

The other man raised his shaggy eyebrows. "Not many spacemen stop here these days."

"Spaceman. I was born on Earth. Kansas."

The white-haired man grunted. "I don't think you're in Kansas anymore, Toto." He set a black bag on the deck and opened it. Alex twisted his head to look inside. "Are you a doctor?"

"No, I'm a plumber. Lie still. Of course, I'm a doctor. Will Waxman, M.D. We're not irresponsible, you know. We knew you might be hurt; so I came along."

"Sorry."

"It was the house call that probably fooled you," he said, unfastening the space suit.

Alex watched him reach inside the bag and pull out a stethoscope. The black bag didn't float away like Newton said it should. It stayed put. Gravity field. He would have to remember that. Things wouldn't behave naturally groundside. His reflexes would be all wrong. He wondered how Earthlings could teach physics properly, hampered by gravity that way; then he remembered that they probably didn't bother anymore.

"Breathe slow and deep."

He did, and gritted his teeth at sudden pain. Waxman listened to whatever it was that doctors listened to when they did that. Alex had heard all the jokes about the cold feel of stethoscopes. This one had been carried across a glacier.

"Hurts when you breathe?"

"Yes." He tried to sound blasé.

"Couple cracked ribs." Waxman put the stethoscope away. "Don't worry, though. Lungs aren't punctured. We'll tape you up, and in a few weeks you ought to be good as new."

Alex grunted. Good news from all over. What the hell; he was due for some good news. "Doc, how's Gordon? Have you looked at him yet?" The stilyagi was his responsibility. He was the captain; and if it hadn't been for his stupid pride, Gordon would be sitting warm and snug and conscious back in *Freedom.*

"Gordon? Ah, your copilot. I checked him first. Concussion. No broken bones, no bleeding, no shock. Your people upstairs say there's nothing wrong internally, but we'll be careful until we can get you to a clinic. How does the arm feel?"

"What? Oh, a little numb. Is it broken?"

Waxman ran his hands down the left arm, squeezing gently. When he reached the wrist, Alex sucked his breath in. Waxman nodded. "Sprain, I'd say. We'll tape that up, too. Sherrine, could you help me here with his ribs?"

A woman came around from behind the pilot's seat. Her parka was unzipped and its hood was thrown back, revealing the loveliest woman Alex had ever seen. Tall and thin, even under layers of sweaters, with prominent, fragile bones. "Hi. Sherrine Hartley," she said in a low, throaty voice.

"Alex MacLeod." He managed to reach up to take her hand despite the gravity. It was a hell of an effort, but worth it; but he couldn't hold it up long. She patted his hand with a firm, but gentle touch.

"Welcome to Earth."

"Meeting you makes it almost worth the trip."

She blushed, as if unused to hearing such compliments. How could that be, Alex wondered? A woman as tall and gangly as Sherrine must hear them every day. He studied her as she helped the Doc tape him up. She leaned close into his face as she ran the tape behind his back. How did men and women do it in a gravity field, he wondered? They probably did not need to use Velcro. Gravity would keep everything aligned.

When they lifted him out of the scoopship Alex saw what had happened. *Piranha* had come in hot, melting an ever deeper trough across the Ice as she slowed to a halt. In the end, she had sunk into the glacier like a hot iron and rested now half-buried in a cave of snow and ice. The giant they called Thor was using a snow blower to put a light covering of ice on top of the scoopship.

Nearby were two sledges rigged to snowmobiles. That accounted for the motors he had heard earlier. Both sledges and snowmobiles were festooned with miscellaneous items of equipment and jerry cans exuding a chemical smell.

Sherrine was suited up now, hiding her figure. "That was a piece of luck, wasn't it?" she said, pointing to the half-buried ship. "Thor figured you'd be melted into the Ice; that's why we brought Pop-pop's snow blower. The 'danes will never spot your ship unless they're right on top of it. Even the landing path blends into the glare of the Ice if you're not looking for it."

"Danes?" Alex was startled. "We were nowhere near Greenland!"

"No, not Danes. Apostrophe-danes, as in 'mundanes.' People with no imagination. People who couldn't imagine space travel even *after* it had happened. The 'danes have inherited the Earth."

He sensed bitterness in her voice and gave her an appraising look while her friends strapped him into a sledge. He was already wearing her grandfather's parka. Now they wrapped him in blankets and covered him over with a white bedsheet. A pair of wrap-around sunglasses cut the intensely white glare.

"What now?" Thor said. "Those suits. You going to wear them?"

"No way," Bruce said. "One look at those and the dumbest cop would know where we got them."

"They're not easy to get out of," Alex said.

"They are if we cut you out." Thor had a huge knife in his hand.

Alex felt a moment of panic. His suit was not replaceable. Nor was Gordon's. When the suits were gone they weren't space pilots any more.

And so what? You can't go to space without a spaceship. We're not going back, not now, not ever, so we don't need pressure suits.

"All right. Be careful with Gordon—"

"We will," Doc said. "You worry about the gear. What are we taking, what do we leave?"

"Antenna," Alex said. He pointed to something that looked like a megaphone. "Directional. Not too well focussed, but good enough. Otherwise they'll hear us. When you cut Gordon out of his suit, be sure to get the radio system out of his helmet. And leave it turned off. Should I explain? The suit-to-suit radios broadcast all around; anyone listening will hear and can lock in to trace us. The suit-to-ship radio can be hooked up through the directional antenna so you'd have to be more or less in front of it to catch the signal—"

"Gotcha," Mike said. "We'll get the stuff. You relax."

Relax while a giant named Thor cuts me out of my suit. Sure.

They wrapped them in blankets. Sherrine and Thor had to carry him to the sled. He couldn't walk, and could barely stand. Gordon was still out. They carried him over as well. Sherrine settled him onto the sled and put on more blankets, then a white sheet. "Should I?" she asked.

"Should you what?"

"Like the way the 'danes run things."

Alex tried to shrug under the blankets. "It's not my world; but they did try to shoot me down."

Mike Glider—he called himself "Mycroft"—loomed over him. "They did more than try, Gabe-boy," he said. "They did it."

"That they did." *If I'd turned back, after the first missile— But damn all, we needed the nitrogen.* "My name's Alex, not 'Gabe.'" Talking wasn't easy. The air was cold, horribly cold.

The fat man spread his arms out. "Code names. You're Gabriel; the kid is Raphael. Two angels. Get it?" He took his place on the sledge runners.

Alex wondered how any human being could become as fat as Mike. Perhaps it was an adaptation to the ice age. Heat loss was proportional to surface area; and the sphere had the lowest surface area to volume ratio of any solid.

"Saint Michael was an angel, too," he pointed out.

Mike brightened. "Hey, that's right. Do you think I could go up with you guys when they come to get you?"

Alex didn't say anything. MacLeod's First Rule of Wilderness Survival: Don't piss off your rescuers. But Lonny would never take someone like Mike aboard. Whatever Mike's intellect and training, he was just too damn big. It would take too many resources to fuel that much mass.

They're not coming down for us anyway. We are here for keeps, and Mike is a hell of a lot better adapted to local conditions than I am. "Where to now?" he asked.

"Back to my grandparents' place," Sherrine answered. "So we can return the equipment they loaned us. Bob's waiting for us there with the van." She shook out a bedsheet and hauled it over her head. A slit cut in the middle let her wear it like a poncho. Alex saw that the others were doing the same. But the sheets were too thin to give much warmth, so why—?

"To hide yourselves," he said. "Right?"

She paused and grinned at him. "It was my idea," she said. "Camouflage. Not even Bruce thought of it. This way, if a search plane flies over, we'll be hard to spot. Gran said it would be worth the work sewing the sheets back up if it meant getting you two safely off the Ice."

"Your grandparents sound like good folks."

"They are. Gran was a plant geneticist before they outlawed it. Pop-pop was a farmer. They still do a little bootleg bioengineering in their basement. Developed a cold-resistant strain of wheat that let them bring in a crop for three years after their neighbors went under. They had to stop last year, though. Gran seeded a rust virus that killed off their crop."

"What? Why? If they'd continued— Sherrine, it's going to get a lot colder before it ever gets warmer."

She looked away; beat her mittens together. "Hungrier, too." Her voice was hard and angry. "But their neighbors—their good, kindly, salt-of-the-earth neighbors were starting to talk about witchcraft. They couldn't imagine any other reason why my grandparents' wheat thrived while theirs died. Peasants always believe in witchcraft." She seated herself on the snowmobile attached to his sledge. Her back was turned and he could not see her face.

Bruce Hyde, code-named "Robert," planted himself behind the other sledge. "Everybody ready?" he asked. Doc Waxman took the second snowmobile. Thor and Steve Mews, the black man, were on cross-country skis. They adjusted their sunglasses and waved. Bruce checked his Navstar transponder and circled his arm above his head. "Warp factor five, Mr. Sulu!"

The snowmobiles started with a roar. *Searchers might find us hard to see,* Alex thought, *but we sure as hell would be easy to hear.*

And, dammit, they would stick out for sure on an IR screen. Eight warm-bodied needles in a very cold haystack. And the two snowmobile engines would glow like spotlights.

Alex tried to scan the skies for search planes, but found himself oddly disoriented. The sky was white and the ground was white, and it was hard to tell which was which. "White-out," Mike had called it. "Sky" was "forward," the direction along the acceleration vector. Yet, the visual cues—the ice sliding past the sledge—were at right angles to his sense of acceleration. He began to feel dizzy. He closed his eyes. Give it time, he thought. Let the reflexes catch up to his intellectual awareness. The old-time astronauts had always readjusted quickly to gravity.

Except they hadn't been in free fall as many years as he had. The stations had drugs to compensate for calcium losses, and two tethered ships that spun to make a quarter gee, but it wasn't the real thing. Besides, everyone hated it.

Alex looked at his watch. "Aim this thing south." He indicated the antenna. "South and up. It's not too directional, just get it aimed in the right general direction. We have a relay in geosynch."

Sherrine nodded. None of them wanted to talk. It was too cold.

He tongued his uplink. "Big Momma, this is *Piranha.*" More hiss and crackle. "Big Momma, this is *Piranha.*" Sherrine looked the question at him. He shook his head. "Big Momma, this is *Piranha.*"

"*Piranha*, da. Eto *Mir*. We relay you. Please to be standink by."

He waited. *Freedom* would be below the horizon. Fortunately, there was always something in the sky. The RCA communications satellites, capable of relaying half the long-distance calls of the world, only the world didn't want them anymore. Now this splendid system, capable of thousands of simultaneous calls, served the space stations and the few people on Earth who wanted to talk to them.

"Alex, this is Mary. What is it?" Alex thought she sounded tired, and who could blame her? She had been standing by in Mission Control ever since the launch. She must have been catnapping right at the console. Quickly and concisely, he told her of their IR visibility.

"I don't know what we can do about that, Alex, except to keep you posted on troop movements so you can avoid them. Their search planes have been quartering steadily southeast toward your position."

"Give them decoys."

"Say again?"

"Give them bogeys. I've got it scoped out. Have SUNSAT beam down a few hotspots here and there around the glacier. If they're looking for IR targets, let's give 'em their heart's desire."

Mary fell silent and Alex could sense her working through the calculations. Power was the one thing besides people that the habitats could spare. Space was full of power, supplied by a friendly, all-natural nuclear fusion generator. All you had to do was catch it. . . .

SUNSAT did that. The U.S. government had nearly completed a demonstration power satellite before the Congress changed their minds and proxmired it. They'd needed the money for dairy farm subsidies or corporate bailouts or something else real useful. The entire space budget, start to finish, was less than what HEW had spent in a decade, less than the cost *overruns* at the Defense Department; but space was "frills," so they always cut there first. The station had floated in orbit, nickels and dimes away from being operational, until the crunch came and the habitats decided to cut loose from Earth.

Peace and *Freedom* had pooled their resources and finished SUNSAT, so light, heat and power were the few things that Mary never worried about. The space habitats might starve, or asphyxiate, or die in a solar flare; but they would have power.

"Roger, *Piranha*," Mary said finally. "I will check with Winnipeg Rectenna Farm on power demand and see how much we can divert."

Alex could tell when Lonny entered the comm room from the way Mary talked. When she was alone, he was Alex. When Lonny was there, he was *Piranha*. *Piranha non grata*.

"Winnipeg Rectenna is down, I say again, Winnipeg Rectenna will not be operational for three days." Knocked out by an eco-terrorist bomb thirty hours before Alex took the scoopship down. He'd read about it and wondered if that was significant to his mission. It wouldn't be operational yet. The bomb had done in some of the electronics.

Winnipeg was the only human habitation still functioning that far north, except along the ice-free Alaska Corridor. It had held out so long because of the powersat ground station, built by the Canadian end of the original staging corporation. They had heat and power in plenty, but they couldn't hold the Ice at bay forever; there were too many tons encircling them. And when Winnipeg finally went under, would the U.S. take in the survivors? It was well known in orbit that the Last of the Canadians were also the last friends of the habitats, which did not make them popular in the U.S.A.

"Understood, *Piranha*. I will let you know."

Alex cut contact. So far, Lonny Hopkins, Grand El Jefe and Lord High Naff-naff of *Freedom Station* had not deigned to speak to him directly, which was fine by Alex. Lonny had a grudge against him and, in all fairness, if Mary had been his wife he might have felt the same way. But Lonny had no quarrel with Gordon, nor with Gordon's family, who had powerful connections on *Peace*; nor with the Earthlings who were helping out. So, while Lonny might not go out of his way to help, he would not stand in the way, either. Alex sighed. It wasn't so much that you could depend on him to do the right thing; but Lonny was *very* careful not to do the wrong thing.

Good old Lon. No wonder he loved him so much.

The first search planes broke the southwestern horizon to the right a half hour later. Tiny black specks in the white sky drifted slowly back and forth as they circled. Sherrine throttled back on the snowmobile and watched them.

"They look like vultures," she said.

Alex wasn't sure what a vulture was, but it sounded unpleasant. "Are they coming this way?" He asked in a whisper, not because he thought the search planes could overhear, but because the cold air had made his throat hoarse.

"No," said Mike, the sledge driver. "But that's the good news."

"What's the bad news?" Alex asked.

"The search planes are moving west," said Sherrine. "Whether they know it or not, they've cut us off from Pop-pop's farm. Damn! Another half hour and we'd have been home."

"Can we go around them somehow? Or head somewhere else?"

She shook her head. "Bob and the van are waiting at the farm. If we go somewhere else, how will he know where to find us?"

"Oh, that part is easy," Alex said. "Pick some coordinates —does Bob have a Navstar link, too? No? Then pick a place that he'll know how to find. I'll tell Big Momma; and Big Momma can tightbeam the contact person—"

"The Oregon Ghost."

Whatever that meant. "And then this ghost can call Bob at your grandparents' place."

"That's easy?"

Alex grinned. "Sure. Maybe not straightforward, but easy. There's a difference."

"All right. I'll tell the others." She pointed to the other sledge. "Your friend's awake."

Gordon was watching Alex from within his cocoon of blankets on the other sledge. Alex tried to grin, but his face was nearly frozen.

"We live," Gordon said.

"Da. How're you feeling?"

"Not good," Gordon said. "These are droogs?"

"Da. Good friends." *And they can hear anything I say, so I can't tell him Mission Control says they may be a trifle weird.*

"It was—almost good landing," Gordon said. "I read once that any landing you walk away from is good. But we do not walk."

"Not just yet."

"It is cold. I see why you laugh when I think that because it only freezes water it is not cold. It is very cold." With an effort Gordon pulled a scarf over his face.

"I didn't mean to laugh—" *No response.* Alex drew his own scarf over his mouth so that only his eyes, protected by sunglasses, were exposed, and turned his head away from the wind. *Can't blame him if he's a bit surly. All my goddam fault we're here. But we needed the goddam nitrogen.*

So what about the nitrogen that was already in the tanks? Eh, Lonny?

"Is difficult to move," Gordon said. Alex could barely hear him. "How do people live in this? I try to sleep now."

He didn't, though. Alex could see that. Gordon wrapped himself up, but he watched everything.

The conference ended and Mike and Sherrine returned to the sledge.

"Problem?" he asked.

"We have a place. I don't like it," Sherrine said. "But it's the only possible one."

Steve Mews and Thor set their goggles, dug their poles into the ice, and whisked forth. Their job was to scout ahead for crevasses and other obstacles. "So where to?" Alex asked Sherrine when she resumed her seat.

"Brandon."

"How far is that?"

"About a hundred fifty kilometers across the Ice."

Alex didn't say anything for a while, doing some arithmetic in his head. About ten hours' travel, assuming a reasonable pace. He glanced at the sun, wondering how many hours of daylight were left. It was already high in the sky, and the earth seemed to be spinning awfully fast. When was sunset for this latitude and season? He closed his eyes and tried to picture the globe as he was used to seeing it. What was it like on the Ice at night? Cold. Colder than it was already. "Don't fret," he said aloud. "It's only water ice."

When Alex reestablished the link, Mary wasn't at the comm anymore. It was a woman he did not know. Well, Mary had to crash sooner or later. Lonny might have suggested that she was spending too much time downlinking.

Talk was cheap. The delta vee might cost too much for a rescue trip; but the solar power for the comm links was practically free. He and Mary could talk until Hell froze over; which, judging by his surroundings, would be real soon now.

He let Gordo handle the comm. Not that he was sulking over Mary's absence, but he felt it was about time that the kid took a hand in his own rescue. Alex listened in.

"Skazhitye, Big Momma," he heard him say. "Team Leader 'Robert' points out that, uh, Fargo Gap is uzkiy—is a choke point, and sure to be roadblocked by now. He requests that you contact their driver, code-named 'Pins,' by secure channel and tell him to 'meet us at the gas station.' Tell 'The Ghost' that 'Pins' can be reached at 'FemmeFan's Gramp.' Katya, did any of that make sense to you?"

"Obkhodímiy, Gordon. As long as makes sense to you and to contact. We are lettink you know transponder frequency soon."

Mike told Alex that "Pins" was Bob Needleton. "Pins and Needles, get it? Just like 'Robert' is 'the Bruce.'"

Alex wondered what the point was of having code

names if Mike kept explaining what they meant. Don't mean anything. *It's a game to Mike. High stakes, but still just a game.*

The decision to head for Brandon obviously pleased no one, but there was little choice in the matter. As Bruce explained it, they could not return to Mapleton; they could not risk running the road block at Fargo Gap; and they could not easily set up a rendezvous with Bob Needleton short of a landmark they all knew about. From the glum expressions, they must know they'd still be on the Ice after sunset. Alex wondered if they were having second thoughts about the rescue.

Alex knew that rivers were free-flowing streams of water propelled by gravity rather than pressure. He had seen pictures. He could even close his eyes and remember them. He had swum in one once, a majestically slow stream with banks choked by trees, as close to weightlessness as he had come in those days. But memory did not prepare him for the sight of the Red River from atop the Dakota Glacier.

Sherrine stopped the sledge at the head of a vast ramp of ice while Thor and Steve probed ahead for crevasses. Mike pointed downward. "There she is," he said. "The Red River of the North. It carries warmer water from the south into New Lake Aggaziz. If it weren't for the river and the rectenna farm, Winnipeg would be under the Ice by now."

Alex looked where he pointed. The valley was partially filled in, with ice and snow forming a broad shallow U. The river itself gleamed a perfect silver, the sunlight dancing on it where it showed between the choking ice floes. At first the river seemed merely large; but the nearby hills and ice banks gradually brought it into scale in his mind. The largest free-flowing stream he had seen in recent years was when the laundry basin in the day-care center had plugged up and the rinse water overflowed. He'd gotten three kinds of hell over it and spent a day and a half sponging loose globules out of the air.

What he saw now was vast beyond belief. *Hundreds* of liters of water, at the very least!

He shivered, and not from the cold. Even the trip across the glacier had not prepared him for this sight. The white sky and white land had blended together, destroying all sense of distance. He had halfway convinced himself that he was in a small, sterile room. Now an immense vista opened below him, and—oddly—he felt more dwarfed than during an EVA.

Sherrine must have seen him studying the river because she asked him what he thought.

Alex shook his head. "I've never seen anything so big." He laughed nervously. "In fact, I'm feeling a touch of agoraphobia."

"You're kidding," said Mike. "You live in orbit. You should be used to wide open spaces."

"Well, yes and no," Alex answered him. He kept his gaze fixed on the panorama below him, forcing his mind to accept it. "Inside the habitats, everything is cramped; outside, everything is so vast you can't even relate to it. Life consists of things you can reach out and touch and things you could never touch in a lifetime of reaching. Somehow this intermediate scale *seems* much bigger."

Sherrine laughed. "You should see the Mississippi."

"He may," said Mike. "When the Great Ice builds up enough weight, it'll tip the North American Plate and the Mississippi'll start running north. I'd hate to be in California when that happens. The whole tectonic boundary'll go at once." He dismounted from the sledge and trudged across the Ice to where Bruce Hyde stood watching the skiers through a pair of binoculars.

Alex turned to Sherrine. "Is he always like that?" he asked.

"Mike? Sure. We call him the 'Round Mound of Profound.'" She was perched tailor-fashion atop the snowmobile engine housing, taking advantage of the break to warm herself from the engine heat. "He'll talk about anything and everything. Sometimes he even knows what he's talking about."

Alex shook his head. "Why do you put up with it?"

She gave him a look of surprise. "Fen are a tolerant bunch. You'd be shocked at some of what we put up with. Besides, every now and then he comes up with something useful."

"So, where to now?" he asked. It was irritating to sit bundled in the sledge while others took charge. He knew he should be used to that. *MacLeod do this. MacLeod do that. Don't forget to clean up. Help the kids put their toys away. Try to be useful for a change.* But piloting *Piranha* had wakened something. For a short time he had been making the decisions. Poor ones maybe; but *his* decisions.

Sherrine twisted and faced the river valley. Directly east was the sheer wall of another glacier, higher than the one they were on. "Over there," she said, pointing. "The Minnesota Glacier." For a time she stared silently into the valley. Then, "When I was a little girl, the Red was a 'mean and cantankerous river.' It was either too high or too low. Mostly too low. Filled with sandbars and driftwood. And, oh God, the mosquitoes! They were this big!" She held her hands out an improbable length. "The riverbanks were lined with thick strands of chokeberry and pussywillow, some box elder and elm, even a little cottonwood here and there." She sighed. "It's all gone now. Living in the Minneapolis heat sink, it's easy to forget how much has already been swallowed up under tons of ice. The trees, the fish, even the damn mosquitoes. Whole environments. Soon, the river will be gone, too. It'll freeze and become just another tongue of the glacier.

"So fast," she said. "It came on so fast. Positive feedback. Once it gets started, it runs away before you know it's begun." She turned and looked at him over her shoulder; gave a little shrug. "Sometimes it gets me down, you know what I mean?"

Bruce and Mike were walking back to the sledges, waving their arms. Sherrine and Doc resumed their seats in the snowmobiles. "It's ironic, don't you think," she asked him before starting the engine, "that the biggest environmental disaster in history was caused by environmentalism?"

✫   ✫   ✫

The Valley was as quiet as a Christmas postcard scene. Everything was shrouded in a blanket of light powdery snow. There were ghostly hummocks from which protruded the odd chimney or tree branch. Steve spotted an automobile embedded in the side wall of the glacier itself, its tail end protruding several meters past ground level.

Alex remembered reading about the mammoths found frozen in the Siberian glaciers of an earlier ice age and wondered what future generations would make of this relic when and if the Ice released its grip.

Thor shucked his skis, climbed the ice wall, and pierced the car's gas tank from underneath with an ice pick. Using a funnel attached to a syphon hose, he refilled one of the depleted jerry cans with what gasohol remained in the tank.

So easy. With gravity to help, the fuel didn't have to be pumped; it just streamed toward the Earth's center. But why were Sherrine's fists clenched into tight balls while she watched Thor work?

He asked. She said, "If he slips, he could break his neck."

Right. It was just as well that he was strapped into the sledge. Free to help, he'd be worse than useless. He'd be an embarrassment. Thirty years of conditioned reflexes could not be forgotten overnight. If it had been him scavenging the gasohol, he would have tried to jump over to the car and stand on the ice wall. *You can't stand on walls in a gravity field, Alex. The car didn't just drift there, it must have been lifted and held by the ice.* And, if Thor lost his grip, he would not simply float away in a slow spin; he would accelerate to the ground. It did not seem a terribly long way to fall, but what did he know about falling?

When they set forth again, Thor lagged behind a bit as if reluctant to leave. He kept glancing back over his shoulder. Then he set his poles and pushed off hard, racing past Steve Mews, who had taken the point. Steve gave him a curious glance as he slid past, but did not quicken his own deliberate pace to catch up.

I-29 was poorly maintained. It had been plowed in places, but long stretches had been engulfed by the Dakota Glacier just as the car had been. Alex could see where another highway—US 83—had been cleared as an alternate route wherever the interstate was impassable.

"They don't spend as much effort on this road as they do on I-94," Mike explained. "There are only a couple of towns in the Valley still open"—he waved a mittened hand north—"and only Winnipeg at the dead end."

They halted at the riverbank. Sherrine turned off the snowmobile's engine and stared at the turgid water choked with "pancake" ice and slush—an open expanse of water even vaster than Alex had imagined from the glacier overlook. The scale of the planet was just beginning to hit him. It was huge; everything in it was immense. And it was convex. He held on tightly to his boyhood memories. At one time he had regarded all this as normal.

He wondered how Gordon was taking it. The gravity and the scale were completely new to him. When Alex glanced over at the other sledge, he saw Doc Waxman was bent over Gordon. "Gordo?" Alex fumbled for a moment with the tongue switch, then thought better of it. No point in sending a beacon for someone to home in on. "Are you all right, Gordon?" he shouted.

"Nye khorosho, Alex. Leave me alone." He moaned.

"Doc," Alex called out. "What's wrong with Gordon?"

Waxman turned his bushy, white patriarch's beard toward him. "Motion sickness," he said. "He threw up and it froze all over him. He'll be fine once he gets used to things down here." He shook his head. "I've heard of people getting motion sickness in free fall. First time I ever saw it work the other way."

No one ever died from motion sickness; they only wished they could. Yes, Gordon would get over it, just as Alex already had. It was a matter of synchronizing the sense of balance with visual perception. Gordon was born in free fall and a constant acceleration frame screwed

up his motion cues a lot worse than it did Alex's. Like
everyone else, he'd gone to "Spinning Kiddies." The
centrifuge sessions were required for children—for bone
development, Alex thought. But stilyagi like Gordon generally dropped out, and most adults avoided spin exercises when they could. Alex considered his own condition.
Gone to flab, with bones of rubber, and he'd been born
down here.

"There's no way across that," said Mike, pointing toward the river of slush. "We'll have to turn south."

"Can't do that," said Bruce from the other sledge.
"South takes us to the interchange at Fargo Gap. There's
a police barricade there now. Besides, Bob is waiting for
us at Brandon."

"Pins," Mike corrected him. "Use the code names,
like we agreed."

Bruce gave him a look. "There ain't nobody here but
us tribbles; so who gives a—"

"And Gabe can call Big Momma and change the
rendez—"

"The code name idea was stupid, anyway—"

Doc Waxman stepped between them. "This isn't helping us cross the Red," he said.

They both fell silent. Thor and Steve shuffled their
skis back and forth across the ice. "We can't stay here,"
Thor said. "We'll freeze." He looked back the way we
had come.

Mike studied the river. "Maybe we could leap from
floe to floe. You know. Like Eliza crossing the ice in
Uncle Tom's Cabin."

"Why, Mike," said Bruce, "what a wonderful idea. Did
you hear that, Alex? You can leap from floe to floe."

Alex smiled weakly. "I'm game, but I don't think the
snowmobiles are up to it."

"Well, now, wait," said Mike. "Sure the plan has a
hole in it, but—"

Sherrine: "Not just a hole, Mike. A black hole."

Thor: "Yeah, the plan sucks."

Mike stuck his chin out. "You have a better plan,
maybe?"

Steve Mews interrupted. "I do. Head north."

They all looked at one another. "North," said Bruce. "You mean go to Winnipeg? But that's a dead end."

Steve clapped his mittens together. "Hey, maybe I'm wrong. I don't know the local geography. But didn't that Engineer captain at Fargo tell us that the Red was frozen north of Perley? Well, that's gotta be north of here, right?"

Alex never saw so many mouths hang open at once.

Crossing the Red was easy, Alex thought, if you didn't count holding your breath while doing it. The river was frozen; but the ice was ragged and cracked. A rough ride, and if the ice had given way—

Well, he didn't want to think about that. He supposed he was in less danger than he had been in *Piranha*. A hot ship, miles high, hypersonic speeds. Even without a missile up the arse, there were a million things that could have gone wrong. But it was one thing to face danger with your hands around the stick. It was another thing to face it while bundled into a sledge, dependent on another's skills. It was the impotence, he decided; not the danger.

The glaciers on both sides of the river growled and popped as they flowed south—an odd and disconcerting sound. Every snap made him jerk, thinking it was the river ice breaking up beneath them. He had not expected sounds. But then, he didn't suppose a mountain range of ice could slide across the landscape in silence. He wondered whether, if the glacier sounds were recorded and played back at high speed, they would sound like a rushing river.

CHAPTER FIVE

"In the Hands of Crazy People"

Bruce called a rest break atop the Minnesota glacier. Satellite recon had located a path up the side, but it had been an arduous climb. Thor and Steve were winded. The others stood around the two snowmobiles, slapping themselves with their arms, warming themselves with the meager engine heat. Everyone seemed drawn and introspective.

"I tell you," said Bruce, "that Engineer captain had to be a closet fan. Why else would he have told us about the river being frozen?"

"That doesn't make sense," Mike said. "How would he have known what we were up to?"

"He might have guessed from your questions about the Angels. One fan knows another."

Warmly wrapped and trundled by sledge, Alex chafed at his helplessness while others did the work of rescue. "I'm just not used to being so useless," he told Sherrine. *Actually, I'm here because I was expendable.* He thought of telling her that, but he didn't want to.

Sherrine laughed. "Alex, sitting in that sledge, you've done more to help us than anyone standing up."

The Angel flushed. "I'm a link to *Freedom*, that's all. They do the work."

Sherrine shook her head. "Don't be modest." Was Alex serious, she wondered, or was it just the usual macho self-deprecation? It seemed as if the older space pilot never missed a chance to put himself down, since putting himself down on Earth. And the kid spent most of his time in a kind of sullen silence. And these were space heroes?

Be fair, she chided herself. They were injured and in shock. Give them time to recover.

She said, "Who had Big Momma beam down the IR decoys? Who arranged the rendezvous with Bob when we couldn't go back to Mapleton? Who had the old Hubble pinpoint the best route up onto this glacier?"

"It was a rough climb anyhow. Almost too steep for the snowmobiles."

"It would have been rougher if we'd had to find our own way up, or just climb straight up the sheer wall."

Alex grunted. "We also serve who only lie and wait."

She patted him on his shoulder. "That's the spirit. Don't worry. Steve will have you on your feet in no time once we get off the Ice."

"Steve?"

"Steve's a bodybuilder. Didn't you notice his muscles?"

He had. Steve seemed grotesque, thick and bulging, like a creature from another world; but they *all* looked like that, more or less. "What's he going to do? Lend us a few?"

He liked the sound of her laugh. "You'll have to ask him."

"Hey!"

"What?"

"You're breathing rainbows!"

"I'm what?"

"Breathing rainbows!" She was. Sparkling circles of color came out of her mouth every time she exhaled. They reminded him of radar pulses. He said, "You're magical."

"So are you!" She bent closer to his face. "Hey, guys, look at this! Rainbow smoke rings."

Soon, everyone was laughing and puffing rainbows into the air. Even Gordon was smiling, for the first time since the crash. Steve tried to make patterns in the air by moving his head around.

"We're a lot higher here than on the Dakota," Mike announced. "It's so cold that the moisture in our breath freezes as soon as we exhale. That creates a cloud of millions of tiny ice particles." His own beard glistened with frost as he spoke.

Bruce made a snowball and threw it at Mike. Sherrine grinned and made a rainbow ring. "A lot of my mundane friends," she said to Alex, "think that explaining a phenomenon 'ruins the magic.' I think the explanations just make it more magical than before. 'Danes live in a world where everything happens on the surface; where everything is a symptom—like the rainbows. But a cloud of microscopic crystal prisms is as magical as an unexplained rainbow any day."

When they set out again, Bruce and Mike took the skis to give Steve and Thor a rest. The tall, brawny Thor took over as Alex's sledge driver. He seemed drawn and introspective. He was the only one who had not joined in the rainbow making. His breath sparkled with colors the same as everyone else's, but it didn't seem to delight him.

After a few minutes of riding, Alex leaned his head back and studied Thor's face. "Do you want to tell me what's wrong?" he asked.

"Wrong?" Thor wouldn't meet his eyes.

"You've been acting distracted ever since we left the Valley."

The hum of the snowmobile motor and the hiss of the sledge runners over the ice were the only sounds, until Thor said, "There was a family in that car."

Alex remembered tail fins protruding from an ice wall. "People? Dead?"

"Sure, dead. I got a look in while the tank was draining. The front seats had filled in with snow and ice, but I could see the shoulders and the backs of the parents' heads. The back seats—" He paused and swallowed.

"The back seats were clear. There were two kids there. A boy and a girl; maybe six and four. I don't know. They were lying there with their eyes wide open, as white as parchment, coated with frost. There was ice around their eyes where they'd been crying.

"Nothing decays in this endless cold. If it weren't for the frozen tears, I might have thought they were staring back at me."

Alex glanced at Sherrine driving the snowmobile. She did not seem to be listening. He remembered thinking about mammoths earlier. He pitched his voice low. "You didn't tell the others."

"No. Would you have?"

"We should have done something."

Thor nodded thoughtfully. "See if you can describe it."

"I don't know. Dig them out. Bury them?" On Earth, he'd heard they buried their dead. It seemed a waste of organics to Alex, but "custom is king of all."

"The glacier will bury them," said Thor. "The job's half done."

"It doesn't seem right to just leave them there."

"No, it doesn't. But what could we have done? Broken our necks trying to get them out? What would we have dug the graves with? Inside the car, at least they're safe from wolves. You know what bothers me the most?"

"No, what?"

"The accident must have happened ten, twelve years ago, when most of these towns were evacuated. Hundreds of cars must have driven past. My mother told me that this country once spent millions of dollars to free two whales trapped in the Arctic ice. Why didn't anyone stop to help those people back then? *Those children might have still been alive!*"

Alex couldn't think of any way to answer him. It wasn't his planet. He hadn't been there. He wondered what the evacuation had been like. A panicked flight? A black, depressing recessional? A car skids off the glassy roadway and plows into a snowbank. No one stops. No one cares enough to stop. The country has turned its back on technology. Small is beautiful, but small is also poor; and the country could no longer afford to care.

As the sun dropped toward the horizon, a curious green tint came over everything. The ice and the clouds, perfect white but moments before, glowed like emeralds. To the right, the sky itself was green from the horizon halfway to the zenith. Sherrine and Doc stopped their snowmobiles and everyone stared.

"The sky looks like a lawn in spring," said Sherrine.

"Yeah," said Thor. "And the clouds look like bushy summer treetops. It's a floating forest."

Green was not a color Alex was used to seeing. Black, white, silver, yes. But green was the color of control panel lights; of shoulder patches; the plant rooms, of course, and the spider plants in every compartment; and a few corridor walls here and there. Still, of all the places he had thought to see green, the heart of a glacier was not one.

He asked Sherrine, "Is sunset always like this?"

She turned in her saddle. "No. Sunsets are normally red. I'd heard it was different when you got far enough onto the Ice. Nobody knows why."

Mike was uncharacteristically silent. He muttered something about static discharge, but neither too loudly nor too confidently. Finally, Bruce shouted. "Come on! This isn't getting us any closer to Brandon." His voice was harsh and had a ragged edge to it. When the others looked at him, he turned his head and looked abruptly away.

"Right," said Steve. "Doc, rev it up. It'll be dark soon." The other sledge pulled out ahead and Sherrine fell into line behind.

"Alex?"

For a moment, Alex could not figure who had called him. Then he realized that it was Gordon on the comm link. The kid was finally communicating. He tongued his radio. "Yeah?"

"How much farther must we go?"

Alex shook his head; but Gordon couldn't see him

from his sledge. "I don't know. I've lost track. Should we be broadcasting?"

"Is low power. Carries how far?"

"Don't know. I guess it's all right. We're a long way from anything."

"I think the one they call Robert is worried."

"Yeah." Alex thought he knew why. Bruce had been keeping track of their progress. The others might get distracted by rainbows and green skies, but Bruce always kept the goal firmly in mind.

"I'm cold," said Gordon. "But my readouts tell me it's only minus fifteen degrees Celsius. That doesn't make any sense. Neg fifteen isn't very cold."

"Ever hear of wind chill, Gordo?"

"Wind chill. No, what is?"

Oh, Gordo, Gordo. Of course he didn't know. The only wind in *Freedom* was Lonny Hopkins making a speech. "Gordon, the human body cools by convection, right? We dump excess heat into the surrounding air."

"Yes? Is why we need radiators on the station."

"Uh-huh." The main problem in the habitats was to keep from roasting. No one ever heard of too cold. "Well, what if the air around your body was constantly moved away and replaced by fresh, unheated air. It would seem colder, wouldn't it?"

Gordon thought that one over. "I guess so."

"Look, as your body heat warms the surrounding air, it reduces the heat fall and the rate of heat loss slows. So you feel warmer. But keep the cold air coming in and you'll dump your excess calories faster. It's— What did you say, minus fifteen degrees Celsius? The wind is strong enough to lift granular ice particles. Call it forty kilometers per hour. So the temperature feels as if it were, oh, minus thirty-seven degrees Celsius."

"Alex."

"What?"

"Well, it doesn't help me feel any warmer, but at least when I freeze to death, I'll know why."

Okay, Gordo, be a snot. But he's right. We are not going to make it. It was too cold, and Brandon was too far. The space suits, with their heaters, had been left behind with the scoopship. They would have been incriminating, too hard to dispose of; and the trip was supposed to have been a short one. The suits wouldn't have saved them anyway. Sherrine and the others would freeze; Gordon and Alex could wait on their backs until the batteries gave out. Better that they all go together.

It was getting colder and the wind was picking up. And it wasn't just Gordo depending on him. There were these downers as well. It was his fault they were out here. Sure, he was going to freeze along with them; but do passengers *really* feel better because the captain went down with his ship? Soon enough, he and his friends would be frozen as solid as those children in the car.

"It's not a bad way to go," Thor said softly.

Alex looked up. Thor knew. He had the most experience with the Ice, and he knew.

"You get sleepier and sleepier. Then you don't wake up," Thor said. "They say it's even easier if you don't fight it."

"And do you give up?"

Thor shrugged. "I probably won't. But I won't last much longer than you do."

The glacier at night was as dark as the leeside of *Freedom Station*. But *Freedom Station* could turn on the spotlights for EVA work. Alex didn't think any of the rescue party had realized how dark it would be. They hadn't expected to still be on the Ice come nightfall; so he couldn't blame them for not bringing any flashlights. They had only the two that Sherrine's grandfather kept in the kits strapped to each sledge, and a small trouble light salvaged from *Piranha*. They didn't make much light; but, with them and with ropes tying everyone together, Bruce could hope that no one would get lost in the dark. If only there were some way to turn on the spotlights.

Spotlights. By God!

"Something interesting?" Thor asked.

"Damn right, if I can raise the ship. You don't need the Sun to get heat from the sky."

"Onk?"

"You'll see. I hope. Aim the antenna for me, due south. Big Momma. Big Momma, Big Momma, this is *Piranha*. Priority One. Mayday."

Sherrine looked around with a frown.

"Alex—"

"Shut up, Gordon! Big Momma, Big Momma, this is *Piranha*. Mayday."

☆ ☆ ☆

Captain Lee Arteria relaxed in a chair well to the side of the meeting room, the better to watch the proceedings. One should always have a clear field of fire, just in case. Several of the other attendees threw repeated glances in that direction. Arteria, returning their gazes, could almost read their minds. Slim and fine-featured, pointed chin; short-cropped red hair; noncommittal first name, and a grip like a junkyard dog. Gay man or butch woman? They couldn't tell. It made them uneasy.

Arteria parted her lips in a thin faint smile. They were bothered less by the thought that she might be skew than by not knowing the direction of skew. They liked to put people in categories, even unorthodox categories. It was more comfortable than dealing with individuals and their idiosyncrasies. Deny them that and you put them at a disadvantage. Arteria liked to leave it like that. It was always sound tactics to leave your opponents at a disadvantage.

"Can we take it then," said Ike Redden, "that the subjects have died on the Ice?" Redden represented the INS on the Special Task Force. He was also the chair. Inter-service wrangling and high-level compromise had left the Immigration and Naturalization Service in nominal charge of the search. The space stations had declared their independence almost a generation ago; so their residents were, *ipso facto*, aliens. And illegal immigration was, according to counsel, the most impeccable grounds for apprehension of the stranded astronauts. Still, Arteria was sure that all the task force members were looking for ways to bend the mission to their own advantages.

The State Police captain shook his head. "I don't see

how they could have gotten off the Ice before nightfall without being apprehended."

Arteria could think of three or four ways. She kept her peace. The others were paid to do the thinking.

"There was no one aboard the spacecraft when we found it." Air Force was reluctant to mention finding the craft; no doubt because it had taken so long to do so. Never mind that the shuttle was painted a reflective silver; that it blended into the surrounding ice; that it had apparently been deliberately buried. The failure to achieve instant results was always ammunition for one's opponents. "We assume that the astronauts wandered out onto the Ice and froze. We've done IR scans of the immediate area and found no trace of them. So their bodies must have cooled to ambient. We may never find them."

"They are not dead."

Captain Arteria sighed quietly. Staff meetings were always tedious, especially to the worker bees; but even tedium was better than listening to Shirley Johnson. Redden sucked on his lips and exchanged glances with the State Police and Air Force representatives. "Why do you say that, Johnson?" he asked.

"Ice is a crystal, and crystals focus the life power. Yes, yes, I know people have frozen on the Ice in spite of that; but all sickness comes from negative thinking. One must be open to the life-affirming powers of the crystal."

"The aliens are technophiles," pointed out Jheri Moorkith, the Green representative, "and therefore life-denying. However, I agree that they have escaped. Why else would the techno-scientific elite in their artificial worlds have beamed their death rays at the search teams?"

"There *were* tracks in the snow," State Police admitted, "weren't there, Captain Arteria?"

"There certainly were." Arteria's voice was a husky contralto. No sexual clues there, either. Nor clues of any sort. Arteria intended to participate as little as possible in the conference. The Angels weren't any threat to the United States, and tracking them down was using resources better employed for something else.

"The tracks came to the spaceship from the south. We lost them on the hard ice," State Police continued. "But they were headed toward the interior. There's no chance of finding tracks at night, but come morning we'll start a search pattern around the projected route. The tracks looked like dogsleds, though."

Air Force spoke up. "One of our IR searches turned up a bogey to the east, on the Minnesota Glacier; but close overflight positively identified it as an Eskimo band. Those dogsled tracks are probably another band that saw the ship come down and mushed over to investigate."

State Police: "There have been a number of Eskimo sightings around here over the last few months. There was a fight over poaching out by Anamoose. The white folks chased them off."

"Eskimos," said Moorkith, rubbing his chin. "Good. Native Americans live close to nature. They respect the other lifeforms with which we share this fragile planet. I'm sure they will help us locate the polluting technocrats."

The Angels had help, thought Arteria. Someone came up from the south and took them away to the east. Probably not Eskimos, if they came from the south. That should be obvious, even to this crowd. So. If not Eskimos, who? Given the timing involved, it had to have been impromptu. And, if they had been caught—

People who would risk anything to rescue spacemen, instantly, knowing the government would be searching, too. People who could head straight for the spacecraft without aerial spotters. People who could call down power beams from the stations.

People who thought they could improvise a rescue on the Ice on the spur of the moment and pull it off without getting caught.

Fanac! It had to be fanac.

And if you could think like a fan again, Arteria thought, *you might figure out where they'd show up next.* She smiled wolfishly.

        ★   ★   ★

The response was faint, almost lost in the hiss of static. "Da, we readink, *Piranha*. Chto khochesh? What want?"

"Thank God. Big Momma, it's cold here. We're going to freeze, all of us. We need heat. Can you give us a microwave spotlight? Have SUNSAT lock one of its projectors onto our transponder frequency and track us across the ice."

"Skazhiyte. One moment." Alex waited while Big Momma conferred—probably with the *Peace Station* chief and the SUNSAT engineer. Sherrine asked him what he was doing and he told her. She and Thor exchanged glances.

"Is that possible?" she asked. "To beam enough microwave energy down to keep us from freezing?"

"Sure."

"It won't be, uh, too much, will it?"

Alex grinned. "I'll have them set it for thaw, not bake. Seriously, the beam density is only twenty-three milliwatts per square centimeter at the center of the rectenna farm. I figure if we keep it to a couple of milliwatts, it will take the edge off the cold without cooking us. We'll have to take off whatever rings or jewelry we're wearing, wrap them in cloth; maybe pack them in snow. Belt buckles. Anything metal. Microwaves penetrate meat, wood or plastic, but metal absorbs them. If you kept your ring on, Sherrine, it would probably burn your finger."

Thor grinned. "I'm not sure I'd mind if it did cook us." He looked over his shoulder. "Ever since we found that car. When Bruce raised this expedition, it sounded like good fanac. The ultimate sercon. A quick dash onto the ice and back off. They'd be filking about it for generations."

Alex made a mental note to find out later what language Thor was speaking.

"The trouble was, we didn't make any contingency plans. Heck. We didn't make *any* plans." Thor grinned. "Well, Ghu takes care of idiots, small children, and fen. Who knows what the Great Roscoe has in store for us next?"

"Roscoe?" Alex asked, but they didn't hear him.

Alex barely managed to confirm the beam density with

the Angels before losing contact completely. They must have been at the very fringe of the scoopship relay's range. When he had completed the message, Alex sighed and spat out the tongue switch. "Well, that's that," he said.

"Do you think they got the message?" Sherrine asked. "About the microwaves?"

Alex's eyes were dull with exhaustion and the endless acceleration. "I hope so. They're supposed to lock onto the transponder location and track it all the way to Brandon. We should be warm as toast in a while. If not—" Shrugging would be too much effort.

As they picked their way across the ice, Sherrine waited for evidence of microwave warming. She worried about their equipment. The sledges contained little metal. Her grandfather had made them of wood poles and hide lashings. The two snowmobiles were largely fiberglass, but she wondered what microwave heating would do to the metal engines. Probably nothing. Engines run at high temperatures anyway. *But suppose they can't take it? Better than freezing.* . . .

After a while, she began to feel warm. Was it the microwaves? Or was it only her anxiety? Or just the heat from the snowmobile engine? She saw a crevasse that Mike had flagged and steered around it. *Cans of gasohol. What will microwave heat do to those?*

The moon rose, half full, over the eastern horizon, creating a startling amount of light on the icy landscape. The crust of snow, reflecting the moonlight, seemed to glow from within itself. She breathed out slowly and saw the flickering rainbow of her breath. She was happy. Even if they died here, it had still been worth the attempt.

Astronauts down. Crashed. She loosened the collar on her parka. Hunted by the government. What else would a trufan have done? Fen loved their bickering and fannish politics. Pohl and Sykora *still* wouldn't talk to each other; but take a few years off them and they would both have been here on the Ice together, because it was the right thing to do. Fandom, after all, was a Way of Life.

She unzipped her parka. 'Tis a proud and lonely thing to be a fan. She was glad to be back. When she thought of all the years she had wasted in the "danelaw". . . .

"Sherrine?"

"Yes. Alex?" She kept her eye glued on Mike's back where he broke trail ahead of her.

"Could you take a blanket or two off me?"

She turned around. "What? Oh!" Alex's face was damp with sweat. She realized that she was perspiring heavily herself. She brought her snowmobile to a halt just as Will stopped his and jumped off into the snow and began stuffing ice in his mouth. Now what?

"Fillings," Will mumbled. "Gold caps, teef." He settled back on his heels and breathed a sigh of relief.

"I'm sorry," Alex said. "The calculations must have been off slightly."

"Can you do something about it?" Will asked. "It's like using hot coffee for mouthwash."

Thor rubbed his jaw and agreed. Mike, who had returned from the point and overheard, grinned. "Makes me glad I have plastic fillings. No metal in my mouth."

"Me neither," Sherrine agreed. "But *I'm* glad I'm not wearing braces anymore." The others laughed.

"Very funny," said Doc, chewing on a snowball. Thor and Bruce were sucking in cold air. Sherrine winced. Whenever she did that, it hurt her teeth.

"No good," said Alex, spitting out his communicator once more. "Damn thing's *hot*. I can't raise them. Either we're out of range or the radio finally went kaput."

"No big deal," said Doc. "I'll just keep a mouth full of snow." He took off his parka. "Meanwhile," he said, "it's a little warm for this."

The layered look, Sherrine reflected as she removed her own parka, had its advantages. She unstrapped Alex and pulled a blanket off him. Microwaves created heat by friction. They agitated the molecules of an object, penetrating to a certain depth, depending on the material. When the microwaves were shut off, the object continued to heat by conduction to greater depths. She suspected that she would be removing another sweater or two as the night went on.

"Say," said Mike, "you know what we forgot to bring?"

Thor gave him a suspicious look. "What?"

"Beach umbrellas. Aluminum beach umbrellas. In case it gets too hot."

Doc studied the snowball in his hand, looked at Mike, shook his head and stuck the snowball back in his mouth. Sherrine grinned. Mike had a point. Later, they might wish they had a means of reflecting the microwaves. They laughed and moved on.

"Hey, guys," said Bruce. "Don't look now, but we got company."

Sherrine looked to the sky. "Oh, God—"

"No," said Bruce. "Not up there. Over here."

She looked. Eskimos.

In retrospect, it was probably something she should have expected. Eskimos lived on the ice and the ice was flowing south, so why shouldn't there be Inuit in Minnesota? She said as much to Mike about the small, ragged band that had appeared suddenly in the ghost-light created by the flashlights and the ice-reflected stars and moon. Mike shrugged, scratched his beard and dug into his limitless store of miscellany.

"Maybe," he said. "But the Inuit are a coastal folk. Except for the caribou-hunting bands, they don't live inland. If anything, the Ice should have driven them west along the coast into Alaska, not south into the heart of the glacier."

Krumangapik's face was a deep copper, creased into a permanent squint. He had thrown back the hood of his parka, showing straight-cropped black hair. His own sledge and dog team waited nearby with his partner and their families. Krumangapik grinned, showing the gaps in his teeth.

He smiled at Bruce and the others. The Angels, he wasn't sure of. He kept giving them quick glances from the corners of his eyes.

He said, "You must not thank for the meat. It is bad manners to thank."

Bruce seemed flustered. "I didn't mean to give offense," he said.

"It is our people's custom to thank for gifts," said Sherrine.

Krumangapik did not look at her. Sherrine thought he wasn't sure if she was a woman or not. By his standards, she was too thin to be female; but he evidently had no wish to take chances. Bruce had facial hair and was obviously the leader, so he spoke exclusively to Bruce.

"We do not give gifts. I know that it is different among the *upernatleet;* but in this land, no one wishes to be dependent upon another. 'With gifts you make slaves; as with whips you make dogs.'"

"Then why," asked Mike, "have you shared your meat?"

The old *inuk* seemed puzzled by the question. "You have shared your magical heat so that we are all wonderously warm." His breath made frosty clouds in the icy darkness, so Sherrine guessed that warm depended on what you were used to. "What could I offer in return but these poor scraps of meat. Offal that has been dirtied by the dogs! I am ashamed to offer it to such excellent guests."

Mike and Steve looked thoughtfully at the skewers in their hands. Sherrine hissed at them. "Not literally! If gift-giving makes slaves, you have to disparage the gift." They looked relieved and Steve took a bite and chewed.

"It is really very good meat," he said. "Tasty. What is it, walrus?"

"Dog," said Krumangapik. "But it was a very sick dog," he added hastily. "Mangy. We have lost most of our team on this journey."

Steve gave a journeyman grin. "Delicious," he said.

Krumangapik's band had intended to camp, but when Bruce told them that he was going to press on to Brandon, they elected to join up. "It is safer to travel together," he said. "You carry the warmth with you; and the sooner we get off this wretched ice, the better."

"Get off the Ice?" Steve seemed surprised. "This is your world, isn't it? The land at the top of the world."

Mala, the other hunter, laughed and the old man shook his head. "It is ours because neither the Indians nor the whites want it. The legends say that when we first came into this country, many ages ago, it was already inhabited by those you call Indians. In the white man's school, we learned that these folk were called the Athabascans and the Crees. We fought mightily to take the land from them. The grass ran red with their gore. Ah, there were massacres to whet even the wildest fancy! Even today, to cry 'Indians!' among the Greenlanders is enough to throw everyone into a panic; even though the word has long lost its meaning there. But the Indians were crueler and wiser in the ways of war than we; and, even though the forests were spreading north, there was not room in them for both peoples, and we retreated before them. Soon we came to a strange, white land where the Indian would not follow. Life there became a contest with death, but we learned that if we followed the proper customs, we could live. Later, we found that Sila had arranged all this to harden us against the day of our vengeance. Now, the ice is bringing us back again into the land that was ours." The old man scratched his chin and asked in a perfectly matter-of-fact voice, "You have not seen any Cree, have you?"

Sherrine could not be sure whether old Krumangapik was putting them on. By his own admission, he had been to the white schools. He would have learned there about the ice ages and about ancient folkways. How much of his tale was genuine Inuit legend and how much embellishment to entertain guests? "Why did you say it would be safer if we traveled together?" she asked.

Once again, the old man spoke to Bruce and not to her. It was irritating. "Because of the cannibals," said Krumangapik.

Even Mike was speechless.

"Cannibals?" asked Bruce in a strained voice.

"Yes. Two hunters named Minik and Mattak who accompanied us at first from Baffinland. They were the strongest, so they always took bigger portions of the food than they were entitled to. Every day as we crossed the ice they grew more savage. Several days ago, while we were hunting, Minik and Mattak returned to the camp and attacked the women and children. Oomiliak, my son, fought well and lost an eye." He put an arm around a small boy with an empty eyesocket who stood beside him. "But his sister and mother were stabbed to death and dragged away to be eaten. When Mala and I returned to camp and learned what had happened, we tried to take vengeance, but the dogs were too weak to chase them across the ice."

Bruce swallowed and looked out into the surrounding night. "Where are they now?"

The old man shrugged. "Somewhere out there. Perhaps they are following us. Or perhaps they have gone elsewhere." His face closed up and he looked away, into the night.

For a man, one of whose wives had been killed and eaten along with his daughter, Sherrine thought Krumangapik was taking his loss remarkably well. She wondered if Eskimos felt tragedy differently than other folk.

And the Angels? Alex did not appear shocked at Krumangapik's casual attitude. Why not?

Bruce let the Eskimos take the point. They knew more about traveling on the Ice and would be more aware of dangerous conditions, especially in the dark. Sherrine thought Bruce was more than a little glad to have someone else shoulder the responsibility for a while. Now and then he consulted the transponder and sent word to Krumangapik to alter course. The old Eskimo never revealed what he thought of these directions; but Sherrine suspected that if he ever disagreed with them, he and his band would simply strike out on their own.

Two hours later, they stopped again to shed clothes. The heat, mild as it was, was working its way through their bodies. Sherrine tried to balance the heat and the clothing against the windchill and found, much to her surprise, that she was dressed for a walk on a brisk spring day.

We're in the heart of the Minnesota glacier, she thought, *and I'm dressed lighter than in my own home.* If only there were more SUNSATs in orbit.

When Krumangapik and his band began stripping, Sherrine's jaw dropped. The Eskimos shed their parkas and even their undergarments. She noticed that all of them, hunters and women, wore long johns from Sears. Krumangapik was not the unspoiled savage he liked to pretend. Soon they were standing in the buff.

The two women strung a clothesline between two light poles and hung the discarded clothing to it with pins made of walrus bone. Sherrine had to admit that the younger hunter, Mala, was rather well-hung. Naterk, his wife, was— Well, *round.* She had curves in places where other women did not have places. Sherrine saw Alex and Gordon staring at the woman and turned away. Sooner or later, she knew, they would run into a woman who was not a stick; but they did not have to make such a spectacle of their interest.

Krumangapik invited them to air out their own clothing as well. "Normally, we do this only in the igloo. It is usually not warm enough outside. But with this wonderful heat—" He raised his arms and turned slowly, as if basking in the sun on Miami Beach.

"Aren't you even a little chilly?" she asked.

Krumangapik grinned his gap-toothed grin again. "Better to be chilly," he quoted, "and also be alone inside one's clothing."

Then she noticed that the women were picking through the furs for lice. It figured. There wouldn't be too many opportunities to change on the glacier. They must spend a great many days wearing the same clothes.

Sherrine looked at Thor, who looked at Mike, who looked at Steve, who looked at Doc, who looked at Bruce. No one moved. Then Steve grinned and pulled his sweater over his head. He cried, "Gentlebeings and sapients all, how can you resist? How often do you get a chance to sunbathe on a glacier?"

They stripped down practically to the buff. Sherrine and Doc both drew the line at shucking their underwear.

Thor and Steve did not; but looking at them, they seemed less a pair of naked males than a pair of Greek statues, one in ivory, one in ebony. Nude, not naked. Naterk kept throwing glances at them, like she was inspecting livestock. Thor gave her a look back and ran his fingers through his beard.

"Don't even think it," Mike told him.

Thor raised his eyebrows and leered. "Think what?"

"You know. Adultery is the major cause of murders among Eskimos." He jerked his head at Mala, who had watched the byplay with no expression.

"All the cartoons—"

"This isn't the suburbs. They don't give gifts, remember? Wife-swapping is the way they seal bargains. If Mala makes the offer—and remember that *he* has to make the offer—then you have to help him when he goes hunting. Either that or you have to offer him your wife."

Sherrine was arranging Alex atop a pile of discarded clothing. Alex was trying to smile hard enough to mask the winces caused by the pain in his ribs. She pulled the strap snug, but not tight.

"Thor," she said, "don't even think it." And she whipped around with a snowball in her hand and blasted him on the chest.

Then all fandom was plunged into war. Even the Eskimos joined in. It was such a relief to know that they would not freeze! Sherrine wondered if she might even get a tan out of it. She was laughing and dancing and dodging snowballs when the spotlight from the helicopter caught them dead center.

★   ★   ★

Lieutenant Gil Magruder studied the shapes dancing in the spotlight below. There were two sleds piled high with clothing and blankets. Nestled in the clothing, he saw two naked corpses, long dead of starvation by the looks of them. Cavorting around them in some sort of ritualistic dance were a dozen naked and near naked men and women, including at least two children. When the light hit them, they froze in place and stared up at the helicopter. Magruder pivoted the copter, keeping the beam centered.

"Sergeant. What do you see down there?"

Staff Sergeant Emil Poulenc looked and swallowed his gum. "It looks like some kind of funeral, sir," he said in a Louisiana drawl. "Those are Eskimos, aren't they? But—"

"But they're naked, aren't they, Sergeant. They're on the Ice at thirty below and they're naked."

"Well, that lady there, she has a brassiere and panties on."

Magruder gave him a stare.

"I mean, she's not *completely* naked." Poulenc's voice sounded wistful.

"Sergeant, what possible difference can a pair of pink panties make at thirty degrees below zero?"

Poulenc scratched his chin. "Well, sir, since you put it that way."

Magruder stared at the group on the ground. "HQ ain't never gonna believe this," he muttered. He straightened and adjusted the rotor. "You know what I think we saw, Sergeant?"

"Sir, I can't imagine."

Magruder turned off the spotlight and banked the copter away to the west. "Nothing, Sergeant. I think we saw absolutely nothing at all."

☆　　☆　　☆

The General Mills station at Brandon was a gleaming beacon in the dark for the last few miles of the trip. Alex sighed. The madcap trip across the Ice was nearly over. Sherrine drove the snowmobile down the state highway toward the station, where Alex saw a man—presumably Bob Needleton—sitting in a lawn chair reading a magazine beside a blazing fire he had built in an oil drum. When he heard them coming, he folded the magazine and stood up.

"It's about time you got here," he said. If he thought there was something extraordinary about a procession of naked people coming off the glacier, he did not say. Instead he gave directions for loading the van.

Alex and Gordon were trundled into the back of the van and laid out flat on a pair of old mattresses. The last sight Alex saw before they slid the door closed was a bunch of naked Eskimos dancing around the blazing oil drum. It was probably a measure of how accustomed he had already become to Earth, that the sight seemed perfectly natural. So far, all the Earthlings he had met had behaved oddly.

Maybe gravity pulled blood from the brain. . . .

Bob climbed into the pilot's seat. "That's that," he said. "Sherrine, honey, your grandparents stayed behind in Mapleton just in case you managed to get back there after all. As soon as we find a working telephone we'll call and tell them you're okay and where to find their equipment. Your pal Krumangapik agreed to wait here until they came by, if I would let him have the fire I built in the oil drum." He started the engine. "I guess that takes care of everything."

"Not quite everything," Alex said. "It's going to get cold. We told SUNSAT to turn off the beam when we got to Brandon."

"Sigh," Thor said. "I suppose we'd be too easy to locate if we kept it. But it was nice to be warm."

There was a mad scramble in the back of the van as everyone hastened to don clothes. Conditions were crowded with seven people in the back of the van. Alex didn't mind the occasional elbow or knee as the others pulled on sweaters and pants, because their body heat warmed the place nicely. He supposed that was how Krumangapik and his friends could sit around naked in a house made of snow bricks. Besides, Sherrine took charge of dressing him, and he rather enjoyed it.

☆   ☆   ☆

Alex relaxed to the rhythm of the van over the highway. He closed his eyes. The rescue was over. For the first time since he'd seen the missile on the radar, he knew he would live for one more day.

A couple miles farther on, he felt a hand shake his

shoulder. He opened his eyes and saw Steve's dark face above him.

Steve grinned. "It's too close in here to run through any *asanas*; and you're not up to it physically yet. So let's begin your conditioning with some *pranayama*. I want you to practice breathing."

Alex wondered what it was that his lungs had been doing all his life. "I already know how to breathe," he told him.

"I don't want you to breathe from your diaphragm. I want you to breathe from your little potbelly." He set his hand on Alex's stomach. "Make your stomach go in and out, not your chest."

Steve wasn't kidding. Alex looked at Gordon and Gordon looked at him and he shrugged with his eyebrows. Didn't everyone breathe from their stomachs? He studied the Earthlings surrounding him and, yes, it was indeed their chests that rose and fell. He watched Sherrine's chest more closely, just to make sure. Maybe their rib muscles were better developed. Gravity again, he supposed.

"That's very good!" Steve seemed genuinely surprised and delighted. "Now I want you to breath using only your left nostril."

He still wasn't kidding. Alex looked around the van, but Mike and Sherrine and even Doc Waxman showed no reaction to Steve's bizarre request; and Thor was trying to follow his directions.

"Come on," Steve said in an encouraging voice. "Practice along with me. In through the left nostril. Out through the mouth." When he breathed out he chanted, "Om mane padme om."

Hot damn! thought Alex. *We're in the hands of crazy people.* He had never felt safer.

CHAPTER SIX

". . . . *A Way of Life*"

Where in hell was the Con Committee?

Tradition told that a convention committee could win the bid and then vanish. The Worldcon would happen anyway. Chuck Umber believed it. He'd seen conventions, like Nolacon in New Orleans, where the committee's disappearance would have *saved* the convention. But he didn't believe that *this* committee could *hide* in a crowd of less than sixty!

The Con was ready to go. Fans had been arriving for several days and the official program had already started . . . but Bruce Hyde and the rest of the Con Committee seemed to have vanished into thin air, all but one or two, and they weren't talking. Something was up . . . and even Crazy Eddie seemed to be in on it.

Chuck Umber had published fandom's most successful news magazine for more than twenty years, in formats growing gradually more cryptic and secretive for an audience growing gradually smaller. He'd always kept secrets that had to be kept. He smuggled copies of *Hocus* to closet fans with mundane jobs. He knew where Thor hid out.

He was even pretty sure he knew where the Oregon Ghost was hiding. What kind of secret was it that Edward Two Bats could be trusted with it and Chuck Umber couldn't?

He stalked down the first-floor hallway of the Fielding Mansion, counting the doors as he went. Crazy Eddie had said to try the third door on the right in the west wing. Ordinarily he rated Crazy Eddie's reliability as no better than that of a network newsreader; but so far he was the only person who allowed as how he *might* have seen Bruce Hyde around the mansion.

He opened the third door and stepped inside. "Bruce?"

A semicircle of femmefans twisted in their chairs to stare at him. They were variously dressed in gossamer robes and chain mail bikinis, a sight in which he might ordinarily have shown more interest. Instead, he looked left and right around the room. He stuck his goatee out. "Is Bruce Hyde here?"

The panel moderator, with her short-cropped hair and 15th century breast-and-back plate armor, looked like Joan of Arc as played by Ingrid Bergman. She shook her head. "You want the Con Suite. I think it's on the third floor, south wing. This is a panel on medieval and barbarian costuming. You're welcome to join us, if you want."

"Uh, no, thank you." Chuck apologized for interrupting. He was revising his estimate of Crazy Eddie's reliability.

When he left the room he noticed Fang lounging against the opposite wall of the corridor. Five-eleven, muscular, tough as old leather, Fang was batting a rubber ball tethered to a wooden paddle. He wore a small propeller beanie on his head.

At last, Chuck thought. *Someone reliable*. "Fang!"

"Hey, Chuck." The ball was a blur of motion. Fang frowned at it in concentration.

"Have you seen anybody on the Con Committee?"

"Saw Crazy Eddie."

Arrgh. "How about Bruce? He's the Chair. He's gotta be around someplace."

"Think I saw him. North wing. Second floor." Fang missed a swat on his paddle and the tether ball zigzagged crazily. He fumbled with it for a moment, then tucked paddle and ball into the back pocket of his jeans. "Library? Yeah, the library. I'm sure that was him."

"Thanks, Fang. I owe you one." Chuck turned and strode off toward the stairwell. Fang watched him walk out of sight. When Chuck was gone, Fang rapped three times on the door beside him. Crazy Eddie stuck his head out.

Edward Two Bats was a lean, hawk-faced old man, at least part Indian—although from what tribe he had never said. He had been writing science fiction forever, and movie scripts before that. He wore a yellow nylon jacket, and a red bandanna tied around one leg just above the knee. His beard was stringy like a Chinese mandarin's. His voice was gentle. "Where'd you send him?"

"Library. North wing."

Crazy Eddie ran his hand across his jaw. He had odd hands. The fingers were bigger at the tips than at the knuckles. "Good," he said. "Good. Who's waiting up there?"

"Rowland Shew."

Eddie gave Fang a sharp look. "You didn't tell Shew about this, did you? He isn't very reliable."

Fang shrugged. "He's kept Throop hidden for donkey's years. . . . I didn't tell him anything. Too many in on it already. Shew's helping out because Chuck gave him a bad review once."

Crazy Eddie gazed toward the stairwell. "How long can we keep this going?"

"Not much longer. You know how sharp this crowd is. I feel bad about giving Chuck the runaround. He *should* be in on it."

Eddie clapped him on the shoulder. "Sure, he should. And Wade Curtis and Dick Wolfson and 3MJ and everyone else, including fen who couldn't make it to the con. It's just until the committee decides what to do. More than three people can't keep a secret for very long."

Fang sighed. "There's ten of us already."

* * *

Chuck Umber stepped aside to let the tall, lanky femmefan past. She pushed a wheelchair bearing an even more gaunt-looking fan, a thin young man with a

vaguely Swedish look. Chuck wondered briefly if the
poor kid had myasthenia gravis, like Waldo in Heinlein's
story. Then he looked again at the femme and wondered
if they were brother and sister. Who was she?

He searched through the back of his mind. Ah. A
computer programmer, hiding out, gafiated years ago,
even dropped her subscription to *Hocus*. He'd remember her name presently.

As he turned to continue his mission, his arm was
grasped by a thin man with long, wild brown hair.

"Hi, Chuck. I'm Anthony J. Horowitz the Third," the
man said. "Remember me? I've got two books out on the
samizdat network. My latest is a volume of critical essays,
Vampire Unicorns from Planet Thraxisp. And I have a
novel, *Living Inside*. About the first spaceship to Venus.
Would you like to interview me for *Hocus*? I do wonderful interviews. And I did *Trash World*. It's the ultimate
synthesis between science fiction, cyberpunk, and horror."

The book or the interviews? Chuck shook his head.
"Not now, Tony. I don't have time."

Horowitz said, not too forcefully, "*Anthony*, please. I
gave up trying to write as Tony. . . ."

Umber left Horowitz and entered the foyer by the
main entrance. The foyer had a floor of Mexican tile and
was brightly lit through the tall windows that flanked the
front door. A great crystal chandelier hung from the
two-story cathedral ceiling. A three-foot model of the
space shuttle hung from the chandelier, and below that,
an antique tin Buck Rogers spaceship. Chuck smiled
when he saw that touch. Sometimes dreams did come
true. If you made them.

Three hallways branched off into the three wings of
the mansion and a grand staircase curved up to the
balcony on the second floor. No question about it, Chuck
thought, the Tre-house was a fantastic place.

Without Tremont J. Fielding—3MJ as he was known
to all trufans—and his sprawling mansion, Minicon
might not have come off at all. A public venue was
naturally out of the question; and very few fen owned
homes large enough to house even a small con. Chuck

marvelled, as he often did, that the Fantasy Fund had ever had enough equity to help buy this place. It didn't hurt that 3MJ had inherited some money. Maybe a lot of money.

The Tre-house often served as a station on the Underground Fanway. It was stuffed with SF and fantasy memorabilia, usually hidden in secret vaults in the sub-basement, but they'd brought out a lot of it for the Con. The walls were hung with paintings: the usual ones of dryads and wood elves and other fantasy scenes, but now many of them sported a second picture hung to cover the first. There were prints of old *Astounding* covers, suns and starwisp nebulas in wild colors, spaceships, men in fishbowl helmets and women in brass brassieres menaced by bug-eyed monsters. It was so beautiful Chuck wanted to cry.

Much of the mansion's treasure had been reduced to holograms. Without a projector, they were not incriminating. What was on display here were prints; but Chuck knew that Tremont would never have thrown away the originals. He remembered what the place had been like in its glory days, when everything was out, when you couldn't look anywhere without seeing another marvel. Original paintings. Movie posters for long-forgotten B pictures. The little paperweight made from one of George Pal's models for *War of the Worlds*. The Lensman costume. George Pal's pen.

And once—once Chuck had seen the original typewritten manuscript for *Fahrenheit 451*. That would be well hidden now! He looked around, but they hadn't put out the movie poster. Too dangerous—but sometime over the weekend they'd certainly show the film. Could that be the big secret? But nobody would cause Chuck to miss that. Chuck was Heinlein's *Stranger in a Strange Land*! He had two-thirds of the book memorized perfectly, and could recite most of the rest.

In that far corner had been the original Gort robot from *The Day the Earth Stood Still*. A tyrannosaur model from *King Kong* was there now. There had been so much. Now—now they did their best, but the walls and alcoves seemed empty and forlorn.

And Thor was coming down the east wing, pushing a

wheelchair. Another crippled stranger. What was going on?

"Hey, Thor!" Chuck moved to intercept them.

Thor froze in midstride. "Hi, Chuck."

"Where have you been?"

A blank look. "Here and there."

"Haven't seen you."

A shrug. "You know how it is. The Tre-house is a big place."

"Yeah. It reminds me of a scaled down Noreascon III. Remember that one? Seven thousand fen rattling around a convention center bigger than the Ringworld." He extended his hand to the man in the wheelchair. "Hi. I'm Chuck Umber. I publish *Hocus*."

"Gabe," said the other. "Gabe dell'Angelo."

Gabe's arm was coming up in a helpless jerky wobble. Chuck dropped his own hand. "Sorry," he said. "I didn't know—" He coughed to hide his embarrassment. "Er . . . dell'Angelo, you say. You don't look Italian." In fact, this Gabe looked kind of Swedish, despite the dark hair. Gaunt and thin, with prominent facial bones. Like Max von Sydow without the beard. "Where are you from?"

"I came here from North Dakota."

That explained the Swede look, Chuck thought. A lot of Scandinavians had settled the upper Midwest. "I saw another guy in a wheelchair a few minutes ago. Younger. Looked enough like you to be your brother."

Gabe looked uncomfortable. He seemed to be breathing funny. "That was Rafe. We were in a flying accident."

"Oh. I'm sorry to hear that."

Gabe shrugged philosophically. "With a little therapy, they tell me we should be up and walking in no time."

Chuck nodded. "That's good. So, you're a friend of Thor's, are you? I haven't seen you around before. At cons, I mean. Fandom is a small world these days."

"It seems like a big world to me. I just dropped in recently."

A neofan, then. Chuck grinned and gestured broadly. "And how do you like things so far?"

"Everything is very heavy."

Chuck laughed. "Sercon," he explained. " 'Serious and constructive activities.' Not 'heavy.' You'll have to learn the language if you're going to stay with us. Don't worry. You'll find plenty to entertain you. Not every fan activity is sercon." Chuck looked the question at Thor. *Is this guy all right?* There had been a time when fandom had few secrets, but no more. *Can we trust him?*

"Gabe and his brother haven't been able to get to cons," Thor said. "Too close to high tech. But they've lived in the future."

Chuck smiled. Thor was an undergrounder. Thor knew a lot of people who couldn't let fan sympathies show. And dell'Angelo wouldn't be their real names, either. "You've known them a long time, then?"

It was Thor's turn to grin. "Long enough."

"Great." He put his hand on Gabe's shoulder. "Really good to meet you. Have you met 3MJ yet?"

Gabe looked puzzled. "Not yet. Thor told me that this is his house."

"We call it the Tre-house. Wait'll you see his collection. Movie posters. Props. Costumes. Books. Original manuscripts. You know what 3MJ's greatest attribute is? He's got no taste at all."

The man in the wheelchair blinked his eyes rapidly and said, like a good straight man, "That's good?"

"Yes." Chuck waved an arm down the hallway. "See, he saves anything and everything. He doesn't pick and choose what suits one particular clique or literary style. His whole life is dedicated to SF."

Thor nodded agreement. "Maybe we'll have time to look at some of the collection." His grin faded. "Hope you don't *have* to, though."

"Uh?" Gabe grunted.

"Vaults. Hidden places," Thor said. "High tech priest holes."

These guys must be as hot as Thor! Wish I— Chuck suppressed his curiosity. It was hard to remember that there were some things he really didn't need to know. *He* knew he'd never tell, but—

If the Feds could declare you homeless, they could

help you. Help included all kinds of things: psychotherapy, drugs, electrical brain stimulus. Chuck had seen Henry Stiren after the Department of Welfare caught him hitchhiking with a half-done manuscript in his day pack. He'd been a hell of a promising writer before they helped him. Now he read what he'd once written and asked people if they liked it, and when they said they did, he cried.

Chuck shuddered. "Well, I hope you don't *have* to see it, but if you do get a chance to visit the collection, you'll see cyberpunk next to space opera; hard core next to New Wave. Science fiction, fantasy and horror. This is as close to its 'national archives' as the Imagi-Nation comes. Thor, have you seen Bruce Hyde around anywhere?"

Thor stroked his beard. "Not lately. But I'm sure he's around someplace."

"Then I better be going. Someone thought he saw him upstairs in the library. Glad to have met you, Gabe." He patted the invalid on the shoulder. "Not many neofans drop in on us these days." And he hurried off.

★   ★   ★

Alex watched Chuck climb the stairs. "Can't we trust him?" he asked Thor. The roly-poly man looked like a baby-faced Mephistopheles, complete with goatee; but he had seemed pleasant enough.

"Sure, we can trust him," said Thor. "But it's one more risk. He runs *Hocus Pocus*, the biggest fanzine around. The authorities tolerate it because it's focused on fantasy, but Chuck manages to slip in some good old, technophile SF propaganda now and then."

"So, he's on our side, is he?"

Thor twisted a strand of his beard around his finger. "As much as anybody here. But you guys are Big News, and the Library Advisory Boards all read *Hocus*." Thor's face turned ugly. "I don't know how they get copies. Somebody sold out. But the fewer who know, the better. That minimizes the risk. Not just to us but to Chuck Umber." He chuckled. "One day he'll realize that you answered his every question literally and kick himself."

"What did he mean by the 'Imagi-Nation'?"

Thor released the brake on the wheelchair. "The danelaw is where the mundanes rule. Downers, you called them. The Imagi-Nation is us."

"I see." A small group, persecuted by its government, forced to hide its treasures and meet in secret. Arguably crazy, every one of them he'd seen, except for Sherrine. And they had risked everything, all their treasures, to rescue him from the Ice. It would hardly be polite to let them know that they were Downers, too.

Alex said, "I'm starting to realize what Mary meant."

"Eh?"

"Mission control told us we had strange friends on Earth."

"None stranger," Thor agreed.

"Now I see what you're up against. It's like David facing Goliath."

Thor grunted disparagingly. "Big deal. Remember who won that fight?"

"But why—" He wanted to ask, why would someone like Sherrine do it? These others he could understand. Thor, running away, looking for some way to hit back. The others, some losers, none of them doing anything important—but Sherrine with her looks and brains could do anything. He couldn't say any of that. "Why do you do it?"

Thor shrugged his massive shoulders. "What else can we do? We believe in the future. We don't turn our backs on it, like the 'danes, and pretend that everything will always be the way it is today. Have you ever read science fiction?"

Alex shook his head. "A little."

"Well, you can see it in our stories. Mainstream literature is about Being. For character studies, it's probably the best genre around; but nothing happens, nothing changes. Imaginative literature is about Doing. About making the future, not just bemoaning it. We'll all be living in the future by and by. Some of us like to scout ahead."

"You make it sound like more than just a hobby."

"FIAWOL. Fandom is a way of life."

Alex opened his mouth to say something, but at that

moment a small crowd of people emerged into the foyer
from the west wing. They were pushing a large cardboard carton on a handcart. Inside the carton sat a burly,
bearded man wearing a snorkle. He was grinnning while
the others poured styrofoam packing chips into the carton, chanting, "Kill Seth! Kill Seth!"

The parade circled the base of the staircase, flowing
around both sides of the wheelchair, and disappeared
down the east wing. Silence descended. Alex had trouble
finding his voice for several seconds. Finally, he croaked,
"Er, Thor?"

"Hmm?"

He turned around and looked at the Nordic god.
"What was that?"

Thor checked his watch. "They must be getting ready
for the book auction. Hunh. I didn't think they'd scheduled it this early in the program."

"Book auction? Who were those lunatics?"

They turned right, into the north wing. Thor said, "No
no no. *Lunarians*. A New York fan club. They raffle off
books at the auction. Seth always wins, so now they kill
him at every con so he can't buy any tickets. Last year,
they made him 'The Wicker Man.' "

Alex didn't ask him what "The Wicker Man" was. He
wasn't sure he wanted to know.

When they arrived at the meeting room, Alex saw
Sherrine evicting a group of young women dressed in
outlandish robes and armor. "Costumers," Thor told him,
"preparing for the Masquerade." Neither the fabric nor
the chain mail concealed very much and he noticed
Gordon staring at the women with considerable interest.
Alex stared, too.

The women were not grotesquely fat; but they may
have massed as much as 60 kilos each. Parts of them
bulged and hung in unusual ways. Gravity, he supposed.
Their breasts and hips were nearly as rounded as those
of the Eskimo women. They needed special clothing to
hold their breasts in place. Some wore their hair so long
that it hung to their waists in back.

Only one, a woman dressed in armor, wore hers sensibly short. In fact, if he pretended the armor was a space suit, she looked halfway normal. All in all, he admitted, Earth women did have a vague, exotic appeal. But true beauties like Sherrine were apparently rare down in the Well.

"I'm sorry," Sherrine told the costumers. "There's been a program change. Didn't you get the update? All costuming panels have been moved to the north wing, third floor."

"Third floor! *No*, we weren't told," the panel leader said. "How disorganized is this Con Committee anyway? People have been looking for them all day. If they're hiding, I don't blame them!"

"I'm sorry," Sherrine said again. She pointed to Gordon and Alex. "It's a question of handicapped access. If you'd like to help keep the programming on course, I'll pass your names on to Ops—"

"No thanks. We didn't come here to run errands for Bruce Hyde and his elitist gang." The costumers gathered themselves together and left in a billow of robes.

They settled into the meeting room and waited. The others dribbled in by ones and twos. Everyone behaved so furtively that Alex was sure they would draw attention to themselves. Bruce arrived grinning. "This is the one room," he announced, "where Chuck won't look for us."

Soon most of the rescue party was present. Doc (Sherrine told him) was a costumer himself and was busy on one of the panels; and Bob had to make a guest appearance at his mundane job at the University. Two strangers had joined them; Sherrine introduced them as Fang and Crazy Eddie.

Bruce rapped his chair arm with his knuckles. "Let's get this show on the road. First order of business is: What do we do with our guests, now that they are here?"

Fang tilted his head back. "Excuse me, Bruce; but let's follow form. I'm Con-Guest-of-Honor Chair, so I'd better lead this discussion."

"Find your egoboo on your own time," said Bruce. "The Con Committee rescued the Angels; so the Con Committee is in charge."

Crazy Eddie frowned. He turned to Fang. "Besides,

the Angels aren't Guests of Honor, so your subcommittee's jurisdiction—"

"Sure they're GoH's," Mike interjected. "Who could be more honored at a Worldcon than a pair of spacemen? And they *are* our guests. Ergo: Guests of Honor."

"Spoken like a faaan," said Edward Two Bats. "Can't you understand? This is big. Bigger than Worldcon." His eyes lit up, as if he had had a vision of the Holy Grail. There was a moment of hushed silence.

Alex spoke into it. "Excuse me. Do Gordon and I have any say in this?"

"No," Fang replied after a moment's thought. "You aren't convention members. You don't get a vote."

"Say, that's right," said Mike. "They haven't paid the membership fee."

"That's silly," said Thor. "I'll *lend* them the ten bucks."

"We could DUFF them," Bruce suggested. "Plenty of money in the Down Under Fan Fund."

Fang shook his head. "No, that's to help Australians come to Worldcon. You guys aren't Australians, are you?"

Gordon looked bewildered. Alex shook his head.

Mike tried to look serious. "Well, but at the moment they are Down Under."

This announcement was greeted with respectful silence. Bruce nodded his head slowly. "I like it. I like it." He rapped the arm of his chair. "They are officially the DUFF members of this convention. As Con Chair, I so rule."

Three people spoke at once. "You can't do that! We have to take a vote."

Alex sighed and closed his eyes. Do they ever *settle* anything? He breathed in through his left nostril and out through his right. It didn't help, but he was fascinated to learn he could do it, and it seemed at least as constructive as anything he was watching.

"Look," Crazy Eddie said, "this is serious!"

And yet—things were being settled. It was always a pleasure to watch a master craftsman at his job. Alex began to enjoy the way Bruce ran the meeting. Bruce played the committee the way a jazzman played his sax.

He played Mike and Fang against Eddie Two Bats and against each other. He worked subtly and indirectly, only rarely resorting to direct action. Bruce ran the show. Crazy Eddie tended to forget this every now and then, but nobody made an issue of it. Alex made a whispered comment to Sherrine.

"Bruce is good at this."

She said, "Bruce is SMOF-Three."

"A what?"

"A SMOF is a Secret Master of Fandom. Fen are a quirky and individual bunch and there aren't many who can handle them. Bruce is one. Benjamin Orange is another. Thank goodness *he* isn't here. Could you imagine two SMOFs at one con?"

Incredibly enough, he could. My God, he thought. I actually understood her.

"The first order of business," said Bruce for the fourth time in an hour, "is what do we do with the Angels."

Alex seized the opportunity. "Now that we're members of this committee—"

Fang cut him off. "Only of the Convention, not the committee. But of course as guests you can—"

"This is serious," Crazy Eddie protested. His big eyes were nearly filled with tears. "Can't you understand that?"

"You have a suggestion?" Bruce prompted.

Alex looked around helplessly. "I guess not. We can't really do anything for ourselves until we can move around better."

"Steve's helping them," Sherrine said. "Teaching them *asanas*. For older people."

"Appropriate," Alex said. "We feel old."

"It is an ancient mariner, he stoppeth one of three—" Gordon said.

"Lousy fielding average," Mike said. "No long gray beards, either."

"You have read it!" Gordon exclaimed. "Coleridge and Pushkin, no one reads any more. You have—"

Bruce bellowed, "QUIET!" For an instant the room was shocked silent.

"What's the problem anyway?" Thor asked. "We just keep them hidden until the other Angels send a ship. Then we whisk them off to the rendezvous."

"Well, sure," said Steve. "But how do we keep them hidden? And where? Here in Minneapolis? What if the pickup ship has to land in Arizona? Can we get them there in time?"

Alex glanced at Gordon, who bit his lip and lowered his eyes. *No point putting this off*, he thought. He took a deep breath—from the stomach and through the left nostril. "There won't be a pickup ship," he told the committee.

Sherrine nodded to herself. Bruce's expression didn't change.

"Why not?" Fang demanded.

"They won't come down the Well."

Everyone spoke at once. "Gravity well, Earth is deep in it." "Niven's Belters called planets 'holes.'" "Come off it, they'll come, these are ANGELS!" "I knew we needed contingency plans—"

Bruce made a whistle of his fingers. Into the silence that followed he asked, "What do you mean? The Angels won't come to get you?"

Alex looked around the circle of faces. *Angels. A sulky adolescent stilyagin and a construction worker who can't go Out anymore. Maybe I should have said to hell with it, work EVA until my brains pour out through my nose. Why not?*

"It's impossible," he said.

Sherrine nodded again, a tiny movement. "I thought so. Jesus, I'm sorry."

"But—you're space pilots," Crazy Eddie said. "They need you—"

Gordon laughed. Everyone looked at him. "What's funny?" Fang demanded.

"Alex is hero. They would come for him, but there is no way."

"They don't need me," Alex said. "And it doesn't matter anyway. There is no way for them to come get us."

"Coming down is no problem," Mike said. His voice lost the bantering tone. "Going back up—"

"Exactly," Alex said. "Going back up. We don't have any ships that will land and take off again. We never did."

Sherrine was looking at him strangely. "You knew it all along."

"There never was a time to tell you."

"Why is Alex a hero?" Edward Two Bats demanded.

"Eddie—"

"I'm a novelist, damn it! I'm not sure I ever met a hero before. Gordon?"

"Flare time," Gordon said. "Solar flares expand atmosphere. *Mir* became unstable. Major MacLeod brought a crew from *Freedom* . . ." He sensed incomprehension in the background murmur and the twisted frowns. "I start over.

"Flare on the sun. Too much energy floods day side of Earth. Top of air becomes hot. Atmosphere inflates like vast balloon, reaches far into space, wraps ghostly tendrils around *Mir. Mir Space Station*, made to fall free through vacuum, begins to slow and drift closer to Earth.

"Major MacLeod brought a crew from *Freedom*. They attached booster rockets to lift *Mir* to higher orbit without disruption. With *Mir* safe, he had to return to bolt rockets onto *Freedom*, because *Freedom* was dangered, too. His suit blew out. Had to patch it and use it again. Pressure suit, it must fit more closely than wife. Cannot borrow someone else's." Alex choked back a laugh. Gordon never noticed. "Once, twice, five times his suit spewed air. One can live through that, but not many times.

"Now he cannot go outside again. Alex MacLeod cannot live in vacuum, even short time will kill him."

"But you flew the scoopship!"

"Dipping takes a good pilot," Alex said. "I'm that. Paint stripes on a brick, I can fly it." He liked the look that Sherrine gave him. But—"Dipping wants an expendable pilot. I'm that, too. Look, everyone knew we might not come back."

"So you're here for the duration," Bruce said.

"Looks that way."

Everyone was quiet. Alex looked from face to face. It was beginning to sink in: This wasn't just a short jaunt. These ... *fans* hadn't signed on for a long haul. Pretty soon the novelty would wear off. Some already had second thoughts. *And I can't blame them.*

Sherrine put her hand on his arm. "So you volunteered knowing it might be one way."

He shook his head. "No, this is the first time like this. Usually nothing happens to dippers."

"Except sometimes they don't come back," Mike said. "Yeah, I can see it."

Sherrine hugged them, first Alex, then Gordon. "Orphans of creation," she said. "At least you're stuck among friends." Steve put a hand on each of their shoulders and squeezed gently but didn't say anything. Alex could feel the impression of Sherrine's ribs and cheekbones where she had pressed against him. *Careful,* he cautioned himself. *Sherri is Bob's girl, like Mary was Lonny's. Like borrowing another man's space suit. Look where it got you.*

Bruce looked thoughtful. "This changes things."

"Sure does," Crazy Eddie said.

"Look, I don't blame you," Alex started to say.

Bruce cut him off. "We'll have to find you both a niche here on Earth. Not going to be easy on you. We all read Heinlein's story."

" 'It's Great to Be Back,' " Sherrine said. "Yes. It must be that way. Living among the stars and then stranded on Earth."

Mike said, "First thing you need is Social Security and driver's license."

Gordon looked puzzled. "Driver license? For what, mass driver? Disk drive?"

Mike sighed. "Never mind."

"Identity papers," Alex said.

"Why do we need identity papers?" Gordon asked. "We are all droogs here, no?"

How they knew that "droog" meant "friend," Alex couldn't guess; but Mike actually smiled. "Sure, we're all droogs," he said. "Illegal droogs."

"You need an ID," said Thor, "because 'the Land of the Free and the Home of the Brave' has become 'the Land of the Fee and the Home of the Slave.' "

"Do you have ID?" Alex asked him.

He smiled. "Sure. Three or four."

"Phony?"

"Free enterprise. They're the best kind."

"Sherrine?" Bruce asked.

"Risky. It was easier when I set things up for Thor. Now they have programs to watch for hackers."

"You probably wrote them," Steve said.

"Well, Ted Marshall and I worked on the Bytehound program, and we left a backdoor in, so I can probably manage it— Sure. We can do it, maybe, but it's going to take some time at my terminal, and I have to get hold of Ted."

"He's not coming," Bruce said. "Thinks he's being watched."

"It's important we don't give him away," Crazy Eddie said.

"So we make do until then," Fang said.

"Tricky, though," Thor said.

"What is this Eye Dee?" Gordon asked. "May I see?"

Fang took out a driver's license and handed it to him. Gordon looked at it carefully, turning it over and over in his hands. He read the form on the back. "It says here consent to have organs recycled. You can refuse, then? Very rich place." He held the card up to the light. "Does not look difficult if you have photograph. You do not have scanner and laser printer?"

"No, we have those," Mike said. "Just making a card isn't the problem. Everything's cross-linked now. If we make a bogus driver's license for Alex or Gordon, the IRS computer looks into the DMV computer and wonders why they never paid taxes before." He looked at Alex.

"But it can be done," Bruce said. "Just not easy anymore."

Alex frowned. "Computers are high technology. I thought everyone down here—except you—I thought most Downers hated technology."

Thor laughed. "They hate it all right. Computers, too. But they still use them."

"For themselves," Steve said. "They don't like others having them."

"Is illegal to own computer?" Gordon frowned. "How do—how can people read what you write? Like poetry? Stories?"

"It's illegal to own an unlicensed computer," Sherrine said. "But there are a lot of licensed ones, and—well, the licensing laws are hard to enforce. So there are networks, and some private boards—"

"There are still publishers," Bruce said. "A few good books get out. And like Sherrine says, there are private boards."

"Boards?"

"Computer bulletin boards," Thor said.

"People exchange files. Not so common as they used to be, now that the phone system keeps crashing. But FAPA is still going," Sherrine said.

"I was in line for full membership in the Cult until I had to drop for missing deadlines," Fang said. "But Bruce is—"

"And disks are harder to get," Mike said. "But I still manage to publish *File 880* . . ."

"He's won twelve Hugos," Fang said.

For one glorious minute I thought I understood them—
Crazy Eddie raised his hand and waved it. "I've got an idea."

Bruce looked worried, but nodded at him. "The Chair recognizes Eddie Two Bats."

Crazy Eddie stood and looked across his blade-like nose. "There are still technophiles in Southern California," he said. "Enclaves clustered around the old, defunct aerospace centers. I say we take the Angels there."

There were nods of agreement. "Makes sense," said Steve. "Angels would be welcomed there. Some places."

"That's right, you still live down there," Fang said. "Do you ever get to the Denny's on—"

Bruce tapped his ring on the desk. "Edward Two Bats has the floor."

"I bet it would work!" Sherrine said.

Crazy Eddie nodded vigorously. "Damned straight! Then, after building our strength, we stage a coup! Take over in Sacramento, install the Angels as symbolic governors, and devote the State's resources to building a space shuttle to take them home again."

"So the question is how to get them to California," Bruce said.

"The Angels have to go underground," Fang said. "Work off the books. Doesn't pay so well as out front, but with no taxes you keep more, and nobody checks ID and credit cards." He and Thor exchanged glances. "It ain't so bad."

For a moment Alex felt panic. Then he realized that they took the good parts of Crazy Eddie's ideas and simply ignored the rest. *And we don't have many choices anyway.* "You're used to living underground," Sherrine said. "They're not. Look at them! No, I'll do something—"

"The Greens lynched a hacker in Chicago," Mike said carefully. "Last month, but I think the body's still hanging from the old Water Tower. Of course you know that."

"That was Flash. Flash couldn't resist letting his friends know what he did. So I'm more careful, that's all," Sherrine said.

"No, we can't let you risk that," Alex said. "I mean—"

"Work underground, off books," Mike said. "Great. What can you do?"

Alex grunted. "I fly spaceships."

Bruce grinned. "Right. We'll send out your resume. But what did you do between flights?"

"I write poetry," Gordon said. "I would like to write science fiction."

"So would everyone here," Steve said. "Do you know how many people make a living writing science fiction? There weren't thirty in the whole country, at *peak*. Now, none."

"There's Harry Bean—" someone said.

"He's a whore. He writes for the Greens," Bruce said. "Odd jobs. Alex? What can you do besides fly ships?"

"Construction engineer." He looked at his emaciated

limbs. "And if Steve's right, I'll be able to do that again in about nine years."

"He is also teacher," Gordon said.

"Kindergarten. I was a day-care father," Alex admitted. The main advantage of the truth was that you didn't have to remember a lot of details. There were other advantages, too, he supposed.

Sherrine looked at him closely. *Now she knows*.

Thor shook his head. "Too bad. They do background checks on day-care workers, ever since the witch hunts. Even the centers who pay 'off the books' have to be careful. Lot of work for Sherrine, and you sure can't do that until she sets it up."

In the lengthy silence that followed, everyone looked at each other, but no one said anything. Finally Sherrine sighed.

"I'm not sure I can do it," she said. "Thor's right, they're paranoid about child molesters. I'd have to build you a whole history, everything, traffic tickets, education— Look, it won't work. We can't fit them in, and we can't hide them." Fang and Thor started to object, but Sherrine overrode them. "We've just been over that. Short term, sure; but sooner or later they'd be discovered. No, there's only one option, and it took Crazy Eddie to find it. We've got to find a way to get them back into space."

"We?" said Bruce.

"Sure, Fandom!"

Mike beamed. "Of course. We'll get them high with illegal droogs."

CHAPTER SEVEN

"Black Powder and Alcohol . . ."

"You're going to send us back to space," Alex said.

"Perhaps I don't wish to go," Gordon said.

"Shut up. Look, with all great respect, how do you propose to do this? As far as I know, the only rockets left on Earth are military missiles." *And I can't see sticking one up my arse and riding it out—*

"Exactly! We hide out until we build strength and take over in Sacramento. Then—"

"There's a Saturn Five in Houston." Fang asked, "Will that do?"

Alex blinked and tried to sit up. "Saturn? Damn right. With a Saturn we could reach the moon. But—I didn't know there were any left."

"There aren't," Bruce said. "NASA took a full man-rated Saturn and laid it down as a monument. Alex, that bird will never fly again."

"Oh."

"It's right in front of the old Manned Space Center," Mike said. "Leetle hard to work on without attracting attention."

106

"Could steal it," Crazy Eddie said.

Bruce closed his eyes. "Steal it, Eddie? Do you know how *big* those suckers were?"

"Three hundred and sixty three feet high. Weighed three kilotons."

Bruce spoke patiently. "And you say we should steal it?"

"If we could round up enough pickup trucks," Eddie Two Bats said thoughtfully. "Of course it will be hard to stand it up again. I think we need an engineer."

"I see how it works," Alex said quietly to Sherrine.

"How?"

"It's Crazy Eddie's job to come up with nutty ideas, and Bruce's job to chop him down. Do any of Eddie's notions ever work?"

She shrugged.

"I could cry."

She frowned. "Over Crazy Eddie?"

"No, the rocket. The Saturn Five was the most powerful rocket ever built—Sherrine, it was the most powerful *machine* ever made!"

"A fire in the sky," she said. "I know the song."

"And now it's a lawn ornament."

"I'm sorry," she said. "Monument! They didn't want any competition for the shuttle. They even tried to burn the blueprints—"

"It wasn't your fault."

"I know that, but I'm sorry. Sorry that anyone could ever have been so stupid. And that was NASA! We gave the space program to NASA, and they, and . . . Damn."

"Does anyone else have an idea?" Bruce asked. "No? Then we carry on as before. The fewer who know about the Angels, the safer they'll be. Don't tell anyone without consulting me. The cover is that they're closet fans from North Dakota, people Fang and Thor have known for years. All agreed? Good. So ordered. Do I hear a motion to adjourn? Meeting is adjourned. Next meeting is in Hawkeye's room about nine. Now it's time to enjoy the convention."

☆   ☆   ☆

The room had perhaps been a small ballroom when the house was new. Now it looked crowded despite its size. There were windows along one wall, with couches under them. The window sills were covered with brick-a-brack, photos of people in odd costumes, strangely painted coffee mugs, vases that held improbable plants. That fur rug, patterned in yellow and orange, was neither the shape nor the colors of any of Earth's life forms. A grand piano stood down at one end of the room. It was covered with photographs and paintings and drawings and plastic objects. Books lined two of the walls, and the spaces between the large archways set into the fourth wall.

A large bear of a man with a sunburst of hair encircling his face stood next to the grand piano, one hand resting on it. He was making a speech, and his free hand waved in time with his words. Other people were talking, too, which seemed impolite.

The man stopped in midsentence when Sherrine and Thor wheeled the Angels into the room. People looked around and opened a path, some of those on the floor moving aside, some standing to move chairs, until Alex and Gordon were moved right up front near the speaker. The others moved back again. It looked choreographed.

"See you," Thor said. He seemed in a hurry to leave.

The speaker was in no hurry at all. He struck a pose, as if waiting for something.

Ritual? Alex wondered. Whatever. *Pavana mukthasan* could be practiced as easily in a wheelchair as elsewhere. Alex used both hands to bend his right leg and tuck it into his crotch against the pubic bone. Then he folded his left leg and laid it atop the right. He made circles of his thumbs and index fingers and rested his hands on his knees. He breathed in slowly through his left nostril, repeating the syllable *yam* six times. He wondered when Steve would graduate him to *siddhasan*, or even *padmasan*. Anything was better than the *savasam* "corpse position" he had practiced in the van during the ride across Minnesota. He hadn't known that relaxing was such hard work; but according to Steve, the first order of business was to make his muscles stop *fighting* the gravity.

Gregory Lutenist cleared his throat. "The Thirty-Sixth Ice Age," he said formally. His voice was strong, easily heard throughout the room.

Alex breathed in. *Yam*, he thought to himself. *Yammm*.

"We live in an ice age—" began Gregory Lutenist. When he got to the words "ice age" three people had joined him, speaking in unison with him. Then came a voice from the crowd: "No shit!"

"—and we always have," he continued, imperturbably adjusting his glasses. "During the last seven hundred thousand years there have been eight cycles of cooling and warming. The glaciers retreat, but always they come back; and the warm, interglacial interludes last for only about ten thousand years. Since Ice Age Thirty-Five ended fourteen thousand years ago, the next one must have started four thousand years ago. Most of human history has been lived in an ice age. So why did no one notice?"

"It was too warm!" someone suggested.

Lutenist beamed at him. "Just so. It's hard to convince a man in Bermuda shorts that he's living in an ice age. But consider the halcyon, interglacial world of 4500 BC!" He waved a forefinger in the air.

"In Scandinavia the tree line was above 8000 feet." Three voices again joined him, speaking in unison, as Lutenist continued. "And deciduous trees grew all the way to the Arctic circle. The Sahara was a rain-watered, grassy savannah crossed by mighty rivers and even mightier hunters. We remember that age dimly as a Garden in Eden." Lutenist paused and removed his glasses. He polished the lenses and set them back upon his nose. He paused, sighed, and said, slowly, so that everyone in the room could join in, "But then the sun went out."

Gordon looked to Alex. "*Shto govorit*'? The man is mad, the sun has not gone out."

Lutenist beamed at Gordon. "Ah—"

"Fresh meat!" someone yelled.

"Tell me, my young friend," Lutenist said. "What lights up the sun?"

"Is trick? Fusion. Hydrogen to helium."

"And when the fusion ends, what then?" Lutenist asked.

"Uh—but how can fusion end? There is plenty of hydrogen."

"But it did end," Lutenist said. "And no one noticed."

Bob Needleton stuck his head in between Alex and Gordon. "Where have all the neutrinos gone? Long time passing . . ." He gave Sherrine a quick kiss on the neck.

"Hi, Pins," Alex said. "Welcome back."

"I didn't want to miss Greg's spiel." Bob cupped his hands around his mouth. "There'll be a neutrino scavenger hunt tonight after the program," he announced. "Bring your snipe bags and your Chlorine-37 tanks." The audience responded with boos and catcalls. Lutenist waved to him and Bob waved back. "Hi, Greg. Still thumping the same old drum, I see."

"Excuse me," Gordon said, "but what means spiel about neutrinos?"

Bob pulled a chair up and set it beside Sherrine between the two wheelchairs. He straddled it backwards. "It's simple really."

Alex braced himself. When a physicist says, "it's simple," it usually meant it was time to duck.

"You see, when two protons fuse into a deuterium nucleus they yield a neutrino. There are two ways that can happen, but . . . Well, the details don't matter. Sometimes the deuterium hip-hops through beryllium into lithium and spits out another neutrino, and there are a couple of other reactions that also produce neutrinos; but that's about the gist of it. Fusion spits neutrinos. Get it?"

Gordon looked puzzled. "I get. So?"

Bob held his hands out palms up. "The problem is we never found the neutrinos. A Chlorine-37 detector should register a neutrino flux of eight snew, but all they ever get is two snew."

Gordon's frown deepened. "What's 'snew'?"

Sherrine hid her face in her hands. Bob said, "I dunno, not much. What's snew with you?"

"Thank you for sharing that with us—"

"Sorry, I've never been able to resist that one. Snew is SNU, Solar Neutrino Units. One snew is one neutrino event per 10^{36} atoms per second."

There was a commotion at the other end of the room. A dozen fans, maybe more, came in. "Is this the pro party?"

"Hey," Lutenist said. "I'm not through."

A large man in a bush jacket waved a salute with a bottle of beer. "Go right ahead, Greg. Don't mind us."

"What's up?" Lutenist demanded.

The man shrugged. "Con Committee said to come here, this will be the 'Meet the Pros' party."

"Aw crap," Lutenist said. "This is my lecture!"

"What's to lecture?" Needleton demanded. "It was all simple, and known before 1980. The sun is not producing enough neutrinos. *Ergo*, it is not fusing. Yet, according to the technetium levels in deep molybdenum mines there were plenty of neutrinos passing through the Earth during interglacial and preglacial periods."

"Excuse me, Bob," said Gregory Lutenist, "are you leading this discussion or am I?"

Bob waved a hand. "Sorry, Greg. Go ahead." In a near-whisper, "Gordon, it's a cycle. Fusion stops, the sun cools a bit, shrinks a bit, the core gets denser and hotter, fusion starts again, the new warmth inflates the sun. See? Is that a relief, or what?"

"Maunder Minimum!" someone shouted.

Lutenist beamed. "The sun goes through sunspot cycles. Lots of sunspots, it gets warm here. Few sunspots, colder weather. An astronomer named Maunder recorded sunspots and found that the last time there weren't *any* the planet went through what was known as the Little Ice Age, the Maunder Minimum." He paused dramatically. "And in the 1980s it became certain that the planet was going into a new Maunder Minimum period."

"Yes, yes, we know this," Gordon said. "Sunspots are important to us. But if so important to Earth, why do they not know cold is coming?"

"Bastards did," the man in the bush jacket growled. "But they said Global Warming."

"Grants," Bob said. "There's money in climate studies. All the Ph.D. theses. All that would go if things were so simple—"

A short blond woman, slender by local standards, came in with a large tray. She carried it up to the piano as if thinking to set it down there, looked at the clutter, turned helplessly— "Ah. You're Gabe?"

He smiled and nodded. She said, "Laurie. Hold this while we get a table." She set the tray across the arms of his wheelchair and was gone.

It was covered with small dishes, each with a couple of slices of vegetables. Cucumber, carrot, a bit of lettuce, some cabbage. A stalk of broccoli. Alex felt his mouth begin to water. Fresh vegetables! Of course the people here would be used to them—

Bob Needleton stopped talking about neutrinos and stared at the tray. He gave a long, low whistle. "Dibs on a carrot stick!"

Gregory Lutenist said, "Broccoli for me. Now. It is important to realize that the sun has always burned hotter or cooler during different eras of our planet's history. Greenhouse or Icehouse."

A fan spoke up. "Carrot for me, too. The dinosaurs lived during a greenhouse era, didn't they?"

A voice spoke from the doorway. "Pros get first choice. This is the Meet the Readers Party, right?"

Lutenist nodded as if there had been no interruption. "Dinosaurs, and the Great Mammals, too. In fact, prior to the Pleistocene the world was quite warm. Hippopotami wallowed in the Thames."

He paused a moment. When he continued, half a dozen voices spoke in unison with him. "Then, in the blink of a geological eye, they were replaced by polar bears."

Lutenist beamed.

Alex looked to Sherrine. "What—"

She laughed. "Some of us have heard Gregory before."

Cucumbers, celery, carrots, luxuries beyond his wildest dreams were cradled in Alex's arms. He couldn't eat; he had to share this with the whole room; and he couldn't get his hands on any of it without dropping the tray. Little dark red spheres, little bright red spheres with white inside, were displayed on big green leaves. Where were they with that damn table?

Badges were showing on various chests. Here were tiny oil paintings of alien creatures and landscapes and starscapes, or wheel-shaped and band-shaped artificial habitats infinitely more sophisticated than *Mir* and *Freedom*. A few badges bore angular cartoon faces and elegant calligraphy: CLOSET MUNDANE. KNOWS HARLAN ELLISON (evil smirk). HAS READ MUCH OF DHALGREN (bewilderment).

Lutenist continued. "Human history is so short that, living between the hippopotamus and the polar bear, we thought those conditions were 'normal.'

"After the sun went out, the interglacial ended and the world grew colder and drier. The Sahara rivers dried up, one by one, until only the Nile was left. By 1500 BC, the Scandinavian tree line had dropped to six thousand feet, and broad-leaf trees had disappeared from the Arctic.

"The weather changed. The North African coast was the breadbasket of the Roman Empire. It began to dry up. up. Great migrations began, Huns, Arabs, Navajos, Mongols. There were Viking colonies on Greenland, but the Greenland Glacier began to move south, until it covered them all."

"Tell you another one," the man in the bush jacket said.

"Go ahead, Wade," Lutenist said.

Sherrine looked around. "Wade Curtis. A pro."

"Writer?" Gordon asked. She nodded.

Curtis's voice boomed even in the large room. "In the American Revolutionary War, Colonel Alexander Hamilton brought cannon captured by Ethan Allen at Ticonderoga down to assist General Washington in Haarlem Heights. He brought them across the ice on the frozen Hudson River. By the twentieth century, the Hudson didn't freeze at all, let alone hard enough to carry cannon on!"

Lutenist smiled agreement. "Right! The Little Ice Age was coming to an end! In fact, a warming trend had started around 1200, and lasted for eight centuries. Anyone know why?"

"Hey, let's eat!" someone called.

"Let him finish," Curtis growled. He drained his beer. A bearded man behind him silently handed him another.

Lutenist stabbed a hand into the air. "Why?"

Someone in the audience responded. "Because a farmer doesn't give up his land."

"That's right, Beth. Farmers! Hunters run, which is what our ancestors did during the Thirty-Fifth Ice Age. But the five hundred million settled and civilized humans of the thirteenth century were not going to pull up stakes and move elsewhere. London, Copenhagen, even Moscow were too valuable to abandon. So what did they do?" He paused and stared around the audience.

Several responded in unison. "They threw another log on the fire!"

Lutenist beamed. "Exactly! They fought the cold with heat, soot and CO_2. Air pollution!"

"Smudge pots," Curtis growled.

"Right," Lutenist shouted. "Smudge pots! Greenhouse effect!"

"*Pollution, poll-ooo-tion,*" someone sang.

Everyone shouted. "Jenny! And Harry!"

"The moonbeam's here!"

Alex painfully twisted around to see. The two people who came in through the archway were matched in clothes and height, but in nothing else. The man was enormous, broad of shoulders, large of chest, and much larger of belly. He wore a battered slouch hat, and an oil-stained denim jacket. His boots clumped on the floor. Over one shoulder was slung a huge guitar case. In his hands he carried two nylon bags that clinked as he walked. He set the bags down and opened one, took out a jar, opened it and sipped at the clear liquid. "Finest corn squeezin's Kansas ever produced!" He handed the jar to Curtis.

The woman called Jenny was as tall as Harry, but thin. Her skin might have been leather. Her hair was long and straight, and dead silver-gray. The eyes burned brightly out of the wrinkles. She carried a guitar, but she wasn't playing it. "*Don't drink the water, and don't breathe the air!*" she sang.

Mike got up from his place on the floor. "We'd given up on you two," he said.

"Bike broke down in Wyoming," Jenny said. "Had to sing for our suppers. Some things you can't sing, though . . ."

Harry struck a chord. "*It's minus ten and counting, and time is passing fast, it's minus ten and counting—*"

"O God, don't," Curtis said. The room was still for a moment.

"Yeah," Jenny said. "And you can't sing 'A Fire in the Sky'—"

An older man went over to her and eyed her belligerently. "I know you. Jenny Trout."

"We do NOT use real names," Jenny said.

"You're a goddamned feminist," the man insisted. "What the hell are you doing here—"

He was interrupted by Wade Curtis, who roared with laughter. "Adams, you know Jenny! Sure, the feminists won, they're running the government along with—God almighty. But think about it, she's too damn much anarchist to be inside the government! Any government. Even a Green-Feminist government."

"I'm no goddam Green," Jenny said.

"Sorry." Curtis actually sounded apologetic. "Anyway—"

"Anyway, Adams," Harry said, "she knows who her friends are. So do I. Have a jug of corn. Real moonbeams."

"Jenny likes to feel wanted," Fang said. "She's not comfortable unless she's wanted by the law."

Jenny grinned, and sang,

"*Wanted fan in Luna City, wanted fan on Dune and Down,*
Wanted fan at Ophiuchus, wanted fan in Dydeetown.
All across the sky they want me, am I flattered? Yes I am!
If I could just reach orbit, then I'd be a wanted fan."

". . . and in the midst of the Thirty-Sixth Ice Age, we were lighting global smudge pots. Wood-burning during the Middle Ages was so intensive that the forests of Europe were actually smaller than in the twentieth century. Coal-burning, which began in the fifteenth century, saved the forests and put even more gunk into the air. By the late nineteenth century, most homes were heated by coal furnaces." Lutenist paused and rubbed his hands together, as if imagining heat vents and radiators.

A line had formed. Veggies disappeared as they moved past Alex. Almost everyone who passed put something in Alex's mouth. Dark red was miniature tomatoes; Alex feared the implications. The red-and-white spheroid burned.

Jenny sang,

> *"Wanted fan for mining coal and wanted fan for drilling oil,*
> *I went very fast through Portland, hunted hard like Gully Foyle.*
> *Built reactors in Seattle against every man's advice,*
> *Couldn't do that in Alaska, Fonda says it isn't nice."*

"Nice touch, Jenny. They'll be expecting you to rhyme it with 'ice.' "

"You don't really think the nukes could have saved Alaska, do you, Jenny?"

Alaska had been beneath the Ice for fifteen years.

". . . Then, beginning in the 1950s, we began to clean up our environment. Household coal furnaces gave way to centralized electric heating; and pollution was confined to the power plant areas, instead of belching from every chimney in the city. The famous pea-soup fogs of London disappeared."

Lutenist smiled wanly. "But so did the warm, rainy British winters. Heavy winters became the norm. In 1984 and '85 several campers froze to death when a blizzard struck the Riviera. Atlanta, Georgia, had a week of zero temperatures. Winter snow became common in the southlands. Meanwhile, the Sahara resumed its southward march and Ukrainian grain harvests became less and less reliable. Raindrops need tiny particles around which to condense. So, when you eliminate air pollution, what happens?"

"Less rain!" cried the audience.

"And less cloud cover means the ground loses heat faster. And that means?"

"The Great Ice!"

"Ice day is a'comin'," Jenny and Harry sang softly. *"Hey sinner man, where you gonna run to—"* It made a nice background, now, for Gregory's litany.

"Yes, my friends." Lutenist was walking back and forth in front of the piano. "The elimination of air pollution did not start with the Greens. It started with the Big Power Companies back in the fifties—as a by-product of their program of clean, centralized electrical power generation. But it accelerated with the environmentalist movement. Soon, we were not allowed to burn the leaves we raked off our yards. We had to bag them, in plastic bags, of course! And have them hauled away by trucks to landfills hundreds of miles away. The Green Laws became more and more stringent at the same time that interest in and support for science was waning—not a coincidence, I might add. Even today, with the Great Ice and the Sahara both sliding south, we are not allowed to throw another log on the fire!"

"Damned good thing!" Jenny Trout shouted.

Everyone looked at her.

"It's got to fall," she said. "All the way. *We don't like this world we made! Bring it down! Bring it down!"*

Harry had taken out his guitar. He struck a chord.

"Black powder and alcohol, when your states and cities fall, when your back's against the wall—"

Alex shuddered.

CHAPTER EIGHT

"... Someone's Daydream"

The Phantom of the Paradise leaped out of the TV screen, as the audience, as always, made helpful comments. Sherrine pretended to watch as her thoughts leaped more wildly than the masked phantom.

Sending the Angels home wouldn't be simple even if they had a ship. Some of it she could do. With Bob to analyze the ballistics she ought to be able to write the code. Some would be tougher. Fuel. They'd have to steal that.

First things first. Without a ship, everything else was moot.

Bob came into the lounge. Had he followed her? When he waved at her and headed in her direction, she sighed.

He was wearing his Rotsler badge. A cartoon face studied the SS ROBERT K. NEEDLETON and thought, "Pretentious." The sharp nose partly covered the letters. Bob dropped beside her on the sofa, just close enough to be within her personal space, and put an arm on the back of the sofa behind her. He leaned close to her ear. "Any ideas yet?"

He certainly had ideas. A couple of fen sitting nearby grinned at her. *Oh, Ghu!* she thought. *After tonight, everyone will think we're back together.*

To some men, "no" meant "maybe" and "maybe" meant "yes." She hadn't seen Bob in two months; now she couldn't get rid of him. He was cheerfully impervious to her rebuffs; as if he were not programmed to accept the data. Like Halley's Comet, no matter how shaken up he was at each encounter, he kept coming back. Only he didn't wait seventy-six years.

Not that he was unattractive. He had been among her better lovers, back in the days when she hung out with the spa set. And maybe she only needed to get used to him again. He had known how to do things in a hot tub that ... For that matter, he knew how to talk *with* a woman, not simply at her. He had been as interested in hearing about her computer work—about LISP and LAN's and baud rates—as he was in telling her about his physics. There was only one thing he seemed incapable of understanding.

And that was endings.

Bob was a romantic. Most men were. They thought that a relationship had a beginning and a middle, but no end. Danny, the time traveller in *The Man Who Folded Himself,* had made that mistake. He kept going back and going back, trying to rekindle the romance with Donna; until finally he had kindled disgust and revulsion in her. The secret was to quit while you were at the top; go out like a champion and not fade into an object of pity like a has-been fighter who couldn't quit the ring.

She didn't want that to happen between her and Bob. She liked him too much. So keep it neutral. Keep it professional.

"You know, that Gordon is kind of cute," she said. And how was that for a neutral, professional remark?

His arm made an aborted move toward her shoulder. "Oh?"

"Yes." She spoke in a whisper. "Not just his background

—a space pilot, by Ghu!—but the way he looks. His facial bones and his little potbelly. And his puppy-dog eyes. He always seems so sad and withdrawn, it makes me want to cuddle him and cheer him up."

"Umm. I'm feeling a little sad and withdrawn myself," Bob said hopefully.

She slapped him backfingered on the arm. "Oh, you know what I mean. He seems so lonely, cut off forever from his home and his friends."

"It was his fault they were marooned, you know."

"What?" She had raised her voice slightly and someone sitting in a nearby chair shushed her. She lowered her voice and leaned closer to Bob. Bob helped her do that. "What do you mean?"

"He told me so himself." Bob whispered into her ear as if they were necking; and she flashed back to three nights ago, when he had woken her from the sleep of the innocent to recruit her into the Rescue Party. A good cover, he had said, in case anyone was listening. Yeah, a damned good cover. He probably thought of it himself. "This morning, when I brought them breakfast ... Doc had taken 'Gabe' into the washroom to, uh, well, help him ... you know."

"Yeah. Go on."

"Well, once we were alone, the kid let it all spill out. It seems that during the missile attack, he shouted out a warning in Russian and Alex didn't understand until too late; and that's why they were hit."

"Oh, no! It must be terrible to have to live with that."

Bob shrugged. "He's young. He'll get over it. That's the wonderful thing about being young. The point is, the kid—"

She never learned what Bob's point was. Chuck Umber burst into the room waving a folded-up newspaper in the air. "Angels down!" he announced and flipped the lights on. "A scoopship went down on the Ice yesterday!" He shut off the VCR player.

"Hey!" someone shouted. "Turn the *Phantom* back on."

"No, wait! Look at this." Chuck opened the paper to

the front page and held it up. AIR THIEVES CRASH ON ICE, screamed the headline. He had a bundle of newspapers under his arm and began passing them out.

A storm of voices greeted him. "What? Where?" "How'd it happen?" "Are the Angels okay?" "How come we're just hearing about it?" "Turn the *Phantom* back on."

Bob leaned into her ear. "That tears it," he whispered. "How long before someone figures things out?" Sherrine grabbed a copy of the paper from Chuck as he went by and flipped it open. She and Bob huddled over it. She scanned the story quickly, as much to learn what hadn't been said as to learn what had. It wouldn't do to show too much familiarity with the story.

The newspaper report was reasonably straightforward, a bit long on loaded adjectives and short on detail, but not much worse than the usual news. There was no mention of what had happened to the Angels. A sidebar, entitled DEATH RAYS FROM OUTER SPACE, told of "beams of deadly microwaves aimed at the search parties" and cautioned the reader that "microwaves are a form of radiation, which causes cancer."

Sherrine pointed. "Nice placement on the comma."

Bob just shook his head. "You'd think they'd know the difference between ionizing and non-ionizing radiation. They can't tell one type of asbestos from the other, either."

"Why do you think they don't know the difference?"

He looked at her for a moment. Then he grunted, "You're a worse pessimist than I am," and turned back to the reading. "The 'danes really think the microwaves were aimed at the search parties," he said. "They don't see it as a decoy maneuver."

A shadow fell across the paper. "What makes you think the microwaves were decoys?"

Sherrine looked up and saw Chuck Umber. Bob opened his mouth to speak and thought better of it. Sherrine said, "Just listen, Chuck." She shook the paper and folded it. "'As is so often the case when people rely on computers, none of the death rays actually struck the search parties.'" She gave Chuck a twisted smile. "Chuck, they tell the public that computers are unreliable—"

"Trust the Farce, Luke," Bob interjected.

"—but do you swallow that? If the Angels didn't hit anyone, it means they weren't *aiming* at anyone. Can you think of any other reason why they'd divert part of the power beam from Winnipeg?"

Chuck pursed his lips and presently nodded. "If the targeting system snafued ... No, you're probably right. The microwaves were meant to hide the scoopship's IR footprint. Damnation!" He ground one fist into his palm. "I wish some of us had been there. We'd've gotten the Angels off the Ice before the Government grabbed 'em."

It was a moment before Sherrine found her voice. "Yeah, Chuck. Too bad." She ducked back behind the newspaper.

More people were pouring into the lounge. Dick Wolfson ejected the video cartridge and turned on the all-news channel. "C'mon," someone cried, "it was just getting to the good part, where Beef gets electrocuted." Sherrine thought it must be Dennis, the comics artist who had created *The Niki Birds*. It was said that you could play a contraband copy of *The Phantom of the Paradise* anywhere in the country and Dennis would be there in time for the ending.

"Settle down, everyone!" roared a bull voice. "Let's hear what the 'danes have to say."

The lounge quieted as the fans concentrated on the tube. The impeccably groomed newsreader recited several items of war news. Swedish marines had forced a landing on the Pomeranian coast; but their Russo-Lithuanian allies had suffered a stunning defeat at Ukranian hands. No one had used nukes, yet; but the world was holding its breath.

Must be near the beginning of the headline cycle, Sherrine thought. She felt mildly offended that the Angels were not the top story. *Let's get to the Angels.*

When the next story turned out to be a presidential photo opportunity, she almost screamed.

Finally, the screen displayed a shot of *Piranha* embedded in the ice. "This update on the forced landing of the air scooper from the space habitats. Scoopships are built to steal air from the Earth and take it to the space stations. Many experts blame the cold weather we are having on the loss of this air. Air Defense forced the latest scoopship to land in North Dakota."

The scene moved past the anchorman to a long shot of the glacier looking down the landing path toward the ship. "Experts now believe that the spacemen escaped from the glacier using inappropriate technology."

Bob snorted. "Inappropriate? It worked!"

"Hush, and listen," said Sherrine.

" ... the efforts of the space stations to stop the search with death rays. Meanwhile, the public should be on the lookout for possibly two illegal aliens believed to be on the loose."

Sherrine blinked at the *artist's conception of spacemen*. The spectrally thin creatures in the sketch looked like famine victims who had been stretched upon a rack. Someone in the room snickered. Others applauded.

"The aliens are believed to be very tall because of the unnatural environment they live in. But, because they live in zero gravity—"

"Free fall, damn it; not zero gravity!" That sounded like Wade Curtis.

"—must be extremely strong, as well ..." Onscreen, stock footage from the construction of SUNSAT showed an astronaut handling an enormous solar collector panel. ". . . so citizens are advised to be cautious."

Sherrine did not know who was advising the government searchers, but they could not have helped the Angels more if they had tried. The exaggerated height and leanness, the misinterpretation of the effect of free fall on body strength . . .

The ruling coalition of proxmires, rifkins, falwells and maclaines scorned "the materialist science story." As if there were another kind of science; as if it were something invented, like myth, to be discarded when a better "story" came along. It was hardly surprising that the government had not sought out scientific opinion.

Or had they? Hah! What if they'd asked a closet fan? For that matter the scientists themselves, the pariahs of academe, might not volunteer to educate the very people who shunned them. Sometimes you *want* an opponent to go on sounding like a fool.

S-s-sooo . . . She grinned and hugged Bob, who seemed surprised and not unpleased. Why, the Angels were nearly home free! If people were looking for emaciated supermen, they wouldn't look twice at Gabe and Rafe.

Harry and Jenny began a song.

> "In a tower of flame in Capsule Twelve,
> I was there.
> I know not where they laid my bones,
> it could be anywhere,
> but when fire and smoke had faded,
> the darkness left my sight,
> I found my soul in a spaceship's soul
> riding home on a trail of light.
>
> "For my wings are made of tungsten,
> and my flesh is glass and steel,
> I am the joy of Terra for the power that I wield.
> Once upon a lifetime, I died a pioneer,
> Now I sing within a spaceship's heart,
> Does anybody hear?"

"Anyone having knowledge of the whereabouts of the air pirates should call the police. Do not approach them, they are armed and dangerous."

"We have to do something." A man's voice. Crying.

"What?"

"I don't know, I don't know, but we have to do something—"

"It's too late, by twenty years."

"My thunder rends the morning sky,
yes, I am here.
The loss to flame when I was man,
now I ride her without fear,
for I am more than man now,
and man built me with pride,
I led the way and I lead the way
to man's future in the sky.

"For my wings are made of tungsten,
my flesh of glass and steel,
I am the joy of Terra for the power that I wield.
Once upon a lifetime, I died a pioneer,
Now I sing within a spaceship's heart,
Does anybody hear?
Does anybody hear?"

The song faded out, and the room was quiet, except for Curtis, who stared at the wall and muttered over and over, "God damn them. We were so near. God damn them all."

The room spouted a geyser of talk when the newsreader finished. Most of the fen chattered excitedly to each other; but Sherrine noticed a few thoughtful faces. Chuck Umber was busily scribbling in a pocket notebook. Wade Curtis was sunk into himself, elbows on knees and chin in hands, mouth slack, eyes hooded . . . eyes touched Sherrine's, wandered away, wandered back . . .

Drunk. Can't say I blame him.

"Come on," said Bob, rising from the sofa and tugging her arm. "We've got to tell the others."

She pulled him back down. "I think they already know. Quiet. I want to hear what gets said here."

"This crowd? Why?"

"Ideas. That's what fen are for."

Someone in the room spoke through the din. "What are we going to do about it?"

The chatter died down. "Do? What can we do?"

Chuck Umber took center stage. "Look," he said, "the 'danes say that the Angels escaped. Well, they sure didn't escape on their own. They had to have had help. We've got to find out who's got them and offer to help."

"Maybe the Eskimos have them," Horowitz suggested. "The paper says that there were tracks around the scooper."

"It doesn't matter," Chuck replied. "We'll find out who has them, sooner or later."

Bob tried to sink down lower in the sofa. Sherrine's pressure on his elbow stopped him.

"Maybe we shouldn't try to contact them, Chuck," said Dick Wolfson. "Whoever's got the Angels might have to hide them for a long time. The fewer people who know who and where, the better."

Chuck shook his head. "Not when the people are fen. I'm going to try and reach the Oregon Ghost. He must know something."

"Sure, Chuck. The Ghost runs his own fanzine. You think he'd let a competitor in on whatever scoop he has?"

Chuck stood up taller. "He will. Because this is the biggest thing to hit fandom since *Star Wars* ... or Apollo Thirteen. We've got to transcend factions and feuds and pull together."

Harry and Jenny had started a song, singing softly as background as the others talked. " ... *and he knew he might not make it, for it's never hard to die, but he rode her into history, on a fire in the sky!*"

Wade Curtis uncurled and stretched and said, "They can't hide them."

There was an instant hush when the writer spoke.

Drunk or sober, the hard science fiction writers were supposed to know everything. Fans laughed at them when they made mistakes, but always listened ... and Wade Curtis had a voice that filled every corner.

"Whoever it is, they can't hide the Angels forever. Think it through. No, there's only one thing to do, get the Angels back where they belong. God damn NASA. Where *we all* belong. God damn them, they ate the

dream. For money. For money. The Angels belong up
there. We have to send them back."

"That's crazy." "No, Wade's right." "Hell, he's drunk."
"Wouldn't you be?" "But how?" "They'll need a rocket."
"Where can you find a rocket these days?"

Sherrine clenched Bob's upper arm so hard he winced.
Yes! Yes, where can you find a rocket? She leaned forward, to hear better.

Wade laughed. "The nearest rocket I know of is Ron
Cole's Titan."

Chuck and some of the other older fen laughed, too. A
younger fan spoke up. "What Titan is that?"

Wade flipped a hand. Someone put a drink in it. "Old
fannish legend has it that Ron once cobbled a Titan Two
together from spare parts he bought from government
surplus sales. Cost him less than a thousand dollars, too.
He was on the Board of Trustees for the Metropolitan
Museum of Boston. He wanted it for an exhibit, of
course. The Boston papers caught him trying to get the
motors through the doors. They ran an article calling him
'the world's sixth nuclear power.'"

Sherrine clenched and unclenched her fists. *But where
is it now?* She dared not draw attention to herself. But a
Titan! Titans had lifted the Gemini capsules into orbit.

Chuck laughed. "I remember that article, Wade. Boy,
was Ron mad! He tried to tell the papers that he did *not*
have a nuclear warhead; but you know how 'danes are.
Rockets equals missiles equals weapons equals nukes.
Sometimes I wonder if Ron didn't go ahead and build a
bomb just for the hell of it. As long as everyone thought
he had one . . ."

"Building a warhead isn't as easy as the 'danes think. I
don't care how many TV movies they show with terror-
ists and mad scientists whipping 'em up in their garage.
Uranium hexafloride isn't just radioactive, it's toxic as
hell. Refining U-235 is not something you can do in your
garage; not without an ample supply of disposable terror-
ists," Wade said wistfully.

Chuck ran his fingers through his goatee. "Still, if
anyone could do it, Cole could. He always had something

wonderful in his pocket. A laboratory opal, a big chunk of artificial sapphire for armor, a couple of strips of platinum—"

"Platinum?"

"I never knew why. Some failed project. And once he typed a guy a check on a sheet of soft gold. The first check bounced, see—"

"Not Ron," Wade insisted. "Not a bomb. He *knows* better. But I did hear that he squirreled away a couple of tank cars of RP-1 and LOX. Just in case he decided to take a trip." He shook his head. "Poor guy is mad as a hatter these days. They kept booting him out of one museum after another. Didn't like his technophile leanings. Is it still paranoia when they really are out to get you?"

"Where is he now?" asked Wolfson. Sherrine held her breath.

Wade pursed his lips. "Ron and his Titan wound up in Chicago at the Museum of Science and Industry. Don't know where his fuel trucks went, maybe there. The LOX is long gone anyway, of course, but that's not so hard to make . . ."

Sherrine's heart pounded. Chicago! Why, that was just a short drive across Wisconsin. So close! She tugged on Bob's arm. "Let's get up to the room. We've got to tell the others."

☆   ☆   ☆

Wade Curtis listened with half an ear while Chuck and Dick debated the wisdom of searching for the Angels.

Someone had to know something. Any two people in the country were connected by a chain of no more than two intermediate acquaintances. That was elementary probability. So, he knew someone who knew someone who knew the people who had the Angels. The question was who? He knew a *lot* of someones.

Reason it the other way. Start with the people who had the Angels. Figure out who they had to be.

Government? Possible . . . but then the government would be bragging, the ACLU would be protecting their rights. . . .

Inuit? Maybe, but not for long. The Inuits lived a physical life, and the Angels weren't going to be ready for that.

Some third group. Someone with medical resources, because if they didn't have medical resources the Angels would be dead already. Maybe they were. Assume they weren't, see where that got you. Like in playing bridge, decide what it takes to make the contract; then assume the cards *did* fall that way, and go for it.

Probably somebody here in this room knows. So close! But no, they'd have told me, Wade thought.

No. You're a goddam drunk, and sober you wouldn't trust a drunk with anything this big. Why should they?

He was distracted momentarily by two fans winding their way through the crowd. Bob Needleton, he recognized. Physicist at U-Minn. The other he recalled as a fafiated femmefan he had known years ago. Computer whiz. "What's their big hurry?" he asked, nodding toward the two.

Dick Wolfson grinned. "If you'd've seen them earlier, you wouldn't have to ask. I didn't know Sherrine and Bob were back together. Haven't seen her in years."

Dr. Sherrine Hartley, only Hartley wasn't really her name, it was her first husband's. She'd been active in fandom once.

"Hunh." Chuck Umber seemed miffed. "There are more important issues at hand than that."

"Yeah," said another fan. "Like how to let the Angels know about the Titan."

Wade fell silent while the other fen debated. It was all moot anyway. Until they knew who had the Angels and how to contact them there was no point in composing a message. Someone handed him a drink, and he swallowed mechanically. Besides—"It's the wrong message," he said, but nobody heard.

If the Angels did want to get back upstairs—and Wade could not see where they had any other option—then it was silly to try setting up Ron Cole's old terror weapon. There were better ways anyhow. He narrowed his eyes in thought. Yes, sir. *Much* better ways. But his head hurt. Someone handed him another drink.

★　　★　　★

Alex stared at the two-headed creature with the nubbled lips. Doc had wheeled him upstairs for the meeting, opened the door, and there it was.

"It" was a smallish skeleton. The heads, set at the ends of long, flexible necks, were flat and triangular. Each contained what Alex took for a mouth and an eye socket. Between the necks was a thick bulge of bone. The creature stood on three legs ending in clawed hooves, with the rear leg attached to the spine by a complex hip joint. There was a small plaque attached to it.

Alex gripped the wheels of his chair and rolled himself across the room. He squinted at the plaque.

SIMPSON: RESEARCH AND DESIGN

Contents: ONE MODEL OF PUPPETEER SKELETON (SPECIMEN A)

THIS MODEL, BASED ON A RARE SPECIMEN TRADED FROM THE KZIN, SHOWS THE PUPPETEER JUST BEFORE THE EXTENDED PHASE OF A HIGH-SPEED LOPE . . . .

Alex shook his head. He could just imagine the consternation if, after the fall of civilization, paleontologists of the future were to unearth this ... um ... sculpture.

"Do you like him?" Doc Waxman wheeled Gordon into the room and parked him beside Alex. "He was a gift from Speaker-to-Seafood."

Alex thought he should be used to this sort of thing by now. "Whom?"

"Nat Reynolds, the writer. It's a long story, involving a drunken conversation with a lobster Savannah. I'll tell you about it someday." He whistled cheerfully while he set up a tray with glasses and an ice bucket. Alex couldn't help grinning. Doc was the most determinedly cheerful man he had ever met. He was easily sixty; yet he had not

hesitated to dash out onto the glaciers with the younger
fans, on what might easily have become a fatal mission-
of-mercy for two strangers. You had to like a man like
that.

"You should see my collection ... Hi, Fang, Bruce.
Come on in. You should see my collection of fannish art.
Or rather, you should have seen it. Statues, paintings.
Worlds of the imagination. Kelly Freas ... I have his
Hraani Interpreter. Bonestell. Jainschigg's 'Eifelheim' original. Aulisio's 'Mammy Morgan.' Pat Davis. Her 'Well-
springs of Wonder' can bring tears to my eyes. She's here
at the Con, Davis is. You saw her mermaid costume at
the Meet the Pros?" He shook his head. "A lot of it's
gone now; confiscated at busted cons. Now I only bring
one object with me when I come. We keep the rest
hidden in the bilge."

"What's a bilge?"

You could see the gears adjust in Waxman's head. "My
wife and I live on a houseboat in the Marina. We've
sealed everything into watertight containers and hid 'em
in the, ah, bottom of the boat." He chortled. "Won't
help in a thorough search; but it discourages the casual
pest, now that we're not supposed to treat the sewage
anymore.... Stop by when you get the chance and we'll
haul some pieces out to display."

Alex grinned. "How can I turn down such an invitation?"

"Easy," said Fang opening a can of beer with one
hand. "We're sending you back upstairs, remember? On
a fire in the sky."

Sure, thought Alex. "Have you found a rocket yet?"

Fang scowled at his drink. "No, but ... "

"But we will," Bruce insisted. "Fen are nothing if not
persistent. There are stories. Rumors. We'll trace 'em
down. One or another's bound to be authentic. The
Ghost may know something."

The others came in by ones and twos. Mike. Edward
Two Bats. Steve was glowing, as if he had just finished a
heavy workout, which Alex thought was rather likely.
Thor was wearing faded jeans, with his tin whistle pro-

truding from a back pocket. He had pulled his long, golden hair back into a ponytail. Not too long ago, Alex knew, such hairstyles on men were regarded as outré. Now they were becoming the norm. He wondered if the sudden advent of long hair and beards during the sixties had been an instinctive ecological response to the imminent ice age; like animals growing heavier pelts just before a severe winter.

"Got it," Mike announced. He searched the refreshment tray and came up with a wine bottle.

"Got what?" asked Bruce warily.

"A way to get the Angels upstairs."

The others waited. "Well?"

"Bang Bang." He opened the bottle.

Edward Two Bats looked at him. "Bang Bang?" Light dawned in his eyes. "Oh, no. No."

"Excuse me," said Alex, "but what the hell is Bang Bang?"

Crazy Eddie's hands came up like a fence. "You're crazy, Mike! Orion is fucking radioactive! The whole world made a treaty—"

Mike overrode him. "It's simple. You get a big, thick metal plate. Real thick. You put an H-bomb underneath and set it off. Believe me, that sucker will *move*." He smiled broadly. Edward Two Bats snarled.

Alex looked at Bruce. "He's not serious, is he?"

"Before you can come down again," Mike continued, "you throw another bomb underneath." He held his hand out, palm down, and jerked it upward in steps. "Bang, bang, bang. Get the picture?"

Alex got the picture. He liked his earlier idea about sticking a missile up his ass better. "I think there may be some difficulties with your plan," he said.

"Oh, sure. Details." Detail work, Alex could tell, was not Mike's forté.

Bob and Sherrine arrived, out of breath and flushed. They paused in the doorway, breathing heavily and grinning from ear to ear. "We have a ship," Bob gasped.

Alex felt a shiver run through him. The others stiffened. A rocket ship? They'd found one? But a ship was only half the battle. There was fueling and guidance and ... It was madness. So why should he be shaking?

It was a fragile thing, this imaginary spacecraft, and Alex feared to touch it. He asked, "What sort of bird is it? What kind of shape is it in?"

"We overheard Wade Curtis down in the movie lounge." Sherrine sank into a chair. "Thanks." She took the tea that Doc handed her. "They were listening to the news and jabbering about it and ol' Wade, Ghu bless him, he cut right to the heart of it. The Angels can't hide out indefinitely. And he mentioned that Ron Cole had a rocket, and—"

Bruce snapped his fingers. "Cole! That's right! There were stories, years and years ago. I didn't think they were true, though. Isn't he in Washington, at the Smithsonian?"

Sherrine shook her head. "No. The rocket is at the Museum of Science and Industry in Chicago. And get this. Wade says Cole has fuel for it!"

They all whooped except Alex. "How much fuel?" he insisted. "And what kind of bird is it? It won't do us any good if it just farts on the launch pad."

Sherrine looked at him. "I don't know how much fuel. Wade said it was a Titan Two. Does it matter?"

"A Titan?" He exchanged glances with Bob and Bruce. "Titans were smaller than the Saturns, weren't they?"

Bob nodded. "A two-stage rocket with a thrust of ... well, enough *oomph* to put a Gemini into orbit. A Gemini held two men. *Freedom's* what ... two hundred fifty miles up? One of the Geminis reached seven hundred, didn't it?"

"A Titan Two has more than enough lift," said Bruce, "*if* there's enough fuel."

"Meet them halfway," suggested Thor.

"Halfway?" said Alex.

Thor had his tin whistle out and was playing an imaginary tune with his fingers. "Seems to me that if we could just get enough fuel to put you on a decent suborbital, the Angels could rendezvous and pick you up. What did Sheppard reach in the first Mercury-Redstone? A hun-

dred fifteen miles or so, wasn't it? That should be do-
able from *Freedom*."

"That's a good idea, Thor," said Sherrine.

The muscular blond smiled. "Baseball," he said.

"Baseball?"

"The Angels can't handle grounders; but I figured
anybody can catch a pop fly."

Mike laughed and shook his head.

"What's so funny?" asked Bruce.

"Certainly not Thor's joke," said Fang.

Mike wiped his eyes. "It just hit me. *Freedom* orbits
two hundred fifty miles straight up, right? *That's less
than the distance from here to Chicago!* We have to
travel farther to get the rocket than we would travel in
the rocket itself."

"There's a little more to it than that," Alex said.
"Velocity matching is tricky."

"It's not the distance," Bob said. "It's the energy."

Mike sobered instantly. "I know that." He stuffed his
hands in his pants pockets and wandered to the window.
The blinds were open; and, outside, stars dusted the icy
sky. He stared at the twinkling lights. "I know that," he
said softly.

With the pollution gone, the stars were so clear. You'd
think that was the point of the exercise.

Bruce turned to Alex. "How about it? If Cole doesn't
have enough fuel to reach orbit, could the Angels at least
rendezvous with a suborbital?"

"They could," Alex agreed reluctantly, "if it were high
enough and on the right vector. It's trickier than just
flinging it up, and it would cost fuel—but yeah. They can
do it."

He exchanged glances with Gordon. *Would Lonny
even bother. Good ol' Lonny would weigh the cost of the
fuel for the rendezvous versus the benefit of getting two
duds back; and, no matter how you sliced it, twice zero
did not make for a respectable return on investment.*

Gordon looked worried. He was probably imagining
the trip. Arcing up on a nice smooth parabolic trajectory.
Hitting the top. Earth curves away below, waiting. . . .

Sorry, we just couldn't afford to meet you. And then an equally smooth parabolic trajectory down.

Alex gave him a nod. *Don't worry, Gordo. It'll never come off. So what's to worry?* Gordon twitched a smile.

Mike frowned and half-sat on the window sill. Alex could see the stars over his shoulder; and damn if one of them wasn't moving!

Somebody's home, once his own, was tracing a curve across the black sky. Navstar? *Mir? Freedom* herself? Without an ephemeris, he couldn't tell—looking up from Earth's surface disoriented him—but he was surprised at how much the sight of it ached.

He would have to go back. Have to. Or die trying. And no one was going to come and fetch him. So he would have to do it himself.

He looked at Gordon and saw the hope there. Gordon couldn't guess how many hurdles remained. Just find the bird and light it.

All right, he thought. *Torch it off and I'll fly it. I owe it to the kid to take him back.*

Bruce scowled. "We're just spinning our wheels here. We need a plan of action." He ticked points off on his fingers. "Number One, is the Titan for real? You know how fannish legends can build. For all we know, all Cole ever had were the components."

"Could still use those," said Edward Two Bats.

Bruce blinked at him.

"If we have to, we'll assemble the damned thing ourselves," he explained.

Bruce started to say something, then shrugged. "Second, we need fuel. Does Ron actually have any, or is that just story, too? If so, how much of it does he have and where is it and how do we load it aboard?"

Thor grinned. He pulled a rubber hose from his pocket. "Same way we fueled Bob's van."

Alex had a mental picture: Crazy Eddie with a giant syphon drawing off LOX from a convenient tank. Don't suck too hard on that hose. . . .

"Third," continued Bruce, "we need a launch site where we can erect the Titan. And fourth, we need to get the Angels there, fuel the bird, and then light it off without being noticed or caught by the authorities."

Crazy Eddie rubbed his hands together. "Piece of cake," he said.

☆ ☆ ☆

Bed-time exercises, Alex thought. He bent way back with his arms stretched out above his head so that his body formed a perfect bow. He could see the ceiling of the third-floor room he and Gordon shared in the mansion. His legs felt like rubber. Steve supported him with a hand beneath his shoulders.

"There, you see?" said Steve. "The muscles are there. It just takes some getting used to. Even falling free, you use your muscles to move things around; you still have to overcome the inertia. The difference down here is your legs have to learn to keep your body upright all the time, without conscious thought."

"If you say so," Alex responded.

"Think of it as bench-pressing one hundred eighty pounds all day long."

"Piece of cake." Alex suddenly realized that Steve was not supporting his shoulders anymore. He wobbled and semaphored with his arms.

"Steady," said Steve again putting a hand behind his shoulder blades. "Now, I'm going to take you through a simplified *soorya namaskar*. You let me know if anything overtaxes you. Now, exhale and bend all the way forward until your hands touch the floor. It's okay if you bend your knees. You, too, Gordon. That's right. No, in line with the feet. Good. Ordinarily, I'd have you tuck your head between your knees, but ... Now, hold that position."

"I think I'm being overtaxed," said Alex. His arms and legs felt like bands of fire. His thigh muscles quivered.

"No, not yet. You're fooling yourself. You're working out, and your body says, 'That's enough, I can't take anymore.' But it's just trying to con you. If you quit, the rest of the day you'll hear your body laughing at you."

Alex's muscles were on fire, and the speech wasn't helping. He looked at Gordon. The kid was holding the pose and grinning. Smart-ass. Just because he was younger ... Alex kept staring at him until he saw the leg muscles tremble. Then he gave Gordon a smirk in return.

Steve took them through a series of twelve poses. Each one forced Alex to extend a muscle group that he was unaccustomed to using. Getting around at the bottom of the Well was certainly different from getting around in orbit. Upstairs, when he kicked off a wall surface, or flexed to a landing on another, he used those same leg muscles to oppose the same body mass. But here he had to do so constantly, not just at kickoff and touchdown. Just as if he were in the centrifuge or aboard an accelerating ship.

It was uncomfortable, but not exactly unpleasant. In fact, living in an acceleration frame had its advantages. Drinking was easier, for one thing. Objects stayed where you put them. And he always woke up in the same place he went to sleep, even without using straps.

That's the spirit! I'm a stranger in a strange land full of wonders and delights. What was the point of being marooned if you couldn't enjoy it? He needed to embrace Doc Waxman's attitude; or Steve's, or even Mike's. The Round Mound paraded his seemingly inexhaustible store of knowledge with the same sort of delight as the kids Alex knew in the day-care center. *Gee, Mister MacLeod, look what I found! Mister Mac! Mister Mac, look at this! Isn't it neat!* That was Mike. Each nugget of information was fascinating. The world was full of new-found marvels and he wanted to share the excitement with everybody. They all did. They had a certain sense. It wasn't a sense of ennui or cynicism. It was . . .

A sense of wonder.

That was it. A sense of wonder, in the fine old original meaning of the word. They wondered *at* their world. Because when you did that, everything was wonder-full.

Later, after Steve had gone, Alex lay abed in the dark, breathing slowly and naturally, imagining the *prana* from the air streaming into his body, strengthening it. *Prana* was the universal energy, manifesting itself in gravitation, electricity, nerve currents, thought. A kind of Hindu unified field theory. It was nonsense, of course. There was no such energy, and Steve knew it as well as Alex did.

Still, the mind-body interface was a funny thing and nobody really knew how it worked. As a metaphor, a mental focus, *prana* worked quite well. He tried to imagine a ball of light in his body, with glowing strands coming from his mouth and nostrils connecting with the sun and distant stars. Images were the tools of the mind, and a practical person used whatever tools came to hand. Sometimes what was important was not what was true, but what you believed was true.

Like cobbling together a spaceship and flying into space.

Believing wouldn't make it happen; but not believing would make it not happen. *Everything starts as somebody's daydream.*

"Alex?"

"What?" He turned his head. In the dark he could not see Gordon, but he could sense the youngster's presence in the other bed.

"About . . . About the dip trip . . ."

"What? That again?" *Couldn't the kid let it be? I'd like to have seen him do better.* "What about it?" he snapped.

"I'm sorry I didn't speak English."

". . . When?"

Gordon twisted around, painfully, to look at him. "When? In final innocent carefree moment before missile shred *Piranha's* fin!"

Idiot. "Gordon, it was too late. The missile must have been in flight before I, before, hell. I should have torched off and gone home. They'd *found* us. We *knew* it."

Silence.

"Maybe we could have made another orbit. Only, we don't carry all that much oxygen. And we needed the nitrogen, we *did*, that's not . . . not just Lonny talking."

"Then it wasn't what I said. Or didn't."

It had really been bothering Gordon. The stilyagin

must have flunked some math courses. "What do you picture me *doing* about anything, with a couple of seconds to work with? What kind of acceleration is *that* to move a mass like *Piranha*, with three tiny embarrassed fins and the scoop dragging us, too?"

Silence filled the blackness between them. Finally, Gordon spoke again. "Alex, do you think this Titan business will work?"

Alex crossed his arms behind his head and stared at the ceiling. Blackness should have stars in it, he thought. "I don't know. If there is a ship and if we can find fuel ... What do you think?"

He heard a heavy sigh in the darkness. "If we can rendezvous, no problem. If they have to come and snatch us as we go past ... They will not do it."

"No, I don't think they would."

Gordon hesitated. "Maybe my family can ..."

"Maybe they could what? Overrule Lonny or Sergei? Not a chance. They can count as well as we can. They've got enough fingers. Hell, you know it's not the personal danger. Not a Floater in orbit would hesitate to risk his life to save another. But when we use common resources, the entire station is at risk, and we have to draw the line. Start making exceptions and where do you stop? When everyone is dying because too much has been used up?"

He was beginning to sound unpleasantly like Lonny Hopkins. "No, your folks will cry as you arc past"—*Which is more than anyone will do for me*—"and they'll curse God that they can't come out and snag you; but they won't jeopardize the station for no other gain than two more mouths to feed."

Alex remembered the old Eskimo on the glacier describing how his wife and daughter had been killed and eaten by his erstwhile comrades. And he hadn't chased after the cannibals and he hadn't wasted any tears. Old Krumangapik hadn't been cruel or heartless. Alex had seen the pain in the old man's eyes. But when you lived on the edge, you learned to cut your losses. Krumangapik had never heard of cost-benefit ratios, but he knew that in his milieu he could waste nothing, not even tears.

Eskimos abandoned their aged and infirm to the Ice. Krumangapik had done it. During their nighttime trek across the Ice, warmed by that invisible beam of *prana* from SUNSAT, he had told of building his mother's Final Igloo.

She was old and frail and she had insisted. She even picked the spot. When it was completed, they had hugged each other and said good-bye; and Krumangapik had sealed the entryway to keep the wolves out and left her there and never looked back.

Alex shivered as he remembered. "A duty to die." How long would it be before elderly Floaters took themselves to the airlocks out of a similar sense of duty? Yes. That was how they would do it. No injections, because they had to conserve the medicines. No slashed wrists, no blood droplets to purge from the air system. They would climb into the airlock, nude, so as not to lose the fabric of their clothing. They would just turn on the pumps to evacuate the chamber. Alex remembered dying such a death. Later, a detail would reenter the airlock and salvage the valuable organics.

Perhaps that was the most unfortunate consequence of the new era of shortages, both in Orbit and down in the Well. That it forced them all, Downer and Floater alike, to be unkind.

"Is it right to string them along?"

Alex jumped. He'd thought Gordon was asleep. "What do you mean, Gordo?"

"These Downers. Fandom. They're risking a lot to help us, aren't they? Shouldn't we tell them they're wasting their time?"

"Don't burn bridges, Gordo. There might be enough fuel to reach orbit on our own."

"Or no fuel at all. Meanwhile, she puts her neck at risk for us. Maybe we should contact Big Momma for instructions."

"No!" Alex spoke sharply. "No," he repeated more softly. "We'd have to make contact through this Oregon

Ghost character. If we do, the fans will know how iffy the whole scheme is and then . . ."

"And then?"

"And then they might give the effort up. Do you want to be stuck down here the rest of your life?"

"No, but—"

"Look. They're already in deep enough for what they've already done. We'll just let things go long enough to see if there is *any* chance at all. Then . . . Then, we'll decide."

"All right, Alex," Gordon said doubtfully. "You're the boss."

Alex relaxed into the pillow and closed his eyes. The room did not become any darker. He listened to his pulse pushing the blood through his arteries. "Gordon?"

"Yeah?"

"She's too old for you."

Gordon didn't answer right away. "She's younger than she looks, Alex," he said after a moment. "Gravity."

"Go to sleep, Gordo." Alex tried to roll over on his side. He almost made it. Good news from all over.

CHAPTER NINE

"Please, Sir, May I Have Some More?"

Alex dreamed he had been strapped down in a runaway centrifuge. The module spun faster and faster. G-forces sat on his bones like mountains. Under the steady pull his face dripped away and pooled around his naked skull. He kept trying to cry out that he wanted off *now;* but he couldn't speak.

Then he heard drapes slithering, and sunlight warmed his face. "Wake up!" a cheerful voice insisted. "Time for *soorya namaskar!*" Alex kept his eyes closed and practiced the *savasam* pose. Go away, Steve, I'm dead.

But the man would not be put off. He shook Alex by the shoulder. "Come on, you two. Discipline is the key. You've got to work at this every day."

Alex opened one eye. Steve stood between the two beds, legs akimbo and hands balled on his hips. He reminded Alex of a coiled spring. If the Downers could only find a way to tap Steve's energy, they could use it to melt the glaciers.

Beyond him, Alex saw Doc setting up two trays. Tall

glasses of milk. A high-calcium diet. "Whatever happened to privacy?" he asked.

"Alex," said Gordon. "It snowed last night."

He opened both eyes and turned to see Gordon standing (standing!) with his hands braced on the window sill. His breath made little clouds in the air and steamed the glass. Alex stifled a groan. If Gordon could do it . . . He pushed the comforter and the blankets off his body. With that much weight removed he felt as if he could float out of bed. *Careful, Alex. Watch those reflexes.* Slowly, he swung his legs out over the edge of the bed and pushed himself to a sitting position.

"That's very good," said Steve, and Alex felt like one of his day-care charges who had just gotten a star on his forehead.

"They tell me it snows a little every night up here," said Doc. He brought the milk over. "Even during the summer. It's colder in California than it used to be; but L.A. only gets snow a couple times a year. Here, drink this. It's good for you."

Alex took the glass with both hands and drank. Milk was good stuff. Too bad they didn't have milk in the habitats. That mix-it-with-water powder didn't count, and they would run out of it sooner or later. Sooner or later they would run out of everything, including time. He clenched his fists around the glass. He was probably better off on Earth. You could still run out of things on Earth, you could still die; but the margin for error was not nearly so thin.

There was a knock on the door. "Come on in," Alex called. "Everybody else has."

It was Mike Glider. He waved. "Good morning, all." He found the most comfortable chair in the room and sank into it. "Bad news," he announced. "Bruce tried to contact Ron Cole last night through the Oregon Ghost. No go. The Ghost says Cole is reachable only through the Museum switchboard and no one wants to say anything over a line where there might be listeners. The Ghost says he can't vouch for the Titan, either. He says he heard the stories, too, back in the old days; but he doesn't know how close to the truth they were."

Doc looked up. "What are we going to do, then?"

Mike shrugged. "Bruce wants to take Bob and me down to Chi to check things out in person."

Alex grunted and noticed how his breath smoked. It was not cold, exactly; not like it had been on the glacier. But it was chilly. Pleasantly cool, actually. More comfortable than the shirtsleeve warm habitats. There was no problem dumping waste heat on *this* habitat! "Is it always this nippy in the morning?" he asked. Yesterday, he had been too groggy from the van ride to notice.

Steve struck a pose. " 'To conserve, we all should strive. Thermostats at fifty-five,' " he quoted. "It'll warm up later. Body heat from fifty-odd fans."

"Some of them very odd," said Mike. "Steve, who was that fellow who used the thermostat law to commit murder? What was it . . . two, three years ago?"

"Don't recall his name anymore. Papers on the Coast didn't play it up very big. Massachusetts?"

"Hyannis."

"What are you two talking about?" Gordon demanded.

"There was a rich old man and an impatient young heir," Mike explained. "The old man had pneumonia. EPA said to turn our thermostats down; so the nephew did it. He was just being a good citizen." He scratched his beard thoughtfully. "He must have inherited enough money to hire a good lawyer, because it never came to trial."

"Government wouldn't want it to come to trial," said Steve. "Good-intentioned laws aren't *allowed* to have bad spin-offs."

Mike shrugged. "Whichever. The DA was really frosted, though."

Steve led them through their *asanas*. Stretch. Bend. Rest. Stretch. Bend. Rest. "I am your transcendental drill sergeant," Steve declaimed. "Meditate, you slugs! *Yam*, two, three, four!" As Alex came out of the Eight-

Pointed Repose, he noticed that Doc was performing the *asanas* along with them.

He had to admit that he felt much better afterward. However, he and Gordon were so exhausted by the mild workout that they took refuge once more in their wheelchairs. "Don't worry about it," Steve told them. "Each day you'll be able to stay on your feet a little longer."

"That's right," said Doc. "You should have seen me before Steve took me in hand." He squeezed his left bicep with his right hand. "Muscles had gone soft. I tired easily. Now, I've never felt better."

Steve looked at him. "There's more to yoga than physical conditioning."

"Breakfast time," said Sherrine. She pushed her way through the door backward, her hands gripping a tray stacked with steaming dishes. Alex admired the view. Then he noticed Gordon watching and scowled. Neither of them were up to *that* sort of exercise; but Gordon would beat him to it.

Sherrine set the tray on the lamp table. Mike tried to look over her shoulder to see what she had brought. "The kitchen is a madhouse," she said. "Ol' 3MJ is down there flipping flapjacks himself. But Shew and Wolfson and Curtis and a couple of others are helping out, too."

"Damn," Sherrine said.

"What?" Steve asked.

"Just remembering. Nat Reynolds used to make Irish coffee at conventions. Long time ago. What happened to him?"

"Exiled," Steve said. "After he got busted and they were all set to charge him with subversion—"

"Subversion how?" Alex asked. "I thought—isn't the Constitution still in effect?"

"For most things," Mike said dryly. "There's freedom of speech for politics and so forth. But no one has the right to deceive people. Back in the '90s one of the Green organizations sued the publisher of a science fiction book and won. Didn't cost the publisher much, but the author was held liable as well. So after Reynolds wrote *The Sun Guns*—"

"I read this," Gordon said. "About satellite power plants to stop the Ice?"

"Yep, that's it," Mike said. "Well, Friends of Man and the Earth sued him. Class action suit for fifty million bucks for deceiving the people. Got a preliminary judgment suppressing publication of the book. Reynolds wouldn't take that and let the book be published anyway, and that was contempt of court, so then they wanted him on criminal charges."

Sherrine shuddered. "And once you're a criminal, they can do anything to you. Reeducation. Community service."

"Well, they caught him, but he and his lawyers worked out a deal. Reynolds gave up U.S. citizenship and was deported to Australia. The Aussies always did like him. He didn't want to go, but he didn't really have much choice."

"Things are pretty rough down there, too," Doc said. "But better than here. Hell, everywhere is better than here."

They were quiet for a moment, then Mike said, "The important thing is, is anybody making waffles?"

Sherrine held a plate out to him. "Here. I brought you some." She gave plates to Alex and Gordon. Alex studied his meal and nearly wept. These people had no idea how wealthy and fortunate they were. Eggs. *Real* eggs from a real hen. And porridge made from cereal grain. None of it powdered or freeze dried or reconstituted or resurrected or derived from a vat of green slime. He savored a spoonful of oatmeal.

"That's one of the things I missed while I was fafiated," Sherrine continued.

Mike looked puzzled. "What? Crowded kitchens?"

"No, it's the way fans pitch in and help spontaneously. 3MJ didn't have to ask a single person for assistance."

Doc nodded. "They seen their duty and they done it."

"Out in the danelaw, nobody helps out unless there's something in it for them. I always had to watch my back at the University. You wouldn't believe the bureaucratic in-fighting that goes on there, and the goddam union laws—"

"I would," said Mike, wagging an impaled fragment of waffle. "That's why I left the IRS. The grunts at the P.O.D.'s were okay. They were just trying to do their jobs—almost impossible, considering how convoluted the law is—but the political hacks . . ." He shook his head.

Alex could sympathize with him. Lonny Hopkins was a son of a bitch; but, to give the devil his due, he was a perfectly sincere son of a bitch. And up there, you did your part or you died. If you screwed up, maybe you killed someone whose relatives resented it, maybe you killed yourself, maybe something else, but the margins were too thin for drones.

Down here they were rich enough to support useless people, but there were so many! All concerned about their own careers and perks in the midst of the struggle for survival.

"Fen are different," Doc said. "At least since the fringe fans gafiated. That was one benefit of government intimidation. A lot of the cuttle fish are gone." His voice took on an edge. "You know the ones I mean. The exhibitionists. And the so-called fans who abused 3MJ's hospitality by stealing his memorabilia. Nowadays the camaraderie is more like it was during First Fandom. It's a smaller group, but closer knit."

"The Few, the Proud, the Fen," said Mike.

Steve nodded. "FIAWOL," he agreed.

Alex held up his bowl. "More gruel, please."

Gordon laughed. "No, no, it is 'Please sir, may I have some more?'"

Mike roared. "You like that stuff? Don't you have 'gruel' where you come from?"

"Oh, sure," Alex retorted. "We make it from the wheat we harvest on our limitless acres."

"Well, if it's cereal you want," said Sherrine, "you've come to the right place. What Wall Street is to junk bonds, Minneapolis is to cereal grain."

Mike scratched his beard again. "Take some home with you, why don't you? I'm sure we could stick a case of Quaker Oats or Cream of Wheat into the Titan with you. A gift from Earth."

"Hey!" said Sherrine. They all looked at her and she spread her arms apart. "Why not?"

"Why not what?"

She stood up and bounced to the center of the room. "If we're going to loft a rocket, we should *pack* it with gifts. As much as it will take. Not just oatmeal, but ... Oh, everything. Anything! Anything we've got down here that the Angels need!"

Doc raised his eyebrows. "That's a great idea, Sherri. It'll show the Angels that they've still got a few friends down here. What sort of stuff do your folks need, Alex?"

"What do we need? What *don't* we need?" Alex wondered how well-informed the fans were about conditions in the habitats. Not very, he suspected. "Bacon and eggs. Meats of any sort. Milk. Carrots, broccoli, everything you were serving at the Meet the Readers Party. Hell, *any* vegetable. You have foodstuffs down here that some of our folks have never seen, let alone eaten."

"Chitlins and collard greens?" asked Steve.

"Sure."

"You guys must *really* be desperate."

"Have you ever lived on a diet of lettuce and mustard greens? Zucchini, sometimes. We do grow vegetables, but there are never enough. You can't eat spider plants! And some of our plant species have died off. We synthesize a lot of vitamins, but nutritional deficiencies are one of our biggest worries." *Along with solar flares, nitrogen outgassing, shortages of metals and plastics, and you name it. But let's not disillusion anyone.*

"Food, then," said Mike. "Geez, we should name the ship *The Flying Greengrocer*."

"Seeds, Mike," said Sherrine. "Not live plants. Call it *Johnny Appleseed*." She went to the small lamp table and rummaged in its drawer, emerging with a pencil and a small pad of note paper.

Mike scowled. "I knew that. I *am* the county ag agent, you know. Not that I know a damn thing about it—"

"Then how the hell did you get the job?" Doc demanded. "As if I didn't know."

"Seniority, of course. I was able to bump out someone else. Helps that I can claim minority ancestry."

"What kind of minority, white man?" Steve asked.

"Yes, just so. Native American," Mike said. "Doesn't show, does it?" He shrugged. "But we can claim it, so I do. The point is, I may be able to get stuff, and I can sure get access to the library records."

He pushed himself out of his armchair and paced the room, rubbing his fist with his hand. "You'll want plants to satisfy three needs," he continued, thinking aloud. "Hot damn! Who would ever have thought that a county agent and the space program ... Well, okay, nutrition is one. You want maximum food value for minimum energy input. Oxygen production and CO_2 scrubbing is another. And radiation hardening. So ..." He paused and rubbed his face. "I should sit down and put together a list, balancing all three needs. But for a start ... Sherrine, write these down: green leafy vegetables and yellow vegetables. Sweet potatoes, carrots, spinach."

"Why them?" asked Gordon.

"They're great sources of vitamin A," Doc told him. "Important for bone growth, and radiation resistance."

"Tocopherol, vitamin E. That's good for radiation, too," said Steve.

"Sure. We can include a couple of bulk bottles of concentrated multivitamins."

"And tomatoes," Mike added. "Rich in vitamin A and they're easy to grow hydroponically."

"We have some of those," Alex said. "But they went bad. Started making people sick. We still grow tomatoes, but we make fertilizer out of them, mulch for the moon rock soil."

"Tomato seeds. Several varieties." Sherrine wrote rapidly. "You must need hydroponic chemicals, too. Even with closed loop recovery, there have to be losses. What do you need for that?"

"Nitrogen, for one thing," Alex said.

"Potassium nitrate," said Gordon. They all looked at him in surprise. "Potassium nitrate," he repeated. "You know. Saltpeter."

"Flower seeds," said Steve.

Alex looked at him in surprise. "Can't eat flowers," he said.

Steve shook his head. "Not for food. But as long as you need plants to produce oxygen, some of them might as well be pretty."

"Pretty is fine," Gordon said. "But pretty takes time, too." He shrugged. "Here you are rich. So much to eat. Not made of algae."

"Green slime," Alex said. "Good stuff. Bubble waste water through a vat of green slime. Takes out the ketones. Dissolve the carbon dioxide. It grows, and you can bake it into bread. . . ."

"Okay," said Steve. "We send up everything we can get, though. Why not? Seeds are small. They weigh next to nothing; and they'll keep practically forever."

"Is good," Gordon said. "When we know how much mass we can take up, we can ask station commander what is needed. I think is not proper to ask until—"

The room fell silent. "Until you believe in this," Sherrine said. "Don't get their hopes up."

"Something like that," Alex said. "I mean—we're grateful, and you're risking everything, and—"

"But it's pretty mad to talk about finding an old Titan, fueling it up, and lighting it off," Doc said. "Of course it is. But—" He held up a finger. The others joined in unison as he said, "It's the Only Game in Town." Doc's eyes lit. "Spices. Pepper. Thyme. Savory. Oregano. Sweet Basil. Dill—parsley, sage, rosemary, and thyme. . . ."

Alex's mouth watered. Mythical flavors from childhood. "Ketchup," he remembered. "And mustard. Peanuts. Gordon, you have never tasted peanut butter. And not just foodstuffs, either." As long as he was daydreaming, why not daydream big. "We could use all sorts of materials. Machine tools, too."

"Plastics," said Gordon. "They can be shredded and remolded. Could always use more."

Alex shook his head. "Plastics would be too bulky to lift in useful quantities. We need things that are small and valuable."

"Don't rule anything out, yet," said Sherrine. "We're brainstorming."

"Too bad you can't grow plastic from seeds," said Doc. "Like you can plants."

"But you can!" Mike said suddenly.

"What?"

"Well, not quite; but ... There was an experimental field—in Iowa?—where they grew plastic corn. *Alcaligenes eutrophus* is a bacterium that produces a brittle polymer. Eighty percent of its dry weight is a naturally grown plastic: PHB, poly-beta-hydroxybutyrate. ..."

"Contains only *natural* ingredients!" declared Steve with a grin.

"Researchers found they could coax the bug into producing a more flexible plastic by adding a few organic acids to the glucose 'soup.' They cloned the polymer-producing enzymes—oh, 1987 or so—and spliced them into *E. coli*. Later, they spliced them into turnips, and finally corn. That was the bonanza. The mother lode of plastic. The corn grew plastic kernels. Think of it: plastic corn on the cob," he chuckled. "Shuck the cobs and you get pellets. Perfect for melting in a forming machine hopper."

Doc frowned. "And you plant some of the plastic seed corn and grow more? That doesn't sound right."

Mike shook his head. "No, that was the problem, plastic seeds don't germinate. So you'd still need the original bugs, but you can breed them in vats and harvest the polymers directly. Not as efficient as the corn, but ... They were *this* close to cracking the sterility problem when the National Scientific Research Advisory Board halted all testing."

"It sounds fantastic," said Alex. "Where can you find this bug?"

"*A. eutrophus*? In the hold of the *Flying Dutchman*. It's just a story that ag agents pass around. The test plot was abandoned when genetic engineering was outlawed. Later, it was burned by a Green hit squad."

Doc grunted. "Hunh. Burning plastic corn? I'll bet it released a toxic smoke cloud."

"Sure. But *that* was the fault of the scientists, not the arsonists. They burned one of the scientists, too."

"My grandmother would know," said Sherrine.

Heads turned.

"My grandmother. She's a genetic engineer, remember? If anyone knows where we could lay hands on a culture of this *A. eutrophus*, she would."

Alex felt a tingle in his limbs. They weren't just joking around any more. They could make it work. Foodstuff. Seeds. Vitamins. Spices. *Plasti-facient bacteria, for crying out loud!* They could actually make it happen. They knew where to find the stuff. Or they knew people who knew. He glanced at Gordon, who was looking straight at him, reading the hope in his eyes.

Sure. Make the payload valuable enough and Lonny Hopkins himself would fly out and grab it, Alex MacLeod and all.

"How would you handle meat, though?" asked Doc. "No seeds. No pills."

"Small animals. Rabbits. They breed fast and they're relatively meaty for their size."

"Guinea pigs? The Incas used those."

"Chickens."

"Hold it. Hold it. This rocket is starting to sound like a Central American bus."

"Forget the chickens," said Mike. "Take fertilized eggs. They take up less space. Hatch 'em in an incubator. Use the hens for egg production. Keep a rooster or two for breeding stock and use the rest for meat."

"But we don't have a chicken incubator," said Gordon.

"Build one. We can put the design and operating manual on a disc."

"Hell's bells," interjected Doc. "Give 'em a whole library on disc. SF, too, of course. They must be getting tired of reading the same books over and over. As for the rabbits and guinea pigs, just take the germ plasm. You have a sperm bank, don't you?"

"Well, uh, yes. For humans."

"Good. Frozen sperm, then. Frozen ova, too. Mix 'em

in vitro. Though you'll still want to take a few females along, just in case. Ova are more delicate than sperm."

"Is diversity problem in sperm bank," said Gordon thoughtfully. "Gene pool is limited."

"*Mars Needs Women!*" shouted Mike. Sherrine looked up from her notepad and blushed a deep crimson. Before she could say anything, Bruce Hyde spoke from the doorway.

"Do I want to know what this discussion is about?"

Sherrine and the others told him, all talking at once. He looked at Alex. "Will it work?"

Alex shrugged. "Why fly an empty truck? As long as we have enough fuel to lift the mass." *And that would be a pretty problem! Trading altitude for cargo.* There had to be enough cargo to make a rendezvous cost-effective. The more, the better. But more cargo, less altitude; and Lonny would have to use more fuel to match orbits, and . . . Where was the break-even point? It was a question of minimizing the rendezvous costs while maximizing the cargo value. A minimax problem. But it wouldn't do any good to try and calculate an answer. Too many indeterminates—Lonny would be making his own decisions anyway.

"Alex?" Steve was waving a hand at him.

"I'm sorry. What did you say?"

"I asked about spare parts and fittings," said Steve.

"We can fabricate most of what we need," Alex told him, "if we have the materials and the machine tools." Maintenance was the one activity in the habitats that was absolutely crucial. "We can scavenge and salvage most materials, although we're always short and more would always be welcome; but machine tools and dies for the machine shop are essential. Some of our blades and drill bits and molds have been reground or resharpened until they're useless."

"Machine tools would be small," said Mike, "but heavy."

"No critiques, yet," Sherrine reminded him as she wrote. "What else?"

"Surgical implements," said Doc. "I'm sure people up

there still suffer injury and illness." He shuddered. "I'm trying to imagine resharpened scalpels and hypodermics."

Alex nodded. "You're right. I'd forgotten. Shots *hurt*."

"And medicines," continued Doc. "All sorts. You must have to ration what medicines you have mighty close."

Doc might as well have pierced him with one of his scalpels. Rationing . . . In a society of scarcity there was always rationing; and some people were on top of the rationing list and others were at the bottom. If Lonny or Mary or hydroponics chief Ginjer Hu fell sick, there would be medicine available. "Essential personnel." If Alex MacLeod fell sick . . .

And if he did climb back into orbit with a rocketful of goodies, would his name move up the list? More to the point, how much could they realistically take with them in a Titan, anyway? Brooding, Alex dropped out of the brainstorming session.

"Not only medicines," said Sherrine, "but other chemicals, too. 3MJ has chlorine for his pool right here. He might let us have some."

"Metals, too," said Gordon. ". . . Nah. Too heavy. We would not lift enough metal to matter."

Bruce laughed. "What do you suppose the Titan is made of? If we can loft it hard enough, we can put the booster into a recoverable orbit. Then your people can mine it to their heart's content."

Later, when they were alone for a few minutes, Gordon looked at him with widened eyes. "It cannot work, but they believe—do you believe, too?"

Alex arranged the blanket around his legs. He smoothed the green plaid cloth, tucking the folds out of sight. Experimentally, he pulled on the chair's wheels and was pleased to see that he could roll himself across the room. As Doc had told him, the upper body strength would come first. It was the muscles needed for standing and walking that needed the training. That and replenishing the bone calcium. He looked at Gordon.

—"I think it *could* work. The essence of trade is 'Cheap here; dear there.' Make the cargo valuable enough and get the rocket close enough and, yes, it damn well could work." Gordon's blanket was a dull monochrome, which secretly pleased Alex.

"But, there are so many things that could go wrong. . . ."

Alex slashed the air with his hand. "Of course there are! Don't teach your grandmother to suck eggs—"

"Sorry, Alex."

"—We don't even know if we have a ship. Or whether we can fuel it. Or a thousand other things. We don't know how much cargo we can load; or what kind and how much will convince the station to bring us in. It's got to be the right stuff. And we can't ask Big Momma without tipping our hand and maybe losing the fans' help. There are a thousand details, and if any one of them fails, the whole idea collapses like a burnt-out star. So what do you want to do? Give up and stay down here in the Well for the rest of your life?"

"No, but you don't have to prove—"

"What do you know what I have to prove?"

Gordon pressed his lips together and looked away. "Nichevo."

"Damn right." Alex turned his wheelchair away. So, why was he being so hard on the kid? Deep down, he knew that they were cut off from home forever. This business with the Titan was just half-baked wish fulfillment. What did the shrinks call it? Denial? Crash a scoopship, did you? Stupid dipper fell into the Well? Hey, no problem. We'll just patch together an old derelict missile; stuff it with a cornucopia of wonderful goods, and sail home to triumph. Lonny Hopkins will be humiliated, and Mary will be so enchanted that she will finally leave him and we will all live happily ever after.

"Ah, cheer up, Gordo," he said. "The damned rocket will probably blow up on the launch pad anyway."

"Blankets."

He turned his head. "Hunh?"

Gordon tugged at his lap warmer. "Blankets. Cloth. How many times can you repatch worn-out shorts or halters?"

"Oh. Sure, sure. Tell Sherrine when she comes back."

"Alex?"

"What?"

"I didn't want to ask before, but what is corn on the cob?"

A flicker of images like an old silent movie. Golden corn glistening with melted butter. Picnic table spread on a bright summer's day. The merest of chills in the air, the distant kiss of infant glaciers. Hot dogs on the barbecue. Mom and Dad laughing to each other across the picnic table. The tangy smell of baked beans.

"Don't worry about it. We'll have a picnic and you'll see for yourself. Spread a blanket and ..." He stopped suddenly and studied his lap blanket. Not just plaid. Light and dark green, with yellow and red pinstripes. It was the MacLeod tartan. And Gordon Tanner's blanket was ... a solid tan.

He laughed suddenly and Gordon gave him an odd look. So, launching them back into orbit involved thousands of details, did it? He felt a sudden illogical surge of optimism. These fans were people who *cared* about details. "Gordo," he said, "we've got to approach this whole thing in a more positive frame."

"What do you mean?"

"Why, there are a thousand things that could go right!"

CHAPTER TEN

". . . . One of the Forces of Nature"

Sherrine held the door of the van open while Bob
rolled the tub of powdered chlorine inside. He put it in
place against the wall and mopped his head with a ker-
chief, glancing back over his shoulder at the tarp-shrouded
swimming pool. "This is stupid."

"Tremont said we could take as much as we wanted.
He doesn't think it will ever be warm enough to use the
pool again." She followed his gaze to the pool. A layer of
ice encrusted the tarp. One day soon, it would never
melt. It was sad, knowing that the pool was doomed, that
no one would ever laugh and splash in it again.

"That wasn't what I meant."

Sherrine folded her arms against the chill. "So?"

"Lugging this crap all the way to Chicago. It's the kind
of thing Crazy Eddie would come up with."

"Alex told us that the Angels need all sorts of chemicals. The space stations aren't perfectly closed systems.
You know that. They were never designed for permanent, isolated habitation—and there's no chlorine on the
moon. You're just jealous because you weren't there and

you didn't think of it." And why did Bob have to throw cold water on her idea? He himself had pulled her into this.

He leaned back against the van and stuffed his hands in his jacket pockets. "We don't know yet if Cole even has a rocket," he said. "And if he does, we can't just climb aboard and take off from downtown Chicago with a bucket of chlorine powder aboard. So, we don't have to load up—on chlorine or anything else—right now."

She shrugged. "Where's the harm?"

Bob rubbed his shoulders. "It's heavy."

She didn't answer him. She huddled deeper in her coat, squinting at the snow flurries stirred up by the wind. The breeze hummed like a tenor pipe where it blew across the archway between the main building and the garage and parking apron. *Like a ghost*, she thought. The Ghost of Minneapolis Past.

"Cold?" asked Bob.

"No," she said.

His mouth twitched and he stuck his hand back in his pocket. "Me neither." After a few beats, he spoke again. "Is Bruce going to tell the rest of the Con what's going on? I had to teach a thermo class this morning, so I missed whatever you decided at the meeting. The traffic was tied up around the fraternity houses. They're getting ready for some sort of Greekfest."

"Call in sick, like I did."

He shook his head. "I owe them."

"Who, the University?"

"No, my students. It takes a lot of guts to sign up for a science course these days. To put up with the taunts and harassment. As long as they show up, I'll show up."

"I'm glad I'm staff, not faculty."

"The Dean insists that we add creationism and crystal theory and spiritualism to the curriculum."

"They already have those—"

"Not as equal time in the physics and chemistry departments."

Sherrine whistled low.

"Yep," Bob said. "The science departments are resisting —we had a meeting after my class—but it's a question of marketing and sales. Of putting warm bodies behind desks. We told the Dean that there was no objective evidence for any of that crap. You know what he said?"

The sky was a slate gray; the cloud deck, low and oppressive. Sherrine stared up into the gloom. "No. What?"

"He said that the alleged objectivity of materialist science was an invention of heterosexual, white males, so we shouldn't use that as a basis for judgment."

She looked sharply into his face. For a change, he was not laughing. "What did you tell him?"

"Nothing."

All the fire had gone out of him, even the anger. Ominous. She said, "And?"

"I said nothing. It was like I'd been caught explaining something to a door, or a telephone recording. I felt like such a fool."

"That's why I love working with computers. They're logical. Rational. They do exactly what you program them to do. And that forces *you* to be logical, too." She shook her head. "But the anthropomorphic nonsense I have to put up with from users . . ."

"I thought you were happy in your little niche."

She gave him a fierce look. "I was, damn you. I was happy! Thank you, Robert K. Needleton, for prying me out into this cold, mean, miserable world."

"Do you want to go back?"

She shook her head. "You can never go back. As long as you keep your eyes shut tight, you can pretend whatever you like. But once you open them, all your pretenses are gone. Even if you shut them again, you *know*. I was getting along, day by day. Nothing was too right; but nothing was too wrong, either. Now, you and your Angels and—" She waved an arm at the Tre-house. "—all this. It's reminded me how gray and awful things have become. People ask me what my 'sign' is. It used to be a joke; but they're *serious*. We have a Supreme Court justice now who consults the stars instead of the Constitution. And the Luddites. Anytime someone suggests *doing* anything, it's 'this might happen' and 'that might happen' and 'think of the risks involved.' But you can't do nothing, either. Oh, sometimes I just want to shuck it all. Go somewhere else."

"Where?"

She looked back up into the sky and hummed softly. "*And that was one small step, and a fire in the sky . . .*"

"Sorry, all those trains have been cancelled."

"Except one."

"Maybe." He placed one mittened hand on her shoulder. "Sherrine. People like us, we should stay here and fight."

"And lose."

"Losing is better than running."

She jerked her shoulder away from him. "I wasn't talking about running." *Yes, you were.* "I'm not like you. I can't laugh about it. I can't make jokes. It depresses me. You'll be making wisecracks about crystal-heads and proxmires until the day they hang you for technophilia—"

"They don't hang you for that. They send you to reeducation camps."

"Whatever. But, for me . . . I can't go back; so I've got to go on."

He nudged her with his elbow. "Here comes Chuck. You never did tell me what you guys decided this morning. What do we tell the others?"

"Oh. It's still a secret. Just us and the Ghost. What they don't know can't get them in trouble." She straightened and stepped away from the van. "Hi, Chuck."

Chuck Umber was agitated. His beard jutted out. "The Con is busted," he said. "The cops are on their way."

Sherrine stiffened. The police were coming? They would catch her here, among fans. She would lose her job. She would . . . "How do you know?" she asked.

"Secret source."

A closet fan in the police department. She remembered a civilian analyst who'd been active before. Probably a secret *Hocus* subscriber—

"Look, you've got to leave *now*," Umber said. "There's still time before they get here."

She turned to climb in the van. Bob grabbed her arm.

"Wait! Gabe and Rafe!" She looked into his eyes. "We've got to find them," he said.

"They're with Thor and Steve," she told him. "They'll get them out."

"Gabe and Rafe," Chuck said. "Dell 'Angelo. A pair of angels?"

"Chuck—"

"Don't worry," Chuck said. "I didn't hear a thing. We'll get them out. Now go! The fewer people in your van, the less suspicious you'll look at the roadblocks."

"Roadblocks?"

"Yeah. This isn't any ordinary bust. The 'danes are out in force. They're looking for something. This isn't just the cops, the Air Force is in it."

Again she traded looks with Bob.

"But I still don't know how the Air Force knew where to look," Umber said. "Hey, get going! Now. And get the badge off, Bob!"

The Rotsler cartoon badge. Bob dropped it in a pocket. "Don't have it on you," Chuck said.

Sherrine said, "How will we find our friends?"

"I said don't worry," Chuck told her. "I've got it all scoped out. Always map escape routes first thing. Head for River Road just south of the big curve near the Bell Museum. Your friends will meet you there."

"Can you get them out in time?"

Chuck grinned. "Did I ever fail to get *Hocus* out on time? Then I won't fail to get this issue out, either."

She climbed into the passenger seat and Chuck slammed the door on her. Bob started the van and they pulled out of the parking apron. "Sherrine, where's your badge?"

"*My*—? Back at the apartment."

"Good thing," Bob said. He pulled on the radio panel. It opened, and he dropped his badge into the cluttered cavity.

SHERRINE HARTLEY, her badge said, and the little William Rotsler figure looked fondly up at the letters, thinking, "Infatuation Object." It wasn't hidden in her apartment. She'd thought it too dangerous. She'd thrown it away.

The chlorine buckets in back rolled and thumped.

Sherrine twisted in her seat and looked out the back window at Chuck. He was already running back toward the Tre-house. She straightened and stared through the windshield. Her hands were clenched in her lap.

"What is it?" Bob asked.

"Nothing," she said. She was thinking of all the times her issue of *Hocus* had come late.

☆　　　☆　　　☆

The Tre-house was in confusion. Fans grasping duffel bags and knapsacks scampered up one corridor and down another. Tremont J. Fielding stood in the tiled foyer giving directions, dividing the flow of fannish refugees so that they did not bottleneck at any one exit. He wore a long, flowing cape—his trademark—and indicated one corridor or another with his malacca walking stick. Wolfson was at the far end of the west hallway, near the carport entrance, hustling them along. Some of the fans were still in their hall costumes: elves, warriors, ancient gods, aliens and spacemen.

3MJ allowed himself a moment to appreciate Pat Davis's mermaid. The tail was split so she could walk. She seemed to swim along the corridor. Much skin was showing, and much more implied. Her fine blond hair bobbed and waved almost as if she were underwater.

Priorities. Who had to run, who could stay? The nature people were safe. The Greens didn't hate them, except for their association with technophiles. The kids were all right, too young to worry the cops. Students would get lectures, maybe some remedial reading on Ecodisasters, but students could get away with a lot.

People with mundane jobs were in trouble. Get them out first, since even if they weren't arrested, they could lose their jobs. And the pros. Most of them had judgments hanging over their heads. They could be sentenced to "community service" for not paying their debts.

Wolfson raised a circled thumb and forefinger. Good. All the pros were hidden in the vaults below. So far no one had ever found those. *Of course, there's a first time for anything.*

OK. The people are safe. Now our treasures. Most of the high tech posters were already gone, leaving the paintings of wizards and elves and witches and fairies. Over there! A medal, stamped in aluminum from the original Apollo 11 capsule and given to people who had worked on the program! Priceless. He plucked it and put it in his pocket. None of this stuff was worth dying for, but this— The bell rang insistently. 3MJ took a deep breath and opened it.

There were at least a dozen cops, eight blues and several greens. Behind them was a squad of Air Police at parade rest, and behind them were more airmen with rifles. An Air Force captain was pointing to a group of students who had run away. "Catch them and check their ID. You know what we're looking for." The sergeant nodded grimly and led four men at double time.

Tremont pretended not to notice the Air Force and Greens and turned to the leader of the local police. "Yes, Officer?" he said politely. The name badge read Sergeant Pyle.

"Sorry to bother you, sir. Are you the householder?"

Tremont smiled grimly. "You know who I am, Sergeant. Yes, I'm Tremont Fielding."

"Yes, sir. Mr. Fielding, we're serving a complaint." He pulled a warrant from his jacket pocket and handed it over. "Public nuisance. One of your neighbors complained about the noise from the party."

Tremont studied the warrant. "I see. Yes, this is all in order. But, Sergeant, I *know* the noise wasn't loud enough to disturb my neighbors."

Pyle exchanged looks with his Green partner, a Sergeant Zaftig. "And how do you 'know' that, sir?" asked Zaftig.

3MJ spread his hands guilelessly. "I throw a great many parties, officer. Charity affairs. All those bodies, it's an easy way to warm the house. As you know, I'm a firm supporter of the Patrolman's Benevolent Association. Hope you liked the party last month—"

"Yes, sir." Pyle frowned. "So?"

"Like everyone else, I am concerned about pollution;

especially noise pollution from my many affairs. So the edge of my property is ringed with sound meters that record the noise levels. I checked them earlier tonight, and the decibel readings have been no higher than normal background noise. Certainly not as high as they were during the PBA benefit last month."

"Sound meters," said Zaftig. The Green looked triumphant.

"Yes. I rent them from the EPA through the local Nader franchise. I have them calibrated there every two months." He turned to Pyle. "I'll be glad to apologize to any neighbor who has been offended, but really, any disturbance must have come from somewhere else. Is there anything else, Sergeant?"

Pyle sighed. "Yes, sir—" He fished in his uniform pocket and pulled out a second warrant and unfolded it carefully, then held it out for Tremont to read. "All right, then. Suspicion of harboring dangerous fugitives."

"Fugitives. May I ask who these fugitives are?"

"Read it."

Tremont adjusted his glasses. He took hold of the warrant in one hand but the policeman refused to relinquish it. Tremont raised an eyebrow, Spock-fashion.

"Sorry, Mr. Fielding," Pyle muttered. "I've got to show it to you, but I can't let you have it."

"I see." Tremont took his time reading the warrant. The longer he stalled, the better for everyone. "There's nothing about who the fugitives are."

"Classified."

"Oh. And the space for the judge's signature is blank," he observed. "Just an 'X.' "

"The judge's name is classified, too." Zaftig looked triumphant. "The mark on the warrant is witnessed," the Green sergeant said, "and the signature is on file at the courthouse."

"I knew we had literacy problems—"

Pyle looked uncomfortable. "There's precedent," he explained.

Tremont nodded. "The Steve Jackson affair. Yes, I understand." Jackson's game company had been seized by the Secret Service under just such an unsigned warrant. His computers, modems, files. Even his printers. Suspicion of hacking. And private ownership of unregistered modems had been legal back then.

"Move aside," Zaftig said. "We'll be searching this place."

Pyle looked at him. "He knows that."

Tremont knew he had stalled long enough. He stepped away from the door. "Very well, Officers. But please be careful. As you know, I have a number of valuable and fragile *objects d'art* about the house."

Zaftig smirked. "Yeah. I heard."

Tremont sighed and resigned himself. There would certainly be vandalism and pilferage. It was grand larceny that worried him. Fortunately, most of the things he considered valuable would be thought trash by the Greens.

The Greens never had liked him, but then they didn't like anybody; they reserved their affection for animals and birds and plants, constituencies that couldn't vote them out of office. They'd steal what they could, and destroy other stuff on general principles. The local police would try not to cause much damage unless they found something truly criminal going on. Tremont J. Fielding had worked for years to raise his standing in the community. His charity balls and fund-raisers helped a lot. Still, he was a known technophile. So were some of the police. But not the Greens, and they had seized control of much of the bureaucracy.

It was the Air Force that worried him. Why were they here? Just who were these fugitives they wanted? He had a pretty good guess. The dell 'Angelo brothers. Wheel chairs, neofans made into instant guests: it had to be them. What were they wanted for? He edged closer to the Air Force people.

It was clear that they were really in charge. They'd let the local cops speak for them, but when it came to giving orders— The Air Force captain stepped forward.

The name tag said ARTERIA. The officer was tall, thin, with long muscles. The helmet strap was buckled, hiding part of the face. The hands were gloved. The grips on the holstered pistol had been customized, and the weapon seemed well worn.

Arteria faced the troops. "We'll conduct this search systematically." The voice was a slightly fruity contralto. "Start on the third floor and work your way down. Remember what the description flyer says: 'spectrally tall supermen.' So be careful." Arteria handed out sketches which Tremont recognized from the television broadcast the night before. "And remember, the Government wants them intact and unharmed."

Spacemen. Dell 'Angelo. Angels. Of course. For a moment Tremont felt hurt that the Con Committee hadn't told him. What difference would it have made? They were welcome here, whatever the cost.

The soldiers clattered up the stairs and fanned down the three wings. Tremont could hear them stamping about overhead. He sighed, but did not leave the foyer. The head cops—Air Force blue, darker police blue, and green—huddled together and argued in fierce whispers. Tremont shook his head as he watched them. Probably arguing about jurisdiction. He could not overhear and did not want to appear nosy.

Wolfson approached and, tugging at his sleeve, drew him aside. Tremont bowed his head so Wolfson could whisper into his ear. "They're all gone or in the hideaway, except for the Lunarians and the two neos in the wheelchairs. There wasn't enough room down below."

Tremont raised his head and blinked rapidly. "Oh, dear." *The Angels! And no one had known to put them below first.*

"Shew and Curtis volunteered to give up their slots in the vault; but, hell, Tremont, those guys are *published*. The cops have their names and pictures on their list."

Tremont touched his arm. "Don't worry. Tell the Lunarians to execute Plan Two. They'll know what to do. Chuck Umber laid it all out before he left."

Wolfson licked his lips. He watched the police barking into their wrist coms. "All right," he said. "I won't worry."

*   *   *

When they hauled out the Pierson's puppeteer skeleton, Tremont kept his face stoically composed; but inwardly his heart cracked as he wondered what he would say to Will Waxman. The puppeteer was his prize possession. Tremont pulled his cape closed and changed his grip on his walking stick. Will knew the risks involved in attending a con. He would buy Doc a drink the next time their paths crossed and they would both shake their heads over their losses.

"Look at that crap," said one of the cops, pointing to the puppeteer.

And that really was too much. He turned to the policeman. "Crap, sir? Crap? Do you comprehend the creativity and art that went into the fashioning of that artifact? An anatomically correct and self-consistent realization of an imaginary beast." *Careful,* he told himself. *It's a Monster, not an Alien.* Fantasy was still marginally acceptable; but just barely so. He hoped the policeman would not read the provenance plaque. Maybe Will had managed to pocket it.

"Art," the cop grunted. "I don't see no NEA sticker."

"It was made before—before NEA approval was necessary. Even today not all art is government subsidized." *And the National Endowment for the Arts had never given a grant to fantasy or science fiction art.*

"Some of the stuff you got here glorifies technology," the Green cop insisted. As if Tremont did not already know it. "You don't want to glorify technology, do you?"

"Maybe he needs some education," another Green said. "Community service."

"Mr. Fielding is all right," a policeman said. "Good law and order man. Come on, lay off."

And I should leave it at that— He couldn't. "Do you dislike all technology? Such as the technology that made the cloth for your uniforms, or developed the electric cars you drove here?"

The Green looked surprised. "That's appropriate technology," he said.

*   *   *

The foyer was empty again, except for the three head cops, when the Lunarians made their move. Most of the searchers were still scattered across the two upper floors, but Arteria and the two sergeants stood in a cluster at the foot of the grand staircase taking reports from their squads over their wrist coms. Those, too, were "appropriate." As were the guns they carried.

The rumble of casters caught their attention, and they turned just as Hal Blandings and three other Lunarians emerged from the north wing pushing a handcart with a large cardboard box on it. They headed straight across the foyer toward the front door. Tremont was stunned. The sheer audacity of it! Lunarian fanac always inspired a certain amount of awe among the more circumspect fen. But this . . . He realized that his fingers were crossed and quickly uncrossed them. When he saw the tip of the snorkel protruding from the styrofoam, he held his breath. Did they have both Angels in there?

The three cops stared for a moment, then Zaftig shouted. "Hey, you four!"

The Lunarians halted just at the front door. Zaftig grabbed Hal by the arm. "Got you, you technomaniac." He pointed at the cardboard box. "That there's styrofoam," he announced. "You know better than that. Wasting valuable resources." He grinned. "Or maybe you don't know better. You will, though."

"Sergeant Zaftig," said Arteria, "that is not why we are here."

The Green turned to the Air Force captain. "You stay out of this, Captain. Environmental laws are *my* jurisdiction. Anyplace, anytime." He faced Blandings. "What've you got to say for yourself, techie?"

The west hallway door opened on cue. Pat Davis emerged into the foyer crossed to the east hallway. Since she was still wearing her mermaid costume, every male eye in the foyer followed her progress—except Zaftig, who was reading the Lunarians their rights, and Arteria, who evidently did not care for that sort of thing. Pyle took after her.

"Sergeant Pyle!" Arteria snapped.

Pyle muttered something about the Helms Law and kept going. Tremont smiled thinly. Enforcing the obscenity statutes was tricky business. The courts had imposed intricate guidelines. Pyle would no doubt have to study the costume for a considerable time and from many angles before he could decide what to do.

Meanwhile, back at the front door, one of the Lunarians was showing Zaftig a certificate proclaiming that the styrofoam in the box was 100 percent recycled material. So was the box. "Recycling! It's important! The paper they use in some of those fast-food places, that's from trees! They cut down trees for that! And we can recycle styrofoam. You know how much energy it takes to recycle styrofoam? Not much. But trees, it takes a long time to grow trees! Owls roost in trees! Trees are important. Sergeant, aren't you for *ecology?*"

The tip of the snorkel sank deeper into the chips.

Zaftig sprang. "There's someone hiding in this box."

Arteria stiffened and looked at Tremont. "Smuggling out a fugitive, are you? That was a pretty clumsy maneuver."

The way the AP captain said it, it sounded almost like a rebuke and Tremont wanted to apologize. *We didn't have time to be particularly clever.* Arteria walked to the carton just as Zaftig grabbed the end of the snorkel.

Wolfson tapped his arm and pointed silently to the top of the staircase. Tremont looked and saw Anthony Horowitz tiptoeing down. He scowled. If there was no room in the cellars for Harry and Jenny, there sure wasn't for a neopro like Horowitz. He'd been left to take his chances— but Tony might just make it. He must have evaded the AP's on the second floor. The two cops in the foyer had their backs to the stairs and the west wing.

Harry and Jenny. Where were they? Jenny was sure the police were after her. She never quite said what for. Tremont didn't know about Harry. No room for them in the hiding holes, and their bike wouldn't start. They'd gone toward the kitchen. . . .

Horowitz made it to the bottom of the stairs. No one had noticed. He'd never have a better chance. Tremont

shook his head. It was a helluva con. Better than Nycon
I.

Zaftig yanked on the snorkel and its wearer emerged
dripping plastic chips, a fish hoisted from the styro-
foamy sea. The burly, bushy-haired Seth looked around
the foyer, wide-eyed. He took the snorkel from his mouth.
"Is the book auction over already?"

Zaftig grabbed him by the wrist. "Is this one of them?"
he asked Arteria.

The AP captain scowled. "Does this look like a 'spectrally thin superman' to you?" A grunt of disgust, but
before Arteria could turn away, Horowitz had blocked
the way.

Horowitz stuck out his hand. "Hi, do you do interviews? I'm Tony Horowitz. I'm an up-and-coming pro
science fiction writer. I've got several books out already,
but I need to boost my circulation."

"A sci-fi pro?" said Zaftig. He grinned. "I think your
circulation just dropped to zero." His eyes dropped
then, and the grin went away.

Horowitz smiled beatifically. "Yes, but think of the
notoriety. Jailed writers always sell more."

Zaftig's eyes were locked on Horowitz's badge. A sly
and dissolute cartoon face, and HAVE SEX OUTSIDE MY
SPECIES. The cop was unlikely to recognize a literary
reference and if he took it at face value ... the law
wouldn't permit him to take it into consideration.

With visible effort Zaftig wrenched his eyes off the
badge. "You ain't no writer. You do sci-fi."

"We'll let *The New York Times* decide."

Jenny and Harry came in from the kitchen. Jenny had
found the maid's uniform. When Tremont's wife was still
alive he'd employed a housekeeper who liked wearing
uniforms because that way Tremont paid for her work
clothes. Now Jenny was wearing it, a conventional black
and white pinafore that looked ridiculous on someone
of Jenny's age and bearing. She'd even put on the silly
bonnet.

Harry was wearing his own clothes, except they were
dirtier and more torn than Tremont remembered.

"I'm sorry, sir," Jenny said. "I'd let this poor man out the back door, but the soldiers won't let me. Here, it's this way—" She led Harry toward the front door.

"Where the hell are you going?" one of the soldiers demanded. "Who is this dude?"

"He's *homeless*," Jenny said. "I gave him a hot meal."

"A bum, you mean," the corporal said.

"Homeless! Are you a monster?" Jenny demanded. She turned to Arteria. "Sir, how can you let your men talk that way? I think there are laws. Don't the racism laws cover this? They can't say such things—"

Pyle was off chasing mermaids. Arteria was buttonholed by Horowitz. Jenny was screaming at the Greens. Zaftig was encumbered with Seth and the Lunarians. Everyone was shouting at the top of their voices—and everyone but Tremont had their backs to the foyer. The north wing door opened, and two wheelchairs rolled swiftly and silently down the ramp. Thor and Fang pushed them into the west wing.

Toward the carport.

3MJ saluted with his walking stick. Fang waved back and vanished out the door with the others. Then Tremont swung his stick up and rested it jauntily across his shoulder. He turned a military about-face and watched the ruckus by the door. He smiled at the back of Arteria's head. *We had just enough time to be just clever enough.*

★   ★   ★

Sherrine rolled down the passenger window of the van and looked behind, up River Road. From where the van was parked she could see the Bell Museum of Natural History. The University buildings lined the left side of the road, while the Mississippi—this far upstream, a human-scale river—curved past on the right in a gentle crescent. Directly upstream, she could see St. Anthony Falls. University students, bundled against the chill, stood in knots along the roadside laughing and talking and swigging beer. Ice patches glistened in the afternoon sun.

"Roll the window up," said Bob. "You're wasting heat."

"I don't see them yet." She faced forward and rolled

the window back up. Crossing her arms over her chest, she stuck her hands under her armpits. Bob had turned the motor off; there was no heat. "It's not that cold, anyway," she said.

"Cold enough."

"Where I was, it was so cold our breath turned colors." She cocked her head and watched the side mirror. No one. The students were waiting for something, but what? Not the Angels, surely.

"Sherrine, someone had to stay with the van. We thought it would just be a short run on and off the Ice. So—"

"You don't have to make excuses."

"I'm not making excuses, dammit!"

"What if they can't find us?"

He paused and groped for the conversational tennis ball. "They'll find us. Chuck arranged everything."

She turned and looked at him. "And who is Chuck Umber that we should put our faith in him?"

Bob draped one arm across the steering wheel and half turned in the seat. "What's bothering you, Sherrine?"

"Nothing. I just don't know if this fanac is going to come off."

"You don't like running off and leaving the Angels behind."

"I noticed you jumped into the van mighty quick." But it wasn't that way at all, she remembered. Not at all. Chuck had come running out with the news and her first thoughts had been for herself; and for her job; and that she mustn't be found here, among fans. It was Bob who had asked about the Angels, when she was already halfway into the passenger's seat. And now . . . What if she'd lost them? What if she'd lost them?

Bob shrugged. "I trust Chuck. It's that convoluted, intricate mind of his. He knew there wouldn't be time to find Alex and Gordon and load them *and* their wheelchairs in the van and leave before the police arrived. It was a near thing as it was. The roadblock on University Avenue would have had them." He shook his head and looked stubborn. "No, we could not and should not have taken them with us. Chuck has something else in mind.

Something to disguise the Angels' feeble condition in a way the police won't question."

"It's not that. It's . . ."

"What?"

She closed up. "Never mind." *But it doesn't matter what I could have done or should have done. It's what I didn't even think of doing.* Damn it all, when Bob had called that night, she should have stayed in bed.

Like those students coming down River Road.

She blinked and hunched forward, staring into the side-view mirror. *What the hell?* She cranked down the window once more.

"What is it?" asked Bob.

"Look behind us." She popped the passenger door and jumped out. The students who had been waiting along the roadside were lined up now, cheering and clapping. Some of them were waving pennants with gophers and Greek letters on them. Farther up the road she saw a fleet of beds, a flotilla of four-posters and brass rails weaving toward her, white sheets flapping like spinnakers.

She went to the rear of the van for a better view. Bob joined her there. "It's a bed race," he said.

The student crowd was growing thicker. Spectators were running alongside the street to keep abreast of the racers. They were yelling and shouting encouragement. She could see now that each bed had a passenger and was being pushed by a crew of three. Did that make them triremes, she wondered? The bedsheets flaunted more Greek letters than a math convention.

"It must be a fraternity event," Bob decided.

"Why, Holmes, how clever of you!"

"Alimentary, my dear Watson. I had a gut feeling."

She stamped her feet. How would the Angels find them in this crowd, local guide or no local guide? Chuck was from the Bay Area, he wouldn't have known about this. So, should she go looking for them or should she stay put?

One of the beds hit an icy spot and skidded, forcing the bed next to it to swerve. The other racers shouted epithets and laughed as they sprinted by. Sherrine imagined the beds cartwheeling and bursting into flame like

stock cars going out of control. Then she realized that
the two stray beds were headed straight toward her. The
students around her parted and fled.

"Hey!" She grabbed Bob by the sleeve and yanked
him aside. They tumbled to the frosted grass together,
rolling tipsy-topsy in a snarl of arms and legs, and Bob
naturally contrived to wind up on top. There was a crash
of metal and a few shouts. Plastic crunched and Bob
leapt up, leaving her prone.

"That's my van!" he cried. "They smashed the tail
light!"

"Thanks for helping me up, Bob," she said.

"What? Oh. Sorry." He hoisted her to her feet and
watched while she brushed herself off. "I always said I
wanted to die jumping into bed with you; but this wasn't
quite what I had in mind. Damn, that light's *broken.*
Hey, you bloody vandals!"

She laughed. When he gave her a look, she said, "I'm
sorry. A hit-and-run accident with a brass bed? What'll
your insurance company say?"

The race had passed by, with most of the spectators;
but the two wrecked beds and their crews remained.
They were hunched over the beds, tending to the occupants. "All right," Bob said to them, "what do you think
you're up to?"

One of them turned around. It was Bruce. "We think
we're making a getaway. What do you think?"

Sherrine's knees almost gave way. Alex grinned up
from his place in one of the beds. "Hi, pretty girl," he
said. "Is that the way fraternity kids talk?"

"We are all droogs here," Gordon said.

"Yep," Mike said. "We didn't have enough money
to bribe the cops. But droogs will get you through
times of no money much better than money will get you
through . . ."

They loaded the Angels into the van. "I was sure
they'd caught you," Sherrine said.

"Not a chance," said Bruce. "Chuck had it all scoped
out. I don't know how he knew about the race—"

"Fans are everywhere," Crazy Eddie said. "Actually, it was fun. How'd you guys like the race?"

Gordon smiled weakly. "I wish I was back in the scoopship, where it is safer."

Alex grimaced. "We crashed that one, too, remember?"

Gordon's smile flickered. "Third time lucky?"

"Come on," said Bruce. "Thor, Steve, Mike. Help me load them into the van before someone comes back to find out what's going on."

"You should have seen it," said Thor, as he and Mike lifted Gordon into the side door. Fang and Eddie were inside, helping. "It was the slickest fanac you'd ever hope to see. Dick Wolfson and 3MJ orchestrated it like a goddam ballet. With a little help from the Lunarians and Tony Horowitz and Jenny."

Mike chuckled as he helped Alex into the van. "It's like 3MJ always says. 'You've got to use your Imagi-Nation.' "

Bruce nodded. "Or like Wallace Stevens wrote. 'In the world of words the imagination is one of the forces of nature.' "

Fang and Eddie hopped out of the van. "All secure," said Fang. "We figure to stay here and dismantle the beds. Shlep the stuff back to the frat house. You guys can put the Angels up for the night. Tomorrow we'll head for Chi-town."

Bob shook his head. "Whatever. You know you could have hurt Sherri and me, ramming into the van like that."

"Yeah," said Mike. "Didn't you see us coming?"

"Not until you were headed right for us."

"No. You mean you didn't read the frat logo on our sail?"

Bob's eyes went round in horror, even as he whipped around toward the beds.

Mike grabbed the edge of a sheet. He flapped it ("Olé'!") and the breeze lifted it from the bed and spread it out like a flag. Sherrine read the letters and laughed. Of course, she should have known. Who else would belong to the Psi Phi fraternity?

Ψ Φ

CHAPTER ELEVEN

"... The Lumber of the World"

Sherrine watched the brown, sere grasslands of Wisconsin slide past the windows of the van. It seemed as if she had spent half her life in Bob's vehicle. First, the drive to Fargo; now this. The gentle shaking of the suspension; the lullaby hum of the tires. And another two days out of her life.

Bruce and Mike had flown to Chicago. She could have gone with them. There were still flights from Minneapolis to Chicago every Monday, Wednesday and Friday; and the ticket prices were not completely out of her range. But ...

She turned and looked into the back, where Alex and Gordon lay on air mattresses, practicing their yoga under Steve's guidance. Flying the Angels on a commercial flight would be risky. Eye-catching. Two gaunt, skinny beanpoles who couldn't walk ... Bob had suggested splitting them up to make them less conspicuous, but Gordon had gone into a panic at the idea and Alex had said no, definitely not, out of the question. Sherrine wondered at that. The Angels hadn't seemed to be on friendly terms.

At least they were speaking to each other again. But Gordon tended to slip into morose silences that needed all of Steve's cheery prodding to dissipate. Alex was no help there. Gordon's silences seemed to disgust him. There was a hardness to Alex, a kind of intolerance for failure that was almost Darwinian.

She turned forward and resumed her study of the dreary Wisconsin countryside. Oh, well. At least this time she got to sit in the shotgun seat; and the van was not quite so crowded. Just Steve and the Angels and Thor and Fang. And the running motor kept them warm.

Wooden rail fences topped by barbed wire paralleled both sides of the two-lane blacktop road. Beyond the fences, a jumble of kames, eskers, and moraines; and nine thousand lakes strewn carelessly behind by yesteryear's glaciers; soon to be gathered and scoured by today's. Sparse, wilted grass sagged against the rolling dells of farm pastures. A corporal's guard of bony cattle, rib-bound and yellow-faced, chewed with half a heart. Some-one had brought in a strain of Highland cattle, more ox than cow, hairy like the yak, with huge horns. Their fur gave them advantages, but they didn't look happy either. Their hooves kicked up dust from the bare spots. Her eyes locked with one; and they stared at each other, human to bovine, until the van had rolled past.

The road was draftsman straight. The rural roads of Wisconsin had been laid out by a maniac armed with T squares and straight edges. It stretched toward the vanishing point on the horizon, where it converged with the fence lines on either side. Sherrine had the sudden, disorienting notion that it was the road that was fenced in, and they drove along a long, thin, blacktopped pasture.

A weathered sign dangled at the roadside. JUNCTION, COUNTY ROADS F AND CC. Wisconsin county roads bore letters. A, B, C; AA, BB, CC. Steve had joked that if they found Route KKK he'd just as soon turn back.

They came on the intersection, right-angled as she had

known it would be, and Bob spun the wheel and they turned right, leaving the Interstate farther behind.

It made sense to assume that the Interstate Highways out of Minneapolis would be watched; sure it made sense to take back roads. But she was tired of watching the richest dairylands in the world turning into desert; she was tired of watching patiently starving milch cows convert the last of the northern prairie into cow pats and methane. Every year, more and more water was locked into the Ice. The prairie lands at the foot of the glaciers were becoming scrub desert. Like West Texas, only cold.

"Cornish game hens," Fang said suddenly.

Her head came up. "What?"

"Alex! How about Cornish game hens? For the ship. They're small, but they're great eating."

The Angel grunted. "They sound delicious."

"They taste like chicken."

Sherrine heard the wistful humor in the older man's voice. "I'm sure they do."

"Say, Alex," said Thor. "Don't just take female animals up with you. Take *pregnant* female animals. Embryos don't weigh anything and you get two critters for the mass of one."

Bob braked suddenly and Sherrine jerked into her harness and then bounced against the headrest. Steve, who had been sitting lotus-fashion in the back, caught himself on the back of her seat. "What the hell?"

"What happened?" asked Alex.

Sherrine turned. "Are you guys all right?"

"I'm sorry," said Bob. "The bridge is out."

Sherrine followed his finger. The road bed crossed a crumbling concrete slab. Holes gaped in the paving and corroded reinforcing bars showed through. The bridge abutments looked as if they had come loose from the earth embankment. Off to the left the dirt had been chewed into muddy ruts by truck tires. Matching ruts corrugated the farther bank. "Doesn't look like anyone has used that bridge for a while," Sherrine said.

Bob hopped from the van and walked to the edge of the creek bank. "Ford over here. Doesn't look deep."

Sherrine left the van and joined Bob at the bridge. Where was the county road crew? How bad had the infrastructure gone that they hadn't had the time or resources to fix this bridge? She ran her glove along the crumbling masonry. Not for a long time.

Thor and Fang joined them.

"I think the van can make it across," Bob said.

Fang walked out onto the bridge span. "Slab bridge," he commented. He crouched with his hands on his knees peering at the cracks and holes. Then he jumped across one gaping hole to the other side, and Sherrine held her breath, afraid that he might fall through.

Thor said, "It looks bombed. Maybe we've driven into a war?"

"No. Spalling," Fang called back. "Worst case of spalling I ever saw."

"What causes it?"

"Water and salt get down cracks in the concrete. The salt corrodes the steel reinforcing rods. Then the water freezes and expands. Concrete chunks pop right out of the road surface."

And the freezing season has grown a lot longer, Sherrine thought, *and they salt the roads a lot more.*

Fang danced back to the bank where Thor waited. "So what do we do?" asked Thor. Fang looked at Bob.

Bob said, "Drive across the ford."

Fang ran one of his outsize fingers along his nose. "Maybe. But if we try to cross and get stuck, we won't be up the creek, we'll be *in* it."

Bob worked his lips; then he sighed. "Yeah, you're right. Jesus, can you imagine being stuck out here in the middle of nowhere? It's so empty. I haven't seen a soul for the last score of miles."

"Don't you believe it," said Thor. "There were eyes in every one of those farmhouses watching us as we went past. They don't like or trust strangers out here. If you ain't white and Protestant, you ain't shit. Sorry, Steve."

Stephen Mews was standing by the opened side door of the van. He shrugged. "It isn't exactly news to me."

Sherrine waited, shivering. It was worse than that.

This was Proxmire country. These were the people who had elected and reelected the nation's premier technophobe to the Senate, where he could give his Golden Fleece Award every month to some especially vulnerable example of scientific research.

Most of the targets he had drawn bead on had cost less than a single Washington bureaucrat. So how would these people react to a band of technophiles travelling in their midst? The Senator had always voted for dairy price supports. Hundreds of millions of taxpayer dollars. She supposed that if she had been a Wisconsin farmer she might have voted for him, too. Farm subsidies never won the Golden Fleece.

Bob nodded. "Okay. We'll look for a detour. Maybe the next road over goes across." He patted his jacket. "At least we can't get lost while we have the transponder. We know which way we want to go. It's just a matter of finding a road that will cooperate."

They trudged back toward the vehicle. "Sure hope so," said Fang.

"Yeah," said Bob. "I'm tired of zigzagging all over Pierce County."

Sherrine took hold of the handle to hoist herself back into the van. Fang shook his head. "Ah, sightseeing, I don't mind. It's the blizzard that bothers me." He pointed skyward with his chin.

Sherrine jerked her eyes upward. Black clouds huddled on the northern horizon. The wind blew cold and from the north. There was a taste of ice in the air.

Yeah, she thought. *Thor and Fang have no jobs. They didn't have to call in and take vacation days. They could have trucked the Angels themselves, if Bob would lend them his van. But that sunuvabitch, Bob, he had to go and volunteer to do the driving.* She dropped into her seat and pulled the door shut with a slam. Was she in a contest with Bob to see who would take the most risks?

She stole another glance at the northern clouds while Bob made a U-turn on the county road. *Risky business*, she thought. *I sure hope I'm back at my desk next week.* Not that she didn't have more vacation days coming, but

... Risky business, she thought again, *but at least they don't know I'm involved with the Angels*.

☆   ☆   ☆

The INS was late for the meeting and Lee Arteria spent the time waiting by doodling on the scratch pad. All the seats around the table had scratch pads and pencils in front of them. Arteria had never seen anything useful recorded on one. The pencil traced a light circle, slightly oblate. Arteria studied it, grinned and added two smaller circles on the sides. Chipmunk cheeks. A tiny pout of a mouth. Two large, little kid eyes, with eyebrows twisted to give the caricature a credulous look. Not too bad for a quick sketch. Sometimes Arteria missed the art world.

"Not bad," said Jheri Moorkith over her shoulder. He stole a glance at Shirley Johnson, then whispered, "But maybe make her a trifle plumper."

And you're next. Moorkith was a good-looking man, square-jawed, square-shouldered. Arteria would have sketched him as a Flash Gordon-style hero ... but her sketches never came out flattering, somehow. She changed her mind and tossed the pencil to the table. "Where's Redden? I don't have time to waste in these meetings."

Moorkith shrugged. "None of us do. But this is INS's way of reminding us who's in charge." He leaned closer and whispered, "I checked your Air Force file."

"Ah. That is illegal, isn't it?"

Another shrug. "I was curious. I like to know who I'm working with."

"Whom."

"Whatever. Didn't do any good, though. Couldn't get access. You must have some good codesmiths on your team. But I was able to look at your credit report."

"That's illegal, too." *But he wants me to know he can do it*.

"Yeah. The box where it asked for sex. You wrote 'Yes.' "

Arteria grunted and half-swiveled the chair to get a better look at Moorkith. "So?"

"So, why didn't you put down the right answer?"

"I did."

"You did."

"Think about it."

He frowned. "Oh. But did you mean *Yes, I have a sex.* Or, *Yes, I want sex?*"

"Whichever way you want to take it."

Moorkith paused and stepped back. He licked his lip. Arteria knew what he was thinking: *Do I make the pass? What if I guess wrong and she's a he?* Or he's a she. Arteria had no idea which way Moorkith swung, and so had no idea which alternative intimidated him.

Which way would he jump? Lee Arteria sent no signals; but she never bluffed.

He hadn't made his move when INS arrived. *Ah, well. He who hesitates is lost.*

"We don't even know if the spacemen were in Minneapolis," Ike Redden insisted. "All you did, Captain Arteria, was bust a few sci-fi crazies holding an illegal meeting."

"Strictly speaking, Mr. Redden," Arteria responded, "the meeting itself was not illegal. The warrant was for harboring fugitives."

"Sci-fi nuts," said Moorkith. "Technophiles. It *should* be illegal."

"Nevertheless, there is the First Amendment."

"You tell him," said the Army rep.

"Maybe we need another exception. After all, Flag-burning and disrespectful singing of the Anthem are not covered by the First. The destruction of Mother Earth is at least as important as those issues." Moorkith smiled thinly. "Got a couple of technophiles to volunteer for reeducation, anyway."

Arteria hid a wry smile. *And from what I could see of those two fans, it's going to be interesting as to who educates whom.*

Redden rapped the table. "Please. That is not the business of this task force." He ran a hand through his hair. "We are searching for two aliens who entered the country illegally. If we don't locate them quickly, we will all look very foolish."

Translation, thought Arteria: *You will look very foolish.* What must it be like to mold your entire life around bureaucratic ladder climbing? To interpret every issue in terms of attaboys and awshits on your performance appraisal? Couldn't Redden see that there were *principles* at stake here? At least Moorkith had principles. Wrongheaded, but principles.

"The spacemen must be in Minneapolis," insisted the State Police commander. "It's the only big city reachable from the crash site. They had to head there. They would be too conspicuous in a small town. Our man at Fargo Gap told us that a van from Minneapolis drove through there the night of the crash, and they were asking about the air scooper."

Army frowned. "The same night? How did they know about it?"

"There was a girl with them. She claimed that her grandparents lived nearby. They'd seen it come down and phoned her."

"You think they were technophile subversives going to pick up the spacemen?"

State Police hesitated. "It seems likely," he admitted and hastily added: "In hindsight."

"Got an ID on the girl?" Arteria asked.

"No. We might have, but it wasn't our detail. One of your people was in charge."

"Who?"

"An engineer captain named Scithers."

Scithers. That explains some things.

"Didn't you search the van," asked Moorkith, "when they came back? You had roadblocks up by then, surely."

State Police bristled at the implied insult. "Once we were informed that the spacemen were not in their vessel, we had to take that into account, yes. A maroon van did leave North Dakota, but there was just one man in it. It may not have been the same van."

Redden looked at the ceiling. "Two maroon vans trav-

elling Fargo Gap in opposite directions the same night,"
he said to no one in particular.

"Then the others in the van must have gone west,"
said Shirley Johnson. "Or north, to Winnipeg."

Army grunted. "The Winnies would shelter them, all
right."

"No," said State Police. "The tracks across the glacier
were headed east. That's why we checked out all known
technophiles in Minneapolis." He looked at Arteria.
"With that sci-fi outfit meeting it looked good. Damn it,
it still looks good."

"Agreed. We didn't find them, though," Arteria said.
They were there, though. I wonder how they worked it?

Redden waved a hand in dismissal. "The tracks were
Eskimos. Illegals who crossed over from Canada. We
found them in Brandon, looting." He turned to State
Police. "But this van. You claim that a whole load of
them went west through the Gap but only one came
back?"

"That's what the trooper remembers. He was almost
sure it was the same van."

"Almost sure," said Moorkith with a smirk.

Redden held up a hand to forestall any argument.
"And they asked about the air scooper. We should follow
up on it. Lord knows, we have few enough leads. Have
you identified the van, yet?"

The State Police captain shook his head. "Just the
color—maroon. The license plate was a fake. Belonged
to a car registered in Brandon."

"Fake. Why didn't you arrest him, then?" Moorkith
demanded.

"The computer was down. No way to check it until too
late."

"Computer was down," Arteria mused. *But lots of
citizens switched plates. Too many nitpicking regulations, like an eternal swarm of mosquitos. The police had
nearly stopped noticing.*

"What about the girl?" Redden asked.

"Okay, *what about* the girl?"

Redden gave an exasperated sigh, and looked again at

the ceiling, as if he expected to find allies there. "Are you checking for grandparents near the crash site?"

State Police set his jaw. "No, sir. That's in North Dakota."

"Fuck North Dakota. What is this, a state's rights convention? This is a national security matter. If we don't show some results soon, the task will be taken out of our hands."

And that won't look good on your record, will it? Whoever found the downed spacemen would shine like a star in this crowd.

Not the Minnesota State Police. The search would be outside his balliwick. It probably was already, but these fools didn't see it yet. . . .

Wait, now. Army, across the table from Arteria, was smiling like the cat that ate the 500 pound canary. He's on to something; or he thinks he is. And he's got a national writ, like the Air Force; so state borders don't bother him. And Johnson, she would try to track their quarries by channeling to some two-million-year-old avatar.

Where was the FBI? Was Redden keeping them out for jurisdictional reasons; or were they running their own search? Or both. Wouldn't that be a hell of a note, if the FBI found them first! There wouldn't be any interdepartmental squabbles to hold them up.

"We can make a request to the North Dakota State Police," said the state cop. "We can ask them to run a cross-check of local residents against Minnesota van owners. If we find a last name match . . ."

"Better check it against all residents of Minneapolis," said Moorkith. "It's a grand*daughter*, remember? And she wasn't driving the van."

Redden shook his head. "I've got a better idea. Our people will cross-check Fargo residents against the 'suspicious background' files."

"Why?"

He gave them a superior smile. "Someone passed the word to Minneapolis about the air scooper crashing. Why would a good citizen leak a national security issue?"

"Maybe they didn't know it was national security?" suggested Army.

"It was out of the ordinary. It's always safest to assume that such things involve national security unless the government says otherwise."

"Say," State Police brightened. "Why not check long-distance telephone calls between Fargo and Minneapolis?"

Arteria listened passively and continued doodling. Everyone had a channel to try. Everyone had an angle that might give results. Hell, who knew? Maybe Shirley Johnson's avatar would pass the word. They would find out who had the spacemen. And everyone would try to keep it a secret from everyone else, so they would not have to share credit. That's what teamwork was all about.

Redden would try to hunt from his desk. He would wait for printouts and summaries to be brought to him. No one ever found anything by tracking paperwork but more paper. He would only find the "Angels" by piggybacking on someone else. Someone who did the grunt work of questioning witnesses and following clues.

That'll be me. Or the FBI.

The Worldcon had seemed a good bet. Hell, it *was* a good bet. The spacemen were there; they were smuggled out under our noses. That man, Tremont Fielding, he knew. I could see it in the way he looked at me. But where had they gone?

Not west; not back to the crash site. There was no percentage in that. Not north, either. Fans were bright, if feckless. So, east? Into Wisconsin? Maybe. They'd have to take the back roads. The Wisconsin Glacier had eaten the Interstate past Eau Claire. So: where could they find shelter in Wisconsin?

Arteria smiled. *Of course.*

✶   ✶   ✶

The snowflakes impacting the windshield were no longer melting. They built into fluffy white masses shoved aside by the impatient, ice-encrusted wiper blades. The black-top ahead of them was turning as gray as the heavens. Gravid snow clouds piled up above them. Flickers of static electricity played along and within them as they rubbed against the sky. Bob was hunched over his wheel, peering into the gathering gloom.

They were in the hill country below Prairie du Chien now, after hours of racing the snow clouds south. The snow clouds were winning. The roads in this part of the state were twistier; the farms were tucked into dells and hollows. Property values had boomed after it became known that this corner of Wisconsin had been free of glaciers the last time around.

Steve and the Angels were staring delightedly out the side window. Steve had never seen a storm like this in California; and the Angels had never seen snow falling. Sherrine chatted brightly with them, as if there were nothing to worry about.

Thor leaned over the seat between her and Bob. "Turn right up ahead," he said. "There's a farm down that road where I did some work last spring."

"So what? You want to make a social call? The Interstate's to the left."

"The hell with you, Bob. I want us to get to shelter, *now*."

"Shelter?"

"Yeah. It's snowing. Or haven't you noticed?"

"I noticed."

"So. Do you know what a plains blizzard can be like when the black clouds roll down from the northlands? They call it a 'norther' around here. Temperatures can crash forty degrees in the blink of an eye; snow drifts man-high in heartbeats. Damn it, Bob, you know what a blizzard can be like in Minneapolis; imagine what can happen out here in the country, beyond the heat sink. I've heard tales about cattle suffocated when the wind blew the snow up their nostrils so hard and fast they couldn't breathe. Farmers don't joke about shit like that."

Bob rubbed the steering wheel with his mittens. He glanced at Sherrine. Then he looked back at Thor. "Are you trying to scare me?"

"Yeah."

He nodded. "Which way is this farm? And how do you know they'll take us in?"

Thor shrugged. "I don't. But it's our best chance. Sherrine, let me take your seat so I can navigate."

Bob stopped the van while they exchanged seats. Sherrine unbuckled. "You have the comm, Mr. Sulu." She crawled into the back—her familiar seat—and Bob put the van back in gear.

"Is it really as bad as Thor said?" asked Alex. Sherrine twisted and looked at him. He looked concerned; Gordon, frankly frightened. Steve, sitting lotus between them, was using yoga techniques to calm himself.

She nodded. "It could be." Never pull your punches; never sugarcoat the truth. What you don't know can hurt you bad. "It could blow over, too; but it's better to play it safe and find a way station where we can hole up."

"Is *that* safe? The authorities are hunting Angels . . ."

"Look, Alex. Gordon. A blizzard can be fatal. We used to have weather satellites that gave us advance warning. Now, folks get caught by surprise. Like Thor said, you don't want to get caught outdoors in a norther. And neither do the cops!"

The snow began falling faster, piling up on the windshield, melting from the heat of the van, and freezing into an impenetrable slush faster than the wipers could handle. The countryside was a blur in the icy lens. Bob turned right and Sherrine felt the wheels go off the road. Bob put the van into first and recovered. He rolled down his window and scraped at the ice with his glove. The wind spray-painted his beard with snow.

If we can make it in time, she thought. And if they'll take us in.

☆   ☆   ☆

Ike Redden held the telephone away from his head and stared at it. Then he put it back against his ear. "What do you mean, you can't get north of Lancaster? A blizzard? Impossible. This is September. How do you know? I see. A truck pulled into Patch Grove with snow on its roof. No, you can't argue with evidence like that."

Wherever the hell Patch Grove is. He glanced at the Air Force Intelligence captain fiddling with a pen on the other side of the desk and shrugged helplessly.

"Yes, I understand," he said into the phone. "But we received a report about a maroon van with Minnesota plates somewhere in your vicinity, and we thought— No, I'm afraid I can't. Yes, we're asking all the counties, on both sides of the River. Certainly. I'm sure you will do your best. Thank you." He hung up and leaned back in his seat. "County sheriffs," he said to no one in particular.

"Do you plan to check out every van in Minnesota and Wisconsin?" Lee Arteria asked idly.

"I suppose you have a better lead, Captain?" Arteria smiled but said nothing and Redden made a steeple of his fingers. *Does that mean the Air Force has a lead and they're not going to tell me? Or does it mean the Air Force wants me to think they have a lead?*

"You could wait for the information from the DMV," Arteria suggested. "At least, it would narrow the list of vans."

Redden waved a disparaging hand. "Ahh. It's been three days already. Some sort of bug in the computer. They're still trying to straighten it out. Goddamn DMV can't find its own asshole if they used both hands."

Arteria considered that in silence, then nodded. "Any word on possible contacts in the Fargo area?"

"Not yet. That moron, Moorkith, is supposed to be running a cross-check through the technophile file . . ." Redden blinked and looked puzzled. "Techno—phile—file," he repeated slowly. "The Greens are supposed to keep it up to date for the House Un-American Activities Committee, but . . . It's just an alphabetical listing of names. They have to re-sort it by addresses and then merge it with another file or something. I don't know anything about computers." He waved his hand airily, as if he were bragging about an accomplishment. "A team of GS-5's could have gone through the list by hand by now." He took another report from his in-basket and studied it. Another goddamned van. This one on US 52

near Rochester. But it was blue and its occupants had
checked out.

Arteria grunted humorlessly, stood and stretched. The
side wall of the office was taken up by a large-scale map
of the upper Midwest. Arteria studied it carefully, running a finger from Fargo to Minneapolis and beyond.
"Where was that van spotted?"

"Which one? We've had two dozen reports."

"The last one; where you put a bug up that badger
sheriff's ass."

"Oh. Crawford County."

Arteria traced a route. "And heading southeast?"

Redden frowned. "On 18. Is that significant?"

Arteria straightened. "Probably not."

Meaning it probably is, Redden thought. What was
Arteria's lead? Damn it, didn't the Air Force believe in
teamwork? Everyone was concerned about getting credit
for the arrest. That Army colonel, he had something
going on the side, too. Some connection with Winnipeg.
This was supposed to be a Team effort; the Team would
share the credit. And Redden was chairman of the Team.

*Well, Ms. Arteria, we'll see just how smart you think
you are.* "If they went that direction," he said, "they
drove straight into a blizzard. If we can believe the hicks.
Probably just a light dusting. You know how the square-
heads like to yank our chains."

"I don't know. Weather is something farmers don't
joke about; especially nowadays. A blizzard, out in the
country; that's a life or death issue."

"Well, if the van Wilson spotted was our quarry, there's
no rush."

"Why not?"

"It's been three days since the blizzard hit. They'll be
froze dead by now."

*   *   *

Deputy Andy Atwood kicked at the back end of the
van with his snowshoe. The crusted, half-melted snow
slid off into a pile on the ground. "Minnesota plates, all
right," he said to his partner. He straightened and looked

around. There were several vans and trucks clustered around the white, clapboard church. St. Olaf in the Fields. He turned up his fur collar. "Come on. Let's check this out."

The snow was two-, three-feet deep. Even with the snowshoes he found it rough going. His feet broke through the crust and he sank several inches into the cold, wet powder beneath. It must have been a hell of a storm this end of the county. It was melting now; but it would never melt all the way. Not 'till spring. If then. He glanced behind to see his partner following in his footsteps.

They were met at the door of the church by a crusty old man in a red-checkered lumberman's cap. He was racking a pair of cross-country skis against the side of the church. "Yes, deputies," he said. "Can I help you?"

"We'll see, old timer." Atwood nodded toward the church. "What's going on in there? It isn't Sunday."

"Nope. Funeral. We hold a few of those after it snows." He worked his jaws, as if he were chewing tobacco and was wondering where to spit. "We don't get much heating oil in these parts anymore," he went on. "Not like you folks in the cities, where the newspapers and teevee cameras are. So when it freezes here ..." And again there was a drawn out, introspective silence and when he resumed speaking, it was in a lower, quieter voice. "When it freezes hereabouts, why we've all got to huddle right quick. Some folks don't make it in time. This time it was a feller did some chores for me. He and a couple of his friends."

"I see. Do you mind if we check it out, Mr. .... ?"

"Wallace. Enoch Wallace." The old man held out a heavily bundled mitt and the deputy touched it briefly with his own. "It's God's house, aina? All are welcome." He held the door open for them.

The deputies stamped the snow off their snowshoes in the narthex. There was a thin layer of snow on the wooden floor, unmelted and trod hard by a great many boots. They unstrapped their snowshoes and hung them on pegs on the wall. Atwood noticed several other pairs of snowshoes, as well as a few more skis. One pair of skis he recognized as the high-tech fiber glass Alpine type. A family heirloom, no doubt, from the days when people skied for fun.

"Huddle," he said. It was not quite a question. He had heard stories. In Grant County, you heard stories.

Wallace tugged off his mittens and stuffed them in his heavy wool jacket. "For the warmth, deputy. For the warmth. Every farmstead hereabout has a huddle room or a shut bed where folks can gather when the cold hits. Folks lie in, under the blankets, hugging each other until it gets warm again outdoors. Those on the outside of the huddle are generally a bit colder; and those on the inside have got to be mighty tolerant of body odor. You don't get much sleep, but you don't freeze, neither."

"Jesus Christ. What do you do during the winter?" Atwood's partner was a young kid new to the force. A town boy. He would see enough before the winter was over.

Wallace seemed not to mind the swearing, even standing in the narthex of a church. "We huddle all winter, deputy," he said with flint in his voice. "Every man-jack, woman and child in the township. We come right here t' St. Olaf's and we huddle."

"Like hibernating bears?"

The old man's eyes were hard as coal. "We don't quite hibernate. Come spring we're mighty thin. And some of us are ready to do murder and some are ready to get married, but mostly we're still alive." He opened the door to the nave. "Mostly," he repeated. "My handyman and some friends of his got caught in the open by Friday's storm. They didn't all make it."

Wallace preceded them into the church. Atwood grabbed his partner's arm before following. "Look, Bill. About huddling all winter. You don't have to say anything back in town. It would only get folks distressed. The townies complain about the thermostat law; but these farm folk, they would be glad to turn their thermostats up to fifty-five."

"But, Jesus, Andy. We should do something for them."

"There's one thing we could do."

"What's that?"

"Drill for oil."

Bill waited to see if he were joking. Then he blurted, "But that's inappropriate technology."

Atwood followed Wallace into the church. "Yeah."

There were three coffins, one of them supported by six bearers. A dozen or so mourners were scattered through the pews. Atwood walked slowly up the aisle, looking left, then right. He didn't see any seven-foot supermen. Spectrally thin, the flyer had said. No one present fit that description. There was one woman, tall and skinny, though not seven feet by any stretch. How did the government know if the aliens were men or women?

The woman locked gazes with him. Her eyes were red-rimmed and wet with tears. Her nose was running and her cheeks were puffy. Embarrassed, Atwood let his gaze drop. He turned to his partner. "Come on, they aren't here."

"What about the van with the Minnesota plates?" Bill whispered.

"Heh. The border isn't that far. You can see Minnesota from the bluffs. Families have got relatives on both sides of the river. You see anybody here who's seven feet tall?"

Atwood winced as Bill gripped his arm tight. He saw his partner pointing surreptitiously at belt level so the mourners could not see. Pointing at the coffins. Atwood sucked in his breath. One of the coffins was easily long enough to hold a seven footer. He stepped over to it and ran his hand along the plain pine wood top. Looking up, he located Wallace.

"Look, I really hate to ask you this, Mr. Wallace; but I'm afraid you'll have to open this up. National security."

"National security?" The old man seemed amused. Atwood wondered if he would ask to see a warrant. Folks seldom did anymore.

"I can't tell you any more than that, sir." He smiled

apologetically and scratched his beard. "They didn't tell me much more. This one isn't your handyman, is it?"

Wallace shook his head. "One of his friends, from out of state."

Atwood nodded. "Then you can't vouch for his identity."

Wallace gazed silently at the coffin. "The lumber of the world," he said.

"Eh?"

The old man looked at him. "The dead are the lumber of the world. Their bones are the ribbing and shoring that hold it up."

Atwood waited while Wallace located a claw hammer. He could feel the eyes of the mourners on his back. Watching with a dull anger. Atwood gritted his teeth. It was a lousy duty to pull.

The nails groaned as they came out of the coffin lid. Atwood remembered tales of elaborate, plush-lined coffins of shiny mahogany. There were special people, funeral directors, whose sole job was to manage an elaborate and impressive funeral display. Today there were just too many funerals. Sometimes the coffin was a canvas bag. Sometimes, not even that.

The lid came off and Atwood gazed into the box. The light was bad; the angle, wrong. He stood aside to get a better view.

A tall man, but not seven feet. So thin he looked almost wasted. He had the skin of a youngish man, yet with the hint of age around the eyes. Atwood glanced at the hands folded across the breast. Long, bony fingers, blackened with frostbite at the end, as were the nose and ears. He sniffed. The corpse had been washed, but the smell of death was there.

Atwood stepped back. "All right." A wave of the hand. "Nail it back up." He brushed his hands vigorously, although he hadn't touched anything. "Come on, Bill. We've bothered these people enough."

Wallace did not follow them out. In the narthex, they pulled on their outdoor gear, strapped the snowshoes to their feet. "Was that one of them?" Bill asked. "The corpse?"

Atwood shrugged. "He was tall enough and skinny enough to fit the profile."

"Aren't there supposed to be two of them? And what about the people who are supposed to be helping them escape?"

Escape to where? he wondered. "We'll pass the van's VIN along and let Minnesota check it out. But you heard what Wallace said. His handyman and a couple of friends. You saw the frostbite, didn't you? Jesus. No heating oil. No gas. They've been written off by the government. They've got to move south or die, and they're too stubborn to move. You wanted to do something for them, Bill? Then let them bury each other in peace."

☆   ☆   ☆

The six pallbearers watched the deputies leave. The whole time the long coffin had been searched, they had held the shorter coffin aloft. Alex was growing tired. His arms ached from hanging onto the coffin handles and he was sure the four men holding the corners were just as tired. After all, they were bearing his weight and Gordon's and the coffin's, too.

"They're gone," said Wallace's wife at the back of the church.

Alex sighed and relaxed. He slumped gratefully to the floor. Thor, Bob, Fang and Steve lowered the coffin to its cart. Bob groaned and rubbed his shoulders. "I thought they'd never leave."

Gordon, leaning on the middle handle on the other side, had to be pried loose, his grip had grown so tight. They led him to one of the pews and let him stretch out.

Alex pushed himself to a crawling position. Sherrine left her pew and helped him back upright. Then he walked in slow, careful steps to the nearest pew and dropped into the hard, wooden seat. He kneaded his thigh muscles. One thing about being snowed in for three days at Wallace's farm—he and Gordon could now stand upright and walk, at least for short periods. Like Steve said, practice every day. Still, what if the security

officer had noticed him hanging onto the coffin instead
of lifting it?

Enoch leaned over him. "You all right, Gabe?"

"I'll be fine. That's the longest I've stood up in . . ." *In
thirty-odd years*, he realized.

Sherrine patted his shoulder. "Before you know it,
you'll be walking across the room on your own."

Alex laughed. Who would have thought that walking
required the mastery of such complex skills? He had
walked as a child, but could not remember the learning
of it. He would look on pedestrians in the future with a
certain amount of awe.

"It was good of you to take us in like that," Alex told
the farmer.

Wallace grunted. "Seven warm bodies during a norther?
My wife and I would have froze to death without you.
Like poor Jed and his friends."

Alex glanced at the coffins. "Yeah."

Enoch had been waiting for the handyman and his
friends to come to his huddling place when Thor appeared on his front porch. After the storm had subsided,
they had all gone out looking and found the bodies only a
few hundred meters from the farmhouse. Judging from
the tracks that had not filled in with snow it appeared
that the three had been walking in a circle. "It happens,"
Enoch had said. "When the wind blows the snow up,
everything whites out and you lose all your sense of
direction." Thor, who had known the handyman, had
insisted on staying for the funeral.

"What next?" asked Alex.

"On to Chicago," Bob told him.

Wallace shook his head. "That deputy copied down
your license plate. Just routine, I suppose. But, if I were
engaged in anything a shade less than perfectly normal—
not that I am, mind you, or that I suggest that anyone
else is—I might be a touch wary of driving that vehicle
over the roads. Folks don't travel so much these days,
what with fuel so hard to get. So anyone far enough from
home might strike the government as suspicious."

Bob frowned and ran a hand though his beard. "You're

right." He looked at Sherrine, then back at Wallace. "What should we do?"

Wallace smiled. "Why don't you folks follow me over to Hiram's shop. We'll see if he can tinker something up."

They followed him outside into the bright, frozen sunlight. Alex found himself walking beside Wallace. Sherri supported him on one side, but mostly he carried his own mass. He walked like a two-year old and felt like two hundred; but he was moving under his own power. "Hiram's shop," he said. "Your friend is not a farmer, then?"

"Heh. No, he's a tinker. He fixes things. It's a knack he has. Snowblowers, radios, TV's." He gave Alex a sly wink. "Maybe even a computer or two, if anyone owned such a thing, which I'm not saying they do."

Alex raised his eyebrows. He exchanged glances with Sherri. "You don't talk like a technophobe," he ventured.

Wallace laughed without humor. "You ever try farming without technology? It's a lot more charming in those old woodcuts than it is in the flesh. In a good year, we get nothing to eat but cheese and beef. Cook the beef good. No antibiotics. If you could lay your hands on a supply of good medicine for cows it would be worth its weight in cheese."

Alex chuckled politely. But why would cheese be valuable in Wisconsin? He would have felt stupid asking. Instead he asked, "What do you do in a bad year?"

Wallace grunted and his voice hardened. "In a bad year we starve."

☆   ☆   ☆

Sherrine found she could not let go of her suspicions. Granted, Wallace had saved them from the storm, and he had helped them fool the sheriff's deputies, too; but that might have been from a sense of duty. After all, their body heat had helped save Wallace and his wife, as well; and the country folk had no great love for a government that had effectively abandoned them. Still . . .

They followed Wallace's pickup down the country lanes

behind Millville. Sherrine sat in the back with Alex and the others. The road undulated through the rumpled hills, whose trees, fooled by the glaciers, were rusted and yellow. An oddly disorienting layer of fallen leaves lay atop the snow, as if the seasons had gotten jumbled by the storm. Some trees stood blizzard-stripped, stark and wintry against the sky. They came out onto a high bluff from which she could see the confluence of the Wisconsin and Mississippi. The rivers sparkled in the sunlight. They flowed sluggishly, with so many of their sources locked into ice.

It was only when Wallace honked and pointed to the driveway of the ramshackle building that Sherrine relaxed. There was a handpainted sign nailed to a post by the roadside. Bright red letters on a large plywood panel:

BIG FRONT YARD SALE
HIRAM TAINE, TINKER

Of course, she thought. *Of course*. They were among friends. She saw Fang grin and nudge Thor with his elbow. Thor smiled quietly, as if at a well-orchestrated surprise. Sherrine started to laugh, earning an odd glance from Alex.

All that time she had been worried about being in Proxmire country. She had forgotten they were in Clifford Simak country, too.

CHAPTER TWELVE

"The Best of All Physicians . . ."

The van was dark and cold and stank with a stale pungency Alex MacLeod could never get used to. Worse than a spaceship! He sat huddled under blankets with the others in the back of the van, sharing his warmth. The only light was the feeble glow of a flashlight. Alex took a breath of damp, moldy air. He wished Bob could start the engine so they could warm up; but, of course, that was impossible.

Sherrine was a goblin face half-lit by the weary flashlight. "This is cozy," she said. "I used to read science fiction books like this—under my blankets with a light. Always with an ear cocked for the sound of my parents coming."

"Did they ever catch you?" asked Gordon.

"Oh, sure. I got a lecture the first time. The second time, they spanked me. They never caught me again. Maybe they got tired of watching. I always looked forward to the summers, though, when they'd send me to Gram's farm. Pop-pop kept two cartons full of old paperbacks hidden in a corner of the root cellar. I could read them in daylight."

199

Gordon laughed. "It sounds like fun."

"Yeah, lots of fun," said Alex. "How long are we going to be stuck here?"

Bob shrugged and the blankets shrugged with him. "I don't know."

"Relax," said Fang. "Here. It's cheddar."

It was a half-pound wedge. Alex felt his throat close up. "No thanks," he said. "I'm going to be heartily sick of cheese by the time we get to Chicago."

"Cheese is fermented milk curd," Fang volunteered. "The Orientals think of it as 'rotten milk.'"

Sherrine turned to him. "Thank you for sharing that thought with us."

"Well," said Thor. "Where there's a curd, there's a whey."

"Seriously," Alex insisted. "How long will we be stuck inside this trailer?" Surrounded by cheese. Encastled by cheesy ramparts. Breathing cheese with every breath. Sure, it saved gas on the van; sure, it hid them from the sheriff's deputies; but it seemed as if he had been buried in a tomb of . . . of fermented curds.

Fang nibbled on the wedge, looking for all the world like an oversized mouse. "How long?" he said. "Hard to say. The trailer takes the back roads to avoid the monties."

"The Mounties?"

"Monties . . . Montereys. They high-jack cheese."

Gordon cocked his head. "High-jack cheese? Poche— Why would anyone do that?"

Fang held his wedge up and turned it so it caught the pale light. "Supply and demand," he said. "South and east of Chicago this stuff is rare. Infrastructure collapsing. Bridges, culverts, embankments. Roads are near impassible. Can't hardly get gas anywhere in Wisconsin. So not much cheese ever gets out of the state. Not until the farmers can hoard enough fuel to make a run like this one. Naturally, the monties are on the lookout. One cheese truck taken to . . . oh, Pittsburgh or St. Louis, could set you up for life."

"I've heard," said Sherrine, "that in some places they

stamp the cheese wheels with official seals and use them
for money."

Thor laughed. "I've heard that. What would you do for
a wallet?"

"No, no," said Fang. "You put the cheese in a larder—"

"Fort Cheddar!"

"—and issue certificates—"

"Backed by the full faith and credit of—"

"Issue certificates," Fang repeated more loudly. "Pay
to the bearer on demand, so many pounds of cheese.
Pound notes!"

"Would a Swiss cheese pound note be worth more
than a cheddar?"

"Sure, you know how reliable those Swiss cheese bank-
ers are. . . ."

"How many Gorgonzolas to a Colby?" asked Steve.
"What's the exchange rate?"

"Excuse me, sir," said Sherrine to Thor, "but do you
have change for a Roquefort?"

"Keep your stinking money."

"Hey," said Bob laughing. "At least the money would
be backed by *something*."

"Maybe," Thor ventured, "they could use jellies and
jams . . . backed by the Federal Preserve Bank."

Alex simply could not believe it. Van and all they were
riding in the back of a cheese-filled eighteen-wheeler
trailer, rolling through territory infested by highway bandits, and his companions made . . . cheesy jokes. "It
seems to me," he said, "that this is an awfully risky way
to escape Wisconsin."

The others looked at him with their mouths half-open
in smiles, waiting for his punch line. Alex plowed reso-
lutely on. "I mean the montereys. They're real?"

"Sure, but . . ."

"Alex," said Sherrine. "The police are looking for a van."

"Hiram Taine gave us new plates and painted us
orange."

"All the more reason not to risk being stopped."

"Besides," interjected Thor, "there's something I've
always wanted to say."

Alex frowned at him. "What's that?"

"Cheese it! The cops!"

Everyone broke into laughter again. Alex scowled and shifted his right foot to a more comfortable *siddhasan* position. His companions couldn't seem to take things seriously. They had to make jokes. Just how dependable was this rescue? Was this to be his fate, his punishment for screwing up that one last time? To be shuttled aimlessly across the planet for the rest of his life?

Sherrine touched his arm and leaned past Thor who was cracking yet another joke to Steve. "Alex," she said. "We could never have scrounged enough gas for the van to drive out on our own. The farmers there have been saving fuel for a long time to send just this one truck out and back. They made a tremendous sacrifice by putting *us* back here instead of the same volume in cheese."

"It's not that, Sherrine. It's . . ."

"It's what?"

Alex sighed and she leaned closer. He could smell the sweetness of her breath. "It's . . ." What *was* bugging him? Was it that the optimism he had felt at the Tree-house had leached out of him? That his resolution to enjoy his exile had foundered against huddling places and blizzards and crumbling roads and funerals? He jerked his head toward the other fans. "Don't they realize the gravity of our situation?" he whispered to her.

She whispered back, "You fight gravity with levity."

Later, as they dozed under the blankets, Alex was jarred awake. He raised himself on his elbows, momentarily delighted that he *could* raise himself on his elbows, and looked around. Not that he could see anything. Under a pile of blankets inside a van that was chocked up inside a trailer. It gave the word "dark" new meaning. He lay still and listened. The familiar grumble of the motor and the gentle rocking and bouncing were missing.

The truck had stopped.

"What is it?" Sherrine's voice sleepy beside him. He flashed a momentary fancy that they shared a bunk together, somewhere hidden from their five chaperones.

"Nothing," he said. "The truck stopped, is all. Rest break, maybe."

"Oh, good. I could use a rest break myself. Should we get out, do you think?"

"Wait." Doors slammed and the engine roared to life. "Changing drivers, I guess." First gear ground and caught. "The two guys up front must have switched seats."

"I hope we get there soon, or this van is going to smell like a New York subway station."

"Please," said Bob, yawning in the darkness, "if you have to go, go outside."

"On the *cheese*?"

"I really miss my space suit," said Alex.

"Eh? Why?"

"It had a catheter," he said dreamily.

☆   ☆   ☆

Lee Arteria studied the list that Moorkith had passed around the table. It was several pages long. Eight- by fourteen-inch computer pages. Names and addresses ranked in severe columns. Not even alphabetized! Maybe it was sorted by address? No, there was no logical order to the sequence at all. A random dump. Maybe no one on Moorkith's staff knew how to run a sort.

That seemed likely. Computers might be necessary, but they were a necessary evil. Learn too much about them and you might be seduced into technophilia. Besides, competency was elitist. It was easy to imagine Moorkith's people gingerly pressing buttons and leaping back lest they be defiled by the touch.

"This is a lot of subversives for a small area like Fargo." The state policewoman was a new member of the Team, representing North Dakota. Arteria supposed that the various state jurisdictions had decided to pool their resources so they would not be left off the Team and miss out on the collar.

"I wouldn't know," said Moorkith. "But I believe it would be wise to investigate each lead for possible connections with Minneapolis technophiles."

Arteria stifled a grin. Pompous ass. They would be a long time checking out some of these leads. Verne, Jules. Gernsback, Hugo. Wells, Herbert George. Even Jefferson, Tom and Carver, G.W. Technophiles, all. Had Moorkith even *looked* at the printout before distributing it? No, he simply assumed it was correct. For someone who professed to disparage technology, he had a naive and trusting attitude toward it.

How long had Moorkith's database been compromised? Arteria would dearly have loved to know. A hack years old would have nothing to do with the current mission. A recent hack might be intended to muddy the search for the spacemen. In either case, the choice of phony names pointed straight toward fandom.

Arteria smiled. So far, no one else seemed to have noticed a fannish flavor to this mission. They might suspect sci-fi fans on general principle—"technophiles is technophiles"—but their general attitude was that fans were hare-brained and ineffectual adolescent nerds. A dangerous assumption, sometimes correct, but sometimes wildly off. *Heh. I can crack this one solo and keep all the credit. Might even be good for a promotion.*

✫   ✫   ✫

The back door of the van was thrown open and raw sunlight filtered into the back of the trailer. Alex crouched with the others next to Bob's van, peering through the pallets of cheese that screened them from view. There were loud voices and shouted orders and the sound of an engine.

Thor scratched his beard and frowned. "Enoch said his friends would release us inside a warehouse before they drove the trailer to the cheese market."

Bob scratched his beard. "Maybe there's been a change in plans."

"Don't like it," said Fang shaking his head.

"What should we do?" asked Gordon.

"Can't run. Can't hide. Might as well enjoy the view."

The forklift pulled the cheese pallet from in front of them. A gang of men in heavy flannel shirts was counting and stacking the cheese wheels. They froze suddenly and stared at the trailer. The leader of the stevedores looked up from his clipboard and an unlit stogie fell from his lips. "Who the hell are you?" he demanded.

Thor studied the skyline. Gray, sooty clouds lowered over squat, blocky buildings. In the distance, twin spires of black smoke twisted skyward. He shook his head. "We're not in Chicago, gang."

"Welcome to Kilbourntown, gentlemen and lady." The Alderman graced them with a benign smile from atop his fur-lined throne. He was nearly as wide as he was tall. He wore a tawny-and-white cloak of fox skins. Aides and servants hovered around him like launch debris around a satellite. A number of the men wore sidearms and crossed bandoleers, but Alex also spotted swords here and there. A young girl, scantily clad, lounged insolently on the steps below the dais. Body odor was a miasma in the room.

Like a barbarian court, Alex thought. He stood wobble-kneed with his friends, still unsure if they were prisoners or not.

Thor gave him his elbow to hang onto. "Great Ghu," he whispered out of the side of his mouth, "we're in Hyperborea. Where's Conan?"

The Alderman lifted a huge, carved stein toward them. "Have a beer," he said formally.

It was a signal. His aides rushed to hand out smaller steins to the travelers. Alex studied his stein doubtfully. Scenes of Teutonic pastoralism adorned the sides. A lid closed the top. Now, that was familiar. Open-topped mugs still seemed a trifle odd to him; but how did you drink from the damned thing? There was no nipple.

Alex noticed a little thumb lever that flipped the lid open. Aha. So, what was the point of the lid? They had gravity here. They didn't have to worry about the beer floating away.

The Alderman waited and his ward heeler motioned that they should drink. It was a thin, sour brew with insufficient carbonation. Alex smiled and pretended to drink some more. "It's very good," he said. No point in offending your host; especially one of an uncertain and barbaric temper.

The Alderman nodded his smiling head. "It tastes like horse piss, doesn't it? Oh, one thing. You're new here, so I'll let you get by just this once. But please, do not speak to me unless first spoken to." The voice twisted up at the end, almost like a question. The smile was still there. The jolly eyes still twinkled. Alex felt sweat in his armpits and groin. *I've never been threatened so politely.*

Alex had already opened his jacket. Now he loosened his shirt collar, as well. This was the first time he had felt really warm since the trek across the Ice. Was it really warm in the Alderman's palace—a.k.a. the old Federal Building on Wisconsin Avenue—or was he just nervous about their circumstances? Then he remembered that the stevedores at the loading dock had been working in no more than flannel shirtsleeves.

Odd. Hadn't Thor told him that Milwaukee was closer to the ice fields than any other major city, save Winnipeg? Something about the Lake Effect and the Jet Stream.

Setting his stein down on the tray proffered by his butler, the Alderman gusted a huge sigh and wiped his mouth with his sleeve. He made staccato pointing motions with his hand and the other servants collected the remaining steins. Alex surrendered his willingly; but Fang held onto his and took a second pull from it before releasing the handle. The Alderman shook his head. "You're either a brave old cuss or you got no taste at all." He rubbed his hands together. "Now, to business. Who the hell are you and what were you doing in the cheeser?"

Sherrine exchanged glances with Bob and took a step forward. "May I speak?"

The Alderman raised his eyebrows. "I asked a question, didn't I?"

"I meant, may I make a request?"

The Alderman raised his chin and stroked it slowly with his thumb. "Sure. Why not? I might even grant it, even though you ain't registered voters."

"Two of my friends here are only recently out of

wheelchairs. They cannot stand up for long periods. Would it be all right with you—"

" 'Your honor' is the correct title."

"Thank you, your honor. Would it be all right with your honor if they sat down?"

There was an audible gasp from the assembled servants and courtiers. One of the waiters fumbled her tray and nearly dropped the steins she carried. The Alderman colored slightly; then he grinned. "Hey, sure. This is a democracy, aina?"

Two chairs were brought. Two only, Alex noted. "I can still stand," he told Sherrine.

"Don't be chivalric. Don't push yourself beyond what Steve tells you."

Alex settled himself into the chair. He glanced at Gordon. "Let them handle this," he said.

"I was planning to," Gordon responded.

The Alderman smiled his humorless smile again. "Now. About your presence in the cheeser."

"We—" Sherrine glanced at Bob, who shrugged.

"Go ahead."

"We were stuck in western Wisconsin, your honor. Some friends helped us save gas by letting us piggyback on the cheese delivery."

"That's a real expensive favor. I'm short a couple hundred kilos American because of you."

"There was a blizzard, your honor," Thor explained. "We saved the farmer's life."

"A square-head's life ain't worth his volume in cheese. But he might not know that." He stroked his chin again with his thumb. "You sure you ain't from Juneautown? Nah, I guess not," he answered himself. "If you was playing Trojan horse it woulda been a stupid stunt; and stupid ain't one of Alderman Wlodarczyck's sterling qualities." He shrugged his arms out wide and slapped them down on the arms of his throne.

"But I'm still out the cheese. So what do I do?"

Alex suspected the question was rhetorical; but Thor spoke up anyway.

"I thought the shipment was going to Chicago. Your honor. Did they put us on the wrong truck?"

The courtiers laughed. Even the waiters permitted themselves a supercilious snigger. The Alderman's smile turned tolerant.

"Did I say something funny, your honor?"

"Ah, those square-heads don't know nothing about economics. Sure, they was sending their cheese by Chi-town; but they coulda got a better deal here. So we did 'em a favor."

"You!" Sherrine blurted. "You're behind the monties!"

The Alderman turned a fierce glare on her. "You watch your mouth there, lady. If you wasn't a lady, you'd get six months hard for leeze majesty. We don't steal cheese here. We need it to negotiate with them gangsters in Chi ever since Juneautown cut us off from the Port and the Marina. Chi's gonna get their cheese sooner or later, don't you worry about that; but it might as well do *us* some good along the way."

Alex was having a hard time remaining seated. Float-ers didn't lose the strength in their hands. Alex's hands were hard and sinewy; they could crush the fat Alder-man's throat, if he would hold still for a moment.

An honest man beset by greedy neighbors. Was it simply hypocrisy? Self-deception? Or the lack of any moral code but relativity?

Or was it not so simple as that? The Alderman and his cronies were arrogant bandits at their center of power. But did the smiles seem forced? Did the eyes glitter with a hint of fear? The Ice was sliding down the west side of the Lake faster than anywhere else on the planet. Places like Fox Point and Brown Deer were already engulfed, according to Thor.

Then why was it so warm here?

Milwaukee was no longer a city: the two sides of the river had become separate warring towns. Maybe Alder-man Strauss was just an old-time, city machine politician desperately fending off disaster from his bailiwick, know-ing all the while that it was hopeless. The pressure of that sort of burden could deform a soul past its yield point, maybe even past its breaking point.

Look what it's done to Lonny Hopkins. And that was an odd notion, because it was the first sympathetic thought he had had about the station commander in a long, long time.

All right, Alex. What would *you* do if you were sitting on a plundered restaurant chair, wearing a cloak of animal skins, watching your beloved community be swallowed slowly by glaciers? Anything it took, right? There was nothing like disaster to focus one's loyalties.

"But the farmers, your honor," Sherrine insisted.

Back off, Sherri, he wanted to tell her. These are desperate, ruthless men and women. They aren't stealing cheese for fun. They are trying to save themselves and their families.

"Hey," the Alderman shrugged magnanimously. "They'll get their payment. We ain't thieves. They got more cheese than they know what to do with it. We got beer coming out our—" He grinned. "Well, coming out, anyway. So we'll load up their stinking cheese wagon with enough barrels we figure equals the cheese and send it back by them. Value for value. We ain't got cheese here; they ain't got beer there. They even get their trailer and their drivers back."

"But, your honor, what can they do with a trailer load of beer?"

"Throw a party. Get drunk. What else is there to do in the sticks? They should be happy we're bartering at all. Meanwhile . . ." And he rubbed his hands. "I figured out what to do with you folks. My city clerk will calculate the value of the cheese you displaced from the truck. Then we'll put you to work at standard wage—minus room and board, of course—until you pay it off." He smiled an appeal to them. "That's fair, aina?"

Alex, for one, was not going to tell him otherwise.

The guard who took them to their new duties was full of enthusiasm and civic pride. If it hadn't been for the short sword at his belt and the crossbow on his back,

Alex would have thought him a member of the chamber of commerce. Or maybe he was.

"Ain't the Alderman a piece of work?" he bragged. "I was in the fight when Juneautown burned the Clybourn Street bridge. He was all over the battlefield, rallying the men, leading that last charge to tear down the barricade. A damn shame we lost the battle; but you can't say the Alderman lost his nerve." The guard shook his head. "That harbor belongs to all of Milwaukee, not just the east siders. It ain't right that they keep us out. Same goes for the old City Hall. Juneautown thinks they're hot shit."

The horse cart pulled up at Zeidler Park and the guard ordered them all out. The park was enclosed in an immense plastic tent shored up by a wooden framework. The plastic was translucent, and through it Alex could make out the dim, distorted shapes of people and plants. He climbed down from the cart with the others and stumbled toward the tent. Despite support from Thor and Fang on either arm, each step sent a lance of fire up Alex's thighs.

"Hey, Hobie!" the guard called out. "Got some new temps for you!"

Glancing up, Alex noticed again how gray the cloud deck was that hung over Milwaukee. And the twin plumes of black smoke to the north. "Guard," he asked, "are those fires?"

"Hunh? Oh, sure. That's how we get our steam heat. We're burning buildings down. So does Juneautown; but it was our idea first. Most everything north of Capitol Avenue is gone now."

"What do you do when you run out of city?"

The guard blinked at him. "There are other cities, aina?"

Hobie was the head farmer for Zeidler Park Farm. Once inside the huge, low tent, Alex was assaulted by the warm, moist scent of compost and plant life. The entire park had been turned over to crops. Rows of corn and wheat were mixed with pea vines and bean plants. The plastic sheeting acted as a greenhouse, letting in the solar energy but trapping the ground-reflected heat, which was supplemented by steam hissing from radiators jury-rigged about the grounds. *Shorewood is burning to keep the corn warm,* Alex thought. It was actually warm inside the farm and, for the first time since falling to Earth, Alex saw men and women in shirt sleeves. They were bent silently over the plants, tending them with hoes and rakes. Some were kneeling, grubbing at the dirt with hand claws and weeders. A few of the ... serfs? ... glanced at the newcomers with a studied lack of curiosity.

There had been a popular joke on *Freedom*, started by a man named Calder. Looking down from space, he had said, the dominant life forms on Earth were obviously the cereals and other grasses. They occupied all the most desirable and fertile land; and they had tamed insects and animals to care for them. In particular, they had domesticated the bipeds to nurture and cultivate them and to save and plant their seed. Now, watching the farmers, Alex could easily imagine that they were worshiping and genuflecting before their masters.

Hobie looked them over. "New temps," he said. "Heh, heh."

"That's right," said Bob. "Just until we pay off the fine."

"And what fine is that, sonny?"

"Well, we were in the back of a cheese truck and ..."

Hobie cackled. "Heh, heh, heh. In a cheeser, was you? And you gotta pay the Boss back for the cheese he couldn't steal because you was back there instead? Heh, heh."

Bob scowled. "What's funny?"

"Well, you may be here a while."

"That's slavery," Bob pointed out without any real surprise.

Hobie affected a look of astonishment. "Why, so it is, sonny!" He leaned forward confidentially and added, "You want we should go tell the Boss? Maybe he'll stop it oncet he knows how illegal it all is. Heh."

Bob's face sagged. He turned to Sherrine and put his

arm around her. "I'm sorry I got you mixed up in this," he said. "I truly am."

Sherrine leaned against him. "I'm a big girl. I make my own decisions. But come Monday when I don't show up for work . . ."

"What?"

She shrugged. "They'll probably start looking for me; but who would ever think to look here?"

Gordon said, "I would like to sit down."

"Ain't too much sitting down here, sonny," Hobie told him. "Lots of bending and squatting though. Heh." Fang and Steve helped Gordon hobble over to the rude desk that was apparently Hobie's business office. Gordon sat against it, taking the weight off his legs. "Hey!" Hobie called, "you a farmer, too?"

Gordon's head hung down on his chest. He shook it wearily from side to side. "No. No, I'm not a farmer. I was a hydroponic tech for a week; and I screwed that up, too."

"If you ain't a farmer," Hobie insisted, "why'd they lame you?"

"What?"

Hobie stooped and made a slitting motion with the blade of his hand against the back of his leg. "These city boys don't know from soil and growin' things. They're much better at burning stuff down. So any farmers they catch they hamstring so we don't try to run away." The telephone on the desk rang and, as if to demonstrate his last remark, Hobie went to answer it. He walked with a curious shuffling gait, almost dragging his left foot. Sherrine shoved her fist in her mouth and even Fang looked ill. Hobie picked up the receiver. He looked at the group.

"Ah, don't look so sad. It don't bother me no more. They just cut the one leg. They don't want us to be cripples."

The milk of human kindness, thought Alex. Great Ghu, he had just begun to gain the use of his legs. Was this barbaric chieftain going to take them away again?

"Yes, Edna?" Hobie spoke into the receiver. He lowered himself into an old swivel chair. The padding was old and ragged and the ticking stuck out from ripped seams. "Okay, put 'er through ... Hey, Terri, you old bug stomper, what's up? Yeah. Yeah, they're here; they just got here. You need to what? Well, that's a new one on me. Naw, they don't look lousy to me; but if you say so, I'll send 'em right over." He hooked the phone and stared at it, pulling his lip. "Terri says you gotta come over by her place for delousing. Says she heard tell of the typhus over by Greenfield and West Allis. Your truck come through that way, so she's gotta check you out. The drivers have already been dusted. Now it's your turn."

And so back into the wagon. Go here; no, go there. Autocrats usually gave "efficiency" as the reason for centralizing the decision making. Good ol' Lonny sure enough did; and Alex was sure that Alderman Strauss did, too. But why did the underlings always have to cut and paste to make things work?

Terri Whitehead ran a pest control operation from a building alongside the Milwaukee River. As the guard said driving them over, you could wave to the guards on the Juneautown side and they could count how many fingers you used. The guard let the horse go at a walk. "You ain't in no hurry to start weeding, are you?" he asked. He wasn't in any hurry, either. He had pulled an easy duty and saw no reason not to relax while he had the chance.

Alex lay on his back in the wagon and stared up at the brown smudge of a sky. Bob, squatting beside him, followed his gaze.

"Filthy, isn't it?" he said. "All that soot and carbon from the fires. This may be the only city in North America with a smog problem, worse luck."

"Worse luck? Why?"

"Because if everybody was lighting fires and putting carbon dioxide into the air it would be a damn sight warmer. Like it used to be before they cleaned up the atmosphere."

Bob gestured with his head. "Take a look around you," he whispered. "Wisconsin has been devastated by the Ice more than any other state, except maybe Michigan. Yet Milwaukee is almost a tropic oasis. Why? Because, whether they admit it to themselves or not, the locals are trying to restore the Greenhouse Effect. They threw another log on the fire."

Steve had been listening quietly to Bob's whispered lecture. He leaned over to Alex and said *sotto voce:* "Burn a log and see it through, with heat and soot and CO_2!"

"We're here," announced Sherrine. "And—" She stopped abruptly.

"And what?" Bob asked, twisting to his feet. He stood silently for a moment, swallowing laughter.

Alex grabbed the side of the buckboard and pulled himself to his knees. They were hitched before a wide storefront with double-paned plate glass windows. A wooden sign nailed above the entrance was painted in bright red and gold letters:

YNGVI'S DE-LOUSING AND PEST CONTROL CENTER

The guard finished hitching the horse to the rail and scowled at them. "All right, why's everyone grinning?"

My question exactly, thought Alex.

Terri Whitehead was a short, muscular woman with long, black hair and owlish glasses. She wore jeans and a man's dress shirt with rolled up sleeves, and elbow-length gloves. When she spoke, it was in a husky contralto.

She took care of the guard first. "Because you may have picked up lice from being around the new temps." She made him take off all his clothing and dusted it with malathion powder. Searched through his underwear, and recoiled in horror.

"What?" he demanded.

She held up forceps. "Louse, aina? I'll have to see if it's carrying anything." There was a microscope by the window. She put the insect on a slide and studied it. "You're lucky. This one's healthy. Get back to barracks and take a hot shower. Here's a prescription. Tell 'em I said *hot* water. Use this stuff." She handed him a small bottle of green liquid. "Use it good, all the hairy parts of your body. Scrub like hell. You'll be all right."

"Uh, Doc—"

"Typhus," she said. "Dehydration. Babbling. High fever. After a while you dry up and die. You won't like it."

"Jesus, Doc—"

"You'll be all right. One thing, if you itch, don't scratch. Don't crush lice. That's really bad. Just wash them off. Then powder yourself. As for your clothes, change clothes. Take your old ones where they're doing a fire and get 'em good and hot, then smoke them good. Real good."

"Yeah, I will, but, Doc—"

"You're all right now. I can tell. You don't have it. Get going before you do."

"What about them?"

She laughed and was suddenly holding a pistol, quite casually. "No problem. Now get going."

"Yes, ma'am."

By this time Alex could feel tiny life forms crawling over his body looking for blood to drink. He kept his hands rigidly by his side. Life under Lonny Hopkins had its drawbacks; but at least lice wasn't one of them.

When Terri faced them, she was laughing. "Yngvi is a louse," she said.

"FIAWOL," Bob replied.

"FIJAGH," she responded. Then she and Sherrine and Bob and the other fans joined in a happy embrace.

Sherrine said, "A sensitive fannish face! I *knew*—"

"There isn't time," Terri told them. "We have maybe an hour before they send another guard. Follow me." She led them to the back of the building and out the rear door. "Don't worry about the typhus," she said. "That was just to get you over here. It's a good thing you have that transponder, Bob. The Ghost knew right where you were." She paused and looked at them. "You guys must be awfully important." No one said anything and she shrugged. "None of my business, right? Come on, this way."

A path led across the ragged yard to the river bank, where a small sailboat bobbed at a decaying, wooden wharf. "Seamus will take you from here. Seamus deBaol. You may remember him. He used to publish a line of SF books in the old days. 'Books by deBaol'? He'll take you down the river as soon as he ties me up back in the shop."

Sherrine took her by the arm. "Aren't you coming with us?"

Terri shook her head. "No, someone's got to stay behind and give you an alibi. I can tell them how you overpowered me and headed west out St. Paul Avenue. My friend Allis Place belongs to Psi Phi Fraternity over by the University. They'll report some horses stolen, so the Alderman's stooges will go chasing off that direction. I'll tell them you're gonna die of typhus anyway. The Alderman will think you're a blessing. Maybe you'll go to Juneautown and start a plague."

"But—you won't come, then?"

"This is my home," she said. "Such as it is. What if other fen find themselves in need of help someday?"

Sherrine hugged her. "It must be awful, living life undercover like that. Aren't you afraid of exposure?"

Terri grinned. "That's why I stay under the covers. Being a fan was a lot simpler in the old days; now we've all got new destinies to pursue. Here." She handed them a paper sack. "You'll need money. Take this. It's filled with cheese. Sorry, no apple pie. 'The best of all physicians is apple pie and cheese.' Quick, now. Into the boat. Seamus, hurry! You've still got to tie me up."

The short, bearded man grinned at them as he jogged past up to the house. "Some parts of this job, I like."

It was a gaff-rigged catboat with plenty of room aboard. The mast was stepped well forward and wore a single quadrilateral sail.

The boat pushed off from shore, and the sail caught the wind. It heeled dangerously, then settled on course. They huddled in the bottom of the boat, out of the chill wind, and Alex managed to be next to Sherrine.

"How did you know she was a friend?"

"The sign. 'Yngvi is a louse'—well, it's a quote from an

old fantasy, and it got to be sort of a catch phrase among fans. As soon as I saw 'Yngvi De-Lousing . . .'"

Alex nodded. "I see. FIAWOL I know, but what means that other one?"

She grinned. "FIJAGH. Fandom Is Just A Goddamn Hobby."

☆   ☆   ☆

The Museum of Science and Industry was located on the shore of Lake Michigan in Jackson Park on Chicago's south side. Seamus maneuvered the catboat to a spit of land just north of the museum and ran the bow aground. "Are you sure you want off here?" he asked.

"Yes," Sherrine told him. "We are supposed to meet someone."

Seamus glanced up at the imposing building. He ran a hand through his beard. "Well, be careful. It's not the museum it used to be. Time was this was Chi-Town's biggest tourist attraction. Four million people a year came to look at Science and Technology exhibits. Like a damn city come to visit. A lot of the displays have been changed over now. They only left a few, and they don't keep the homeless out."

Alex wobbled as he stepped ashore. His legs felt like rubber and he grabbed Thor's shoulders to stay upright. "Sorry," he muttered. "I seem to have lost it." The long, leisurely sail down the Milwaukee River and then along the shore of Lake Michigan had, with its gentle rolling motion, put him back into a state of near weightlessness. Now the earth heaved to and fro as if tossed by waves.

Seamus waved to them as he cast off. The wind was off the lake, abeam to his course both coming and going. "Sailor's wind," he called. "Good luck."

"FIAWOL," Alex said tentatively.

"Don't you just know it," Seamus called. He hauled in the sheets and the boat moved rapidly away.

Bob and Sherrine disappeared and reappeared a short while later with a pair of wheelchairs with C.M.S.A.T. stenciled in yellow ink across the back. "Here you go, guys," Sherrine said. "You wouldn't believe what they wanted for a deposit on these things."

Bob led the way to the front of the building. The façade consisted of tall, fluted columns with voluted capitals. Statues of the Muses gazed serenely down. "It's a huge building," he said. "Covers five and a half hectares. It was built originally for the 1893 World Colombian Exposition; then rebuilt in the 1930s as the museum."

"Where would this Cole character have his Titan?" asked Alex.

"There used to be a wing called the Henry Crown Space Center. It had Schirra's Aurora Seven Mercury capsule and the Apollo Eight, the first craft to orbit the moon. The Titan is probably back there. I figured maybe we could mount the Apollo on the Titan somehow. It seats three."

"Which means," Sherrine interjected, "that you could even take a friend with you. No, guess not. Seeds and stuff—"

"The Titan was rigged for a Gemini," said Bob, "but I figured we should be able to . . ." His voice trailed off. Alex suspected that Bob was just beginning to appreciate the magnitude of the proposed rescue. As long as it was blue sky dream, there were no problems; but the closer they came, the more the difficult details emerged.

People didn't really build spacecraft in their backyards, or in museums. That was just science fiction.

So far so good!

They went up the handicapped ramp to the left of the main entrance. The mass of the building was beginning to get to Alex. *Peace* and *Freedom* were frail metal balloons next to this concrete habitat. It was, he thought, like being in a hollowed-out asteroid.

Bob secured a map of the museum and they huddled over it. The logo read, "Chicago Museum of Science and Appropriate Technology," with a footnote explaining that "science" did not mean only "materialist science."

Now, what might "non-materialist science" be? Alex wondered. Plasma physics?

"Here it is." Bob pointed. "I'll be damned. It's still in the same old spot. Henry Crown Space Center. What does it say in the description?" He bent closer. "This exhibit has been preserved as it was in the past as an example of Big Technology. Astonishing as it may seem, billions of dollars were once spent in outer space rather than here on Earth. See the actual capsules that were used to give a few military pilots joyrides at taxpayer expense."

"I don't understand, Bob," Alex said. "How could they spend money in space? There were no stores there back in those days."

"That's not what they meant, Gabe," Bob replied.

Thor spoke gently. "They meant that the money was spent on the space program rather than on Earthly problems."

Sherrine burst out, "They got so much from the space program! Fireproofing. Weather forecasting. Dammit, these"—she kicked Alex's wheelchair—"lightweight wheelchairs we're pushing around. Sorry."

Alex started to laugh. Sherrine said, "Sorry. My *God*, it's been so long since I could *say* this kind of thing!"

"Did these chairs really—"

"Waste-water treatments. Medical instruments. Most people had no *idea* that any of that came out of the space program. Or for that matter, that it even existed. A new design, lightweight wheelchair doesn't make the kind of headlines that a scrubbed launch or a flawed mirror makes, even if the structural analysis techniques and composite materials used to make the damn thing were aerospace from the beginning. What is everyone grinning at?"

"Welcome back," Steve said.

"Thanks. Oh, Bob, there was nobody to *talk* to."

Steve said, "All that stuff was just 'spin-off,' you know. Science happens because one day a scientist wakes up and says, 'Today I'm going to invent toothpaste.' If he didn't *plan* to invent a better wheelchair, he can't take credit for it."

"Come on," said Bob. "We're wasting time here. Let's get back to the Crown Center."

He led them through several exhibits on the way to the back room where the space exhibit was stashed. One was a Hall of Minerals that featured all sorts of crystals, together with detailed descriptions of the powers of each for " . . . clearing away negative attitudes, centering personal energies, enhancing communications, promoting healing, opening the heart to love and courage, simplifying decision making, balancing the spirit, focusing the mind, tapping into psychic powers, and using chakras and colors."

Another exhibit was entitled "Origins of the Earth." There were seven panels, one for each day. One large poster read, "The Speed of Light: A Test of Faith?" and explained how light created "already on the way" could give the impression of a universe much larger and older than it really was.

There was a Green exhibit on alternate energy sources. Windmills, passive solar. Biomass. "Biomass?"

Bob said, "Burn wheat and corn. Real efficient. Well, at least they don't have an exhibit on generating energy by squeezing crystals."

"Why the grin, Alex?" Thor asked as they entered a stairwell and turned right into a dimly lit corridor. A faded sign on the wall read, "This way to Henry Crown Space Center."

Alex chuckled. "We grow perfect crystals in our electronics lab in *Freedom*. I could be rich if I had brought a handful with me."

The Crown Center was housed in a separate wing that could be reached only through a long, narrow corridor. A homeless pair huddled in a niche near the doorway. They were bundled up in torn blankets that covered everything but their eyes.

"Hey, man, you got any change?"

No one looked at them. Eye contact might humanize them. . . .

Half the lights in the hallway were out and the edges at the floor and ceiling were thick with nitre and cobwebs. This was a part of the building long—and deliberately—neglected.

The center itself was dimly lit. The two space capsules were shadowy shapes suspended from the ceiling. A couple of teenaged boys who had found their way in were standing beneath the Mercury capsule. ". . . and all they ever brought back was a bunch of dumb moon rocks," Alex heard the one tell his companion. He turned to them as he was wheeled past.

"Did you ever ask what those rocks were made of?" he asked.

The two kids gave him a wary look. "Rocks is rocks," the older said.

"Right, kid," murmured Thor. "Aluminum, titanium, zirconium, calcium. If we had mined the moon like some people wanted, we wouldn't have to disturb Mother Earth and ruin the environment here."

The younger kid stuck his chin out. "Yeah, but then we woulda ruined the moon's ecology."

Thor smiled. "I can't argue with that," he said mildly. "Mighty important, that lunar ecology."

One of the boys nodded solemnly. The other muttered something under his breath.

The two teenagers left casting a few careful glances behind. "You better be careful, you come back here," the younger one called. "Or the spook'll get you!"

"All right," said Bob when they were gone. "Let's spread out and see if we can find Cole."

They split into groups and explored the corners of the hall. Alex saw a shuttle simulator, now padlocked. A sign told how much taxpayer money had been spent so astronauts could play "computer games."

"Over here!" Sherrine shouted. "The Titan!"

They converged on her voice. A tall cylinder stood in an ill-lit corner of the room, a majestic shadow among the shadows. "I can't believe it," Bob said, his head tilted back to seek its top. "We actually found it!"

Fang approached the behemoth in awe and fear. He ran his hand over its skin. He looked at his hand. He studied the ill-lit surface a few moments more, and said, "I'm going to be sick."

Alex yanked on his chair's wheels and rolled up to the artifact. Closer now, he could see rust spots, popped welds, holes where fittings should have been. There were no main thrusters mounted at the base.

Alex noticed a dark horizontal line running across the booster about halfway up. His own belly lurched and tried to turn over. The bird had been cut in half, he realized. Cut in half, to transport it or to get it through a door. He remembered that Bob had described Cole's rocket as a kind of Flying Dutchman, wandering from museum to museum.

This ship would never fly. It never could have flown.

I never thought it could. Never in a million years. Then why was he so disappointed? Why was he biting his lip so hard that he could taste blood? He heard a sob to his right and turned in time to see Gordon stagger out of his wheelchair and lean against the Titan. His arms stretched out to embrace it and he placed his cheek against its cool skin. Tears had pooled in his eyes.

"It won't work, Alex, will it? It won't fly. We'll be marooned down here forever. Crushed and tripping and staggering like drunken fools until they finally catch us. Never to see my semya again; never to plavat in the old ESO module. Never drift my broomstick on lazy orbit to *Peace*. If only—" Gordon sagged and Steve grabbed him under the armpits to keep him from falling.

"If only what?" Alex snapped at him. "If only what? I'd strangle fucking Lonny if my arms were long enough, but it wouldn't change anything. If only I'd waited another orbit! We could have scooped our air on the next pass."

He tried to jerk his arm away from Thor, who was trying to calm him down. If Thor noticed, he didn't react. Sherrine stepped between them, saying something that Alex refused to hear. "We are stuck down here, Gordo," he persisted. "Stuck. Forever. It doesn't matter whose fault—"

"Quiet, there! Quiet, I say!"

The sudden voice came from above. Alex looked up with the rest and saw wild hair and a long New Englander face, pasty white in the uncertain fluorescent light, staring down at them from an opening high up in the Titan. The face showed nothing. He said, "Get away from that. It's not yours."

Nobody moved.

A knotted rope snaked down from above and the tall, thin man came down hand over hand. He landed too hard, staggered, recovered. He took his place before the Titan, in no evident hurry.

"I bought the parts and put it together and held it together for forty years. You're not going to hurt it."

Thor stepped up to him and reached for his arm. "Ron? Ron Cole? Is that you?" His hand stopped, because that was a gun in Cole's hand.

The creature looked at him. "Yes." He squinted at Thor's face. "I know you. Don't I?" His other hand stroked the discolored flank of the Titan. He held the gun with evident negligence, but it was still pointed at Thor's belly.

"They took away her boosters, they did. Her boosters. Too dangerous, they said. Hah! What did they know? Without the fuel ..." His lips clamped into a straight line.

Thor had backed away a bit. "What fuel is that, Ron?"

Cole backed against the Titan, shaking his head. "No, no. Things are seldom as they seem; skim milk masque ... masquerades as cream." He nodded his head wisely. His gun hand drooped.

"Ron, what happened to you?" Thor demanded.

"Heh. One Flew over the Cuckoo's Nest—"

"Electro shock," Fang said. "And drugs. They must have helped him, in one of the mental health centers."

When Thor turned back, Alex could see tears staining his beard. "I knew Ron," he said. "I knew Ron back in the old days, in Boston. We had dinner together at a Thai restaurant there. He told me stories, wonderful stories. About how the *Boston Globe* made him the world's sixth nuclear power; about Wade Curtis and the

machete; and Reynolds and the Great Duel. . . . He was
the brightest man I ever knew, and look what they've
done to him. Look what they've done." He bowed his
head and Steve stepped to his side and put an arm
around his shoulder.

It had all been in vain, Alex realized. The harrowing
trip across Wisconsin; the blizzard; the narrow escape
from slavery . . . All for nothing. The shining vision of the
old Titan had gone before them like a pillar of fire in the
desert night. And at the end, they had found only junk
and an old man who had been helped by mental health
professionals.

No one said anything. Bob studied the Titan, checking
out every part of it; as if he could will it into flight
worthiness, as if he could somehow find something they
had overlooked that would make everything all right.
Steve consoled Thor, while Sherrine comforted a weeping Gordon. Even Fang seemed bereft of ideas.

Alex watched Gordon cry. Thor had lost his friend.
Sherrine had lost her job; or would when she failed to
show up for work in the morning. Bob had lost his van,
and probably his job, too. But Gordon cried uncontrollably. *Okay, for Gordo this is a totally alien planet. I could
acclimate myself. I was born here. I loved Kansas; I cried
when my parents took me up. I could learn to love it here
again. I could convince myself that I was only coming
home again.*

The Titan had given their sojourn a purpose. They had
had a goal, as quixotic as that goal had been. Now, they
had nothing.

CHAPTER THIRTEEN

"See What Free Men Can Do. . ."

"She's dead, then," Bob said. "Goddam. The rumor was right. Cole had a rocket. Maybe it was alive, once."

"For all the good it does us," Sherrine said bitterly. "Oh bloody hell, I'm sorry. I'm really sorry."

"Don't look now," Bob said. He jerked his thumb toward the entrance. The homeless pair who had claimed the corridor were now in the room, still wearing their blankets. Sherrine wondered if they had clothes on under them. The pair seemed to be hustling a girl in her teens. The girl tried to move away from them, but the pair followed, evidently begging.

The pantomime dance was curving them toward the rocket. Cole eyed the three warily and took a tentative step to place himself between them and it.

One of the blanketed figures began to sing, very softly. The other joined in, then the girl they had been begging from. Even as close as they were, they could barely be heard.

"Star fire! Star fire!
It's singing in my blood, I know it well!

We can know the promise of the stars.
Star fire! Star fire!
The promise of the universe is ours—"

"Harry?" Bob said quietly.

"Nobody else," Harry said. "Been waiting for you. 'Lo, Ron."

" 'Lo, Harry," Cole said. "Wade send you?"

"Yup. Says it's getting on for time to move on."

Some of the mad glint faded from Cole's eyes.

"Harry, what are you doing here?" Bob demanded.

"Better yet, what are you talking about?" Sherrine said.

"Shh," Jenny said. "Come on where we can talk." She eyed the two spacemen. "Huh. You're walking now! You had me fooled."

"Not me," Harry said. "I guessed in Minneapolis. Come on—"

Thor looked at Harry and shook his head. "Same old bullshit. Like hell you guessed." He looked suspiciously at the girl who had come in with Harry and Jenny. "Who's this?"

She had dark hair, soft brown eyes, exotic features. Sherrine thought that with a little makeup and some attention to her hair she would be beautiful. As it was, she seemed to want to look plain: no makeup at all, not even lipstick, hair brushed severely back and tied in a bun. She wore a skirt and sweater, both drab brown, with black leggings and ugly leg warmers over those.

"Who's this?" Thor demanded again.

"Violetta Brown," Harry said. He looked around the room, saw no one, and lowered his voice. "Oliver Brown's daughter."

"Oh," Sherrine said. "Pleased to meet you, Violetta. Is your father—"

"Waiting for us," Violetta said. "Come on. Harry has a lot to tell you."

"That I do," Harry said. He turned to Cole. "You, too, Ron. Wade says it's time. Said you'd know what I meant."

Ron Cole nodded slowly. "And past time. You'll be back?"

"Tomorrow," Harry promised. "Maybe tonight."

"Let's get out of here," Thor said. Outside he turned to Harry. "You get picked up as homeless—"

"Lots," Harry said.

"But you're no crazier than you ever were. Why?" He stabbed an arm back toward the dimly lit space center. "Why the hell did they do that to Ron? And not you."

Harry shrugged. "He was interesting."

"Interesting?"

"Yeah," Jenny said. "The last thing you want to be is different. Those mental health centers are filled up with graduate students, all just alike, no future, unless they can find an interesting case to write a thesis about."

"Ron couldn't be ordinary no matter how hard he tried," Thor said. "Yeah. I see."

Harry said, "Some of us hide it better than others."

☆   ☆   ☆

Captain Lee Arteria opened the folder and removed the single sheet of paper it contained. *Do all files start as innocuously as this?* One sheet; but destined to multiply, like a bacterial colony. *Trees die so that we may keep dossiers.*

Arteria looked up and caught the eye of Captain Machtley, the North Dakota liaison. The State Police agencies, fearful of being left out in the cold in the pursuit of the spacemen, had agreed to be coordinated through Arteria's Air Police.

"Why don't you fill us in on what this says, Captain?"

Machtley cleared her throat. "Her name is Sherrine Hartley. She lives in Minneapolis, but her grandparents live near the crash site; and the telephone company's records show that she called them the night of the crash."

"Well. That certainly sounds suspicious. Calling your grandparents."

"In the middle of the night? Besides, there's more," Machtley said happily.

Arteria replaced the sheet in the folder and closed it. "Tell me."

Machtley looked around the table at the others. *That's right*, thought Arteria. *Share and share alike.*

"Dakota Bell's data banks were scrambled the next day. If the off-line backup hadn't been done first thing in the morning, there would have been no record of Hartley contacting her grandparents. We suspect that the Legion of Doom was involved."

Lee was unconvinced. "The Legion of Doom has been sparring with the phone company since Day One. It might not be related."

"We would never have found the grandparents," Machtley insisted, "if we hadn't gone door to door. It was a neighbor who told us about the granddaughter in Minneapolis."

Arteria smiled. "I've always said that good old-fashioned police legwork beats these computerized searches for useful results. Moorkith and his Green Police are going nuts trying to straighten out their records. They're too damn lazy to hit the bricks."

"Don't forget the Motor Vehicle data banks," said Captain Conte, the Minnesota liaison. "They were scrambled, too. Remember when we tried to ID the maroon van?"

Machtley nodded. "That's an interesting point. Hartley's grandparents would have been on Moorkith's un-Green list, too; if *it* hadn't been hacked up. They are not the milk and cookie type at all. The old lady is a former gene-tamperer."

There was a general stirring around the table. "You're right," Arteria said. "Gene tampering does not sound good at all."

"It violates God's law," put in Captain Traxler, the Wisconsin liaison. "And it harms the ecology. Satan's work."

"We've started checking up on the Hartley woman," said Conte. "She was once reported as active in the science fiction underground."

Aha. "By whom?"

"Her ex-husband."

"Ex-husband. Was the report substantiated, or was it just a messy divorce?"

Conte shook his head. "Nothing was proven; and the

records say she's kept her nose clean the last few years. But still, where there's smoke, there's usually fire."

Oh, well, thought Lee Arteria, *we never needed a Fourth Amendment, anyway.* Start making exceptions in the need for probable cause and where did you stop? Not at sobriety checkpoints. "Does anyone else have anything concrete to add?"

Nobody spoke. After a moment, Arteria nodded. "Very well, Captains. Scrambling three separate databases relating to Hartley, her grandparents and the van. Machtley, that was good work. It would be one hell of a thick coincidence." *And there is a definite whiff of fannishness about Hartley. Gafiated years ago, but still has connections.* "Hartley *may* have been the woman in the van at Fargo Gap. It's worth following up. Captain Conte?"

"Yes?"

"I think we should pay this Sherrine Hartley a visit, don't you? And . . ." Arteria leaned back in the chair and contemplated the ceiling. "I don't think there is any reason to let the Green Police or the INS into this quite yet. Let's wait until we have more to show before we let them share the credit."

The grins of the other captains showed that they knew quite well how to share credit.

☆   ☆   ☆

Oliver Brown had the entire fourth floor of an older apartment building. There was no elevator. They carried the Angels up the stairs using sheets for hammocks.

The building looked old and run down, but the apartment was light and clean. Books were stacked everywhere, in book cases, in piles on the floor, on every flat surface.

Violetta introduced her father. He was a little taller than Sherrine, portly, with dark hair and a distracted expression. He tended to mutter to himself when he wasn't talking. Like Samuel Johnson, Sherrine thought. He ushered them through the living room to another room piled high with even more books.

Bruce and Mike were there.

"I see Harry found you," Bruce said.

"Yes. He said Wade Curtis sent him," Bob said.

"I work for Wade," Harry said.

"Doing what?"

"Gopher. Booklegger. Postman. Whatever needs doing." Harry grinned. "He said go hang around Ron Cole and see if anyone from Minicon shows up."

"But why—"

"He guessed?" Sherrine asked.

"Suspected," Jenny said. "He said maybe someone would come looking for a rocket ship."

"If somebody from Minicon comes looking for a rocket ship, tell 'em where to find one. That's what he told me to do. So here you are," said Harry.

"It doesn't work!" Sherrine said. She was near tears. "It never would have worked!"

"That pile of junk? Naw."

"Until we got here you didn't know that any better than the rest of us," Jenny said sharply.

Harry gave Jenny a pained look. "I knew it wouldn't work. Anyway, we got here just ahead of Bruce and Mike, and they said you were coming. Only you didn't come, and they couldn't wait for you at the museum."

Mike patted his ample bulk. "Too conspicuous."

"What happened to you?" Bruce asked.

"Long story," Fang said.

"So Jenny and I moved in," Harry said. He fished into his pockets and held out a handful of change and a couple of bills. "Not too bad a location. Some people still care. A little."

They heard footsteps outside. Violetta opened the apartment door. "Hi, Mom."

Mrs. Brown was bundled up against the cold so that she looked larger than her husband. She looked at the crowd sprawled around her living room and smiled thinly. "More of your godfather's friends?" she asked Violetta. "Glad to meet you, but I'm afraid I can't feed you all. We—" She hesitated.

"Helga works at the university clinic," Oliver Brown said. "And I write science fiction. She doesn't get paid

much but it's more than I make. What she's too embarrassed to say is that we can't afford to feed you."

"Will this help?" Sherrine handed her bag of cheese to
Helga Brown.

"Cheese? Wisconsin cheese? Ollie! It's real, the real
thing— But there's too much! I can trade this for a
lot—"

"Go see what you can get for half of it," Oliver said.
"Violetta, go with your mother."

"Maybe I better go, too," Harry said. "Tough neighborhood—"

"You have to tell your story," Violetta said. "I'll get
Roland. My boyfriend, he lives next door. He'll come
with us."

"Fan?" Bob asked.

Violetta laughed. "My father is Oliver Brown, my mother
is Helga Brown, my godfather is Wade Curtis. You figure
it out."

"All right," Thor said. "Just what the hell is going on?
We've chased all across Wisconsin. Lived through a blizzard, almost got enslaved by a crazy alderman, damn
near caught by the cops, just so we can find out that Ron
Cole is mad as a hatter and his rocket never was any
good. Now you tell us—what in hell is it you want to tell
us, Harry Czescu?"

"If you'll shut up for a minute, maybe he can say it,"
Jenny said.

Thor glared at her.

"Wade says—"

"*Wade* says," Thor said. "Look, Wade Curtis hasn't
been sober in ten years. Maybe he's not raving like Cole,
but he sent us here! He believed in Cole's rocket, just
like you did, and I did and—Oh, God, Damn, It."

"Got a letter," Harry said.

Bruce asked, "Letter for whom?"

"Maybe you." Harry took off his left boot. "Wade said
I should give it to—I should give it to somebody I
thought he'd trust." The inner lining wasn't properly

sewn to the boot shell. Harry reached between the two leathers and took out a dirty envelope.

"What does it say."

Harry said, "It's sealed." The hurt barely showed. "Wade said I should burn this if nobody from Minicon showed up looking for Cole, but if anybody did, give it to somebody with judgment." He looked around the group. Finally he held the paper out to Oliver Brown. "Reckon he trusts you."

Oliver took the paper. "What Harry is carefully not saying is that Wade and I are still collaborating on a book. Harry brought me two new chapters yesterday."

He went over to his desk and got a letter opener. He was maddeningly slow, and Sherrine wanted to scream as he smoothed out the envelope's wrinkles, then carefully inserted the letter opener and slit the paper. There was a single sheet inside, and he took it out slowly.

"I haven't seen Wade, haven't seen Wade for years," Oliver muttered. "Afraid it will cost Helga her job. If they knew. But they do know. They have to. Maybe they don't, though." He spread the paper out and began to read. "Ah. Hmm. Mmmh hmmmh. Yes. Yes."

"For God's sake!" Bob shouted. "What?"

"I'll read it," Oliver said. He cleared his throat. " 'King David is in the high desert. It's a Doherty project. My wings are made of tungsten, my flesh of glass and steel. Explorers—' "

"That's a song," Sherrine said.

Brown looked up. In the silence Harry sang, "*I am the joy of Terra for the power that I wield—*"

Sherrine and Jenny were with him. "*Once upon a lifetime, I died a pioneer. Now I sing within a spaceship's heart, does anybody hear?*"

" 'The Phoenix,' " Harry said with just the trace of a bow. "Julia Ecklar."

"Damn drunk," Thor said. "Told you he's just a drunk. Doesn't make any sense at all."

" 'Explorers in the desert keep bottle shops,' " Roland read. " 'Skim milk masquerades as cream. It is time for the merry soul to move on, to see what free men can do.

What man has done, man can aspire to. Love and plenty kisses. W.' "

"That's it?" Sherrine asked.

Oliver nodded. "I hope it means something to you."

"We were hoping it would mean something to you," Mike said. "Harry, he thought we'd understand this?"

"Thought it was important enough to send me here with it," Harry said.

Which might mean he wanted you out of the way? Sherrine rejected that with a violent headshake. "Start with what we know. He thought someone from the Con would be here. Why? Nobody's come here for years. Because—because he'd talked about Ron Cole's Titan at the Con."

Mike: "Someone might have overheard—"

Bruce: "—and told the Angels!"

"So it's a message for us," Sherrine said. "Why in code?"

"Drunk," Thor said.

"What if Harry got picked up?" Fang suggested.

"No, I was carrying a manuscript for Oliver," Harry said. His big shoulders rolled, free of that weight. "They'd have sent me to mental health for that, letter or no."

"He wasn't protecting Harry and me," Jenny said. "What, then?"

"Who the hell cares what he thinks?" Thor demanded. He looked to Fang. "Maybe it's time to move on."

"No, it's time for the merry soul to move on," Mike said. "That's Cole, of course. Not that it would be so obvious if we hadn't just seen him."

"Skim milk—Cole said that, too," Sherrine said. "Harry, you had a message for Cole!"

"And what were you supposed to do once you'd found us all and delivered the messages?" Bruce asked.

"I can tell you exactly what he said," Harry said. He looked uncomfortable.

"What?" Bruce said.

Harry looked out the window.

"Want me to tell them?" Jenny asked.

"No. No, I'll do it." Harry stuffed his hands deep into

his jeans pockets. "Wade said, 'Harry, I trust your honor with my life, but I don't trust your judgment to go buy the beer. If nobody shows up, forget all this and meet me in—well, where we meet, next month. If anybody from Minicon shows up, go tell Oliver Brown, then deliver the messages, and stand by to help people. I think they'll want help.'"

"And that's all?"

Harry shrugged. "That's all."

"Where is Curtis now?" Mike asked.

Harry shook his head. "I don't know, and I guess I wouldn't tell you if I did."

"Great," Thor said. "So we have this nonsense from a drunk writer, and a messenger he doesn't trust with his drunken ravings, and we're supposed to get all excited."

Fang said, "Thor, it's a *puzzle*."

"Wade always did drink a lot," Oliver Brown said. "But he turned out the stories. He used to be in the space program, you know. Other things. Were you ever in his study before they burned it down? Big place. Books. And a signed picture of *Voyager*— Hey!"

"What?" Bruce demanded.

"'See what free men can do.' That was the inscription on the photo. By, by the man who built it—Dick Rhutan! Who flew *Voyager* around the world on one tank of gas. *That Voyager*."

"Rhutan. *Voyager*. King David in the desert!" Mike said.

"Mike?"

"*King David's Spaceship!* It's a book title. And the Rhutan brothers were working on a spaceship. A spaceship called—" He paused dramatically, holding a wide grin. "Wait for it. It was called *Phoenix*. They were working on it in the Mojave desert."

"Be damned," Bruce muttered. "That was that thing that looked like an inverted styrofoam cup—"

"Single stage to orbit, vertical take off and landing," Oliver Brown said. "SSTO VTOL."

Mike was frowning. "Sure, we all saw the briefing at a Worldcon. Long time ago. Nolacon? Somewhere in there.

Wait a minute and I'll come up with the name of the guy who was in charge of the *Phoenix* project."

"Hudson," Oliver Brown said. "An old friend of Wade's."

"Hudson. An explorer in the desert," Mike said. "Yup. Well, there's no question what Wade was talking about. *Phoenix*."

"A spaceship. Where have I heard this before?" asked Alex. But his blood was beginning to sing. Again.

"Yes, I know," Sherrine said. "But—but *Phoenix* was real! They spent tens of millions of dollars on it. And *Voyager* was real, it flew around the world!"

Steve got up from the floor. As usual he seemed to float up, as if he could turn off the gravity. "*Phoenix* is real, all right," he said. "I've seen it. It's in a museum in Mojave."

"Another museum," Gordon said. "I think perhaps this time we do not bother?"

"Suit yourself," Steve said. "But *Phoenix* flew once. I saw it."

"Flew!" Alex tried to stand. Fang noticed and helped him. "Flew?"

"Not to orbit," Steve said. "The *Phoenix* was just too heavy. Hudson had to make too many compromises. But it could have gone around the world, like *Voyager*, if NASA hadn't stopped him."

Thor said, "Like the *Spruce Goose*? There's always a reason why it didn't work."

Steve's muscles were bunching. Thor was getting to him, though he may not have been aware of it. "NASA said it had to do with flight safety. Gary Hudson got to take the *Phoenix* straight up fifty miles and dump most of his fuel and come straight back down. Then the budget cuts came, and the Green Initiatives passed, and the Greens got in control."

"So where is this *Phoenix* now?" Alex demanded.

"In a hangar on what used to be Edwards Air Force Base in California. It's been preserved as a reminder of Big Bad Science, just like the Space Center here. Actually, I think the military may have had ideas they could use it. They didn't have the money to fix it, but they never throw anything away either. It's out there 'as a monument.' People are supposed to go out and be scandalized; but . . . When I was there, a lot of the tourists had tears in their eyes."

"Probably for all the money that was wasted," said Fang sarcastically.

Steve nodded. "Truer than you think. I shed a few myself at the waste. That's where I met Hudson. They've got him conducting the tour."

Bruce jumped. "Himself? Why—"

"I thought the Single Stage Experimental Lifter was never finished," Thor said belligerently. "They proxmired the whole space program. They even outlawed private ventures, like Hudson's."

"That's what Gary said when I took the tour," Steve agreed. "*SSX Phoenix* was never finished. Just flew the once. Never fly again, he said. Over and over. One thing, though."

"What's that?" asked Bob.

Steve sighed and smiled dreamily. "It seats ten."

Sherrine felt her heart begin to pound. Seats ten, she thought. Seats ten. "Never finished," she said. "*Phoenix* is too big to hide. Hah!"

"Hah?" Mike said.

"Bottle shop," she said. " 'Explorers in the high desert keep bottle shops.' "

Smiles began to form. Bruce said, "Ah. A bottle shop sells miracles, and is not what it seems. . . ."

"And the proprietor of a bottle shop usually lies. So what do we have? A rocket ship, in plain sight, and Gary Hudson who helped *design* the bird makes sure he tells everyone that it can never fly again." *And it seats ten! It seats ten!*

"I do not believe it," Gordon said. "It is one more goose to chase. A chimera."

"Me, either," Thor said. "People, it's been fun, but I am not chasing off to California after another rocket ship."

"So what do we do with the Angels?" Bruce asked.

Thor shrugged. "Not my problem. The Con's over.

You're Chairman. You take care of the pass-on. You don't need Fang and me for that. Time for us to move on—"

Fang said, "Guests are my responsibility."

Thor shrugged. "Suit yourself."

"We all have places to be," Bruce said. "Except you and Fang. Steve, how are you getting back to California?"

"Amtrack. I have a ticket. Don't think I can get anymore. Maybe they'll be watching the stations anyway."

Harry had been uncharacteristically quiet. "Jenny and me, we're headed that way. Maybe we could steal another bike—"

"We have a little money," Bruce said.

"Yeah, but—" Harry shook his head. "It's a rough trip, riding double. Don't think the Angels would make it."

Gordon laughed. "Nor do I, Harry!"

"It's all crazy anyway," Alex said. "You know where there is a ship. Single stage to orbit, seats ten. Assume it works, that unlike that ancient Titan, it has been well maintained. I don't believe it, but assume that. It will need—I'm guessing—half a million pounds of fuel? Liquid oxygen and liquid hydrogen. They don't leave that stuff lying around."

There was no answer.

"Fine. You don't have the foggiest notion of how to get the fuel, or how to move it if you did—"

"Details," Mike said.

"Dreams," Gordon said.

"I'm with Gordon," Alex said. "Look, we are very grateful, but it is time to give up the dreams. We have to look for ways we can hide. Forever, I guess."

Silence descended within the Brown household. Presently Mike Glider said, "We can get you ID, I think. Permanent convention guests. God knows fans will help."

"Given ID," Bruce said. "Sherrine?"

"If I lose my job—and I will if I'm not back tomorrow morning—there won't be anything I can do." *It's just a dream. A dream that seats ten. Oh, damn—*

"Then we have to get you back to Minneapolis. Fast," Bruce said. "That needs working on. Meanwhile, can they hide here? Oliver?"

Brown nodded eagerly. "I would be honored. I suppose you won't mind telling me about life in space?"

"OK," Bruce said.

But what if I don't want to go back? Oh, that's crazy. Let them find a way. I go home, I go back to my job. I get Ted on-line and we work out the ID. And I go back to work, doing what I always did, my neat career and I have some memories.

"Sherrine's not the only hacker in fandom," Steve said conversationally.

They all looked at her. "Yes, of course," she said. "There's Ted Marshall. And—"

"And?" Mike demanded.

"RMS himself," Sherrine said. "Nobody knows anything but his initials. Ever hear of *emacs*?"

"The programmer's editor? Sure, I use it," Bob said.

"He wrote it."

"Could he arrange fake ID for the Angels?" Bruce asked.

Sherrine nodded. "If it can be hacked, he can hack it."

"Would he?"

"For space pilots? Oh, yes."

"Why don't we know him?" Mike asked.

"Oh, RMS has been wanted forever," Sherrine said. "Since before the Greens took over! He used to come to Worldcons, but—well, he doesn't stand out in a crowd. Doesn't want to."

"So how do you contact this RMS?" Bruce asked.

Sherrine shrugged. "A million ways. It's just a question of getting the word out on the net. The Legion of Doom will see it and—"

"I used to think I understood you people," Alex said. "Legion of Doom—"

"Super hackers. They—well, they're pretty good, and not always responsible. Some are fans, some aren't. But they listen to RMS, and he's a fan—they'll let him know we want him. The question is, will he believe us? Everyone's after RMS. Pick his brains, jail him, reeducate him, study him in psych labs, he's an odd fish and—"

"Easy," Bob said.

She tried to smile. "*Yes*, we could get him to do it. I don't know why I didn't think of it before. RMS and Marshall, they can do it if anyone can." *It doesn't have to be me. I don't have to stick my neck out. I can crawl back under my covers.*

"So what do we do now?" Bruce said.

"Don't know about you," Harry said. "I've got a message for the merry soul."

"Then what?" Alex demanded. "Why should we care what that crazy man says?"

"He was one hell of a man, once," Thor said.

"A hell of a man who got his brains burned out," Alex said. Strain in his muscles was making him irritable. "So what happens? He tells us another story, and we end up in another stupid chase across the country, more crazy aldermen, cheese trucks, people with guns—"

"Alex, it was not so bad," Gordon said.

"What?"

Gordon shook his head. "Was not fun, then; but think of the stories we tell now. Bed races. Dancing on ice."

Oliver Brown chuckled. "Sure you're not a writer?"

"I wish to be. I have written . . . minor things. But it was not survival-oriented task, so . . ."

Harry shrugged. "I don't know what will happen. Not my job to know what will happen. I know what I was told to do."

"Resent what Wade said, don't you?" Jenny said.

Harry glared at her.

"True, though," she said. "Everybody knows it. Deep down, you do."

Harry tried to grin. "You didn't have to say it."

"Sure we did. I'm still with you, eh? You must do something right—" She caught herself. "Anyway, we got our job straight. Go tell Cole it's time to see what free men can do—oops."

"Yes?" Bruce prompted.

"Without the Angels, why is it time?"

Bruce nodded to himself. "All right, we should all go see Cole."

"Not me," Thor said. "You guys carry them. I'm not going back there."

"That does present a problem," Mike said.

"Maybe not," Bruce said. "Harry—Harry, go find Cole, and bring him here. Make sure you're not followed."

"Maybe he won't come," Harry said.

"He'll come," Oliver Brown said. "He knows the way."

"Oh. Yeah, of course he would," Mike said.

And that would be that, Sherrine thought. They'd take the Angels to California, either to hide them or to try again with *Phoenix*. But that wouldn't matter to her. By tomorrow she would be back home in Minneapolis, safe and snug and not quite warm.

☆   ☆   ☆

The wind blew cold sleet into Captain Lee Arteria's face, stinging her exposed skin with a thousand tiny needles. The Minnesota troopers and the Minneapolis police formed a cordon around the small, one-bedroom house. Neighboring houses winked in the dusk as their inhabitants pulled window shades aside for a glimpse of the goings on. One or two neighbors had bundled up and come out onto their porches. They stood there with their arms thrust under their armpits, bouncing up and down in nervous anticipation.

Lee Arteria had never liked spectators.

A glance into the pulpy sky showed that the storm had hours yet to run. Arteria called to the squad on the Hartley porch. "No answer?"

A pantomime shake of the head.

"Then break the door in, Sergeant Pyle." The policeman hesitated, and Arteria shouted, "It's fucking *cold* out here."

Pyle nodded and raised a boot. Two well-aimed kicks broke the latch and the door swung in and banged against the back wall. Arteria crowded into the hallway with the others.

"Shit," said one of the state troopers. "It ain't that much warmer in here."

Conte stood by Arteria's elbow. "Are you criticizing the thermostat law, Trooper?"

"Uh, no, Captain."

"All right. Spread out and search the place."

"What are we looking for?"

Arteria threw back the military parka's enormous, fur-lined cowl and gave the trooper a grim smile. "You'll know when you find it."

A search did not turn up much. One of the city police located a photograph of Hartley and handed it to Pyle, who showed it to Conte and Arteria. "Horsey looking, ain't she? You'd want to brown bag a date like that."

"That will be all, Sergeant," Arteria said in severe tones. "Homeliness isn't a crime." *Besides, it isn't true. She's attractive enough.*

"Good thing, or she'd be doing hard time." Pyle barked at his own joke and resumed supervision of the search.

Conte studied the picture over Arteria's shoulder. "What do you think, Captain? Is it her?"

Arteria passed the photograph to him. "Probably. Show it to some of those nosy neighbors hanging around out there. Verify her identity. Find out if they know the name of the man in the picture, too."

Conte called to a trooper and gave him the instructions.

"Wait," said Arteria as the man turned to go. "If it is Hartley, have him get copies of the photograph made for distribution."

Lee went from room to room looking for inspiration. Nothing was conspicuously missing from the closet. The toothbrush still hung in its rack above the sink. One toothbrush only. An ice-coated pool of water stood in the sink. A housecoat thrown across the bed. Wherever Sherrine Hartley had gone, she had left in a hurry and had expected to return soon.

That fits. Angels down. Fans to the rescue. She picked up the housecoat. It was quilted; down-filled. Whatever happened to flimsy negligees? Arteria had always liked those. Now you couldn't find them anywhere. Victims of the new, chillier age. Besides, judging from her picture, Hartley had never been the type to wear risqué nighties.

Or was she? *Aah, who ever knew?* Lee dropped the housecoat onto the unmade bed. *What are we doing here, pawing through some poor woman's personal things and laughing?* The people at the University had described her as a loner, a misfit. A talented programmer, they granted, but, really, a nerdette, lacking in the social graces.

And didn't I know a lot of those, boys and girls both, once upon a time? This could be my room, if I'd stayed where— Bit late for that, now. Or is it? How long before one of the searchers found—

The thought was hardly born when a city policewoman, her hands thrust deep underneath the mattress, shouted in triumph. She pulled out three tattered, dog-eared paperback books, looked at the covers, and handed them over to Pyle with a smirk. "She's one of them, all right."

The books were *The Sixth Winter*, *The Man Who Awoke*, and *Fahrenheit 451*.

"Look at this crap, would you," Conte said in disgust. "With all the problems here on Earth, why would anybody waste their time with this escapist stuff? We oughta take these and throw them right into the trash can."

"What're the stories about, anyway?" Arteria took the dry, brittle volumes from Conte and read the back covers. *Won't do to let them know I know already . . .* "Get this. It says here that *The Sixth Winter* is about the sudden onset of an ice age; and *The Man Who Awoke* is about a scientist in 1933 who goes to sleep and wakes up in a future of depleted resources and ruined environments."

Conte took the books back. He scowled at them. "Yeah? What's the third one about?"

"Burning books."

Conte looked uncomfortable and opened his mouth to say something; but he was interrupted by the arrival of Jheri Moorkith and the Green Police.

"Bureaucracy," said Moorkith, shaking his head. "Would you believe it? I never received your memo announcing this raid."

Arteria shrugged. *Okay, let's play head games. First you dribble mine around the floor; then I'll dribble yours.* "It's probably lost somewhere in the interdepartmental mail. The courier will find it stuck in the bottom of his pouch tomorrow."

"Well, no matter." Moorkith dismissed the breach of protocol with a wave of the hand. "I'm here now. What's going down?"

Arteria hated civilians who tried to talk like cops. They always got it wrong anyway. Conte flashed a sympathetic smirk. *I'm glad he's your problem.*

"We're checking on a possible lead. The details were in the memo—"

Arteria was interrupted by the return of the state trooper with the photograph. "Good news, Captain," he said, reporting to Conte. "We've got a definite make on Hartley. Neighbor lady on the west says the fellow in the picture with her is an ex-boyfriend named Robert Needle—or something like that. A university prof. Get this: he's a materialist scientist. He used to hang out with her a lot. We're running a make on him now. But, get this, the neighbor says he drives a maroon van. And he showed up here about two in the morning the night the air thieves went down."

Moorkith sucked in his breath and traded triumphant looks with Conte and Arteria. "I think we're onto something here." He took the photograph from the trooper and studied it.

We? "How can the witness be sure about that early morning business?" Arteria asked.

"She says she sleeps light and the noise of the van woke her up. Me, I think she's a nosy old biddy who likes to spy on her neighbors. But what the hell, a lead's a lead, right?"

Right. And the University said Hartley called in later that morning and took an unscheduled week's vacation. She's supposed to be back tomorrow. When she does, we'll be waiting for her. And then what do I do?

CHAPTER FOURTEEN

"The Sister of Misfortune . . ."

"We'll get him," Harry said. "It may take a while. Ron gets spooked easy."

Oliver Brown nodded. "Well he might. I'm not overly anxious to have him seen here, for that matter."

"We'll be careful." Harry and Jenny left, and Oliver barred the door.

"Do authorities watch this house?" Gordon asked.

"We don't think so," Oliver said. "Helga and I are better known for fantasy. And the SCA."

Alex shook his head. "SCA?"

"Sorry. Society for Creative Anachronism. The Current Middle Ages. I was king, once."

"I think I will let Alex explain later," Gordon said. "May I read now?"

"Certainly," Oliver said. "What would you like?"

Gordon grinned and swept his hand to indicate the disorderly piles of books everywhere. "I think I will find something—I will remember where, and put back there."

"Thank you. Use my big chair if you like, the light's

good there, very good, it's a comfortable place. Alex, you look tired."

"Heh. Considering that I weigh almost a hundred kilos—"

Oliver patted his ample bunk. "Alas, so do I. So do I, but I am more accustomed to it. Perhaps you would like to rest in the spare room?"

"Yes, please."

Oliver led the way. "I'm afraid it will be a bit cold," he said. "We don't heat this room. Hydrogen is scarce." He ushered Alex through the door.

"Hydrogen?"

"Yes, the Greens like to use hydrogen. They pipe it through the old natural gas lines. Alas, much leaks, and is wasted, and since they shut down most of the power plants there is little electricity to make hydrogen."

"But they do make it?"

"Oh, yes. Here we are. As I said, the room is cold. I'll get you a blanket."

The room was cluttered as well as cold. In the habitats, a space this cluttered would be a death trap: masses could crush a man from any direction. Here, gravity . . . then again, gravity was part of the problem. Loose objects had to rest all against the same surface.

There were the inevitable book cases, but here odd tapestries hung on one wall. They showed scenes of dogs chasing deer. Two large steel swords hung in the corner, and below them were two almost identical swords made of wood. A day couch near the window was piled high with—"Costumes?" Alex asked. "Armor?"

"Yes. I mentioned the SCA? We still meet, we still hold tournaments. It is an allowable activity. Indeed, many of the Greens come."

"But what do they—you—do?"

Oliver Brown grinned. "Why, we dress up in medieval costumes and pretend we live in the Middle Ages," he said. "What else? It used to be fun to learn medieval skills, how to live on common, cheap food, fight with swords and spears, and run a civilization with low technology. Now—"

"Yeah. I see."

Oliver piled the stuff from the couch onto a chair. "We don't go often now," he said. "I am afraid someone will get drunk and forget that the Greens are listening." He handed Alex a heavy wool cloak. "Use this as a blanket. I'll call you for dinner."

The window looked out onto gray, mean streets. Other apartment buildings, identical save for their graffiti, lined both sides of the block. The cars were old and in disrepair. One was up on blocks; another, stripped. Street lights flickered uncertainly, then brightened in the growing dusk. Alex looked to the sky, but found it overcast with low-hung, gray clouds. A solitary figure, heavily bundled, walked quickly down the street on the opposite side. He—or she—clutched a cane not needed for walking, and glanced warily left, right, behind.

Get used to it, Alex, my boy. From now on this is home.

Maybe not. *Phoenix!* He remembered the program. A low-cost system, not merely reusable but savable. It could get to orbit even with one engine out. Ran on liquid hydrogen and liquid oxygen.

They make hydrogen. If they make hydrogen, they must have oxygen as well. But—

There was a tap at the door. "Come in."

Gordon came in, frowned at the costumes, swords, and tapestries. "I thought perhaps you might want company."

Gordon found a pair of cushions and lowered himself to the floor, slowly, carefully. "It is tiring, standing upright so long. But, every day grows easier. Perhaps I will like it here. The people are . . . interesting."

Alex smiled and sat on the bed beside Gordon. "Remember what they do to interesting people."

"Is criminal. Alex, is *no* objective evidence for the effectiveness of psychoanalysis. Just replaces conscience, original sin and confessor with superego, id and analyst. In Stalinist times, was used in same way to deal with dissidents. Our way is so obviously right and good that if you disagree you must be crazy."

"I never heard you talk this way before, Gordo."

"I sound angry? I am angry. I like these people, Alex. I am half-Russian. Mental health clinics ... I *know* what they are risking to help us. You saw Cole. I don't wish that to happen to Sherrine, or any of our friends."

"Neither do I. It's simple enough. We let them go home, and we keep moving. No more dreams."

"You must always have dreams." Gordon craned his neck and looked at him. "You do not wish to remain down here, do you?"

Alex rose and walked to the window. He studied the shrouded sky once more. "No."

"Yet, you were born here. This was your home."

A shrug. "That was a long time ago."

"And if we go back? Colonies are doomed. We all know this."

Alex looked around the room.

"You think they listen?"

"No. If these people are listening without permission it would be more than—no. But don't say that where they can hear, Gordon."

"Is pravda, though. More than pravda. Is true."

Alex nodded slowly. "Yeah, I suppose it is, over the long haul. We're running out of everything. The resource base is too small." He laughed bitterly. "Ninety percent of the resources available to the human race, easily available, aren't on Earth, and we *have* them. But the resource base is too small. Not enough people, not enough chlorine, nitrogen—"

"Dr. Lichinsky says give him few more years, he will make chlorine and nitrogen."

"Fusion synthesis. Yeah. And his people have been saying they'd have that Real Soon Now since before you were born, Gordo. Face it, even with chlorine and nitrogen and more genetic materials, there are just too damn few of us!"

"Yet you are eager to return."

"Hell yes! I fought to make *Freedom* a home. Home is the place you would die to save. And that's *not* the bottom of the Well. Not that it matters. We can't go back."

"I think this, too," Gordon said. "But—is not so bad."

"Yeah, yeah," Alex said. "But dammit, the Downers are on a downward spiral, too. They turned their back on the future, and now they've got no more chance than the habitats! Every decade, every year, they're less able to cope. It won't be long before conditions will be like that song, 'Black powder and alcohol. When your states and cities fall—' "

"Orbital decay."

"Eh?"

"Is like *Mir* and *Freedom*, nye pravda? Spiralling downward. Every decade atmosphere drag eats velocity. But perhaps a timely boost can still save them."

Alex scowled and looked away from him. "It's not that easy. We're not talking about a space habitat you can strap booster rockets to."

"No, trajectory of people is harder to change. So. What do we do now? Do you believe in this *Phoenix*?"

Alex worked his lips. "No, but—if there's even the slightest chance."

"Why?"

"Why not? We have to go somewhere. Steve said California was our best chance for going underground, anyway."

"And when *Phoenix* fails to rise from her ashes, you will chase after the next rumor and the next."

"At least I'll still be trying. What else is there to do?"

⋆   ⋆   ⋆

Ron Cole sat in a large stuffed chair in the oversized living room. He looked somehow out of place, and kept casting nervous glances left and right. Jerky movements, like a bird's. Then he sprang from the chair and shoved it into a corner of the wall. After that he sat slightly more at ease, though he still seemed to twitch nervously.

"Is it still paranoia," Thor whispered to Alex, "when they really are out to get you?"

Cole's eyes danced from face to face around the room,

lingering briefly on each. He frowned slightly when he locked gazes with Alex; and nibbled on his lower lip over Harry. "Oliver," he said plaintively, "there are too many."

Helga and Violetta had already returned with several bags of snack foods that they had bartered from the grocery store for the Wisconsin cheese. They broke open bags of chips and trail mix into large bowls and handed them out. Alex raised his eyebrows.

"So much in trade?" he asked her.

"Oh, people will pay far more for the cheese than it is worth," Helga explained. "I suppose that, as long as a single slice can make it out of 'America's Dairyland,' people can tell themselves that things aren't all that bad and they'll return to normal someday."

"Nostalgia has value, doesn't it?" said Sherrine. "Don't we have our own nostalgia? For the way the future was."

"'A Fire in the Sky' . . ." said Bob.

"And we all want a slice of that future, too," said Mike with a grin.

"The *Phoenix*," said Bruce.

Cole jerked and looked at him. "You're not supposed to know about that. What do you know about *Phoenix*? Oliver, I don't know these people."

"Take it easy, Ron. Nobody here but us chickens. Alex and Gordon here are . . ."

"Angels. Yes, yes. That's obvious. Bone structure. Height. Anyone can see that. And Thor. I know Thor. I think. It's so hard to remember sometimes."

Alex exchanged looks with Gordon. Was their origin that obvious? If so, how could they ever hope to maintain a false ID? Or was it—remembering the other people they had encountered along the way—obvious only to someone like Cole?

"You know Harry," said Oliver.

Cole made a face. "Yes. I knew Harry. Know Harry. Oh, thank you."

Violetta had come by with a tray of glasses. Cole took one and sipped it. "Oh my, yes. What is it?"

"Dandelion wine."

Cole licked his lips. He looked sly. "I know where you can get some peach brandy."

"Yes, Ron," said Helga from the kitchen door. "We know. You sell it to us. Harry?"

"Yes, ma'am?"

"Could you help me out in the kitchen for a minute. I'm cutting up the rest of the cheese for hors d'oeuvres."

Harry looked briefly angry, then looked sidelong at Ron Cole. "Yeah, sure."

Jenny took his arm. "Come on. They don't need us here." She led him from the room. At the doorway, she turned. "It really does hurt his feelings, you know. He's not as tough as he likes to act."

Oliver shifted in his seat. "Sure. But, Christ, Jenny, you know him better than any of us. I sent him out for beer once and . . ."

"And the store was closed, so Harry broke a window. I know. He likes to tell that story."

Alex frowned. "He smashed a store window to steal some beer? That doesn't sound—"

"No, he left money for it."

Thor was sitting on the floor with his back to the opposite wall. He rose smoothly and dusted himself. "I guess I'll take a long walk."

Steve said, "Hey, Thor . . ." And Fang reached out and touched the golden giant's arm.

"Sorry, Steve. Fang. But I haven't stayed loose this long by hanging around a bull's-eye. Neither have you."

Fang shook his head. "I'm seeing it through. I finish what I start."

"Let me know what you decide."

When Thor had gone, Cole peered at the group from Minneapolis. Oliver held out a hand. "I'll vouch for them, Ron. You trust my judgment, don't you?"

Cole sucked in his lips and nodded.

"Harry delivered the message?"

"Oh, yes. It's time to move on and see what free men can do."

Silence lengthened. Faintly from the kitchen came song:

*"Nader's Raiders want my freedom, OSHA wants
my scalp and hair,
If I'm wanted in Wisconsin, be damned sure I
won't be there!
If the E-P-A still wants me, I'll avoid them if I can.
They're burning down the cities, so I'll be a wanted
fan!"*

It twitched nerves. Oliver said, "Whatever happened
to escapist literature? Ron, tell us about *Phoenix!*"

"*Phoenix*. A fire in the sky," Ron Cole said. "It flew
once, you know. I was there. Gary was sure it could
circle the Earth. They wouldn't let it fly all the way,
though. They kept her chained. Not everyone wanted
her chained, though." His voice had become nearly normal, and Oliver leaned back, more relaxed now.

"It was politics. NASA and the military," Cole said.
"The cost per pound of payload to low earth orbit was
five to ten kilobucks. Those were the official numbers.
The real cost—well! NASA got five billion a year and
they were lucky to get a launch every two months. If
Gary could fly to orbit for a few million dollars instead of
billions, NASA would look ridiculous."

"I remember," Alex said.

"But the Air Force was going to build it, part of the
strategic defense system, but then the Russians gave up
their empire, and the Air Force wasn't worried anymore
that someone would seize the high ground on them. So
they killed the program, but they hate to throw anything
away. Pack rats, they are. So they decommissioned her
and set her up on a public part of Edwards, so techni-
cally they still have some jurisdiction."

Alex leaned forward. "How did they decommission her?"

Cole chuckled. "They unplugged her. Heh, heh."

Bruce frowned. "What does that mean?"

Cole looked uncertain. "You're sure I can—"

"You can tell us," Oliver assured him.

"They took her ROMs." Cole perked his head up and
beamed at them.

Steve cocked his head. "They took her ROMs?"

"It means," said Alex, "that they pulled all the computer chips with the flight programming and internal controls. Engines, life support. Everything that made the bird alive."

Sherrine sat up straight. "Programming? Why, we should be able to replace that! Bob and Gary can work out the physics. And Tom Marshall and I can do the coding."

Alex smiled thinly. "About 200,000 lines of code, to judge by the birds I've flown? That's 100,000 lines apiece. At 100 lines a day, that would be three years' work."

"That's right," said Mike. "ROM wasn't built in a day."

Sherrine slumped. "Oh."

"Strike one," said Alex, holding up a finger. "Is there anything else, Dr. Cole?"

"There's the IMU, of course. They took that out. Couldn't leave *that* in."

"What's an IMU?" asked Fang.

"It's an inertial platform," Bob explained. "It would be about so big . . ." His hands cut a figure in the air. "Maybe a little bigger than a shoebox."

"I don't suppose you have one on you?" Alex asked Cole.

Cole looked at his hands, as if he expected to find an IMU there. "No. *That* I don't have."

"Strike two." Alex held up a second finger.

"And of course," Cole continued, "there's no fuel."

"Strike three, and we're out." He turned to Gordon. "All I asked for was a chance. But there's no chance here."

Cole blinked rapidly. "Oh, but none of those are insuperable obstacles. No, indeed. Not insuperable, at all."

Oliver Brown nodded slowly. "You don't have the IMU. What is it you have, Ron?"

Cole looked sly. "Well—"

"ROMs. He gave you a copy. For safekeeping," Oliver insisted.

"Yes, yes, you know us both, of course you know that. Yes. I have them, back at the museum. Wrapped in foil. I have them, safe, safe. We thought—we thought once I would go with Gary, but not now, not now. Now I would be a burden."

"Unstrike," Mike Glider said. He held up three fingers, and folded one down. "Now what about the—IMU?"

"Oh, we know where that is. They put it in a safe place." Cole nodded happily.

They waited while Cole continued to nod. A pained look crossed Oliver's face. "Where is it, Ron?"

Cole became suddenly wary. "A very safe place." His eyes slid left and right and he leaned forward and whispered. "It's in the military security area at Edwards AFB."

"Military security area. A safe?" Oliver asked.

"Something like that," Bob said. "We've got security containers at the University. Surplus—"

"That sounds simple enough," said Fang. "Just straightforward B&E and a little burglary. Harry!" he called.

Harry stuck his head in from the kitchen. "Yo."

"You know those things at Bob's university?"

"Look like file cabinets with a big combination lock," Needleton said.

"Sure," Harry said.

"Can you open one?"

"Take about half an hour if you don't mind noise. Couple of hours if anybody's listening."

Mike Glider folded down another finger. "Two."

"And the fuel?" Alex demanded. "Where are we going to find a half million pounds of liquid oxygen and liquid hydrogen?"

They quieted down. Sherrine seemed crestfallen. Bob and Oliver, somber and thoughtful. Steve, folded into a lotus on the floor, vibrated with nervous energy. "Shit," said Fang. "That's a stopper all right."

Cole looked puzzled. "But that's the easy part," he said. "You *make* the fuel."

Alex strained to hear Cole through the resulting babble. The man kept talking in the same low tone of voice despite the noise around him. Finally Bruce put two fingers in his mouth and whistled.

". . . hydrogenation of fats; and of course, there's the TV industry."

Silence.

"Would you mind repeating that, Ron?" said Oliver. "We didn't get it all."

Cole squeezed up his face. "I was simply explaining why, in spite of government craziness and propaganda, there are still plants making hydrogen. The Greens may not like industry, especially the chemical industry; but hydrogen is politically correct. When you burn it, the ash is water vapor. There are things that they want to have—that they need to have. Like television. You can't make television sets without hydrogen."

"Heating, too," Oliver said. "We have hydrogen pipes in this building. It's not very pure, but it's hydrogen."

All true, Alex thought. And the more Cole talked, the saner he became, probably because in talking science he was orbiting in his home module. . . .

"Yes, indeed," Cole said. "All you need is methane and electricity. And steam. Methane—CH_4—is everywhere. Natural gas. Swamp gas. You get some when you crack petroleum or pyrolysize coal. And cow farts."

Mike's jaw dropped. "You're going to make rocket fuel from cow farts?"

"No, of course not. I only meant . . . methane is common. There is hydrogen in the pipelines. There will be a pipe to *Phoenix.*"

"Wait a minute," Alex said. "A hydrogen pipe? Liquid hydrogen?"

"No, no," Cole said. "Just hydrogen. But you compress it, and it will liquify. It is not that difficult."

"And the oxygen? LOX?"

Cole shrugged. "Liquify air, and boil off everything else. It is really very simple." He spread his hands and smiled at them. "And there you have it."

In spreading his hands, Cole revealed two bright glassy marbles. Gordon pointed at them. "Shto eto?" he asked.

"Hmm? Oh, my family jewels. I made them. A long time ago—carbon-12 diamonds." Cole stared at them morosely. "It was my idea, but the big companies took the idea away from me. They make good lasers, you know; but I kept these because they were beautiful."

"All right," said Alex, still not quite believing it. "There are chemical plants operating that make hydrogen—"

"They're small, too. Ten to twenty people."

"And pipe it through the desert. And the LOX you get by compressing air and letting the O_2 boil off. Fine. But a half million pounds—"

Cole shook his head emphatically. "That's the total, not all of that is hydrogen. What you need is 66,500 pounds of hydrogen. It's bulky, but—well, there are ways."

"And the oxygen?" Gordon asked.

"Most of the ship is oxygen," Alex said.

"All right, I bite," Fang said. "How do you liquify air?"

"Turbo expander," Cole said. "Four hundred thousand pounds of oxygen, make it on the spot."

"Where do we get a—turbo expander?" Bruce asked.

Cole shrugged. "I don't know. I haven't cared since they—since they ruined my ship. But Gary will know. Oh yes, Gary will know."

Mike Glider folded his index finger halfway. "Only half a strike left."

Alex found himself nodding, nodding. Half a strike. "Now I'm lost. A—turbo expander. What powers that?"

"It's like a jet engine," Cole said. "Very like a jet engine. In fact, it is a jet engine, but it won't fly—"

"So it needs—"

"JP-4. Kerosene," Cole said.

"A *lot* of kerosene, I expect," Oliver Brown said.

Mike Glider held up one finger again. "Strike—"

"Yes, a lot," Cole said. "But not more than we have."

"What?" Bruce demanded.

Cole grinned widely. "Larry and Curly. You must meet them. Alas, I sold Moe. . . ."

The door on the abandoned warehouse bore a stenciled sign reading *Private Property—Museum of Science and Appropriate Technology*. Rust speckled the metal siding; grass and weeds had punched through the cracks and edges of the concrete truck apron. The shattered windows had been boarded over and covered with graffiti boasting of long-vanished gangs. The cold wind blew off the lake and crystal patches of gray frost nestled unmelted in the shadows.

Cole bent over the padlock and worried it with a key. "This leads back into the bluff underneath the museum. It forms a subbasement where they used to bring exhibits in and out. Hardly used anymore. No sir. Hardly used."

Alex, Bob, Sherrine and Oliver stood behind him, casting occasional wary glances around the open area by the lake and at the museum.

"Ah." Cole grunted in satisfaction and the chain fell away. The doors pulled smoothly up and clicked into place with a satisfying snap. Behind them, two gleaming Peterbilt tractors reared high and proud. The headlights and grillwork had been polished to a sparkle that coruscated from the quiet sun overhead.

"There they are," Cole announced. "Larry and Curley."

Alex stepped into the warehouse. He ran his hand along the bright, cold grillwork. Each tractor was hitched to a long, silver, cylindrical tanker. The logo painted on the side read:

MILKHEIM
LOW-FAT MILK

"These will hold liquid gasses?"

Cole's head bobbed. "Twelve thousand gallons each. I got them war surplus for practically nothing. For peaches . . ." He laughed. "They are filled with RP-4. Enough to power the air converters. Now all you must do is get them to Thunder Ridge."

"Thunder Ridge."

"Edwards Air Force Base," Cole said. "The rocket test stand. Get them there. Gary Hudson will do the rest."

Cole approached the nearest truck—Larry?—and laid his cheek against it. "I've been waiting for this day forever." There were tears in his eyes.

"I don't get it," said Bob. "You've got the ship and you've got Gary to pilot it. You've got the backup ROMs—

maybe—and know where to get the IMU. You know where to find fuel and you've got the trucks to move it. So, tell me one thing, Ron. Why didn't *Phoenix* fly a long time ago?"

Good question, thought Alex.

Cole pointed to Alex. "Because we were waiting for him."

"What?"

"How could you know our scoopship would—"

"Wait!" Oliver held up his hands. "Wait. Ron? Ron, it's all right. It's been years and years. Most of us forgot *Phoenix* ever existed. How did you know Alex was coming?"

"Know Alex was coming? No, that's silly. Alex? Couldn't know. Couldn't know. But we needed Angels to make it fly. Angels to bear her up into heaven, lest she dash her foot upon a stone."

Alex rubbed a hand over his face. *Oh, dear God . . .*

"You see, she won't reach orbit on her own. Gary told me that. Long ago. Before. She's a heavy-duty ship, designed for flight tests. And maybe Gary cut the design too close. She can get to elliptical orbit, but it won't be stable." He turned watery eyes on Alex. "And up to now there's been no way to change that. But you can."

"What in the world is this?" asked Sherrine. She called from the back of the cavernous garage. Alex and the others followed her voice to a dark corner behind the trucks where an immense and convoluted structure of piping stood hissing. Out of one end, small dark droplets of liquid fell into a holding tank. Oliver started to laugh.

"So this is it!" he said.

Cole bounced up and down from his knees, holding a finger over his lips. "Shhhh!"

"What is it?" Sherrine repeated.

Bob frowned at the structure. "It looks familiar. I've seen it somewhere." He started to hold his finger under the dripping liquid, but pulled back. Who knew what that stuff was?

"It's the regenerative cooling system from the old

Titan up in the museum," Oliver explained. "Ron stripped it out and used it to make his still. He distills fruit brandies." He placed a finger under the drip and stuck it in his mouth. "Blackberry. Very tasty. The museum doesn't pay Ron squat."

"I pay *them*," Cole said. "Heh. Apple is best. The trucks were bought with apples and peaches."

Bob started giggling. "*Moonshining* in the basement of the Museum of Science and Industry? I love it!"

Alex smiled. "Yes, but back to the trucks. Is there fuel? Can we get to California? Or is that another detail?"

"Some details are important," Cole said. He pointed to stacks of 55-gallon drums racked against the far wall opposite the still. "Shemp."

Alex blinked. "Shemp?"

"Fourth truck," Cole told him. "Sold it before I sold Moe. Full of JP-4. Kerosene. Heating oil——"

Oliver nodded. "People pay a *lot* for heating oil and they don't ask questions."

Alex blew a cloud of breath into the chill air. "No, I don't suppose they do." He had a sudden, wild image of Cole, his eyes glowing crazy, careening Moe around the streets of Chicago, making clandestine midnight deliveries of black market heating oil. It was a hell of a planet.

☆   ☆   ☆

Bruce was a SMOF. He made a list. SMOFs always make lists.

Sherrine sat on the floor next to Steve, with her knees drawn up under her chin and wondered if she would ever see Gordon and Alex again. She pictured *Phoenix* soaring skyward on a pillar of fire. God, to be there! But she would be back home, and would hear about it only on the news (if they dared run it on the news) and she would smile a secret smile that her coworkers would never understand.

"First," said Bruce, "we need identity papers for the Angels, in case *Phoenix* doesn't work out. Sherrine, Mike, Bob and I will be returning to Minneapolis. Sherrine, you'll link up with Tom Marshall and get *that* ball rolling. Okay?"

Back to Minneapolis. Sherrine nodded. "Sure." Back to the old terminal. It would be tricky, working things out of the University computer center, setting it up so they couldn't trace back to her.

Bruce checked off something on his list. "Good. I'll have The Ghost set up the Great Scavenger Hunt." He looked at Alex. "Fans will come up with stuff we never thought of. You'll have your cornucopia."

Bruce checked off another item on the list. "Mike."

Mike came to abrupt attention—hard to do while slumped in a chair—and snapped a salute. *"Oui, mon capitan!"*

"You find out about the plastic corn at Iowa State."

"Yes, *mon capitan!*" He looked at Sherrine. "I'll need a name," he said.

Sherrine rose. "I can call my grandmother right now. Oliver, can I use your phone?"

"Use a public phone," said Thor. "Always use public phones. It's a rule."

Fang looked at him. "I thought you were quitting this."

Thor shrugged and looked away. "Last reflex twitch of a dying brain."

"Don't do it now," said Bruce. "Wait till we're done here." He studied his list and licked the point of his pencil. "Steve. You've got to get back to California, right?"

Steve, meditating in a full lotus on the floor, answered without opening his eyes. "Right."

"Could you be our point man for the first option? Head up to Edwards and talk to Gary. Get the full picture. Fill *him* in on what's happening. Find out if he'll volunteer his bird."

"He'll volunteer, all right. I only met him the once; but the one thing in life he wants more than anything else is to fly that bucket."

Harry popped the lid of a beer can. "Odds are that Wade has already filled him in."

"Sure, but Wade doesn't know everything. Steve, it can't hurt to make sure."

Steve opened his eyes. "I know that. My dojo can stay closed another few days."

"We're not asking you to go underground," said Bruce, checking another item off the list. "Oliver will hide the Angels until everything is ready."

Oliver bowed. "My honor."

"Especially Gordon," added Violetta, giving the younger Angel a broad smile. "You can make Roland jealous."

Gordon said, "Well, uh . . ."

"Check," said Bruce. "Next item is to get the trucks—"

"Larry and Curley," said Cole.

"—to California. We need drivers." He looked at Thor, Fang and Harry.

"I told you already," Thor said. "Count me out."

Harry shrugged. "I can take one, but the bike will be more useful. You'll need scouts, and Jenny and I do that best."

Fang raised his hand and waved it back and forth. "I want Larry."

Bruce blinked. "Why Larry in particular?"

"Because I always liked him. The Forgotten Stooge. He never got the credit he deserved."

Bruce made a note on his pad. "Fine. Jenny can ride the bike—or can you drive this rig?"

Bob said "She doesn't have to. I'll drive."

Bruce frowned. "Bob? Don't you have to be back at the University?"

"I took care of that. I'm not going back."

Sherrine looked at him. "What happens to your students? I thought you told me you owed it to your students to teach them."

He met her eyes. "I will be teaching them. This will be a lesson they'll never forget."

"Are you contemplating going to orbit?" Alex asked.

"Sure. I'm in good shape, I have a Ph.D in physics, and the rocket seats—what? More than two."

"More than two, da," Gordon said. "But—"

"He's saying don't burn your bridges," Alex said. "Com-

mander Hopkins may not want another physicist. Even if
this *Phoenix* works, which isn't all that damn clear to
me."

"I know that," Bob said. "I didn't quit. On the way
here I called the University and told them I have typhus."

"Typhus?" Thor said.

"Why not?"

Damn you, Sherrine thought. *And I'll be back at my
computer console—*

Bruce tugged on his beard. "Okay, then. Bob and
Fang drive. Harry and Jenny scout ahead. Steve takes
the train to coordinate with Hudson. Now what about
Dr. Cole? Ron, what do you want to do? Stay here?"

"It may not be safe," Cole said. "It has been getting
worse every year. Another year, two at most— No, there
is no reason for me to stay here now."

"Want to go to California?"

"No. It would be too painful," Cole said. "You may
have the tank trucks. I have another, a six-wheeler. If
you will help me load my still on it, I will be all right."

"I'll help," Thor said. "Ron, if you like, I'll go with
you."

Cole looked at him. "I remember you. Yes, I would
like that. Thank you."

Sherrine took a deep breath. "I'm going, too," she
announced.

"What?" said Bob. "Now, wait. You can't take that
chance."

"You are."

Bruce brandished his list. "You've got to go back to
Minneapolis to coordinate the Angels' new IDs," he said.

She shook her head. She had been wondering for days
whether she was risking her job—whatever security she
could count on in poor, doomed Minneapolis—or whether
she was leaving it behind. Now she knew. Damn Bob,
anyway. "You don't need me. The Legion of Doom can
handle this. So I guess it's not so important that I get
back to my job tomorrow—"

"What you're saying," Bob said, "is that you don't
want to go back to your job."

She took another deep breath. "I guess that is what I said, isn't it?"

Sherrine called her grandmother from a phone booth in the candy store on the corner. She used a few tricks to shunt the call through four other trunks just to humor Thor. After she had talked to Gram, she was glad she had.

She must have looked badly shaken up when she left the phone booth because Harry, who had escorted her there, looked concerned. "What's wrong, Sherry?"

"I—" She shook her head. "Take me back, Harry."

Back in the Brown apartment, she handed Mike a slip of paper with a name and phone number. Then she turned to Bob and fell into his arms. "Oh, Bob. We made the right choice, after all." Tears ran down her cheeks. When had she started crying, for Ghu's sake? She didn't like to cry.

"What do you mean?" Bob asked.

"I mean they know about us!"

"Who?"

Bruce rose from his chair. "Who knows what?"

"The police. Gram said they came to her house asking questions. About me. About a maroon van. I— I—" She paused, took a deep breath. "I made some other calls. Tremont says they've got my house staked out and they're asking about Bob around the University."

Bob stepped away from her. He looked a little gray.

Sherrine touched his arm. "We'd both already decided we weren't going back."

"I know. It's just . . ."

"What?"

"Now we *can't* go back. It's different when somebody's following you around burning bridges."

Bruce and Mike exchanged glances. "What about the rest of us? Doc Waxman?"

She shook her head. "I don't know. But why would they have any clues that point to you guys?"

Mike let out his breath and Sherrine knew that she

should be relieved for his sake, as well; but she was simply angry that he was happy to be off the hook.

"Oh, dammit. Dammit." She made fists of her hands. "I never had much; but it's gone now. My house. My car. All my clothes, except what I packed for this 'two-day' excursion. Everything."

Bob shook his head and said, yeah, he was sorry for her, too. And that made her cry even more, because, hell, Bob had lost as much or more as she had, and somehow he could smile. She felt a hand on her shoulder and turned and stared into Ron Cole's crazy eyes.

"Don't worry, dear," he said. "Don't worry. You can always stay in my Titan. The sister of misfortune is hope."

"Oh, Ron Cole. That's the kindest thing anyone has ever said to me."

"Gather round," Bruce said. He sat in front of Oliver Brown's fireplace and tapped the paper against his hand. "I've got a list."

"Why am I not surprised?" Mike asked.

"List?" Harry asked.

"Things we have to do. First thing: Mike, you're the only one who has any right to be at that research place, the one with the bacteria."

"Well, yes . . ."

"It's not far out of our way," Bruce said. "We go there, make sure everything's all right, and Belinda Jenks will meet us in her car and get us back to Minneapolis. The rest of you will go on to St. Louis. The St. Louis people will get you aimed west."

"Right. We're off then," Harry said. "We'll be sure everything's all right."

"What if it isn't?" Mike asked. "What can you do?"

"We can warn you," Harry said.

"How? Telephone?"

Jenny sniffed. "We'll get you the word. If we have to make enough noise that everyone in the country knows—" She patted her oversized handbag.

"Yeah, well that makes sense," Mike said. "But—" He took Harry aside. "Harry, take this. It's a thousand."

"I don't need—"

Mike's voice was low but intense. "Harry, you never ask until you need it right *now*. This time—just take the money, Harry. Think of it as default option money. It's your last gasp. When you run low on funds and Jenny's ready to rob some poor schlub at gunpoint, use the damn money instead."

Harry hadn't taken it. Mike said, "You know her, Harry. Any excuse. 'Bring it down, bring it down—' "

"Yeah." Harry took the money and had it in his boot with a minimum of motion.

CHAPTER FIFTEEN

Treasure Hunt,
or
The Hundredth Dream

<logon>
<Greetings, all, from the Oregon Ghost. Gabe and
Rafe are on their way. Let's all chip in and do what we
can for their going-away present. If you can't deliver it in
person, leave word and I'll find a way to get it there.>

—Ghost, with both hands, you couldn't find your—

<Alter! How did you get out of your dungeon? I don't
have time for you now. There is serious business afoot.>

—That's why I'm here, you pitiful Primary Ego. This
is too serious for me to sit back and watch you screw
things up. Did you think I would stay down there amus-
ing myself by burning those old copies of *The Intergalac-
tic Reporter*—?

<What?! How dare you burn my collection of fanzines?
What would Carol Kovacs say if she knew?>

—Well, an imp has to keep itself warm somehow. If
you would heat the dungeon I wouldn't have had to
ignite that stack of *Lan's Lanterns* last week—

°Shriek°

—Or the *FOSFAXs* or *Mimosas*. They're getting dry and crumbly. Make good tinder—

<All right, Alter. Make your point, if you have one.>

—Point? Point? Oh, very well. Friends, don't trust The Ghost. His minds aren't what they used to be. Send your contributions to the usual places. DUFF, SKIFFY, TAFF, they're all in this. The final drawing hasn't been scheduled yet; but the big prize is still the Trip of a Lifetime. Remember, two Grand Prize winners have already been chosen, but don't let that stop you from giving them the boost they need. They're feeling a little Down.>

<Thank you, Alter. Now get back to your dungeon, like a good little Ego.>

—Don't count on it, Ghost. I'm the Prime Self now. Remember? The fans voted for me in *Galaxy* years ago. Me, not you, Ghost. Eh? No! Not the Spell! Not the Spell! Arrgh!—

<logoff>

*   *   *

<Like what?> Anonymous note on electronic bulletin board.

<You name it; they need it. Make it small and make it light. There's a weight limit on their baggage.> Anonymous reply on same bulletin board.

*   *   *

Captain Doom flashed the light briefly at the big wooden sign. PUTNAM'S WORM FARM. WORMS FOR SOIL CULTIVATION; WORMS FOR BAIT; WORMS FOR ALL PURPOSES. He pondered that, wondering what other purposes worms might have. Then he shrugged and touched his throat mike. "Captain Doom to SMOF-One," he whispered. "I am in position."

"Roger, Captain Doom," he heard Benjamin Orange's voice tinny in his ear. "Go for it."

Captain Doom nodded to his three companions. He grabbed a section of chain-link fence while Mark and Lisha Hartz worked their wire cutters in unison. Then he lifted the loose flap like a trap door. He clapped the third fan on the shoulder. "Chain up! We're going in!"

Andy ducked swiftly forward with a shovel in his hand. Captain Doom began counting in his head. "One one-thousand; two one-thousand; three one-thousand ..." Then he tapped Mark and Lisha, who dropped their bolt cutters, grabbed plastic sacks, and scurried through the hole in the fence.

While his teammates were gone Captain Doom tied twisties to the cut sides of the fence flap. Then he waited. When his mental count reached three minutes the bag carriers slipped back through the fence, followed in another minute by Andy with the shovel. The four plastic sacks bulged and Captain Doom caught a whiff of the contents. "Better double-bag that," he said. "It's a long ride back."

His three companions nodded and slipped away into the darkness. As he fastened the loose fence section back in place with the twisties, Captain Doom triggered his throat mike. "Captain Doom to SMOF-One. Mission accomplished. Have the deodorizers ready."

Captain Doom rejoined the others. Benjamin Orange stood by the open back doors of the panel truck they had come in. Doom's teammates and two other teams were already seated inside the truck, wiping greasepaint from their faces. Orange was garbed in slacks and dress shirt and sported a prominent bow tie in the Black Watch tartan. He wore a headset and throat mike that left his hands free for a clipboard and checklist. SMOFs *always* made lists.

"Can you hear me, Team Gamma? Can you hear me?" He glanced up as Captain Doom approached. "How'd the worm farm go?"

"It went like clockwork, Orange."

"Good." The SMOF nodded. "Good. Wait." He put a hand to his earphone. "Ah, there you are, Henry. I can hear you now. Have you got the bull semen? Yes, I know it's kept cold. We've got a refrigerated container in the truck; so hurry it back here. SMOF-One, out." He grinned at Captain Doom. "Let's see the Lunarians top that one. With that plus the ova from the agricultural school ... if the Angels can't culture a bit of laboratory beef, then we aren't the Fanoclasts."

★   ★   ★

The clerk at the checkout counter raised his eyebrows. "Starting a garden, miss?"

Winnie Null piled more seed packets on the counter. "Sure am."

The clerk studied the packets. "You must have a mighty big plot."

"Big enough."

"You've got too much there, miss. They'll choke each other out."

Winnie sighed. Why did men assume that, because she looked like a covergirl, she did not have a brain in her head? "I know what I'm doing."

"If you'd like a little advice on gardening, I get off at five."

"That's very generous. My husband and I will be glad to have your help." Husbands were useful, she reflected, as the clerk suddenly busied himself with his job. One of these days she would have to get one.

★   ★   ★

Thor waited by the checkout lane at the supermarket, holding a place in line while Fang scurried back and forth with small purchases. That earned him a glare from the lumpy, dough-faced woman who was next in line. Probably upset because, due to Fang's ploy, she was one place behind her rightful place in line. Thor considered letting her go ahead; decided against it. Her shopping basket was piled so high that by the time she was through at the cash register the glaciers would be in the parking lot.

The doughy woman gave him one last glare before, rustling the pages with a flourish, she dived behind the anonymity of a checkout tabloid. This one, called the *International Global Celebrity Tattle-Tail*, featured a lurid headline in 72-point type:

"ICE NUDES ON GLACIER!!!"

It was accompanied by a rather fuzzy photograph of a

nude woman in unidentifiable surroundings. The remainder of the headlines lined the margin of the front page like wallflowers at a school dance. One of them proclaimed a new "Thermal Diet" to help keep one warm and comfortable during the colder winters. From what he could glean, it involved a considerable amount of curry and jalapeño peppers.

The woman caught him reading the front page and, with a sniff of righteous indignation, folded it over and returned it to its rack. Thor wondered what unspoken rule he had transgressed. Could one freeload on a freeloader?

Fang scurried up to him with an armful of spice cans, dumped them into the arm basket Thor held, and dashed off for one more run. Thor scanned Fang's choices. A little bit of everything, with an emphasis on the preservative spices. When the contents were used up, the light tin-plated containers would still be valuable. He considered for a moment sending Fang after some jalapeños, but decided it would take too long to explain.

Where were the Angels by now? Halfway to St. Louis, probably. Thor toyed idly with the spice cans. Was he right to drop out? After all, Fang was sticking with it. He'd be setting out in Larry as soon as they bought the supplies.

But someone had to watch over Ron Cole. And the fewer people hanging around the Angels the better. And the *Phoenix* would never fly anyway.

See what free men—

Thor sighed unhappily. He had really believed in the Cole legend. A naive belief, he saw now. His parents had always been after him to "be realistic." Especially after catching him with "that" literature. So he had always associated realism with a world where dreaming was suspect.

Ninety-nine out of a hundred dreams came crashing down around you. But if life always fell short of your expectations, that was no argument for *lowering* them. There was always the hundredth dream.

The shopper in front of him finished her check through

and Fang returned to line with a jumbo jar of multivitamins just in time. Madam Doughball pointedly did not move aside for Fang, but that didn't stop the crusty old guy. He lobbed it.

Now, there was someone who had the Talent. Fang could dream realistically. The Titan had not fazed him at all. An option had failed to pan out; there were other options.

Fang watched the tally carefully. Programming skills were deteriorating and scanners had been known to commit egregious errors as a result. But all Thor could see in his mind's eye was the magnificent ascent of *Phoenix* from her desert home. With ten berths in her crew cabin module. Eight of them up for grabs. He wondered if any of the others had had the same dream he had.

But it wasn't realistic.

☆   ☆   ☆

Riding in the cab of an eighteen-wheeler tank truck southbound on I-55 for the Gateway City, with the pavement humming beneath their tires and off-highway neon-lit diners flashing past in the darkness, Sherrine had a barely controllable urge to tune into a country/western station. Bob was hunched over the steering wheel, eyes glued on the road ahead. He looked like a trucker. They'd found him a yellow baseball cap with the name of a feed store on it, which he wore pushed back on his head. Between them, Gordon dozed fitfully.

Sherrine had thought that the truck cabin would be crowded with four of them aboard; but she found that the big Peterbilt could fit three across the seat while the fourth could rest in a smaller sleeping compartment behind the cab. The two Angels did not mind the cramped conditions. In fact, they seemed to relax. Sherrine judged that they were accustomed to sleeping quarters not much roomier than the back of the Peterbilt.

They passed the turn-off for Winnemucca, which made her think of Cordwainer Bird. Bird had taken the National Endowment for the Arts advance for *The Very, Very Last Dangerous Visions; Really. And This Time I'm*

Not Foolin' and vanished without a trace. Rumor speculated that he was preparing the ultimate diatribe; the one that would rock the Establishment to its very foundation.

There were stories about Bird. Some of them were true.

I wonder if Bob misses his van. Foolish question. Of course he did. He had had that van a long time and had kept it in careful condition. It was comfortable, like an old slipper. Lots of memories there.

Lots. The quilts and blankets in the back of the van were not entirely meant for insulation. Sherrine gave Bob a sidelong glance. She was not opposed to marriage, in principle. Not for sex, although the new laws made it safer that way, but for the comradeship. She had even tried it once, and it had been the happiest three years of her life . . . though the marriage had lasted five.

Whatever had become of Jake? Had his liaison with Heather lasted? The Cookie had struck her as one who enjoyed the chase more than the prize. Suppose, after dumping his wife for a better looker, Jake had been dumped in turn for a more virile stud?

Or else Jake and Heather were living a life of connubial bliss in a suburban bungalow somewhere, with a miniature Jake and Heather scampering around them.

Well, well. How little we know ourselves. She had not thought about Jake in a long, long time. Yet, the recollection still drove her heart to flutter. Not the end-Jake, but the early Jake. He with the wide, smiling mouth and the perpetually shadowed jaw and the audacity to wander through the timescape of undreamed lands. Somehow, beneath the bitterness, beneath the anger, there was . . . not love, but the shadow of a love that once was.

She was glad when Bob pulled over and turned the wheel over to her. Gordon half-woke, then settled back. Alex climbed out of the sleeper box like a sleepy spider monkey. Bob crawled in. Sherrine put the monster in gear.

The task at hand was to honcho an eighteen-wheeler to St. Louis. Other cars drifted past like windup toys. There weren't many in these early morning hours.

The truck turned majestically, less like a car than a

seagoing liner. A lot of momentum in an eighteen-wheeler. But if they stuck mainly to the interstates she would be okay. No sharp turns. What was it that Bill Vukovich had said after winning his second straight Indy 500? "There's no secret. You just press the accelerator to the floor and keep turning left."

"What did you—?"

"Did I say that out loud? Sorry, Gordon. Back to sleep."

"Can you drive and talk?"

"Sure, Gordon. How are you holding up?"

"I was asked, 'Am I still having fun?' I am. You?"

"I haven't had time to stop and think since Bob rousted me out of bed to pull Angels off the Ice." She remembered the comfort and security of the computer room with a longing that shocked her. There was an animal contentment to living only in the present, snug under the covers and comforters, giving no thought to the future.

The future was a sneaky tense that crept up a day at a time, each tomorrow just a little different from the last, until one day you looked back along the path you had travelled and saw how very, very far you had come from your roots. Safe and secure; but with your dreams cauterized. In the bright light of day, she could see that that path of accumulated tomorrows was a smooth and slippery one that led down, down, down. The bottom of a Well was the point of minimum energy; which was why it was so easy to rest there unmoving.

To move, however ... Ah, that was another matter entirely. There were other paths, other tomorrows. One could choose among them. And she had made her choice.

And having made that choice, having left behind everything in her life but a change of clothes—"Yeah. Yes, Gordon, I'm still having fun."

But both Angels were asleep, slumped into each other as if boneless.

Sherrine felt more at peace than she had had at any time since Jake had left. Yet, all the psychologists would agree that she should be feeling terrible tensions and insecurity. *A body at rest tends to remain at rest, unless acted upon by an outside force.* She had never thought of Newton as a psychologist before.

They passed an interchange. A neon sign on the feeder road below them glided out of the darkness and then faded behind them. HARRY'S ALL NIGHT HAMBURGERS. She felt a sudden passion for cheeseburger and fries.

☆　　☆　　☆

He licked the pencil tip with his tongue, tucked the receiver more firmly against his ear, and held his hand poised over the order pad. "All right, go ahead. You want what? Cornish hens. Fine, ma'am. Yes, we do. All sorts of barnyard animals. A half-dozen? And what? I see. Is there some reason why they should be pregnant? How about a nice rooster, instead? Fine. Yes, you can pay when you pick them up."

☆　　☆　　☆

The clapboard building was falling apart. The porch roof sagged, and the windows were boarded up. Shutters and sidings loose and brittle with time rattled in the prairie wind. Behind the building, black and rotted husks dotted a weed-grown field. Mike Glider gingerly got out of the truck and looked around. "Harry?"

"Here." Harry and Jenny came down from the decaying porch.

"I thought this was the place," Mike said. "Now I'm not so sure."

"This is it," Harry said. He held up a piece of broken board. IOWA STATE COLLEGE AGRICULTURAL RESEA— The end of the sign was charred black.

"Sure is run down," Bruce said.

Mike nodded. "Yeah, but it was once the pride of the Agricultural Service. They did a lot of good work here."

"Closed by court order," Harry said.

"Worse than that," Mike said. "They didn't even wait. A Green flying squad burned the main building out. Killed four of the research staff—and got off as justifiable manslaughter."

"Wasn't the only place that happened," Harry said.

"The big pogrom—lot of scientists killed that year. Okay, what's next?"

"We get shovels," Mike said. "They buried the bacterial cultures out in the cornfield when they heard the mob was coming."

"I better watch the bike," Harry said.

"It's all right, I can see it," Jenny said.

Harry shrugged. "Okay." He looked around at the wasted fields. "Shovels. Dig where?"

"They faxed me a map," Mike said. He grabbed the doorknob and shook it. The door would not budge. "They used student labor during the school year; then used volunteers so they could continue working the land"—again, he tried the door—"into summer sessions. There are probably all sorts of tools—" He kicked the door. "If we can just get inside."

The doorknob was pulled from his grasp. "I came in through the back," Harry said.

Mike looked at Bruce and Bruce looked at Mike. "I would have tried that next," Mike said. He stepped inside the building to the musty smell of cobwebs and rotted wood. A thick layer of dust coated the floor, broken by the tracks of rodents.

The building was a warren of rooms and closets. Abandoned offices. Desks with empty drawers hanging open. File cabinets overturned. Papers scattered about the floor, stained with rodent droppings and the leak of rain through the roof.

"God damn them," Mike said reverently. "They did good work here. Milk. We had a way to synthesize hormones. Natural hormones, what cows make themselves. Give the cows more and get half again as much milk. Only they wouldn't let us use it."

"With people starving?" Jenny demanded. "How long has that been going on?"

"They discovered how to do it back before the turn of the century," Mike said. "In 1987."

"But—why—"

"They're still testing to see if it's safe. That's what the Greens said. The dairy corporations didn't fight very hard. The last thing they need is cheap milk. Oversupply, they called it."

He found Bruce at the back door of the building. The door was hanging loose on its hinges, and the jamb around the latch was broken and splintered. Bruce pointed to the shattered door. "When Harry said he came *through* the back door—"

"He's got a helluva knock, doesn't he?"

Harry approached them from the farther hallway carrying two shovels over his shoulder. "I found a store room," he announced. He gave one shovel to Bruce; the other, to Mike. "And there were just enough shovels."

＊　　＊　　＊

<logon>
<SMOF-One: Bull semen!!!??? The Ghost>
<logoff>

＊　　＊　　＊

The plant manager spoke in such a broad Texan accent that you would never guess he was not originally from Texas. Just as some people were "more Catholic than the Pope," Ron Ellick reflected, others were more Texan than the Texans. Johns even kept a stuffed rattlesnake in his office. It all seemed very strange, because they were in the Pennsylvania coal country, nowhere near Texas. Ellick felt right at home.

The plant manager led him past the beds of enormous NC machines jigged to shape different parts from the base material. All but one were silent and shrouded. The plant was weirdly quiet with only a handful of people at work. The echo of hammer, saw and drill sounded small in its cavernous spaces. "Not very busy, Mr. Johns," Ellick ventured.

"Call me Johnny," the manager said. "And you're right. We aren't very busy, 't all. Because of the all."

"All?"

"Right. Pollution laws won't let anyone drill for all anymore. So, less fuel for the airlines. And they cut back on the number of flights because it might damage the ozone layer. So fewer planes are being built." Johns shrugged. "Bunch of guano, if you ask me. But I'm an interested party. The aerospace people were our biggest customers. Now all we get are maintenance and spares orders. There's an example, on that pallet. See where Mitch is gluing the details in place? Now, what does that remind you of?"

"A bee's honeycomb."

Johns nodded. "Right. We call it structural honeycomb. That there is part of the nose assembly for a 737b."

Ron Ellick studied the part dutifully. He had flown from Minneapolis to Philadelphia, courtesy of 3MJ, on an old 737b. He wasn't sure he wanted to know how much of it was held together with glue. "You work on some mighty big parts, Johnny. Awkward shapes. Must be a problem handling the stuff."

"Oh, not the raw material you were asking about. That comes in blocks. Come on, let me show you."

Johns led him to an area of the plant filled with shelving. Each shelf held a stack of what looked like solid oblong blocks. "The way the industry's been ruined, we have enough honeycomb in stock here to last a generation." Johns shook his head sadly. "Anyhow, the stuff was shipped collapsed into blocks like this. Easier to handle. We set the blocks on an extender, put hooks in each end, and stretch 'em open like an accordion." He pointed to another machine which to Ellick looked like a rack from a medieval torture chamber. His mind toyed with the notion: a modern-day horror story. . . .

"So the original honeycomb block," Johns went on, "takes up hardly any room at all. Ginny, show Ed here what happens when you put a block in water." He nudged Ron Ellick with his elbow. "Watch this."

The worker pulled on a pair of metal reinforced gloves. *Glaives*, thought Ron Ellick. *Chain mail.* It seemed appropriate for someone who worked on a rack. She pulled a block from the shelves and began to lower it end-first into a barrel filled with water.

"This one is aluminum," Johns told him. "But we have

honeycomb in all sorts of metallic and non-metallic composites."

The block was completely immersed in the water now and the level in the barrel had hardly risen at all. "Ninety percent air," Johns assured him. "I doubt there's any structural material on the face of the earth that combines the structural strength with the lightness of honeycomb."

Ron Ellick nodded. *Or off the face of the earth, either.* "How much for the blocks?"

Johns rubbed his chin and looked thoughtful. "The aluminum kind or the—"

"Each."

Johns cited a list of prices from memory. Ron Ellick wrote them down on a notepad. "OK, Johnny, I'll talk to my people. You can ship it to California?"

Johns nodded. "Son, the way the market is right now, I'll *carry* it to California."

☆   ☆   ☆

<logon>
<I have caught the bug. MYCROFT.>
<logoff>

☆   ☆   ☆

Ted Marshall was a young man, round of face and soft of muscle. At 5'11" and 160 pounds, he gave the odd impression of being both skinny and overweight. He had an aversion to athletics of any sort. Every morning he watched a run of joggers pound by his home, lifting them up and putting them down; a peculiarly elaborate form of self-torture. In high school, he had taken remedial gym.

He held the chip up to the light and looked at it. "How many books does it hold?"

"About five hundred," said Will Waxman. The old man with the bushy patriarch's beard laid four more on the table. "This is almost my entire library. The last one, there? That's the Encyclopaedia Britannica."

Ted grunted and laid the first chip down. All five had been modified to look like Nintendo "Game Boy" cartridges. "Cyberbooks. And you want to know if I can duplicate them?"

Will Waxman nodded. "And the reader." He set a Sony Bookman on the table between them. "Maybe a dozen of each?"

Ted picked up the Bookman. "Where did you get this baby? I thought their import was banned."

"It is."

Ted inserted one of the cartridges into the Bookman and touched the "game buttons." "How does it— Never mind, I got it. This is page forward; and this is page back. Hey! You've got the entire Heinlein canon in here! And Asimov and de Camp and . . . What does this button do?"

"It moves the cursor around so you can tab hypertext buttons. Go ahead, move it to the story title you want to read and then press the 'A' button."

Ted did so and smiled when he saw the title page appear on the screen. He glanced at the other cartridges. "This must be a lot of fun when you're browsing through the encyclopedia."

"*Flying* through the encyclopedia," Will corrected him, "like a stone from David's sling skipping over the water. No, more like jaunting in Bester's *The Stars My Destination* or the stepping discs in Niven's *Ringworld*. Did you ever hear Philip José Farmer's definition of a dullard?"

Ted shook his head. "No."

Will grinned. "Someone who looks a thing up in the encyclopedia, turns directly to the entry, reads it, and then closes the book."

Ted laughed. "It's a damn shame they banned these things. The trade problem—"

"Trade friction had nothing to do with it." Will took the Bookman from Ted, saw that it was open to *Pebble in the Sky* and flipped through the electronic pages. "Can you imagine any gadget better designed to seduce the 'Video Generation' into reading?"

Ted frowned. "Nah. Conspiracy theories are fun, but it's usually just ineptitude or—"

"A well-read, educated public is more difficult to lead

around by the nose ring." Will leaned across the table. "Can you duplicate the chips and the reader, Ted? I need to know."

Ted Marshall shook his head. "No, I can't. The programming? No problem. But the chips themselves . . . I'm not a hardware man."

The old man sighed. "I was hoping to keep my originals. Oh, well."

Ted held out a placating hand. "Hold on, Will. I don't know how to duplicate the hardware, but I know someone who knows someone."

Free-lance electrosmithing was almost as incriminating as free-lance programming. Will didn't ask further. Ted Marshall made the Bookman and its chips vanish. "I'll see what I can do. You won't mind if I make copies for myself, will you?"

"Of course not."

"Still. Won't the, uh . . ." He cast his eyes toward the ceiling. "Don't our friends need things like algae for their hydroponics a lot more than they need books?"

Will shook his head. "Man does not live by pond scum alone."

*　　*　　*

\<logon\>
\<Ghost: Honeycomb, won't you be my baby. Batman\>
\<logoff\>

*　　*　　*

"Oh, what a cute little bunny rabbit!" said Adrienne Martine-Barnes, stooping over to peer into the cage. The oversize rodent inside laid her ears back and sniffed. The gnawing incisors lay bucktoothed over the lower lip. "Yes, aren't you cute." And plump, too. Rabbits gave good meat per volume. So did guinea pigs.

"May I help you?" The pet store manager had come up behind her.

Adrienne rose and turned. "Yes, you may." She had the commanding presence of the queen of Olympus. A white streak accented her otherwise black hair, as light-

ning does the night sky. "How much are the rabbits and
the guinea pigs?" The manager told her and she nodded.
She pulled a checkbook from her handbag. "And do you
give quantity discounts?"

☆   ☆   ☆

When they came to the Interstate bridge over the
Mississippi, they slowed, and Harry and Jenny came by
on the motorcycle. Harry held up his hand, thumb and
forefinger in a circle.

"All clear," Bob said. "At least from outside."

Alex could see the St. Louis waterfront laid out below
him. Many of the docks and wharfs along the river stood
dry and inaccessible, since so much of the river's source
water was locked up in northern ice. Starved as she was,
though, the Mississippi was still a mighty stream; and tug
barges and riverboats crowded her like a Manhattan
street. The Missouri, which entered a few miles upstream, was still running near strength, wind and rain
patterns having so far kept her watershed nearly ice-free.

Even so, Alex noticed two barges aground on a mud
bar near the East St. Louis side of the river. Grain
barges from the north, Bob told him. Files of people,
ant-small in the distance, marched on and off the barges,
balancing baskets full of grain on their heads. He wondered how much of the cargo they could salvage before
rats and rot did for the rest.

Gordon, sitting between them, suddenly perked up
and pointed through the windshield. "What is that?" he
asked.

"That is the Gateway Arch," said Bob, taking the exit
onto Memorial Drive. "Our destination."

"But what does it do? What is its function?"

"The Arch? There's an elevator inside that takes you
to an observation platform on top. And there used to be
a Pioneer Museum underneath; that's closed up now for
lack of funds."

"That's all? Not for microwave relay or, your word . . .
weather observation or such?"

"No, it was a tourist attraction. A monument. Why?"

Gordon shook his head in wonder. "I have never seen such an artifact built for no useful purpose. Could make poem about such beauty. Building under constraint of gravity field is like building poem under constraint of sonnet form. Requires craft and artistry."

Alex noticed Gordon's lips move and grunted. The stilyagin was probably trying to compose a poem on the spot. It was that sort of distraction that got him put on probation, then on the dip trip.

But Gordon was right about its beauty. In orbit Alex would not have wondered twice about the Arch. Such construction would have been easy, given the mass . . . which is never given, in orbit. *That's why we need Moonbase so badly. All that free mass!* But in a gravity field . . . how did they keep it up? Its soaring lines seemed to defy gravity. He tried to imagine the forces acting on the arch. The downward vectors must be translated into vectors along the length of the arch itself. A neat problem in basic physics. It was a fascinating planet. His eyes travelled along the sleek parabola until, in an odd echo to his thoughts, he saw what looked like vector arrows pointing down from the top of the Arch. As he watched, the arrowheads swayed slightly in the wind.

"What are those?"

Bob squinted through the windshield. "Beats me." He reached back over his shoulder and rapped on the back of the cab. "Coming up on the Arch," he said.

The panel separating the sleeping cubicle from the cab slid back and Sherrine stuck her face through. "The fan club meets in the underground museum, right?"

"That's what Violetta said. They'll give us a place to spend the night." He pulled to the side of the street and turned on his blinkers. A car and two horse carts drove around him. "All clear," he announced.

Alex heard the door to the sleeping cubicle open and shut. He squirmed a bit in his seat; then he gripped his cane, unlatched the passenger door and slid to the sidewalk.

"Hey," said Bob, "where are you going?"

"With Sherrine," he answered. He flourished his cane. "For the practice. And just in case."

☆   ☆   ☆

Sherrine saw him coming and waited politely on the tiled plaza. She was framed by the gleaming Arch against the backdrop of the river. A barge drifted lazily behind her, keeping carefully to the channel buoys. He was struck again by her fragile beauty; a beauty she herself seemed oddly reluctant to acknowledge. Most Earth girls seemed terribly short and muscular to him; and he had seen enough by now to realize that pudgy and burly were the norm. Yet, Sherrine continued to allure him.

Was it only a physical thing? Or was it a fixation—imprinted like a baby duck!—brought on by the fact that she was the first woman he had seen after Mary had . . . had betrayed him? Now there was a thought!

Betrayed you how, Alex? Because she didn't order you back upstairs after that first missile attack? Because she left it up to your own stupid pride? *If anyone betrayed you, Alex, it was yourself.*

A sudden horn jolted him from his reverie. Two men in a horse jitney shook their fists at him as they pulled around. As if they hadn't the whole street to themselves, Alex thought sourly.

Sherrine said, "Alex? What's up?"

"You don't want me with you?"

Her lips parted to answer him, then she shook her head. "Come on, then. I think the entrance to the old museum is over this way." Alex wondered what she had been about to say. He thought he could make a reasonable guess. Couldn't stick to the flight plan, could you, Alex? And why? To moon along after a woman who . . . He wanted to say that he found her attractive; that he admired the way she had abandoned her career and freedom to help him; that he wanted to get to know her better. But the words stuck awkwardly in his throat. Held down by gravity.

She led him down a concrete ramp festooned with gaily-colored graffiti and handbills. One large poster, plastered overtop the others, announced a closed-circuit TV address by Emil Poulenc, "Discoverer of the Ice

Folk." Whatever that meant. The sun was high in the sky, brushing the shadows from the ramp. Four odd, circular shadows wavered like black spotlights on the paving stones.

Why can't I ever pick a woman who'll choose me back?

Sherrine knocked three times on the boarded-up doors at the bottom of the ramp. A face like a side of beef peered down at her from behind a plywood partition, too high up. With a bit of a stutter she said, "We're knights of Saint Fantony."

His face showed nothing. "Here for the High Crusade?"

"To win victory or sleep with the Angels. By order of Duke Roland."

"Duke Roland" was Oliver Brown.

The giant's face withdrew into shadow. A minute or two later the door opened.

The young man who opened the door was considerably smaller. In the midday brightness he seemed shy and awkward. He blinked up at Alex and held out his hand. "Welcome," he said. "I'm Hugh." He indicated his companion, a giant to rival Thor. "We call him Fafhrd."

"What *are* those things up there?" asked Sherrine, staring up against the glaring sun at the four bundles dangling from the Arch.

The young man looked up, shading his eyes with his hand. "Scientists from the University. They were accused of practicing nuclear physics."

Sherrine stared at Hugh. "They *hanged* them for that? Because they were convicted of being nuclear physicists?"

The young man shook his head. "They weren't convicted. We think they were four of the people who ran the museum here. The place was empty after that, and we moved in." Hugh had led them inside. Alex saw a flash of silver at his left hand, then jumped as a huge hominid shadow caught the corner of his eye.

Hugh had a knife in his left hand. He'd had it ready while his right immobilized Alex, while the giant doorman guarded him from overhead. "Duke Roland says you're to be trusted. I trust my senses when I can. Alex, how do you take a shower in free fall?"

Alex said, "It takes forever to get wet and forever to get dry. Wherever water is, it wants to stay. We don't have enough water anyway. Mostly we— Hugh, how would a Downer know if I was lying?"

"This Downer was a physics teacher at KC High. Milady, I might grant you're an angel, but not an astronaut."

Sherrine smiled and colored. "No. I was one of the rescuers."

"I see." Hugh's arm swept in a circle. "Well, welcome all!" Others came from out of the shadows beyond the entryway. Many people, some in armor. "You have friends?"

"Yes. I'll go for them," Sherrine said, but she didn't move at once. "Hugh, if the locals are hanging scientists, are you safe here?"

Hugh's face closed like a wall . . . and then he said, "We are safe indeed. I am Duke Hugh Bloodcup because I was King Hugh of the Middle Kingdom six years ago. The locals—the Downers—they hanged four scientists here, once. But when others came to disturb us, we buried those bodies and replaced them. The locals see four bodies hanging from the Arch. They never think to examine them, to see if they've been cycled. But there are rumors enough to protect us, and if *they* won't—"

"Yes. I see. Your Grace, Alex MacLeod will need to sit even in your presence—"

"Yes, of course. A chair for our saintly guest! And an escort for Lady Sherrine!"

CHAPTER SIXTEEN

The Last Shuttle

"I tell you, Captain," Lieutenant Billings insisted, "*something* is going on. There's been increased activity in the fannish underground over the past few days. Weird activity."

Lee Arteria nodded to the AP lieutenant standing stiffly before the desk; reached out and riffed through the thick stack of reports. "Yes. Though how can you tell when fannish activity is weird?"

"They've been quiet for so long. The timing must be significant, wouldn't you agree, ma'am?"

"True."

"Someone must be hiding the spacemen, or we would have found them by now."

"But sci-fi fans? Really, Lieutenant. Could a bunch of nerds and geeks have slipped the aliens past the search parties on the Ice? With virtually no notice, mind you." She grinned. "Maybe the Ice Folk have them."

Billings made a face: "Ice Folk. Supermarket tabloid nonsense. A newly evolved race of humans who can live naked on the Ice? And there's that Sherrine Hartley. She never reported back to work. And her boyfriend with the maroon van called in to report he has typhus. Typhus! And vanished. Captain Arteria, this other fannish activity must be related to the spacemen, too."

"Cornish game hens, Lieutenant? How will that help hide the fugitives?"

"I don't know, ma'am. They might be stocking a hidden hideaway with food."

"Bull semen, Lieutenant? Earthworms?" Arteria leaned forward, hands placed flat upon the desk. "Dung?"

Billings turned red. "Maybe they're hiding on a ranch or a farm."

"Could be, actually. Anyway, you've convinced me. Something's up. Get reports on all unusual activity by known or suspected fans. Let's get 'em!"

"Yes, ma'am!"

Lee Arteria thumbed idly through the file folders. *They're up to something. But what?* Fans were technophiles, so they were watched; but they were mostly flakes, so the effort was sporadic and incomplete. And they kept trying to recruit the cops, lecturing them, giving them reading material, driving them crazy.

More fanac would surface presently. Bull semen, earthworms, dung, game hens? Worse than the Stardust Motel Westercon Banquet! *Bouncing potatoes, bouncing potatoes—* A known fan in Portland bought rabbits. One buck and several females. How did that fit the pattern? Impregnating rabbits with bull semen? A secret gengineering project? But to what purpose? *You'll come a-bouncing potatoes with me!*

Angels down. Fans to the rescue. *That, said the waitress, is roast beef and a salad, too! You'll come a-bouncing potatoes with me!* But what would they want with Cornish game hens?

☆   ☆   ☆

The St. Louis Society for Creative Anachronism were not exactly fans. But there was considerable overlap between SCA and fandom; and Oliver Brown had been

King Roland II, which made him a Royal Duke, and the SCA people were deferential to their aristocracy. The place was used by fans; but it was an SCA fief.

The museum was a large, low-ceilinged space broken up by partitions and display cases into quasi-rooms ill-lit by kerosene lanterns and candles. Men practiced with padded weapons in cleared spaces. Women showed each other intricate ways of making cloth with their fingers. Men, women, children huddled around the light sources, reading tattered old books; talking and arguing with animated gestures; or, in a few cases, writing intently on smudged tablets of lined paper.

Two knights brought Gordon inside, one at each elbow, and helped him to a chair. He was pale with effort . . . no, Gordon was stronger than that now. Pale with shock. He'd walked under four corpses.

Alex said, "Still think the Well is worth saving, tovaritch?"

Gordon nodded. "Desperately so."

"Where's Sherrine?"

"Helping Pins with docking maneuvers. A squire has shown them where to hide the truck. Why, are you lonely, Alex?"

"We're to meet the King all together. Never mind, that must be them." There was activity at the door. Passwords were exchanged, while the silent giant Fafhrd took his defense position. Duke Hugh ushered them in: Sherrine, Bob Needleton, Harry Czescu and Jenny Trout. Gordon and Alex stood to join them. Duke Hugh whispered instructions before they were led to meet the King.

The procession was short. All eyes were on them. Alex enjoyed having Sherrine on his arm, though she was supporting him. The King was a large young man whose nose had once been smashed flat against his face. It was fun to watch him try to balance hero worship against his royal dignity. Still, he was the man who had beaten every other fighter in St. Louis; that was how you got to be King. The four bowed, with Sherrine and Bob supporting the Angels.

They were turned loose into a party that was just
starting to turn raucous.

Harry and Jenny stayed behind, by invitation of the
King. Some of the court settled in a circle. Some had
lutes or tubes that turned out to be musical instruments.
Alex listened for a bit. Songs of past and future—

> *"Wanted fan for plain sedition, like the singing of
> this tune.*
> *If NASA hadn't failed us we'd have cities on the moon.*
> *If it weren't for fucking NASA we'd at least have
> walked on Mars.*
> *If I never can make orbit, then I'll never reach the stars."*

Never can make orbit . . . Harry and Jenny were singing to Alex's soul. Alex wasn't in the mood for that much
gloom. He moved away, toward laughter.

Jenny's voice followed him. "How's this, Majesty?

> *"Wanted fan for mining coal and wanted fan for
> building nukes;*
> *Wanted fan by William Proxmire and a maddened
> horde of kooks.*
> *Washington, D.C., still wants me 'cause I tried to
> build a dam.*
> *If they're tearing down the cities I'll help any way I can."*

"Yeah, Jenny, I know you would . . ."

Gordon gravitated to one of the fans who was writing
furiously on a legal pad. He stood a little aside so as not
to distract the woman; but Alex could see that she was
aware of the Angel's hovering presence.

Alex wandered among mannequins dressed in the style
of mountain man, Plains Indian, cowboy. They stood
ghostly sentinel amid prairie dioramas and reconstructed
Conestogas. Sunbonnets and calico and flintlocks. A mold-
board plow. A *la riata* coiled to loop over a steer's horns.
Chaps and Stetson hat. Buckskin shirt and leggings done
up with beads and quillwork. A birchbark canoe bearing

a *coureur de bois*. The opened diary of a woman who had crossed the Plains in an 1840's wagon train. Alex tried to read what was written there, but the light was too dim.

All the ages interfaced. No wonder fans were comfortable here.

Gordon, he saw, was deep in conversation with an aspiring writer named Georgina. The stilyagin was sitting lotus beside her on the floor and was pointing to something on her pad. They had gathered a small audience—all femmefans, Alex noted—and she was nodding with a very serious look on her face to whatever Gordon was saying.

Alex found a chair and sagged into it, a bit too tired to be sociable.

Somebody brought him a pewter flagon of fairly powerful punch. A younger fan brought an elderly couple over and introduced them as Buz and Jenn. "Have you made much use of the shuttle tank?" Jenn asked. "The one that went up with the last shuttle?"

Alex nodded. *Noblesse oblige.* "We couldn't live without it. And the other one. I've heard the story, of how the pilots and a friend in Mission Control brought the first tank to orbit. It was supposed to splash, but the pilots pulled the circuit breakers for the separation charge igniters."

Buz nodded. "The astronauts and cosmonauts had already decided to try to build a civilization. They had to have the tanks for living space."

"You were in on that?" Alex asked.

"A little," Jenn said. "They couldn't do that but once, though. Then came—"

"The Last Shuttle," Buz said.

"Yeah. I was in it," Alex said.

"We know," Jenn said. "How are Ian and Alicia?"

"You knew them?"

"Yes."

"Dad was killed in a blowout nine years ago," Alex said. "Mother died last year. Heart."

"Oh. I'm sorry," Jenn said. She turned to her husband. "They had twenty years together. Up there."

"And we're still here," Buz said. He turned to Alex. "It was Ian and Alicia or us," he said. "When the astronauts decided to take the last shuttle up. The space program was winding down, and we thought it would be important to get more people into the habitats. *Peace* and *Freedom.* Cooperation between U.S. and Russia. Symbols of peace and progress. They already had a shuttle tank in orbit, and we wanted to send another, but mostly we wanted to send up families. Jenn and I were candidates. So were Ian and Alicia, and you, only you didn't know it. You were about six, as I recall, and your mother was small, so the two of you weighed less than I do."

Georgina and Gordon had come to listen, and others gathered around. "What happened to the last shuttle?" Georgina asked. "You still have it, don't you?"

"Sure. It can't reenter. It was damaged."

"I heard—there was a riot at the launch," a fan said. He was younger than Gordon, a small round teenager with thick glasses. "I read about it—"

"It was *Enterprise Two,*" Alex said. "Like Buz said. There had been regular supply runs, but—maybe Buz should tell this."

"I've told it before," Buz said. "Let's hear how you tell it."

"I was six," Alex said. "My father and mother were mission specialists. Engineers. They'd heard the space program was being closed down, and thought—they thought that if there were families in space, Americans as well as Russians, it would shame the government into supporting them. So they all volunteered to go. They thought there would be other ships. The NASA ground crew swore they'd stay on the job, refurbish the ship and send her back up with supplies. It wasn't supposed to be the last one."

"Some group had tried to get a court order to stop the launch," Jenn said. "Said there was a chance that a bad launch could fall on pleasure boats out in the ocean. Then they sent most of their membership down to man a fleet downrange of the pads."

Their audience had formed up in a circle. The younger fans were wide-eyed. A man in medievals, a troubadours outfit, with a lute slung across his shoulder, was jotting notes. Older fans, hanging farther back, showed a blacker mood. It wasn't just a yarn to them. They remembered.

"That was Earth First," Buz said.

Jenn snorted. "You mean Earth Only."

"Earth Last," another muttered. "Bastards."

"Nobody worried about their court order," Alex said. "But then the word leaked out that the launch was on, and a mob gathered around the perimeter. They tried to tear down the fences, but there was another group, the L-5 Society, supporters, trying to protect the ship. Not enough of them. There was fighting. Mom wouldn't let me watch. She had a death grip on me until she could get us aboard."

Alex noticed he was rubbing his arm, and stopped. "We squeezed into one couch. Everything was going wrong, Dad said half the control board was red, but they launched anyway. I remember the acceleration. Mother was holding onto me, the couch wasn't big enough, other kids were screaming, but Dad was grinning like a thief; I'll never forget his face. Or Mother's.

"On the way up there was a *clonk* and a lurch. Didn't feel any worse than what was happening till I saw Dad's face. Scared. *Snarling* with fear."

"An eco-fascist Stinger," Jenn said. "It was a near miss. Ripped a shitload of tiles off her nose."

Alex nodded. "Punched nearly through. I've seen it. But we made it. Mission Control kept feeding corrections to the main computer. They're the real heroes, the NASA ground crew. I never knew their names."

"Why them?" asked one of the young fans.

"Because they stayed at their posts."

"But—"

"The mob broke through."

"Oh."

"The fighting in Mission Control was hand to hand," Buz said. Long, hard muscles were jumping in the old man's arms. He'd learned to fight ... but afterward, Alex thought. "The mob had baseball bats. Two had handguns. Some of the ground crew held them at the door until they took bullets and went down." He turned to the woman beside him and took her gnarled hand in his and stroked it. "The mob swelled inside, swinging bats and smashing panels. The crew held on, nobody left, nobody left a console until *Enterprise Two* was up." He sighed and looked at the floor. "The police showed up then; but it was too late to save anything."

"The MP's were pissed," said Jenn. "They'd been ordered to stand down because the organizers had assured everyone that the 'demonstration' would be peaceful; and an MP cordon would have been 'too provocative.' Not that the politicians needed much assurance. California and Florida both had Green governors."

"Skazhitye," said Gordon. "But how do you know so much about it?"

The elderly couple glanced at each other. Jenn said, "Jim here was Launch Control and SBR Separation. I was Flight Path Planning and RSO."

"You—" Alex felt a lump rise in his throat. Buz's voice—a younger Buz's voice—had been the last words from Earth he had heard, fed through the speakers into the passenger cabin in the silence after the engines shut down. *Good luck, Enterprise. Our dreams are going with you.* Alex took a step toward them and they rose from their chairs. A moment's awkward hesitation gave way to an embrace. Alex's cheeks were hot with tears.

"You knew, didn't you," he said, hugging the old woman. "You knew it would be the Last Shuttle up."

She said nothing, but he could feel her head nodding. "We knew we'd never see another," said Buz. "Not in our lifetimes. But we're still the lucky ones. Come."

He led them through the exhibits, past the trappers, the cowboys, the sod busters. Pioneers, Alex thought. Pioneers all.

Buz led them to a small case near the back of the museum. It was nothing but a scroll, done up on pseudo-vellum. One-inch-square photographs had been mounted beside a list of names. The lettering was an intricate Old English calligraphy.

𝔖𝔱𝔞𝔯 𝔇𝔞𝔱𝔢 670127 𝔙𝔦𝔯𝔤𝔦𝔩 𝔍. [𝔊𝔲𝔰] 𝔊𝔯𝔦𝔰𝔰𝔬𝔪
𝔐𝔬𝔤𝔢𝔯 ℭ𝔥𝔞𝔣𝔣𝔢𝔢
𝔈𝔡𝔴𝔞𝔯𝔡 ℌ. 𝔚𝔥𝔦𝔱𝔢 𝔍𝔍
670424 𝔙𝔩𝔞𝔡𝔦𝔪𝔦𝔯 𝔎𝔬𝔪𝔞𝔯𝔬𝔟

710629 Vladislav Volkov
Georgi Dobrobolsky
Viktor Patsayev
860128 Francis R. Scobee
Michael J. Smith
Judith A. Resnik
Ronald E. McNair
Ellison S. Onizuka
Gregory B. Jarvis
Christa McAuliffe

Alex woke groggy on a museum bench.

Gordon sat in a plastic shell of a chair hunched over a scarred and warped desk. He was staring off into space with his mouth half-open. Writing a love poem? Sure. And to whom, Alex thought he could guess. Shoeless, he padded up silently behind Gordon and read over his shoulder:

The scoopship's cabin was a sounding box for vibrations far below the ears' grasp; as, high over the northern hemisphere, her hull began to sing a bass dirge. My bones could feel . . .

Gordon jerked suddenly and turned in his seat. "Alex, I did not hear you come." He covered the tablet with his forearm.

Alex grinned. "Does the hero get the girl?"

Gordon flushed a deeper crimson. "It is not that kind of story. Are no heroes. It is story about belonging; about one's place in the world. About being at home."

Alex's eyes flicked toward the hidden sky.

"No, Alyosha. Not home like that. Not accident of birth. Home is where, when you have to go there, they have to take you in. Sometimes you find it in places you don't expect."

"That's fine, Gordon." Gordon did have a way of putting words together. Not just a subsonic hum, but a "dirge." The hum and the sweetness of flight—yet with a touch of ominous anticipation. When Alex wrote, the words fell like stones in line: solid, serviceable prose for memos and technical reports and the occasionally informative letter; but it never sang like Gordon's did.

"May I ask you a question, Alex?"

"Sure. I can't sleep; and we'll be leaving soon anyway. Ask away."

"About Sherrine." He looked up, locked eyes with Alex for a fraction, then looked away. "Alex. I burn. Sherrine . . , She is as Roethke wrote: 'I knew a woman, lovely in her bones, / When small birds sighed, she would sigh back at them . . .' But I . . . she and I . . ." He shook his head abruptly. "Nyet. I cannot assert myself. The time is not right." He turned and looked again at Alex. "What if she does not care for me?"

Alex almost laughed. "Is that what you wanted to ask me about? You want her, but does she want you? How would I know? Ask Bob. She doesn't confide her love life to me." Alex forced the words out between his teeth, surprised at how much they hurt. "Things are a lot looser down here in the Well, you know."

Gordon looked at him strangely. "I thought you . . ."

"You thought I what?"

Gordon shook his head. "Nichevo."

Alex shrugged and tried to recover his broken sleep. What was with Gordon, anyhow? Lost on frozen Earth, the authorities searching for him, and there he sat writing fiction in the middle of the night. A novel no one would read.

☆   ☆   ☆

Sherrine drove the rig while Bob slept in the back. The hill country of southwest Missouri, trees shorn prematurely of their leaves, swept past on both sides of the nearly abandoned interstate. The setting sun nagged at the edges of her vision, not quite dead ahead and too low for the visor to help, painting the pastel clouds that hugged the horizon. She kept her speed down; from fear of the cops, but also because she had to watch each overpass as she came upon it.

Here the Ice was only a distant whisper beyond the horizon, borne on summer breezes that had become crisp and cool. The fall came earlier, and the winter blizzards were more frequent.

And none of the overpasses had quite collapsed. But they were shedding. What had Fang called it? Spalling? Sometimes she had to steer the truck around chunks of concrete lying in the roadway under an overpass; and she sweated when she drove across a bridge. The dreadful blizzards of the smog-free 19th century Plains once more shrouded the heartland in winter, freezing and cracking the works of mankind.

Alex was crumpled against a pillow jammed between the passenger door and the seat back. He slumped loosely, dozing, bent like a contortionist, or a marionette. From time to time he would blink and raise his head and gaze around himself as if baffled before nodding off once more to the gentle rocking of the truck's suspension.

Gordon sat between them quietly reading a book. He had found it at the clubhouse in St. Louis and had pounced on it with unconcealed delight. A thick squat paperback with cracked and dog-eared covers. *The Portable Kipling*. The fans had made him a gift of it.

He closed it now, because it had grown too dark to read. Gordon gazed out the windshield into the gathering dusk, where sunset stained the western horizon. He whispered so as not to wake Alex. "I saw nothing like this in *Freedom*. Always we see sunsets from above."

Sherrine was glad of conversation. Driving in silence disembodied you. It was talk that made you real. "I've seen the old pictures, looking down on the Earth. They made my heart ache."

"Each place has its own beauties. We can learn to love the one, and still yearn for the other."

"What were you reading?"

"A story. A character sketch. 'Lispeth.' It tells of Indian hill country girl raised by English missionaries. She wears English dress and acts in English manner. When a young official of the Raj passes through, she falls in love. He swears he will return and marry her; but he never has such an intention and abandons her without a thought. Finally she realizes truth. So she gives up the mission and returns to her village and her gods and becomes peasant wife."

"A sad story."

"A tragedy." She could hear his smile in the dark. "I am half-Russian. We are not happy without a tragedy. Kipling saw the tragedy of India. Lispeth thought she was English, but the English never did."

"I haven't read much Kipling. His books are hard to find these days."

"Oh, but you must. I will lend you mine. Kipling. And Dickens. And London. And Twain. Wonderful writers. I have. . . . No. I have only this one book now. Real book, of real paper. Still, you may borrow it."

Sherrine smiled to herself. "You like to read."

"Yes. Yes. Though much I do not understand. References. Shared assumptions of Downers. I read Austen one time; but her world is like alien planet. Still, I laugh and cry with her characters."

"I had a math teacher in college who had read *Pride and Prejudice* fifteen times, in fifteen different languages."

Gordon blinked. "Math professor?"

"Math professors read literature, Gordon. But it's not commutative. Lit profs never read math."

He laughed. "Russian literature is harder than maths. Do you smile, that I find Russian literature difficult? My *matushka* made me read Tolstoy, Gorki, Pushkin. It was so different from my father's Western literature. In the West, novel was biographical. About characters. About Lispeth or David Copperfield. In Russia, was writing about ideas. *War and Peace. Crime and Punishment.* Characters, even central characters like Karenina only illustrate the Idea. Very hard for each people to read the other kind. But my *matushka* said it was important I live in two worlds, the *Rodina* and the West. A new society is evolving in the habitats. Western optimism and Russian gloom."

Sherrine laughed. "It sounds . . . appropriate. It needs a new literature, then. A synthesis. Floater literature."

"Perhaps. Gloomy optimism. Optimistic gloom. I have tried . . ." Silence.

"Light-hearted pessimism. Mark Twain?" She turned on her headlights. Had Gordon said— "You've tried to

write something?" Scratch any eager reader and you'll
find a wannabee writer.

"Nichevo. Story fragments. A few poems. Such things
are not survival-related activity. I must steal time to do
them. So they are not very good. Nothing good enough
for you to hear."

"Have you ever read a fanzine? No, really. I read some
pretty awful stuff in my grandfather's old pulps. Go
ahead. Recite one of your poems for me."

Next to him, Alex stirred and shifted positions.

"No, I cannot," Gordon whispered.

She took a hand from the steering wheel and laid it on
his arm. "Please?"

"I . . . If you will not laugh?"

"I won't laugh. I promise."

"I hold you to promise." Gordon coughed into his fist,
straightened in the seat. He looked off into the black
distance, not meeting her eyes, and spoke gently:

> *"Lying softly, white as snow is snow,*
> *With delicate beauty, borne delightful to the eye,*
> *Reflected in the silver, skydropped moon:*
> *Her face, upturned and smiled on by the stars.*
> *Asleep is she more lovely and at peace;*
> *Her skin would glow a light unsnowlike warm.*
> *She sleeps. Touched by the moon*
> *And me."*

He fell silent; still he would not look at her. *Bashful.*
"Why, that's lovely, Gordon."

He turned at last. "You like it?"

"Certainly." Sherrine probed: "She must have been
pretty."

"*Who?*"

"Your girlfriend. The one you wrote the poem to."

"She is. Very beautiful."

Aha! "Have you ever recited for her?"

"Yeah-da. I did."

Sherrine smiled broadly out the windshield. Gordon
was caught on that cusp where he wanted to keep his

love a deep, delicious secret and shout it to the world at
the same time. She had been caught there once before.
She and Jake. A long time ago, but she could remember
the wonderful glow. With Bob it had been different—
fun, good times, a lot of laughs; but she had never
glowed. "What did she say?"

"She said my poem was lovely."

"Well, that's a pretty tepid response to a love poem."

A long pause, then, "Ah. I had forgotten."

"Forgotten what?"

"You do not live in such close quarters as we do. You
do not have to be so careful to avoid offense or to rub
against your neighbor's feelings. So few of us, and still
there has been murder, because we cannot escape from
one another. One does not speak of love until one is
sure."

"Then how can you ever be sure?"

He may have shrugged in the dark, but he did not answer.
Sherrine returned her attention to the road. She kept it at
thirty and slowed for every shadow in the road. Some
shadows were hard and rigid. Approaching bridges, she
crawled.

Ten minutes or an hour later, something went *click* in
her head.

Oh, no. He means me!

It had been obvious for some time that both Angels
lusted after her. Lord knew why. Tall and skinny was the
Angel ideal, but . . . Lust she could deal with. A little
recreational workout; fun for everyone and no hard feelings. It was impossible to sit between two horny males—
three, counting Bob, who was in a perpetual state of
rut—without picking up the pheromones. She was more
than a little horny herself.

But Gordon was not just horny. He was in love; and
that she could not deal with; because . . .

*Because Jake is still living there, somewhere in the
back of my skull.*

Oh, great. Now she had four men to deal with. Three
live and present; one a ghost. An old rhyme capered
through her thoughts. *It's gude to be merry and wise. /*

*It's gude to be honest and true; / It's gude to be off with
the old love, / Before you are on with the new.*

Was he asleep? Or studying her in the dark?

She said nothing; concentrated on her driving. *He
loves me?* She craned her neck and looked in the large
side-view mirror. A smaller Sherrine, distorted by the
convex shape, stared back. *He loves* me? The truck had a
lot of inertia; a lot of momentum.

Gordon said, "You are offended."

"No!" She paused; spoke again. "No, I'm not. I'm
flattered. It has been a long time since anyone loved me."

Gordon seemed appalled. "*Shto govorish?* How can
that be? There is Bob—"

"He only thinks he's in—"

"And Alex."

The cab was silent except for the older Angel's deep,
regular breathing.

"Alex."

"Yeah-da. You do not see it? He is Earthborn American: more direct than most, but still a Floater. Still, even
he may have been too oblique for you. Alex loves you;
though he writes no poems. Is why I have hesitated so
long to speak. He is my captain, and—and I wish to be
fair." He shook his head again. "Life is complicated for
my generation. If I was all Russian or all American, there
would be no dilemma."

"Fair! And he treats you so badly. I mean, I like Alex,
too; but he's so stern and unforgiving. Especially over
the crash."

Gordon nodded slowly. "That is true."

"And it wasn't really your fault."

"My fault? Oh, no. It is himself he cannot forgive. He
was hero once. Now he feels neglected. After the first
missile we could have aborted to orbit. Alex chose not to.
Because he wished again to be the hero, da? Now he
feels shame. He feels he has failed *Freedom*; has failed
Mary Hopkins; has failed me."

"How would you like some advice, Doctor Freud?"
The voice was low and thick with sleep. Sherrine twisted
her head to look past Gordon. Alex's eyes shone in the

dim, reflected light. The cab fell silent. The tires hummed
on the roadway.

"Mind your own *business*, Gordon." Alex twisted,
punched the pillow into a shapeless lump, and lay back
into it with his back to the rest of the cab.

After a while Gordon leaned over and spoke in a
whisper. "I was wrong. This truck cab is as close quarters
as anywhere in orbit."

Sherrine sucked on her lip. The Interstate was a pale
ribbon under the rising moon. A single car distant in the
northbound lanes was the only movement other than the
wind-tossed trees. It would not do to laugh.

☆　　　☆　　　☆

Arteria stared at the Alderman. The platoon of Air
Police stood by waiting, their weapons held at a casual
order arms. The Alderman's court cast wary eyes at their
visitors and kept their hands away from their own motley
collection of hunting rifles and bows. *Bows!* Outside, the
shoop-shoop of helicopter blades interrupted the silence.
"Well?" Arteria put an edge of menace into the question.

The Alderman looked up from the photographs he had
been given. He licked his lips and looked around at his
ward heelers. The ward heelers would not meet his eyes.

"Yeah. Sure." Alderman Strauss stuck his chin out.
"They was here. What about it?"

"I'm glad to hear you say that, Alderman. It confirms
what we learned from the truck drivers and your own
stevedores." *Though those farmers in Millville were certainly tight-lipped. HAH! "Big Front Yard Sale." And
that van the Kilbournetowners confiscated ... Lieutenant Billings says it's maroon under the new paint job.
Thank God I saw that deputy's report on the funeral in
Millville.* The engine's VIN had matched a van owned by
Robert K. Needleton of Minneapolis, a materialist science professor at U. Minn. Called in sick, with typhus.
Whereabouts unknown.

"Now, where did they go when they left here?" *God,
we should clean out this nest of barbarians, too. Why
haven't they been evacuated south? If the government*

*knew how far they've fallen under the cloak of anarchy
... The Green Weenies would love to arrest an entire
city for air pollution. Unless they don't care, or don't dare
let the rest of the country know what's happened here.*

Arteria studied the bitter and edgy men and women
clustered around the Alderman's throne; smelled the
ripe smell of fear. *Sure. Move them south. And when
conditions to the south worsen, too, move them farther
south. I'm glad it's not my job to do anything about it.
Maybe they've got the right idea. Stay and fight. Like
Scithers and his engineer cadre at Fargo Gap.*

The Alderman tugged at his spade-like beard, clearly
wondering if he should try to hold out for some advantage, but Arteria's face decided him. "They went west,"
he said. "They escaped from the de-lousing station, stole
some horses and rode west. We didn't bother to chase
'em because of the typhus."

West didn't make sense ... though typhus did. If
Needleton had been here ... "Are you sure?"

"Sure, I'm sure. You can ask over at Yngvi De-Lousing,
if you want."

Arteria nodded slowly, eyes hooded. "You're right.
Maybe I should ask over there." Arteria turned to leave,
and the MP platoon followed, not quite relaxing, not
quite turning their backs.

"Hey!" The Alderman's voice stopped them and Arteria
lifted a questioning eyebrow.

"You're from the government, aina?" The Alderman
was out of his seat and the arrogance and contempt had
dropped from his face. "When's the government gonna
come and help us out of this? I've got people dying up
here!"

Arteria said nothing for a long moment. *He still be-
lieves in government bailouts. What can I tell him? That
the government is too busy chasing polluters and nuclear
scientists and secular humanists? And people who cut
wood without permission. That the government can't
afford it any more and wouldn't know how, anyway?*

A curt nod. "I'll let them know the way things stand.
Things are tough all across the northern tier."

The Alderman licked his lips. "Yeah. Sure." He looked around at his cronies. "Things must be a lot worse other places, right? Otherwise they'da gotten to us by now."

Arteria wouldn't meet his eyes. A crafty machine politician. He wasn't fooled. It was the *Titanic* all over again. Not enough lifeboats to go around.

Outside at the command chopper Arteria contacted Redden on the radio. "Your reports seem to have been correct, sir. That's right. We found the van. We can confirm Needleton as well as the Hartley woman. Plus four other males, three Caucasian and one black." *Two of them were tall and skinny and having trouble walking.* Things were getting interesting. "There's a lead here I want to follow up on. No, sir, I don't need anything more. I'll go solo on this."

Arteria rang off and handed the set back to the tech sergeant. The sergeant looked worried. "Do you think that's wise, Captain? You could send one of the troops, instead."

"No, Sergeant, this is something I've got to do personally."

"But you'll be out of touch. Shouldn't you . . . ?"

"Soldier, ask not what my plans might be." Arteria looked left, then right, then added in a lower voice, "It's a crazy idea; and if it doesn't pan out . . ."

The sergeant blinked, then slowly brightened. "I get you. No one will know."

"Right you are. Besides, I won't be any further out of touch than the radio in my car, will I? We'll just have to make sure that the Rapid Deployment Team is ready to go anywhere, anytime, on my signal. Now tell Lieutenant Billings I want a staff meeting in ten minutes."

The sergeant saluted and dogtrotted off to find the platoon commanders. Arteria smiled a slow smile. Solo and in civilian clothes. That was the best way. No committees to second guess and hamper you. Just your own wits and reactions. Follow the clues wherever they led, without a lot of silly debate. Redden and the military brass would want periodic reports; but that was no problem. Moorkith would be worried that he wasn't getting all the skinny; let him stew. If the others wanted the credit of finding the Angels first, they would have to do the same thing. Get off their asses and scour the highways and byways. Especially, the fannish byways.

And who better to scour those byways than a gafiated fan?

Lee parked outside Yngvi's De-Lousing. Her car was plain black, with civilian license plates from Ohio, because this wasn't the first time she'd needed to look like a civilian. She went up to the door and waited to see a sensitive fannish face.

"FIAWOL," Arteria said.

Terri Whitehead gave her a blank look. "What?"

"FIAWOL, and it's damned well true of you if not me."

"I don't know—"

"Look, I don't have a lot of time," Arteria said. "Yngvi is a louse, but throwing a handful of rotten snow at *me* isn't going to get rid of me."

"Who are you?" Terri asked grimly. "The only people here are the Alderman's slaves—and police. And you?"

"Air Force," Arteria said. "I'm in charge of finding the Angels."

"Angels?"

"Look, Dr. Whitehead, if I wanted you in jail I'd have come with a squad and taken you away." Lee took a photograph from her jacket pocket. "Here. Sherrine Hartley and Bob Needleton. They were here. Incidentally, Dr. Needleton called in to his university claiming he had typhus. I suppose he got that idea from you. Ideas are contagious."

"I—"

"So why should you tell me anything?" Lee asked. "Because *they're going to get caught*. Be real clear about it. That picture's being circulated all over the country. If *I* find them, I can help them. And will."

"How do I know that?" Terri asked. She was near tears.

"You don't, but you know damned well nobody else cares," Lee said.

"Who are you—"

"Hah. Got it," Lee said. "WackyCon at Waikiki Beach. Lex Nakashima's convention. You were on a panel with

Will Waxman. The Miracles Panel. Cheap superconductor wire, cold fusion—"

"My God, that was fifteen years ago!" Terri said. "You were there all right. But—you're police now."

"Air Force," Lee said. "Air Police. Office of Special Investigations. Yes. Look, Dr. Whitehead, this is it: you tell me where they went, or—"

"Or?"

"Or I walk out of here, of course, and keep looking on my own. *You're* safe no matter what you do. But you won't know who finds them."

"What will you do with them?"

Lee shook her head. "I won't kid you. I don't know myself. Let me point out that I can always find them. I can go back and take the Tre-house apart. Somebody there knows. Save your friends a lot of trouble, Terri. Where'd they go?"

"I won't tell you."

Lee shrugged. "Ok, but you're making a *lot* of trouble for 3MJ, and the result will be the same no matter what. I sort of like the old boy, but—anyway, good luck." She turned to go.

"Wait."

"Yes?"

"Damn you. Leave the others alone. Chicago. They wanted to go to Chicago, so we took them there. To the museum. The big one, Science and Industry."

"Museum. Right. Thank you. Now we've got one more problem. You'll want to call them. I'm afraid I can't let you do that, so a couple of my troops will sit with you for the rest of the day. You're not under arrest unless you want to be, but you're incommunicado for a few hours." Lee went toward her car, stopped, looked back. "FIJAGH," she said.

CHAPTER SEVENTEEN

". . . Better than a Plan"

Excerpt from the electronic Journal of Surrealistic Housekeeping, *Adrienne Martine-Barnes, ed.:*

If a little lemon juice is good for stains, a bit of gallium and germanium will do wonders for dope. I mean how much flip-flopping can a body take, land's sake? PNP is not a supermarket abbreviation for pineapple, is it? And don't forget heavy metal music, either. (Who could? Such *lovely* melodies. . . .)

Orange is a Taurus, of course. (Boeuf l'Orange!) But what of the rest of the zodiac? What's *your* sign? There is Pisces, after all. How many fish swim in the ocean of night? Or Sagittarius. No, I'm not sure what that means, either. But it must mean *something*! Tap into your cosmic connection and feel the vibes of the universe. I'm sure you'll come up with something useful. Let's see . . . Aquarius is obvious; a bit too obvious, I'm afraid. As for Gemini, they had better quit cloning around. And Aries has taken it on the lamb. Honestly. I wouldn't try to pull the wool over your eyes.

We all know how important the Sweepstakes is, so I know you'll all send your entries in promptly.

Now, the next article on surrealistic housekeeping is one you have all been asking for. How do you keep watches from melting on the arms and backs of your sofas and chairs? Why, it is simplicity itself, provided, of course, that you have enough lace Dalis. . . .

☆　　☆　　☆

Ike Redden threw the printout down in disgust. "All right," he said to Moorkith. "*You* tell me what it means!"

"Captain Arteria seems to understand this stuff," Moorkith said.

"She's on a special assignment," Redden said.

She! "Where?"

"Damned if I know," Redden said. "But she gets results."

☆　　☆　　☆

There was a TV in the lobby of the Museum of Science and Appropriate Technology. Lee Arteria was just showing her credentials to the manager when the newscaster said, "More on the ice nudes, from Winnipeg. Gerald Cornelius and Anthony Rogers were found on foot on the Fargo highway, both suffering from frostbite. They told police of being rescued from their wrecked truck by a tribe of naked and near-naked savages."

All of Lee Arteria's assumptions came crashing down around her ears. They'd done it again, they'd moved the Angels out of the United States across the Ice in a microwave beam to keep them warm—and Lee Arteria was haring south on a wild goose chase. *Well done, Whitehead.*

The broadcast continued. A black-bearded man said, "They were lovely. Thin, almost hairless, and their skin was pale blue. Some of the men offered us their wives. Maybe they were evolved from Eskimos, or maybe they just learned their mores from Eskimos. Their skin was cold to the touch. I mean, when in Rome, sure, but if I had it to do all over again—"

Bruce Hyde. The breath went out of Arteria in a whoosh. So that's where they went, Hyde and Mike Glider, after they tried to get into Sherrine Hartley's house and almost got caught. Over the Ice.

And to hell with them. Lee Arteria was after bigger game.

She looked around the empty garage. "Milkheim Low Fat Milk," she said, and noted it in her casebook. "You're sure about this?"

The maintenance mechanic nodded enthusiastically. "Yes, ma'am, that's what they had painted on them. 'Milkheim.' Means 'Milk Home' in German. Now Mr. Cole, he called them trucks by names, a name for each one of 'em. One of them was Larry, and I disremember the other, but when there was three, one of them was Moe, I remembers that. Set a big store by those trucks, Mr. Cole did. Always taking care of 'em, giving me money to look after them, keep them ready to run, but he never took 'em noplace."

"Tell me about Cole," Arteria said.

He eyed her suspiciously. "What call you got to be asking about Mr. Cole?" he demanded. "He's a nice man. Touched in the head some, yes, ma'am, some people thought he was plumb crazy, but he's a nice man, no trouble at all if'n you didn't mess around with his trucks. Or his rocket ship."

"Rocket ship." Lee smiled. "We just want to help Mr. Cole. Dr. Cole, actually. He was very famous once, did you know that? He has earned a pension from the National Science Foundation, but there was something wrong with the paperwork."

Joe Jefferson nodded sourly. He understood mistakes in paperwork.

"So all I need is his signature, and he can collect his pension," Lee said. "It's not a lot of money, but I bet he can use it. Is he around?"

"No, ma'am, leastways I haven't seen him. He used to sleep in that rocket, but a couple of days ago a lot of people come here and took them trucks away, and his

. . . and some other stuff that belonged to Mr. Cole, and I ain't seen him since."

"A lot of people," Arteria said. She smiled. "Tell me about them."

" 'Milkheim Low Fat Milk.' Two big Peterbilt tanker trucks," Arteria said. "Look, Billings, this is a long shot, we'll really look like idiots if it doesn't work out. I can't afford to look like an idiot, can you? Right. So what I want is a quiet request to State Police to report the location of any truck that says Milkheim and report it to my fax number. Observe and report, but don't stop them. But don't ask Wisconsin or Minnesota or the Dakotas. *Right*, Billings. Do not ask them. Yes, Billings, *exactly* right, it means you have to send out requests to the others one state at a time, and I'm sorry, but you see how it is. Chances are this is nothing, but if it pans out we may both get promotions. Right. Thanks."

★ ★ ★

Fang guided the milk truck through the interchange and onto I-25 South. The Denver skyline glittered before him: tall, boxy, glass towers cut at strange angles. Fang squinted his eyes and tried to imagine that they were a growth of immense quartz crystals set in the midst of the High Plains. By aliens. Uh-huh: aliens. After cutting their teeth on Great Pyramids and Easter Island self-portraits, the space gods had finally hit their stride with this immense crystalline structure. White quartz, black quartz. Quartz as clear as glass; opaque, stony quartz.

Suppose someone discovered Denver's alien origin, *and the aliens were still around*! Disguised as real estate developers. Good. That was good. Who was in a better position to "grow" a crystal city than its developers? Come to think of it, who was more alien? What hidden purposes *did* they have behind their weirdly shaped erections?

Okay. The aliens are metaphors for mindless, runaway development. That made the story literary. So, the aliens realize they've been found. What do they do?

They capture Our Heroes and turn them into bug juice. Alien Cliché number one, vintage 1950.

They capture Our Heroes and take them on a tour of the universe and invite them to join the galactic confederation. Alien Cliché number two, vintage 1980.

Damn Hollywood. No matter what kind of aliens you had, they were already used up.

No, wait. Remember Nancy Kress's "People Like Us?" That's it. The aliens are neither benign nor malevolent. They do what they do for their own reasons . . . like the aliens who built Clarke's *Rama*. Like the Europeans coming to America. The Spaniards came for gold; the Incas were just in the way. The destruction of the Amerind societies was simply a spin-off of Europeans doing European things for European reasons.

Good title: "Spin-off."

He was so deep in the story that he didn't see the flashing red light behind him for several seconds. *Oh shit! But I wasn't speeding, dammit.* He pulled over carefully and stopped on the shoulder.

The Colorado state trooper walked up to the cab window and smiled. "Sorry to stop you, sir, but I noticed one of your brake lights is out. The middle one on the left side."

"Aw, shit. Thank you, Officer, I'll get it fixed at the next truck stop."

"Yes, I think you ought to. OK, just wanted to let you know." The trooper turned away, then turned back again. "Driving alone? Where'd you sleep last?"

"Only ten hours, Officer. Really."

"All right. We're strict on that in Colorado." He walked back to his cruiser.

Fang let out a deep breath. *I am sleepy*, he thought. *And there's sure no hurry, they don't want me to be in Albuquerque until tomorrow afternoon. I'll get that light fixed and catch some z's.* He was careful to accelerate smoothly and level out, his speed just at the limit. After a while the cruiser passed him and went on ahead, leaving him to his thoughts.

So, it's the same with the aliens who are building

Denver—and all the other strange glass-box downtowns. Aliens doing alien things for alien reasons. Only human egocentrism would suppose that they came to conquer or assist *us*.

So Our Heroes discover the aliens and the aliens don't do anything. Who would believe it anyway? They don't even bother to capture the protagonists and tell them ... No, wait. The reader has to know what's coming down, so someone's got to explain. Unless he sent the story to Ted Bistrop at *Fantasy & ...* Nothing was ever explained in the stories *he* published.

☆   ☆   ☆

The fax machine was built into the car's dashboard. It startled Arteria with its "wheep, wheep."

> PETERBILT 18-WHEELER TANKER MARKED MILKHEIM LOW FAT MILK PROCEEDING SOUTH ON I-25 AT DENVER. DRIVER OLD FART WITH BEARD. COLORADO STATE HIGHWAY PO-LICE OBSERVED MINOR SAFETY VIOLATION. NO CITATION ISSUED.   BILLINGS.

Denver. What in hell do they want with a truck full of rocket fuel in Denver? Whatever it is, I've got some driving to do if I'm going to catch up.

Her suitcase was already in the trunk. Her telephone and fax were connected to the cellular phone system, so she didn't have to tell anyone where she was going. She took out maps.

Not Denver. Colorado Springs? USAF Space Command had been there, when there was a Space Command. It was the reason Arteria had joined the Air Force. Fifteen years ago, even ten, you could kid yourself that the United States might go back to space, get moving again, stop retreating from the Ice.

Not now. Now—

The Milwaukee alderman had upset her more than she wanted to admit.

Now I can never go to space. I catch criminals.

It was a job she mostly liked. She was good at it, good

at solving puzzles, and she liked the power that being an OSI Special Agent gave her. Twitching the nerves of the mundanes, she liked that, too.

Not Denver! West of there. Edwards! It came as a sudden flash, as things often did for her, and it took her several minutes to construct what her subconscious had leaped past. Angels Down. Fans to the Rescue. What to do with Angels? Send them back to Heaven. How? Dr. Cole's broken Titan, but that wouldn't do it. What would? What was left?

What was left was the only working rocket ship in the United States. *Phoenix*, sitting on Thunder Ridge at Edwards Air Force Base.

★   ★   ★

Morning in the desert.

Alex watched the sun come up across Bob's shoulder, teasing streamers of fog from the sluggish Washita River that ran parallel to the highway. The fog slithered across the barren, dusty ground and wrapped itself around the sparse stands of Lone Pine and scrub grass that dotted the otherwise empty land. The pale light of dawn created a wash of white, green and brown; a weird, alien vista of mist and grass and sand.

"What do you think of it?" Bob asked. "Quite a sight."

Alex shook his head. "I was just getting used to the green."

"Oh, this part of Oklahoma used to be green, I'm told. You didn't see real hardpan desert until you hit west Texas. Now there's no rain and in a few years there won't be a speck of green left hereabouts."

Alex looked at the sleeping form beside him. "I should wake Gordon up. He could write a poem about it."

There must have been something in his voice, because Bob gave him an odd look. "You have something against poetry?"

Alex shook his head. "Never mind. It's not important." Bob said nothing. Finally, to fill the silence, Alex continued. "Gordon is irresponsible." He looked at the sleeping stilyagin, just to make sure he *was* sleeping. "He likes to write poetry when he should be doing something else."

"Poetry? About what?"

Alex scowled. "Love poetry, mostly. The last time he got inspired, we nearly lost an entire tray of tomatoes. So they put him on probation. That's why he was assigned to the dip trip with me." He rubbed a hand over his face. Two-day stubble scratched his palm. His skin felt oily, dirty. He hoped it was not much farther to the next safe house. He should let his beard grow out, like Gordon was doing. Clean-shaven Downer males were a rarity.

"Look, Bob, I haven't said this before because . . . well, because. But the only people they assign to dip trips are the expendables, like Gordon."

"And yourself?"

"Yeah-da. Me, too. Nothing more useless than yesterday's hero. I'm no good for outside work anymore. I can't even work in the command module because I get the shakes whenever—oh, hell. I don't want your pity. It's probably just as well that I'm stuck down here."

"Don't be too sure of that. Being stuck."

"No, Bob, don't mistake my orbit. I want to get back upstairs more than anything I've ever wanted. Almost anything. Not adventure; not glory. I'm just homesick. *Freedom*'s my hometown, and I miss it. But I really don't expect it to happen. And if it doesn't . . . Well, I *can* make a life for myself down here."

"Hanging around the docks," Bob said with a half-smile.

"What?"

"Never mind. Don't dismiss *Phoenix* out of hand, though."

"I haven't. But there's more to a successful launch than stealing a ship and taking off. Damn, I *know* what's involved. Maybe this Hudson character does have the ROMs. Maybe the IMU isn't locked up so tight as all that. But eighty-eight thousand liters of liquid hydrogen?"

"You want—"

"Forty-four thousand liters of LOX? Someone will notice!"

Bob shrugged. "You want me to tell you it's all worked

out. That we've got a plan? We don't. But, hell, we've got something better than a plan."

Alex didn't ask him what that was.

✱   ✱   ✱

The fax wheeped again. REDDEN AWARE OF MILKHEIM REQUEST AND REPORTS. PLEASE PHONE ME ON SECURE LINE SOONEST. BILLINGS

Aw, crap! She watched for a telephone.

"Billings? Arteria."

"Yes, Captain. I don't know how Redden got onto it, but he found out about your request to the highway patrols. He's got all their reports coming to him, but there's more, he's set a trap in Albuquerque."

"Trap. What kind of trap?"

"I don't know, ma'am. Something about a fannish church, but he sure wasn't going to give *me* any details."

"The fans own a *church*?—Albuquerque, fine. And he's intercepting reports about the trucks."

"Yes, ma'am.

Lee thought for a moment. "All right. Quietly cancel our request for information on those trucks. Do it in a way that makes it look like we're embarrassed about asking. Then see what you can find out about that church. I'm nearly to Sante Fe, I'll get on to Albuquerque. Ask around and get me a clue. Any clue. But don't let them know I'm out here."

"Well—"

"I'm pretty sure I know where they're taking those Angels," Arteria said. "And why all the odd purchases. You were right, Billings, it's fans. Now if we do this my way, the Air Force will get all the credit. That means you and me."

"Yes, ma'am." He sounded enthusiastic.

"When you've got the other stuff done, get my chopper and our crew and take it to George Air Force Base in the Mojave. OSI official investigation."

"George Air Force Base. Bring your helicopter and crew, and come myself. That place is like the back side of the moon, Captain."

"I know."

"All right, ma'am."

"Good man. I'll meet you there."

A fannish church in Albuquerque. There were a lot of fans in New Mexico. Fair number of writers, too. But a church? With luck Billings would find out something.

Lee Arteria drove steadily. She was just passing through Sante Fe when the fax began. "Wheep! Wheep!"

UNIVERSAL BROTHERHOOD OF THE WAY. FORMERLY CHURCH OF SCIENTOLOGY. NORTHEAST AREA ALBUQUER-QUE BASE OF SANDIA MOUNTAINS NEAR TRAMWAY STA-TION. REDDEN AND MOORKITH ON THE WAY. MILKHEIM TRUCK AT OUTSKIRTS ALBUQUERQUE. TRUCK STOP. DRIVER ASLEEP. REDDEN DOESN'T KNOW YET.

Lee smiled faintly to herself. So. Redden can think ahead, too. Good move, setting a trap at that church. The Angels may well stop there on the way west.

If the Angels were caught by Redden and the New Mexico Police, the Air Force wouldn't get any credit at all. What I need, she thought, what I need is to get them to Edwards. Once on an Air Force Base, they're mine. *All* mine.

Which means I ought to do something about this trap . . .

☆   ☆   ☆

Sherrine was almost tired enough to pull Bob out of the bunk alcove. She kept driving because they were already in Albuquerque. The church couldn't be far. A pew would make a hard bed, but a *long* one. Sherrine was looking forward to that. So, she guessed, were the Angels.

The roar of the huge motor changed timbre. Trouble? Something else? Numb in the ears and the mind, she still recognized the sound just before six motorcycles roared up into her rear-view mirror.

She held the truck steady. This ship-on-wheels must be terrifying to a cyclist.

They drove past. All but one. Harry Czescu (why had Harry joined a covey of strange bikers?). He was waving her over, arm windmilling in seeming terror.

There was no place to pull over. At a Y-intersection she angled right, no longer headed for the Universal Brotherhood of the Way. Still looking . . . but Harry was motioning her forward, to follow him.

Sherrine called, "Who's awake?"

"Yeah-da."

"Alex, get Bob up. Shake him if he's settled." Like salad dressing. . . .

Harry led and she followed. Onto the I-40 freeway and onward, west. Flagstaff was three hundred and forty miles away. She'd need fuel much sooner than that.

"Sherrine? What?"

"Harry's got us back on the I-40."

Bob rubbed his eyes. "He wouldn't do that lightly. What happened *exactly*?"

She told him. He said, "The way to read Harry is, he's seen something seriously wrong, and he's right. He'll try to fix it, but badly. So stop when you see a *decent* chance."

She drove. She wondered about Fang and Larry. *Both* trucks had to reach the Mojave. What was going through Harry's mind? A man you couldn't trust to buy the beer . . .

A turnout. She eased into it . . . signal, keep it smooth, don't panic yet. Brought the behemoth to a stop.

Now panic. Sherrine eased out of the cabin and down. Where the hell was Harry? Long gone, it looked like. Nope, that was him coming back. The Angels were sliding out, too, slithering down to the dirt, distrusting gravity.

Harry pulled into the cloud of dust, bringing more. "It's a trap! We've got to keep moving!"

"What about Fang? And Jenny?"

"I left Jenny on watch in case I missed you. I'll have to go back for her. I found Fang sleeping it off while he waited for dark. Jesus. I think I lucked out. After I saw the church, I found a bunch of bikers and pulled into the middle of them. They got me close to Fang. I gave him the word, and then I caught up with the bikes." Harry patted the metal flank of his motorcycle. "*Goood* boy. I don't know if I was followed or not. But someone knows we're here, and someone else must have—Jesus, we've got to get—"

"Harry." Bob's voice was soothing. "We can't outrun anything except on the straightaway. So why don't you tell us about this trap?"

Harry's head sagged. Then his body followed. He was doing a back stretch, hanging from the hip bones. He came up, rolling for full effect. "That's better. Yeah. The church looked fine. I went past it, figuring to park a decent distance away, and I saw the billboard. I saw just enough that I pulled into a Taco Bell and Jenny and I took a pew near a window so we could study it. Here."

He handed across a notepad. The printing was Jenny's:

SERMON BY THE REVEREND NEHEMIAH SCUDDER
IF THIS GOES ON

"Uh . . . *huh*."
"What *is* it?"

The crushing power in an Angel's hand was always a shock. Bob said, "Literary reference, Gordon. Robert Heinlein, 'If This Goes On . . . ,' in which the Reverend Nehemiah Scudder turns the United States into a religious dictatorship . . . incidentally terminating space travel, come to think of it. So it's a definite warning."

"Too bad we can't rescue whoever left it," Harry said, "but those trucks come *first*."

"Yeah. Back aboard. Sherrine sleeps, I drive. Harry, you get Jenny *now*, and then we need the services of the Oregon Ghost. We need a source of gas not much more than eighty miles away, and refuge in Flagstaff."

The Ghost's instructions took them to a fueling station and a decent chili joint in Grants, New Mexico, sixty-five miles east of Albuquerque. Hours later, approaching Flagstaff, they switched from I-40 to the old, worn Route 66. Then to asphalt, then gravel: the roads grew narrower and harder to drive. Why were they being led *here* in eighteen-wheeler trucks?

Bob had to fight the wheel because of potholes. It was midafternoon; he had been driving since dawn, and he was puffing from fatigue and the thin air. Sherrine knew that she didn't have the strength in the arms to spell him.

Motel up ahead: long two-story buildings with porches. A more compact, more ornate structure must be Registration. A few bulbs in the signs were dark. There weren't many cars. The drive-in next door was dead. Nobody had bothered to change the letters on the marquee:

SCI FI   RILLER
OCTO SSY

"The city must have moved a highway on them," Bob said. He was driving dead slow now, hunched like an ape over the wheel. "In Flagstaff they're always doing that. It's slow death for a motel. Or a drive-in." He pulled between paired pillars into the driveway.

"Octocon," Sherrine said, "used to be in Santa Cruz."

Two men were running to meet them ... then a dozen. More. The first were guiding the truck. Bob was muttering to himself as he followed them toward one of the long, windowed buildings ... with a face missing at the narrow end. They guided Curly into the opening, into a shell two stories high.

"Crazy. Do you suppose they never finished it?"

"Smuggling. The customers weren't stopping anymore and import duties kept going up. I'm guessing, of course," Sherrine said. "Pull up to the end. They're lowering some kind of false front behind us."

☆   ☆   ☆

It was not a big con. Four long buildings enclosed brown lawn and a pool. They had taken over just one of the buildings; they stayed clear of the Registration building, including the hotel restaurant, newsstand, etc. Rooms along the side that faced a wall had become the dealer rooms, Con Suite, Art Show, and a couple reserved for programming.

Four people talking on a panel stopped when the
procession hove into view; then the panel followed their
audience over the low railings.

"Welcome to Microcon!" And the fans surged around
them, hugging and shaking hands. Alex had time for one
glimpse of Gordon's bulging eyes before they were borne
away.

"Only Hotel Liaison eats at the hotel restaurant," a fan
said. "We don't want to be too visible, but we do need to
keep track. So far so good: nobody's been asking about
tall supermen."

The rooms were all bedrooms, all the same size; but
doors could be opened between. Three upstairs rooms
were the Con Suite, and that was where everyone was
eating.

There was a punch bowl filled with a pinkish liquid of
uncertain genealogy. Several bottles of homemade wine
lined the windowsills. Tables pushed against the walls
had bowls of popcorn and corn chips and various dips,
and a vat of soup sat on the floor. There was great variety
to the food, and a flavor of panic and improvisation.

"I'm sorry there isn't more," Buck Coulson apologized.
"Times are tight. Be sure to keep your glass handy so
you don't accidentally use someone else's."

Numbers were hard to gauge because the convention
was so broken up, but Alex hadn't counted more than
thirty people.

He was half-reclined in a chair and footstool, delight-
ing in his ability to sprawl. Sprawling was wonderful after
scores of hours of being wedged into a bouncing truck
cabin. He eavesdropped with half his attention, and
watched the women.

Sherrine was asking Tom Degler, "You worked up a
convention just for us?"

"We don't need a good excuse. A bad one is fine."
Degler's face was surrounded by a sunburst of bright,
red hair; full beard, hair tied up in back with a rubber
band. His legs, which Alex could see between the knee
socks and shorts that he wore, were also hairy. *Perfectly
adapted to an ice age*, Alex thought.

"Fast work," Sherrine said.

"Well, but you're still carrying the Navstar transponder, right? And you had to have a place to rest. It's a long drive across Oklahoma and the panhandle. Ever since they caught S. B. O'Rafferty, there's been no safe house on that leg of the Fanway."

Maybe a third of those present were women. All pudgy or burly, of course, in Alex's estimation; but not bad looking. Not bad looking, at all. Either that or it had been a *long* time—

"They caught O'Rafferty? Oh, Tom. The old guy was a past master at staying hidden."

Degler shrugged. "They reeducated him; but no one can tell the difference. He always did see everything skewed sideways and upside down from Tuesday. But of course he's being watched, so we stay clear of him, now." He shook his head sadly. "Anyway, The Ghost let us know when you'd be arriving; so last night I made a few phone calls. Kind of a welcoming party." He looked around the Con Suite, a bedroom with the beds removed, a few chairs, fans sitting on the carpet. "This is all that's left of Suncon and Bubonicon and the others. Slim pickings, eh?"

"Worldcon wasn't much bigger," Sherrine told him.

"Speaking of Worldcon," said Barbara Dinsby, "did you hear? Tony Horowitz got himself arrested to distract the cops during your getaway." Dinsby was a thin woman with long, dark red hair. She wore no makeup and tended to lean toward you when she spoke. Alex considered her the second prettiest woman present. According to Degler she already had several stories on the samizdat network, one of them critically praised.

Bob raised his eyebrows. "Horowitz?"

"Sure. When the chips are down, we all play on the same side."

"Did he make bail?" asked Sherrine.

"Tremont took care of everything. And Tony's book sales have tripled. Everyone on the Network has been downloading his manuscripts; and half the pros are lining up for his shared world project."

Sherrine craned her neck. "So, Tom. Who'd you snag for Guests of Honor?"

Degler beamed. "Well, you, actually."

"What?"

"Sure. Are there any fans more worthy than you and Pins, here?"

Alex grinned at Sherrine's sudden discomfiture. "Don't fight it," he said. And, in a more serious voice, he added, "You deserve it."

"But . . . "

Degler put his hand on Alex's thin shoulder. "Gabe and Rafe, of course, are the Pro GoH's."

Alex looked at him. "Now, wait a—"

"What do we have to do?" asked Gordon.

"Not much," Degler told him. "Just mingle with the guests; talk to them. You get a free con membership . . . "

"*Spasebo*."

" . . . And you have to make a GoH speech later tonight."

Alex opened his mouth to protest, but no words came out.

"Tom," said Bob, "they aren't actually SF pros."

Degler grinned. "They *live* science fiction. That's close enough."

"But I can't come up with a speech, just like that," Alex said. "Not that quickly." After the rescues of *Peace* and *Freedom*, when it was clear that the boosters had restabilized the orbits, and Lonny invited him to address the assembled Floaters from his hospital bed, he had been unable to say anything coherent. Lonny, damn his black heart, had probably known that.

"Don't worry," Degler said. "Just make it up as you go along. You're a spaceman! You could get up there in the pulpit and preach from the Albuquerque phone directory and still get a standing ovation."

Indeed, he could. As the fans milled around his chair, Alex discovered that anything he said was soaked up by his eager listeners. The little orbit-to-orbit "broomsticks" that they rode between the stations? Fascinating. (And five minutes later he heard two fans blocking out a story about witches in space.) The details of hydroponic farming? Endlessly interesting. Especially the painstaking attention to detail that Ginjer Hu demanded.

Filkers were gearing up out by the pool; the laughter was louder than the singing.

Sherrine settled onto the narrow arm of his chair. "Comfy?"

"Very. Next best thing to floating."

"So let's float?"

He peered up at her elvish I've-got-a-secret smile. He said, "If you have antigravity, we've chased our tails a long way for your amusement."

She laughed like bubble-wrap popping. "Alex, it's possible to float in water. The Dinsby just took Gordon out to the spa—"

"*Water*."

"Yeah, water."

"I forget how much water there is. We walked across a frozen river, I've seen the damn Mississippi, I don't know why it keeps hitting me like this—"

"But if Gordon and Barbara Dinsby are out there, every horny male and curious fan is going to be stripping down, too, so if you want to float—"

"Lead me."

It was turning chilly. There was a stack of towels on a webbed recliner. The pool had long been empty, but the spa was bubbling and steaming. It was eight feet across, circular, with people-sized indentations in the rim. Gordon and the red-haired woman were already in, and nestled comfortably close. In the dark around them, fans were stripping down.

Sherrine began to strip off her clothes, standing up. Awesome. Like a dancer, Alex thought, or a gymnast. He sat on one of the webwork recliners to get his shoes and pants off. Bare-assed fans were beginning to slide into the water. Two had kept their underwear on.

"The law speaks," Sherrine said, "as follows: you can

wear anything you want in the spa after dark. Bob really did go in in the top part of a tuxedo once."

Barbara Dinsby was scratching Gordon's back in slow, luxurious circles, while Gordon twisted around to talk to her. Thurlow Helvetian was scratching Barbara's back. Tom Degler slid into the water behind Helvetian, and a short woman moved up behind him. A circle-scratch.

Sherrine, entirely naked and entirely lovely, slid into the water ahead of Gordon. Gordon's hands rose in the air; his fingers flexed like a pianist's. Sherrine waved imperiously to Alex, and Alex slid in ahead of her.

She spoke against his ear, a warm breath within the steam and roar of bubbles: "Scratch or massage?"

Decisions, decisions.

The huckster was a skinny gent with an unruly mop of salt-and-pepper hair; somewhat elderly, but with a twinkle in his eye. He wore a colorful, billowing shirt and stood behind a table stacked high with books from which he importuned passing fans. He wasn't getting much action. They were all wet from the spa, and the night was driving them in.

"Hi," he said to Alex, "I'm Thurlow Helvetian. May I shamelessly try to sell you a book?"

"You can try," Alex allowed as he paused at the table. He was bundled up now, and nearly dry, and still warm. "You'd have better luck with Gordon. I'm not much of a reader. Then again, Gordon's still in the spa."

Helvetian nodded to himself. "Start slow." He rummaged about on the table and emerged triumphantly with a cloth-bound volume. "Here. *A Night on the Town*. This is a fair sampler of my work. All short stories, so you get it in small doses."

Alex studied the book. The cover bore a stamp: Certified Elf-Free! "Fantasy."

"Rational fantasy," Helvetian assured him. "Fantasy with rivets. It means getting the details right, making sure it all hangs together logically."

"My *matushka* once said—" Alex turned and saw that Gordon had come up behind him. Gordon was surrounded by a group of five femmefans, including Barbara and Sherrine. "My *matushka* once said that the secret of realism was to describe the thumb so well that the reader thinks he has seen the entire hand."

Helvetian nodded. "That's right. It's got to be consistent and realistic or you lose the reader."

"What if it's a fantasy?" Alex asked.

"Especially in a fantasy," Helvetian replied.

"Yeah-da." Gordon's head bobbed vigorously. "A dragon you may believe in, or a time traveller, but a time-travelling dragon asks too much of the reader. H.G. Wells never used more than one—"

"Gordon? Save it," Barbara said. "It's time for your speech."

Gordon's mouth opened and closed, and he half-turned to run.

"Alex, isn't it? You're next. Or if Gordon freezes up, you're first. Work it out between you. Thurlow, you're not going to miss the GoH speeches, are you?"

"I didn't used to go to the program items . . ."

The Angels looked at each other. Neither had anything planned. Neither wanted to go first.

"Together," Gordon said.

"*Mir* was old. A tested, fully manned space station, more than the United States ever had, but old," Gordon said. "We had a Buryat shuttle up when everything stopped, but that was useless, not much more than a missile without guidance. We made it part of the habitat and rifled it for parts. There was not much on the moon, but we could work with what there was because of all that lovely working mass free for the taking—"

"And oxygen. There's infinite oxygen in lunar rock."

"So we had Moonbase. We even expanded a little. And in orbit, *Mir* and two shuttle tanks from which to make *Freedom*. One shuttle, ruined. And three NASPS."

The room was filled with rows of chairs. Behind them there was still standing room; the balcony doors were opened wide.

These thirty people were more than he could have

gathered aboard *Freedom*, without leaving crucial functions untended. All these solemn eyes. . . .

"Now, each of the NASPS is different," Alex said, "and neither of them could carry cargo, because each was an experimental hypersonic ramjet airplane. *Piranha* couldn't even reach orbit without an auxiliary tank at takeoff!"

"And of course these were no longer available."

"You get a bubble for two and the rest is fuel tank and motors. So landing it and coming back to orbit—"

Gordon was really enjoying himself. Nobody in *Mir* or *Freedom* had ever looked at him like this. He said, "You would do only for the joy of it, and it would cost in hydrogen and wear. But we found we could convert all three to dive into the atmosphere and return without too much loss of delta-vee. Without that, we would not have nitrogen."

All these solemn eyes. Where was all this support when space was being abandoned like an unwelcome gift? Only thirty, though they seemed like more. But those who gathered on the desert to watch the shuttles land numbered up to a *million*. Where were they?

Running from the Ice.

Gordon was saying, "The scoopship's cabin was a sounding box for vibrations far below the ears' grasp; as, high over the northern hemisphere, her hull began to sing a bass dirge. My bones could feel . . . "

"I've lost track of my cup," Alex said.

"In the old days," Sherrine whispered in Alex's ear, "there would have been plastic or styrofoam cups."

"Nonbiodegradable plastic or styrofoam cups," said Degler, appearing out of nowhere.

"Bullshit," said Sherrine. "Plastics are recyclable. Shred it and melt it and make more. The fact that no one *bothered* gave plastic a bad rep."

"Well, not quite," Degler said, fingering his beard and grinning. "There are EPA rules that forbid the recycling of certain plastics. The styrofoam used by fast-food chains was chemically recyclable; but the EPA forbade it because"—he gave an exaggerated shudder—"because it had once touched food."

"Yeah, and they replaced the stuff with coated paper, that was also nonbiodegradable and nonrecyclable. So the rules had zero impact on the environment and the landfills . . . And why are you laughing, Tom?"

"What if it was on purpose?"

"What do you mean?"

Alex noticed that a small crowd had gathered around them, listening intently to what Degler had to say. He saw Bob Needleton and Barbara Dinsby and the huckster, Thurlow Helvetian; Gordon's head topping them all. *We really do stand out in a crowd.* Gordon had been letting his beard grow ever since St. Louis, but it was not much to speak of yet. Sherrine had called it a beatnik beard, whatever that meant.

Degler glanced left and right, and leaned forward. Everyone else instinctively leaned toward him. "I meant, what if it was on purpose? There was a company in California that bought chemical wastes from other companies; processed the waste and broke it down; and sold the end products as feed stock. Closed loop recycling. The state EPA shut them down."

"Why?" asked Alex.

Degler eyed him, and again glanced conspiratorially around the room. "Because the EPA rules required that chemical wastes be put in fifty-five-gallon drums and stored."

"Why, that is pomyéshanniy," Gordon said. "If we did so on *Freedom*, would soon die. Cannot afford to waste waste. Is too valuable."

If the Downer Greens were serious about recycling and waste reduction, Alex mused, they should be clamoring to communicate with the stations. Who—on Earth or off—knew more about the subject than the Floaters. *It isn't just our quality of life, it's our lives.*

"Exactly," said Degler. "So why do so many environmental regulations wind up *harming* the environment? I say, what if it's on purpose?"

"Can't be," said someone in the crowd. "What purpose?"

"Yeah, who would gain?"

"The Babbage Society?"

"No, the *Greens*. The Greens would gain job security," said someone else.

"Job security how? They're pledged to clean things up."

"No they aren't," said Tom Degler with a grin. "They're pledged to advocate rules whose apparent purpose is to make someone else clean things up."

"That's right. There's a difference. The rules only require actions, not results."

"I have a question," said an elderly fan. "Why did the Greens become so popular back in the '90s, which was *after* the worst pollution had been already cleaned up? None of you kids remembers the old days, when coal smoke blanketed every city and the Cuyahoga River caught fire."

Alex had finally figured out why Degler grinned all the time. He was watching funny pictures inside his head. "This is your hobby, isn't it?"

Degler grinned at him. "What is?"

"Throwing out wild ideas and watching people play with them."

"No, this is my profession. Dropping seed crystals in a supersaturated solution. Plumbing is my hobby."

Chairman Buck Coulson produced a giant cake covered with chocolate frosting, baked in the shape of a manhole cover. He presented it to Degler as Con Chair. Degler wiped a tear from his eye. "I'm touched, folks. I am truly touched."

"Hell, Tom," said Bob. "We've known that for years."

"Okay!" said Buck rubbing his hands. "That's three uses." He pulled a scrap of paper from his pocket and made a note.

Alex looked around for help. He saw Sherrine nearby with a glass of bhlog in her hand and beckoned to her. Sherrine giggled and weaved her way to his side. "What did Buck mean, that's three uses?" He had to lean close to make himself heard over the noise of the room party.

The jostling crowd pressed Sherrine against him just as he bent close. He wasn't about to complain.

"Mmmm," said Sherrine, lingering against him for just a moment, bracing herself with her arm around him. "Egscyooze—I mean, excuse me. I'm sorry."

"I'm not."

"Have some bhlog?" She held her glass up to him.

"No, thanks. I had one. It ripped the top of my head off. What's in that stuff?"

"Oh, I don't know. No one does. It's a closely guarded secret known to no one." Sherrine giggled again.

"You're drunk."

She pressed a finger against her lip. "Shhhhh. Maybe no one will notice." She drank the rest of her bhlog. Then she pointed at the cake. "Chocolate-covered manhole covers are, *is* the only idea Tom ever threw out that never went anywhere. What can you say about chocolate-covered manhole covers?"

Alex smiled. "Not much."

"A cake for Tom, that's three. A source of food on an alien planet, that was first."

"What was the second?"

Her diction became careful and solemn. "The American Dental Association thinks they are bad for children's teeth."

It must have been almost one in the morning. There was only a handful of fans still lolling about in the Video Room. Sherrine sat tailor fashion near the door, talking tête-á-tête with Dinsby. The others had wandered off. Some were dozing on the floor. Buck grew sufficiently bored to turn on the TV. He sat splayed in the sofa changing channels at random with his phaser. Tom Degler snored beside him.

Slouched in the armchair with his head buzzing, Alex let his mind drift with the TV. Buck would not stay on one channel long enough for anything to make sense. If, after five glasses of bhlog, anything could make sense.

"For relief of hemorrhoids," the TV declared, "use —°!°— the President of the United States—°!°—I couldn't

imagine anything more exciting—°|°—building value in
every step of design and construction —°|°—don't miss
all the action—°|°—with Barbie —°|°—But what if Lance
discovers us, darling—°|°—coming up next—°|°—Sherrine
Hartley—°|°—All right, let's move 'em out—°|°—for Cap-
tain Spaulding, the African explorer—"

"Wait!" said Alex suddenly alert. "Buck! Back up a
couple channels."

°|°°|°and a photograph of Bob and Sherrine graced
the screen. "—of those suspected of harboring the fugitives. Hartley is a computer nerd. Her boyfriend,
Needleton, is a scientist. Needleton's van was used in the
getaway. It was found in Milwaukee—"

"See Spot," snarled Buck. "See Spot run. Run, Spot,
run."

"Quiet!"

"—seeing them should contact the State Police. Captain Lee Arteria of the U.S. Air Force Office of Special
Investigations is leading the pursuit." Outdoor shot of a
hard-looking officer in fatigues. "We're piecing the evidence together, Heather," Arteria told the newser. "There
are several promising lines of inquiry—"

Alex grabbed the phaser from Coulson's hands and
stabbed at the buttons until the screen went black.

Bob spoke without turning from the screen. "The
backdrop. It was the Museum of Science and Industry in
Chicago."

Coulson frowned. "Arteria looks familiar. I've seen
him somewhere before. At a con? Art show?" He shook
his head. "A long time ago."

Had Sherrine seen this? Alex twisted and looked by
the door. Barbara and Sherrine were gone. *But they
were there earlier.*

He left the Video Room and wandered down the
corridor. An open room door showed fans carpeting the
beds and floor. Other doors were closed and silent. The
Con was shutting down for the night.

Downstairs in one of the function rooms, he found
Dinsby in a circle of femmefans surrounding Gordon.

". . . syllables, accents or feet," Gordon was saying.

"But English stresses are too strong for syllabic poetry, which is why haiku does not work in English. Accentual poetry is the native English structure. As in Beowulf, which has four beats per line with central pause. Is also the limerick like you hear in nursery rhymes and rap. But accent structure can degenerate into mere 'broken prose,' like free verse, which is basic form used for advertising copy. Was Chaucer who invented the foot, which combines accent and syllable— Yes, Alex, what is it?"

Alex put a hand on a table to steady himself. "I'm looking for Sherrine. Have you seen her?"

"She was with me earlier," Dinsby said. "I came out here for the midnight poetry panel. I saw her leave the room party a few minutes ago. I think she went outside." She pointed to the side door on the right.

Outside, the night air was a knife in his lungs and the stars hung like diamonds on velvet. He exhaled a cloudy breath. Not as cold as it had been up north; but still . . . The moon was low in the west, casting pale, pearly shadows. One of the shadows moved slightly and Alex headed toward it.

She was hunched up with her knees tucked under her chin and her arms wrapped around her legs. Alex hunkered down beside her. She looked at him; looked away and drew her sleeve across her nose.

"You shouldn't cry during an ice age," he told her. "Your eyes will freeze closed."

"Or open. I'd rather have them freeze open. Better to see if anyone's chasing you."

"You saw the news clip, then."

She said nothing, but Alex could sense her nod. "I won't make a very good 'wanted fan,' will I? If they showed Fang or Crazy Eddie on national TV with everyone in the country asked to turn them in . . . they'd throw a party."

"They think they can't be caught. They have faith in their own wits."

"I'm in real trouble, then. My instincts are no damned good."

"Your instincts are the best."

"I'm drunk, and I'm depressed, and I'm cold."

Alex didn't think he could do much about the first two complaints. He put his arm around her. "Do you want to go back inside? It's warmer there."

He could feel her shake her head. "No. I'm fine now." She snuggled against him. "Who would have thought it could get so chilly in the desert?"

Alex pointed to the sky with his left hand. "No clouds. The ground radiates its heat into open space. I bet you could make ice that way."

"You can."

"Ah."

"Look at the moon," she said. It was three-quarters full and just kissing the horizon, swollen by the lens of air. "It's beautiful, isn't it?"

"Not so beautiful as the Earth, looking back."

"Have you ever been there? To the moon."

"No." And now he could never go. *Alex can't go out and play because he might get a nosebleed. I don't even have a suit anymore.*

"I'd like to go there. I've always wanted to go there. Ever since I read *Space Captives of the Golden Men*. I forget who wrote it. A juvenile. These kids are kidnapped by Martians—we could still imagine Martians in those days—and taken to the moon; and I've always wanted to be . . . to be . . . "

She turned and buried her face against him and he hugged her tight. "I'll take you there," he promised. *Don't make promises you can't keep.* "Someday, I'll kidnap you and take you to the moon."

"Oh, Alex." She put her arms around his neck and kissed him. It was a soft, lingering kiss, and Alex felt himself respond to the promise. He shifted his arms and hugged her tight and kissed her back. "Alex, make love to me."

"What, here? Now? It's too cold."

She laid her head on his shoulder. "You don't want to?"

"I—yes, dammit. Yes, I do. But—"

"Then forget your damned courtship rites and your damned propriety. You're in Faerie now. All the habitat rules are suspended."

"Except cold!" he laughed.

She grabbed him and ran her hands down his body. The moon had set and the desert night was as black as death. The galactic spiral was a garland draped across the sky. They fumbled under their clothing, exploring each other; never quite exposed to the night cold and growing warm enough with the effort. Alex discovered that if you were careful and if you wanted something badly enough, you could accomplish anything. None of it was planned.

It was better than a plan.

CHAPTER EIGHTEEN

The LASFS

Steve Mews and George Long pedalled through the decaying neighborhood at dusk. Long looked around and whistled. "Man, this place would make Harlem look like Bel Air!"

Mews grinned. "Yeah, but it's not so bad. Besides, we're the meanest S-O-B's in the valley."

George Long looked it. He was an enormous black giant. Steve had been trying to get him to work out for years, but Long always said, "Hell, I'm a nurse! Sometimes I wonder what a frail old geriatric patient thinks when he sees, or *she* sees, Rosey Grier bearing down on her with a bedpan and a mucking great hypodermic. You get me doing that black-belt stuff and they'll arrest me for breathing."

The house was huge, a six-bedroom mansion built in the 1920s during the Hollywood era. It hadn't been painted in years, and now stood almost isolated. There were houses on both sides of it but they'd sunk even further into decay, not quite abandoned, but inhabited by people who just didn't give a damn. Mews led Long up the driveway to the garage in back. There were other bicycles there. The garage was dimly lit by a single electric bulb.

"Big place," Long said. "I knew Los Angeles fans had a clubhouse, but this is something!"

"Heh, heh. You don't know the half of it." Steve swept his hand around. "There was a freeway going through. The Greens got that stopped, but the whole area had already been condemned. Nobody can get permits to build here, or to tear anything down either. It's all pretty stupid, but it's good for LASFS. Glen Bailey knew it first because he's a Green."

Long shied off a bit. "You've got a tame Green?"

"Glennie's not tame. But he's definitely one of ours, and he got us this house. They're paying *us* a caretaker fee to keep the druggies out!" He grinned. "Of course, they aren't paying the Los Angeles Science Fantasy Society, Inc. They're paying the LA Safety First Society. The checks still read LASFS."

"You're still incorporated?"

"No, they yanked our *Inc.* 'Not in the public interest.' I keep forgetting."

There were more lights at the big house. Steve led the way to the back door and knocked, then stood in the dim pool of light from the porch lamp. After a moment the door opened. " 'Lo, Steve," a large elderly woman said.

" 'Lo, June. This is George Long."

"I know George," she said. "You're a long way from NESFA."

Long nodded. "New England's getting cold. I'm moving out here," he said. "By way of Worldcon."

"I ran into him at Minicon, then on the Amtrak," Steve said.

June opened the door and led them into a kitchen. There were a dozen fans talking, standing in doorways as fans did. Most didn't know George Long, but June was taking care of the introductions. "Is Merlin here yet?" Steve asked.

"Upstairs."

The stairway was ornate, with magnificent wood bannisters. There was mahogany wainscoting in the hallways, and the ceilings were carved plaster. Most of the splendor was in decay, but here and there someone had worked to restore it.

The upstairs room was locked. Steve knocked and waited. Finally the door was opened by a tall man with stringy gray hair and bad teeth. He stood in the doorway. "Steve."

"I need to get on-line."

Merlin Null, LASFS Senior Committeeman, frowned at Mews. "The rules are, you tell me, and I do it if I think it's safe."

"Merlin, this is Stone from Heaven business."

Null thought about it. "Have to check." He came out into the hall, carefully locking the door behind him, and led the way down the hall to another room.

C.C. Miller, often called Cissy for reasons no one remembered, was Chairman of the LASFS. He sat at a table in the old butler's pantry making a list. Miller was a large, round man, gray haired as most LASFASians were. His wife, Ginny, looked half his age, but she always had.

"Steve wants me to log him on," Null said.

Miller nodded knowingly. "It's all right. Steve, when you get done, we've got a package for you."

"Package?"

"Fan Express," Miller said. "From Curtis. Address 'Bottle Shop Keeper, care of Steve Mews.' I gather he wants you to deliver it."

"That figures. See you in a minute."

Back inside the locked computer room there were three people at a poker table. Hands had been dealt, and there were poker chips in front of the players. No one really cared much about illegal gambling, but it was a cover for the locked door.

Null locked the door again, then opened a cabinet. Inside were more poker chips and cards. Null reached past them to open the back of the cabinet, exposing a computer console. Null pulled it out. "OK, what?"

"FAPANET," Steve said. "I need to get on."

Null typed furiously. There were the odd tones of a

modem dialing, then locking on. Finally Null stepped
back. "You got it."

Steve typed gingerly. "They call me Bruce."

<Hello Bruce. Enter your password>:

"I am new in town."

<Welcome Bruce. Down, alter. Down I say! Be a good
Imp and let me talk. Bruce, Pins says they're looking
forward to greatest burgers in the universe for lunch
tomorrow. That is tomorrow. Treasure hunt has gone
well. Time to see the bottle shop wizard.>

"Roger Dodger." Steve stepped back from the console.

"That's it?" Null asked.

"That's a lot," Steve said. "Now I need to see C.C.
again. I'm going to need some help. Starting with a car
and somebody to drive."

The drive from Los Angeles through Mojave took
nearly three hours in C.C. Miller's underpowered car.
Interstate 5, the main north-south California artery, was
still maintained, but when they turned off into the Ante-
lope Valley and headed toward Palmdale the decay in
America's infrastructure was obvious.

They crossed the San Andreas Fault line. "Lucky so
far," Miller said. "We've been expecting The Big One for
years. . . . "

"They said at Minicon that the Ice would definitely
trigger it," Steve said. "Guess that would close the highway for good."

Palmdale was half-deserted. They passed a stand of
dead trees and grapevines. "Can't say I disagree with
the Greens on that one," Steve said. "Sucking water out
of Sacramento to grow Christmas trees and grapes in the
desert never did make sense."

"It would if you had enough electricity to make the
fresh water," C.C. Miller said. "But, hell, that's science
fiction."

They drove through Mojave, past the faded signs proudly
announcing *Phoenix* and *Voyager*. Now Mojave was a
small road town, as it had once been. They turned east.

A sign told them it was twenty-five miles to the turnoff to the Thunder Ridge Air Force Museum.

There had once been a fence and guard post at the North Entrance to Edwards AFB, but the guardhouse was boarded up, and the fence had been knocked down by tumbleweeds piling against it. There had been some maintenance, though. The blacktop road up the ridge from Highway 58 had potholes, but Steve didn't think it was much worse than 58 itself, and 58 still had traffic, if you could call a truck every five minutes traffic. The view across the Mojave Desert to the north was spectacular. So was the Rogers Dry Lake bed to the west. *Where the spaceships used to land. A million people camped out on the desert to watch the first shuttle landing....*

The museum stood at the top of a ridge: several concrete block buildings, a blockhouse, a large concrete pad, and big cylindrical storage tanks. The security shack at the main gate to the facility was empty, but the gate was open. They drove on up to the largest building, a huge structure. Most of the windows were boarded up, but not all, and there was a light inside one office.

Gary Hudson was tall and thin, graying a bit. He wore a silver-tan shirt and a desert hat, and looked a bit like the old films of Indiana Jones when he wasn't carrying a bullwhip and pistol. He came out of the office and watched as C.C. and Steve got out of their car.

"Museum's only open Friday and Saturday," he said. "Sorry, it's a long trip, maybe I can show you a little anyway." He waved toward a big corrugated aluminum structure. "The bird's in that hangar."

"We'd love to see it," Steve said. "Thanks."

Hudson led the way over in silence. The wind whistled off the Mojave Desert and howled around them, rattling the corrugated metal of the hangar building. They went in through the small, people door set in the enormous hangar door. It was almost as loud inside as out, but it was a relief to be out of the wind.

It was gloomy inside. Hudson gave them a moment to

let their eyes adjust. The roof was eighty feet or more above them, held up by a network of girders that looked needlessly complicated just to hold up a roof.

Phoenix stood in the center of the enormous room. It looked like a giant ice cream cone, sixty feet high, standing on its big end. At the slightly rounded base it was half as big across as it was high. It stood alone, with no scaffolding around it.

Hudson threw a switch, and banks of spotlights came on.

The nose was rounded. Holes a foot and a half across ringed the base: not one big rocket motor, but a couple of dozen little ones. There was a small door, high up. The hull was grimy enough to need hosing down, but it didn't seem to have been cut in half or anything. The damn thing even had windows.

Steve stared up at it. Beside him C.C. said, "Your big mistake was, rockets are supposed to be phallic symbols."

Hudson nodded. "Wrong shape. Too short, too. The tailfin on a 747 stood taller than *Phoenix*."

"Yeah, oh, well, the shuttle wasn't any better—"

Normally Steve would have joined in. Somehow he didn't have the heart. There had been scaffolding; it had been wheeled into shadow to display the beast better. Like the last Saturn, laid out horizontally so the tourists could see it better.

"—Saturn, too. What kind of a phallic symbol is it that comes apart during launch?"

"Yeah, but it did *get* there, Gary."

Pause. "Yes. Well, *Phoenix* hasn't been well maintained, as you can see," Hudson said. "She'll never fly again." He looked closely at Steve. "I've seen you before. You came with a tour about two years ago."

Mews nodded. "You must not get many people here."

"Not many black people," Hudson said. "And you cried then, too."

"Oh."

"Can I show you anything else?"

"Yes. What I'd like to see is outside," Mews said. He led the way away from the building, away from where

Phoenix stood under the tin-roofed hangar. Away from the fuel tanks. Off past the parking lot.

Hudson frowned but followed as Steve went out to an empty area. "Safe to talk here?" Steve asked.

Hudson nodded. "Safe everywhere. No bugs here, if there ever were any. Things deteriorate, and nobody cares about a dead bird anyway. She'll never fly again. Talk about what?"

"She sure looks dead." Steve sighed. "But I've got a package for you. Wade Curtis says to tell you it's a Doherty Project."

Gary Hudson's face went quite slack. He shied back a bit from the small parcel Mews pulled from his jacket pocket. "Doherty Project."

"Absolutely."

Hudson took the package and opened it. Inside was a half-pint bottle of clear liquid. "Moonbeams?"

"Seawater," Steve said. "And we took that shipping tag off a compressed air cylinder. It has a poem written on it. It's to be pinned to the ground with a knife."

Hudson stared out across the desert. "For Mare Imbrium," he said slowly. "Yeah. All right, you're real. At least you sure come from Curtis. Like a ghost after all these years. Now what's up?"

"Angels down. You heard about it."

"Sure. So?"

"We rescued them."

"Where? Where are they?"

Mews pointed east. "About ten miles that way. The Astroburger stand, at Cramer's Four Corners. Waiting for you to say it's all clear. They've got two tank trucks of jet fuel, and the ROMs that Cole was keeping for you."

Gary Hudson stared at him. "But—you mean—"

"Hope you've got your bags packed," Steve said. "It's time."

☆   ☆   ☆

The motorcycle came up an hour later. Harry and Jenny got off and stretched elaborately. "Hello, Gary."

"Hello, Harry. OK, you're real, too. Are there really Angels out there—"

"If the chili ortega Astroburgers didn't kill 'em," Harry said. He looked around the facility. "Can we work alone here?"

"Until Friday," Gary said. "And I can close the gate then, if there's good reason."

Harry had a small radio, the kind that used to be sold in pairs as children's toys. He extended the antenna. "Gabriel, this is Rover. All clear." He listened for a second and grinned. "OK. Now, do you have a beer? It's been days. I mean literally."

The tanker trucks wound slowly up the hill. Hudson watched with binoculars. "They look full," he said.

"They are full," Harry said. "One diesel fuel, one JP-4. Enough to make the hydrogen and LOX—"

"For a bird that will never fly," Hudson said.

"Oh, bullshit," Harry said. "You haven't been saying that so long you believe it, have you?"

"Harry—"

Harry shrugged. "Okay, but you're scaring the kids. Look at Steve. He's turning white."

"I am not."

"Get that man a mirror!"

"Harry, there's no launching pad, *nothing*."

"Sure," Harry said. "Gary, one thing, you better let the Angels in on this right away. When they finally set eyes on Cole's Titan, they were ready for self-immolation."

Hudson was sweating, and it wasn't the heat. "Harry, why don't I just put up a neon sign?"

"It's gonna get conspicuous anyway, isn't it?"

"This is just what I've been avoiding for fifteen years. More. Some of the Air Force types like to daydream, but a real launch? If they see . . ."

"You're gonna be conspicuous. That's all. What can you *do* that won't show right away? Making fuel is noisy. Your grocery bill is gonna go up. You'll have to wheel the beast out—"

"No, that's the one thing I don't have to do. Bring them in, Harry. Just bring them."

☆   ☆   ☆

It was crowded with four in the truck. The Angels hadn't wanted to be separated from each other, and Gordon hadn't wanted to travel without Barbara Dinsby. *New love and true love,* Bob Needleton thought. They look cute together. Of course it meant that Sherrine was riding with Fang in the other truck.

And maybe that's all right, too. It was pretty clear that something was happening between Alex and Sherrine. *And we're leaving her behind, too. If that rocket works I am by damn going. I have earned a place. I thought of the rescue!*

Harry was waiting at the turnoff into Edwards. He waved them on, then passed both trucks to lead the way. Bob was glad that the road was twisty and full of holes. He welcomed the distraction.

☆   ☆   ☆

Lee Arteria drove past the turnoff into Edwards and went on for another mile before stopping. Even then she stayed well inside her car, so that the sun wouldn't flash off the binoculars. She watched as the trucks ground slowly up the hill.

So far so good. And Moorkith was still looking for the Angels down by the Mexican border, certain that they were being smuggled out of the country. Arteria grinned wolfishly. *It's too late, Moorkith, my lad. They're on Air Force property now. They're mine.*

☆   ☆   ☆

Gary Hudson shook hands with Alex, then Gordon. He prolonged his grip on Gordon's hand. "Weak arm, strong grip. Do you have any trouble standing?"

Gordon grinned broadly. "Stronger every day. Steve has—"

Hudson pulled his arm to the right and back. Gordon fell over.

Hudson's left arm caught Gordon's elbow and pulled him back upright. Nobody laughed at Gordon's gaping astonishment.

Hudson said, "Sorry. I had to *know*. So. It's decision time."

"What's to decide?" Harry said. "They need to go to orbit, and you have the only rocket ship that will get them there."

"Harry—" Miller said.

"He's right," Fang said. "God damn."

"So I just fire it up and go," Gary said. "So simple. Why didn't I think of that?"

Gordon asked, "Is it real? Will it fly?"

"It's real but—" Gary caught himself. He took a deep breath. "It's a real rocket ship. It really goes straight up on a pillar of fire. It even goes into orbit. Barely. Almost."

Nobody wanted to say it, so they all looked at each other until Jenny Trout said, "What good is that?"

"I don't get much chance to explain this. We have here a *prototype*, and it isn't the whole thing. When we were doing the planning, I took the most optimistic assumptions. Why not? But the FAA had some rules that apply to airplanes. My stockholders wanted a heavier heat shield. The landing legs—"

"Landing legs? Sorry," Alex said. "Of course it has to land. I'm too used to dippers."

"Sure. *Phoenix* comes down on its own tail fire, just like all the old *Analog* covers, just like the LEM. I made the legs so slender it won't stand up unless the fuel tanks are dead empty. But they still have to take a recoil, and my stockholders wanted them beefed up." Hudson's bony shoulders rose and fell. "*Everything* got just a little heavier.

"But, dammit! I'd have put a bigger cabin on the real thing. It'd fire passengers halfway around the world in under two hours. Every president of every company or country would want one. And with the zero stage it could have reached *geosynchronous* orbit, and that would have been . . ."

Nobody had said anything about a "zero stage." Alex was about to comment when Hudson went on. "The zero stage would have been cheap as dirt. Same fuel and oxygen tanks, same pump system, same legs—because of course it lands independently! Half again as many motors and no heat shield. You could serve a dozen *Phoenixes* with two lousy Zeros because they recycle so fast."

"So where is your zero stage?"

"It paid the lawyers for awhile, and then I was bankrupt. The Greens sued me. Poking holes in the ozone layer, yada yada." Hudson shook his head violently. "Sorry. Way off the subject. You want to know what you need *now*."

C.C. said, "Yeah. You can't get to orbit?"

"I can *barely* get into an *elliptical* orbit with the low end eighty miles up. The atmosphere pulls it down fast. But another ship could rendezvous and boost it the rest of the way. That must be what you were planning with the Titan, wasn't it?"

"Yeah. What else do we need?"

"Quite a lot—"

"Will these help?" Bob Needleton held out a package wrapped in foil. "Cole said these are the ROMs."

Gary took the package. "That's a spare set, but yeah, after all these years it's worth doing a program comparison."

"And we brought you the fuel to make the fuel," Sherrine said. "And—fans have been collecting things to go up with the Angels. Seeds, chemicals, supplies, all kinds of things—"

"All that stuff isn't coming up here!" Hudson exclaimed.

"No, no, it's going to a safe place in Los Angeles," Miller said. "We'll bring whatever's needed from there."

Hudson nodded.

"Can—may we see the ship?" Barbara Dinsby asked. She was holding tightly onto Gordon's hand.

Hudson sighed. "Yeah, sure." He led them into the hangar and turned on the lights.

"God, that's beautiful," Jenny said. "Beautiful. Starfire!"

Alex walked slowly over to the ship. He ran his hands along the sides, then stooped to look up into the engine chambers. When he stood again his face had changed.

"You can fly it, Alex?" Gordon asked.

"It doesn't need a pilot," Alex said. "It's up to Mr. Hudson, I think. But it's clear someone has been taking care of this ship." He looked up at the roof scaffolding. "Does that open?"

"Just once," Gary said.

"Once is all we need," Alex said. He looked straight at Hudson. "Commander Hopkins—our leader in the habitats—I'll start over. We thought it would be pointless to say anything to Lonny Hopkins about spaceships. Now . . . does he have a decision to make? Do I call him? I wouldn't want to unless this was all real."

"Let me think about it," Gary said.

"Don't think too long," C.C. Miller said.

Gary frowned at him.

"We heard from Ted Johnstone in Phoenix. He works for the Highway Department. The police are looking for milk trucks. They're being real quiet about it, but they're looking."

"Oh, shit," Fang said.

"The church," Harry said. "That's—"

"That's fine," Jenny said. "So first thing is we get the damn trucks under cover, right? Looks like there's room in here."

"Actually, there's a garage made for tanker trucks," Gary said. "I'll show you." He turned toward the door, then turned back. "Hell, I don't know why I'm stalling. I've been waiting for this all my life. Major MacLeod, you can tell your boss that with any luck we'll be launching you within a week."

Three fans had wheeled the scaffold up to the *Phoenix*. Hudson climbed up to the door, used a key, tried to open it.

By then Alex was up there with him, climbing barefooted, using his toes. He felt no gut-fear climbing this spiderweb of metal, but he didn't trust gravity. He set himself and pulled alongside Hudson, and the oval plug-shaped door swung back.

Three heads poked in: Gary, Alex, Gordon. And a fourth: Sherrine. Sherrine said, "Four."

There were four seats, two with control consoles, two without. There were tanks, and bracing struts, and oxygen lines. Hudson waved and pointed and lectured. "We were set for up to a month in orbit. A lot of this could come out, because we don't need that much oxygen. I could have got another couple of seats in. Of course I don't have the seats, but that's no sweat. Glue in an exercise mat and two pillows for knees and head, that's all it would take. It's a matter of what cargo you're willing to give up."

"Four." Gordon scowled. "I should be reassured that it will not shrink by more yet."

Alex said, "After Chicago, after Titan, I wouldn't have believed *this* much. Gordon, by God, we can get home again!"

"Da."

The stilyagin's enthusiasm left something to be desired. No seat for Barbara? Others must stay, too ... but Gordon wouldn't meet Alex's eyes.

They sat in the large workroom outside Hudson's office. In better times a dozen engineers would have sat at the desks and drafting tables there. C.C. Miller had his notebook and was ready to make a list. "All right. Dr. Hudson, what do we have to do now?"

"Details," Gary said. "First things first. We clean out the tanks. The hydrogen tank won't need a lot of work, but there's a fair amount of work to clean the oxygen tank. We'll need alcohol."

"Alcohol," Miller said. "What kind?"

"Anything would work, but since there will be people working in that tank, we'll want ethanol so we don't poison them."

C.C. wrote it down on his list.

"How much alcohol?" Harry asked.

"Gallons."

"Gallons." Harry shook his head. "All right. I'll see what I can do." He grinned. "Going to be the first time I ever convinced LASFS that they ought to buy me enough to drink. God knows I've tried."

"How many people do we need?" C.C. Miller asked. "To clean the tanks, other stuff?"

"Well, maybe ten," Gary said. "Moving scaffolds, just standing watch, that sort of thing. But they'd have to be reliable."

"They will be," Miller said. "I've got Lee Jacobs rounding up a crew. They'll come up in a van, as soon as some of the other stuff from the treasure hunt comes in. Gary, you may be a bit surprised by some of what they've rounded up."

Hudson said, "Can you keep most of the LASFS away? I'll look conspicuous enough without a horde of fans looking over our shoulders."

"What I can do, *maybe,* is make it official. Announce that anyone who comes brings groceries. I worried about that. What are a dozen of us going to *eat*? Nobody gets in without a bag of groceries per. Nobody will do that twice. Fans can't afford it."

Hudson nodded reluctantly.

"After we clean the tanks," Alex said. "What then?"

"We have to get hydrogen. That's not hard, the pipe-line's already in place, we just tap it off the main pipeline into Mojave. We'll have to go turn it on, but the valve's not guarded."

"Won't anyone notice?" Sherrine asked.

"Not for a couple of weeks," Gary said. "And by then with any luck—"

"Right," Miller said. "What happens after the hydro-gen's flowing?"

"Compression," Hudson said. "We run the turbo com-pressor and liquify the hydrogen. Takes about three days. Make it four to be sure."

"What about the LOX?" Harry asked.

"That takes about three days, too, but it's quieter," Hudson said. "That takes a diesel engine. The hydrogen compressor is run by a jet engine."

"Jet engine," Sherrine said. "Aren't they noisy?"

"A little," Hudson said. "Hell, a lot."

"So we have to run a jet engine for three days," Miller said. "Don't you think someone will notice?"

"I've thought about that for ten years," Hudson said. "I've got a cover story. This is a research facility as well as a museum. We'll say we're doing hydrogen energy research. I can double-talk it. I've even got a grant request to show around. It should work—"

"And if it doesn't work, we're all dead," Alex said.

"Would it help if we had a high ranking Green space cadet up here?" Miller asked.

"Green space cadet? Contradiction in terms," Hudson said.

C.C. Miller grinned. "That's what you think. OK, what comes after you make the fuel?"

"We need the IMU," Hudson said. "I know where it is."

"You're sure?"

"Yeah, I actually get along pretty good with some of the Air Force johnnies over at Dryden. They keep hoping we'll be able to take *Phoenix* up again. But, you know, I'm not exactly a professional thief," Hudson said. "Somebody's got to break in and steal the IMU. I think we do that last thing. I can double-talk the compressor if we get unwanted company, but there's only one thing we could be doing with the IMU."

"How long does it take to install?"

Hudson shrugged. "Half an hour, but it's better if we can run some tests. Four or five hours of tests after installation."

"And then?"

"Launch," Gary said. "And I get to find out what free fall feels like."

"You're going then," Miller said. He made another note.

"Hell yes I'm going," Gary said. "I've waited all my life. Not to mention what they'll do to me for stealing my own ship. I'd take Annie, too, but she's in New York. Laid up for two weeks with a cracked ankle. Lousy timing."

"Makes sense." C.C. wrote rapidly. "So. There's you, and the two Angels. Say about seven hundred pounds. How much more can we lift?"

"Four thousand pounds," Gary said.

"Hah. One seat open, and still room for supplies."

Alex shook his head. "Before you start filling those seats, you better let me talk to Commander Hopkins. He's going to have something to say about that."

"Big Daddy, this is *Piranha*. Big Daddy, this is *Piranha*."

"Da, *Piranha*, we relay you. Be standink by."

"Alex! Are you all right?"

"Better than all right, Mary. Is the Commander there?"

"I'm here, MacLeod. What's your situation?"

"Damned good, that's what my situation is," Alex said. "I feel like singing, that's what."

"Are you drunk?"

"No, sir, not drunk. Not on booze, anyway. Commander, we have a spacecraft."

There was a long pause. "The transponder says you're in the Mojave Desert. *Phoenix*?"

"Yes, sir. *Phoenix*. We can—Gary Hudson says we can lift off in about five days. With cargo. About two tons of cargo. Seeds, computer chips, vegetables, minerals—you name it, they seem to have found it for us."

"Hudson. Gary Hudson. He's still alive?"

"Yes, sir, alive and in charge. You know him?"

"I know about him."

Alex couldn't get any information from the tone of voice. "Sir, he wants to come up with us. But wait until you hear what all we can bring with us. Look, I know Hudson's a little old, and you don't want more crew, but—"

"That's funny," Hopkins said.

"Sir?"

"MacLeod, I'd far rather have Hudson than you. He's a ship designer. And that ship— Is Hudson there?"

"Yes, sir."

"Put him on."

Alex had set up the radio in Hudson's office. He motioned Hudson in and took off the headset. "He wants to talk to you. Commander, this is Gary Hudson. Gary, Commander Lonny Hopkins."

"Hello, Commander." Hudson put on the headset. "Yes. Yes, sir, it's the old *Phoenix*, and I believe she'll work, but it's going to be close. We'll get into an elliptical orbit, but there's not enough fuel to rendezvous. You'll have to come get us."

Alex listened for a moment, then felt useless. Maybe they wouldn't want him to listen? *I'd far rather have Hudson than you.* It made sense, but it still hurt. He went out into the main engineering bay. The others were grinning like crazy, but their faces fell when they saw Alex's expression.

"What did he say?" Gordon asked. "It is impossible after all?"

"Huh? No, as far as I know everything's fine. Last I heard they were talking details, but it didn't sound like anything was a showstopper."

"Then what is eating you?" Sherrine asked. "We're here! It's working!" Her expression didn't match her words. She looked almost as down as Alex did.

"It's—"

"Alex," Hudson called. "Your turn again."

"Yes, sir," Alex said. "Of course I can't tell without really inspecting the ship, but everything looks all right. Gary started the diesel compressor, and that works. We don't want to fire up the jet turbo expander until the hydrogen is flowing, but the unit's in place. I'd say it's just the way Hudson explained it, we make the fuel, steal an IMU, and go. About five days."

"All right," Hopkins said. "And meanwhile there's all that cargo." There was no video link but Alex could see Hopkins rubbing his hands together. "And the ship! The ship!—OK. Now for passengers. I'm told it seats four. I don't have to tell you that we don't really need more drones up here. Hudson's fine. Hudson's wonderful. Gordon's people will be very pleased to get him back. That's two. But then there's a problem."

"Problem, sir? I'm all right, I won't have to do any EVA on this—"

"You might, but that's not the difficulty." Commander

Hopkins paused for a moment. "Major MacLeod, I'll come get you. But bring your own woman."

"Sir?"

"We understand each other, MacLeod. Shall I get Mary in on this loop? I can, and I will if I have to."

"I—"

"MacLeod, I wouldn't risk the fuel for you. You know that, I know that, Mary knows that. But you're bringing up treasure beyond price, and you'll have a new job up here, coordinating with our friends on the ground, because, although you don't seem to have noticed it, I have: that ship can land and take off again. We can send it back down for more supplies."

Son of a bitch, Alex thought. Of course it can. We were so concerned with getting *up* there—"Yes. I see that."

"So someone will coordinate with the ground people. You seem to understand them, and there's nothing else for you to do between flights, so it's you. Only I don't want you hanging around Mary while you do it. She's pregnant, you know."

"No. I didn't know."

"It may be yours. It's not mine."

"Lon—"

"Shut up. I've been sterile since the Lunar reactor flared. I was impotent for a while, too. Now I'm still sterile, but I'm not impotent. And you will stay away from Mary. I want to be sure of that. Bring your own woman, MacLeod."

"So I'm in."

"Yes. Smile?"

Sherrine considered that. "I'll come, of course. But you get to tell Bob."

"Sherrine, there's room for five, or six, or whoever we *have* to take. It's a trade, passenger for cargo—"

"Sure."

"We'll get him aboard. But without you, *I* don't go. And I'm on record, I could live with that. Would you live with me on the ground? Marry me?"

"I'll *come*."

"Why aren't we smiling?"

Sherrine lunged. Alex thought the impact would knock him backward, but she caught her mass and his, too. What muscles she had! And she felt so good. Why hadn't they been doing this ever since Flagstaff? And she buried her face in his throat and said, "It's, I wanted, damn. Four seats. Would you have asked me anyway?"

"When I got up the nerve."

"Time was getting damn short, Alex! How long would you have waited?"

"Oh . . . just about thirty seconds too long, judging by past performance. But it's all right, right? Lonny Hopkins as Cupid." He pulled back to see her face. "It's not okay."

"It's okay," Sherrine said. "I'm tougher than you think."

CHAPTER NINETEEN

"Death Will Not Release You . . ."

Stakeout could be a peaceful, lazy, catch-up time. Arteria hadn't done stakeout in years. She played a box of cassettes from Books by Mail while she watched and waited.

Some science fiction was still approved. The box was labelled as "The Sheep Look Up" by John Brunner.

She had a perfect site, on a hill high above the old Rogers Dry Lake. Her binoculars and telescope camera lenses could see most of Thunder Ridge.

Vehicles came: vans and campers, six to ten passengers each. Numerous grocery bags went into the concrete buildings. Nothing heavy. The tanker trucks had vanished into a garage; they certainly hadn't come down the hill again. Vehicles came and went. Some stayed.

Lot of manpower there. What work would need all those hands? Most of it must be going on in the hangar. Meanwhile, a city of tents and campers was going up on the desert.

It had been like this in the days when the shuttle landed. Much larger crowds then, of course. Several square miles of Nature's own parking lot, with guides to set them in rows. Campers, tents, a line of huckster tent-booths selling food, drink, badges and patches, photos and paintings, commemorative mugs and T-shirts. At night, little coal fires, music, sometimes a whiff of marijuana; tiny parties and profound silences, while hundreds of thousands of people waited for dawn.

Everybody else always saw it first. Then there it was, nose pointed *way* down, the world's boxiest glider. You'd hear *BooBoom*, a double sonic boom from the nose and the awkward bulge at the tail.

Afterward the Air Force raked up their several square miles of garbage and ran a roller over the black spots where fires had been, and it was as if the crowds had never been.

Twenty to thirty of them, now; no more. No spacecraft would be landing tomorrow. Were they singing? Did they tell old stories? Lee Arteria the outsider, the watcher, watched and wondered what she was waiting for.

Wheep! Wheep! Wheep! Captain Lee Arteria tore off the fax sheet and read it.

> WE'RE HERE AT GEORGE AFB. TWO SQUADS AIR POLICE, TWO PILOTS, YOUR HELICOPTER AND ME. STANDING BY FOR ORDERS. COLONEL MURPHY WANTS TO KNOW WHERE THE HELL YOU ARE. I TOLD HIM YOU HAD A BIG CASE BUT I'D FIND OUT.
>
> BILLINGS

Yeah. I'm going to have do something pretty quick or get off the pot. But when? By waiting she got license plates and photographs of conspirators: half a dozen cars and trucks with a dozen people—sensitive fannish faces on Thunder Ridge.

But what good was this doing? Especially now. One call, and the Air Police would surround the place. Her chopper would come. Imagine the consternation when she landed!

So far there were no decisions to make. The astronauts —she was quite certain that was who they were—had

made no attempt to leave the base. Everyone else could
be identified and tracked down.

So what are you waiting for, dear? Lee Arteria had
always liked the chase better than the kill; but this was
different, very different.

The motorcycle started, was coming down the hill
now. Two people on it. The usual overweight bearded
driver. No guitars. It was just dusk, not much light, and
they were moving too fast for her to see the face of the
rider, who was wearing a helmet anyway, but it clearly
wasn't the thin older woman who usually rode back there.

There was a tool kit strapped to the luggage carrier.
The motorcycle reached the bottom of the hill, but instead of turning north onto Rocket Site Road—on her
new map it was labeled Ecology Ruin Drive—the motorcycle turned west. That road led around Rogers Dry
Lake and down to the south entrance of the base, into
the area still guarded by the Air Force. What in the
world would they be doing there? They'd need papers—

When the road turned southwest, the motorcycle continued due west. It passed just under Arteria's hill and
continued out across the dry lake. *Curiouser and curiouser
. . . Night was falling fast now. Maybe this wasn't such a
good idea. What in hell can they be planning?*

She got out her best night glasses. There was just
enough moonlight to let the big binoculars follow the
unlighted motorcycle across the lake—

They stopped about a quarter of a mile from the
fence, left the bike, and went on foot to the fence.

Not quite to the main fence. To a smaller fenced
compound outside the main base. The two figures huddled near the fence on the far side from the base. No
one was likely to see them—no one not watching them in
the first place, anyway. In a few minutes they were
inside the fence and alongside the corrugated aluminum
building. Either the door wasn't locked or they were
good at lockpicking, because it didn't stop them for long.

They went in. Arteria timed it: nine minutes and a
couple of seconds. Then they were out again, out the
door, pause to repair the fence, then out on the lake,

running to the bike. They walked it for half a mile, then started it up and drove without lights. The desert wind covered the sound as they drove back up to Thunder Ridge.

Arteria got out her map of the base. It took a while to find the area that the bandits had visited, but there it was:

HYDROGEN PIPELINE VALVE CONTROL BUILDING

A main hydrogen pipeline led down from the north, across Edwards, and on toward Los Angeles. Two smaller lines branched off at Edwards. One went from the valve building into Dryden. The other went around the dry lake and up to Thunder Ridge.

☆   ☆   ☆

"Slicker'n ary weasel," Harry said. "Got in, broke the lock, turned on the valve, and epoxied the lock back so nobody'll notice even if they look."

"They can find the hole in the fence," C.C. Miller said.

Bob Needleton said, "We did a pretty good job of restoring the fence, too. It's like the lock, if they know to look they'll find it, but that's the only way. The real question is, is the hydrogen coming through?"

"There's pressure," Hudson said. "We're bleeding out air now, but if there's pressure, we'll have hydrogen by morning. OK. Well done. Tomorrow comes the real work."

Harry was weeping. "Shame," he said. "Goddam shame." He crawled out of the tank, painfully, like the first fish that tried to conquer the land. He was wearing white coveralls, white socks, and a big white painter's hat. His face and beard were nearly covered by white cloths, and he wore white gloves. He stood up in the sunlight, leaning heavily on Jenny Trout, and blubbered. "Goddam crying shame."

" 'How horrible. All that scotch.' " Fang's voice echoed like a thousand metal ghosts. His head popped out of the opening, swathed in white like Harry's and smiling a goofy smile. "Liter . . . rary reference."

"It's in a good cause," Hudson said. "Harry, you're supposed to clean that tank, not drink the solvent."

"I didn't drink one damn thing. Not one," Harry blubbered. "Poor LASFS. Nothing to drink anymore. All they had."

"Drink, no," Fang said. "Woosh! But a man's got to breath. Doesn't he? Hee!"

"Anyway, I think that's enough for Harry," Hudson said. "You, too, Fang. Who's next?"

" 'How horrible! All that scotch!' *Mad* magazine, fifties," Fang said. "When the oxygen comes in, we should breathe summa *that*. Hangover."

"I'll take a turn," Jenny said. "I'm with Harry, though. Distilling the alcohol off good scotch and bourbon is a hanging offense." She took Fang's protective garments as he wrestled them off. "Cheer up, Harry. You've never been so drunk, and the LASFS paid the bill."

The noise began at noon, the high-pitched scream of a jet engine. Arteria's camp was fully three miles from Thunder Ridge, but it was still noisy. She swept her binoculars over the area. The fans had clustered around one of the big cylindrical tanks, had opened it up and gone inside two and three at a time. They came out staggering. Now they had the tank sealed off and they'd started the big jet engine on a stand next to the other partially buried tank. Other fans were carrying things into the big hangar that housed the rocket Arteria had never seen.

There was other machinery running, too. A big diesel engine belched smoke on startup, and still put fumes into the air. That one seemed to be attached to the larger of the two fuel cylinders. After a while the lines from the diesel began to smoke.

Not smoke. Condensation, even in this dry air. LOX! They're making LOX, which would explain their working on the tank, cleaning it out. LOX, and hydrogen.

Lee had never seen anyone liquefy gasses, but it was clear that's what they were doing. They must be entirely crazy—like the Jonestown massacre, whole communities *do* go mad, and this little clump of madmen must think— but *why* did they think they could—

The anticipation grows, in the crew that waits below, in the silent burst of stars before the dawn.

*Starfire! Starfire! We can know the promise of the
stars . . .*
Unless I stop it. I'm supposed to stop it.
She was still watching when the Green Police car
drove onto the base.

✶   ✶   ✶

The car glowed iridescent green like a bottlefly. It
wound up the side of the hill toward Thunder Ridge.
Harry dove into his saddlebags and came up with a
pistol. Jenny produced one from her boot.

"No, dammit," C.C. Miller said. "Put the damn hardware away." He had to shout, almost to scream, to be
heard over the sound of the compressor.

"They're police!" Harry said.

C.C. was bobbing and weaving to stay out of the line
of Harry's weaving revolver. Harry hungover wasn't much
better than Harry drunk. "Harry, we don't have time.
Shut up and get yourselves under cover! We'll fix it!"

"We'll be watching," Jenny threatened. She pulled
Harry into the blockhouse.

"So damned close," Hudson said. "Another couple of
days—"

"Come and meet them."

"Oh, joy."

"Meet them on their own territory. At their car. It's
supposed to be reassuring," Miller said.

The Green car pulled up and two men got out. C.C.
Miller waved to one of them, a short man with a beard
so black that it looked dyed. "Hello, Glen!"

"Hello. This is official. Captain Hartwell, Green Police. Dan, this is C.C. Miller. That's Gary Hudson. He's
in charge here."

Hartwell was tall and thin. His look was grim as he
stared at the jet engine. "What is this?" he shouted.

Hudson indicated the office area. "It's quieter in there."
He led them inside. With the door and windows closed
they could almost talk.

"All right," Hartwell said. "What's going on?"

"Hydrogen economy experiments," Hudson said. "We're

liquifying hydrogen and oxygen. Then we'll burn them. If we can increase the efficiency of hydrogen burning by ten percent, we can save enormous amounts of energy. Just enormous. And with the winters getting longer, and everything colder—"

"You mean the glaciers coming," Hartwell said.

"Well, yes, but I wasn't sure you guys believed in them," Hudson said. "I've talked to some—"

"Some fuggheaded Green Police," Hartwell said. "Yeah, but you can't judge us by them! Niven's law. No cause is so noble that it won't attract fuggheads."

"Well—yes," Hudson said. "I wouldn't expect you to believe *that* either."

"We're not all fools," Hartwell said. "Man, that noise pollution is *savage*, and the smoke isn't much better. If you can really justify this, you'd better tell *me*, quick, because someone is sure as hell going to notice."

☆   ☆   ☆

Just as well I didn't move, Captain Arteria thought. *The Greens got there even faster than I'd have guessed. They'd have beat me in.*

And now what? Call the helicopter, go down, and claim them. It's still an Air Force base. Wait ... hell, now who's come to join the party? She swung the binoculars to the point of a dust plume just starting up the hill. *More Greens? Oh, Lord, it's Earth First.*

Black letters on the car's iridescent green flank read REMEMBER THE GREAT ALASKA OIL SPILL!

"They should change that bumper sticker," Sherrine said to C.C. "You knew one of them."

C.C. said, "Glen's ours, roughly speaking—" And then Glen Bailey had nearly reached them. C.C. yelled above the jet roar, "Where's your friend, Glen?"

"Hudson's still lecturing Hartwell. Some fur haters called in a violation in the Mojave, so I grabbed him and came. Hartwell was never in fandom, he just used to read the stuff, so I've got no strings on him, but he kind of caught the bug. He'd wipe out all the polluting factories if we have to, but he'd rather put them in orbit and on the moon where they can't hurt anything and turn the Earth into a park like the good guys wanted to do in *Spirals* and—"

C.C. held up both hands. "Okay, okay. Sherrine, what were you—"

"The bumper sticker," she said.

"So?"

"It looks . . . All right, the Great Alaska Oil Spill. I was in grade school," Sherrine said. "I remember my father shouting at the television and cutting his Exxon credit card into strips. He shouted in my face about greed and profit. The Sound was going to be polluted for years. So the next summer I asked him why the TV people didn't go back to Alaska and show people how polluted it still was. Daddy gave me a funny look and never mentioned it again. The Greatest Oil Spill in History, and it wasn't worth a one-year-later follow-up."

Glen was still looking at her. She said, "Then Saddam Hussein covered the Persian Gulf with oil and made it all moot. So your bumper sticker looks fairly silly, doesn't it, Inspector? And in ten minutes an Earth First police van is going to be up here and on our asses—"

C.C. was shaking his head and smiling while Inspector Bailey said, "You don't get it. Hussein doesn't listen. I mean he's dead, of course, but he didn't listen any better when he was alive, let alone to infidels from Satan's own United States. Why would anyone be yodeling in Iraq's ear when they don't listen? Corporations listen. McDonald's switched from paper to plastic even when it would *hurt* the environment, because the Greens told them to. Remember the boycotts against South Africa? The Soviets made them look like choirboys by any civilized standard, but they just didn't fucking *listen*, so what would be the point in—"

"Enough, Glen," C.C. said. "Did you get enough from Gary? Can you talk to Earth First about hydrogen experiments?"

"Yeah, have some faith, Cissy, I'll have them dying to put their support behind—"

"Yeah, good, good." Then they all ducked as the Earth First van pulled up in a wave of dust.

☆　　☆　　☆

A boy and a girl, both tall and lean and dark-haired and well under twenty, spilled out of the van and pointed and jabbered. Noise! Smoke! See? See? Three uniformed Earth First cops, two women and a man, followed them out more slowly. Glen walked up to join them.

Sherrine said, "Those kids must be the ones who turned us in."

"Sherrine, I don't want to be recognized, but one of us should be there," C.C. said. "We don't want them thinking Glen's a flake."

"Perish the thought!"

"It's not *like* that. He's bright, but there's a glitch in his programming. Too much LDS in the sixties, like Mister Spock." Sherrine laughed, but C.C. went on earnestly. "He can't stop talking by himself. He has to be stopped."

Glen talked. The Earth Firsters nodded. The boy and girl listened, ready to offer what they knew.

Hudson and Hartwell came out of Hudson's office and sauntered toward the Earth First van.

The kids had moved closer to the compressors. The noise was horrendous, and the girl had put her hands over her ears as she stared at the spinning jet turbine. Sherrine watched as the girl moved around toward the front of the engine. The danger area was clearly marked off with a low rope barrier, but it would be easy to step over it. "Hey!" Sherrine screamed and ran toward the girl. "Stop!" The screen over the jet intake would keep out birds, but it might not be strong enough to hold a one-hundred-pound girl. *Talk about mixed emotions!* Sherrine thought.

The boy had moved closer to the exhaust, and now stood with his nose wrinkled as he held his hands over his ears. Eager to be offended. When he saw Hudson and the others gather near the police van, he got the girl and led her over. Good. They did not need an injured civilian.

An Earth First cop talked while Glen smiled and nodded.

Sherrine strolled up; but what would she *say*? How do you talk about hydrogen? The ashes are water vapor, utterly pollution free, and what else is there? Now Glen was talking again. "So, Michael. You were on your way from Las Vegas to L.A. for a, what, a demonstration?"

"Yeah, outside the premiere," the tall boy said. "Anyone wearing fur, she'll at least know what we think of her! The rest of us went on in the other car, but Barb and I thought we'd better report what we saw. Jeez, you can *smell* it, the filth they're putting in the air—"

"Kid," said the male Earth First cop, "have you noticed it's getting chilly lately?"

"Sure, the Ice is coming." The boy named Michael looked elaborately around him at the heat of the desert. "Okay, I've seen them on TV, the glaciers, but they don't affect the principle, they don't affect the blood spilled. Wearing fur was murder when the goddam scientists were still whimpering about global warming, and it's still murder today!"

"I don't question that, but it seems to me," Glen said to the speaker, "that all of your targets are women. Isn't that sexist? I mean, men wear fur, too, not often, but—"

An Earth First policewoman said, "He has a point, kid. Sexism is politically incorrect, too. I think you need to target an equal number of fur-wearing males."

Now Barb was glaring at Michael. The boy said, "Uh . . ."

"And why just fur?" said Glen. "Leather is the skin of a dead animal, too!"

Earth First glanced down at their boots. So did both of the kids. Sherrine hadn't had to say anything at all. Glen let them argue—fur versus leather, wild free beasts versus beasts held prisoner until their deaths, hide and meat versus fur alone. The teens' respect for uniforms was fading. The cops were getting angry.

Glen said, "What we could do is, we should station teams outside biker bars and throw dye on leather-clad *men* as they come out."

The jet motor roared in a sudden silence.

"That would be more correct," the girl called Barb

bellowed. "We'd include men as well as women. And it would show that we care as deeply about homely cows and other leather-producing animals as we care about cute, furry rabbits and minks."

Michael said, "Barb—"

Oh, that *would* be fun, Sherrine thought. Glen was right: the attacks on fur-bearing upper-class women *were* sexist. Let's see what leather-clad bikers do when Michael and Barb spit on their jackets. Sherrine was trying to swallow a grin . . . and Earth First turned to face Hudson and Hartwell with evident relief.

☆   ☆   ☆

Nobody seemed to be under arrest. Just a shouting match. Lee Arteria still didn't see that her presence could swing events one way or another.

She watched the Earth First cops begin a search. Hudson would have his papers in order, of course, assuming the cops even recognized the spacecraft. Presently they drifted back. Still the desert roared and black smoke drifted, and still there were no arrests.

Now the cops got back into their van; the teens argued, then got in, too. The van drove off. Minutes later, the Green car followed.

How the hell did they work that?

And where did it leave Captain Lee Arteria?

Sanity check: they were still liquefying hydrogen and oxygen. They had come to see *Phoenix* . . . possibly they'd had contingency plans, but they'd come to see *Phoenix* first, and what they saw must have looked like a working spacecraft. Crazy amateurs . . . but they had Gary Hudson to tell them whether *Phoenix* was in any way crippled, and they'd judged Hudson sane.

They were planning to launch.

They were still gathering. The grandest gathering of pro-technology buffs ever to pour jet-engine roar and hot kerosene exhaust into clean desert air was still gathering. Fuel and oxydizer, the stranded dipper pilots as passengers, maybe Hudson himself as pilot . . . what else did they need? Cargo? *That's what the fans were up to, all*

that weird stuff! Cargo for the space habitats! There had
been a lot of stuff, boxes, paper bags, at least one cooler.
Course programming: they must have that solved. Copies
of the programs stored away. So. What else would they
need to launch?

Lee Arteria smiled. *Yes!*

> BILLINGS, TELL COLONEL MURPHY THAT WE'RE ABOUT
> TO MAKE THE MOST IMPORTANT ARREST OF THE DECADE.
> BOTH SPACEMEN PLUS THE WHOLE NETWORK THAT SMUG-
> GLED THEM ACROSS THE COUNTRY. USAF AND OSI WILL
> GET EVERY BIT OF THE CREDIT.
>
> TELL HIM TO HANG ON FOR THREE MORE DAYS AND
> WE'RE SET. THIS WILL GET HIM A BRIGADIER'S STARS. NOT
> TO MENTION PROMOTIONS FOR YOU AND ME.
>
> ARTERIA

☆   ☆   ☆

They only turned on the lights in the hangar when
they had to, and never at night. The lighted windows
must be visible for tens of miles. It was near dusk, and
the daylight through the windows was dimming, but
Harry Czescu and Bob Needleton continued to move
cargo. "Sarge" Workman helped for awhile, but he was
the only jet mechanic they had, and they needed him to
keep the turbo expander working properly. Gordon joined
them, got tired and quit.

Nothing was large, nothing was heavy. They climbed
about within the cabin space, tethering everything with
lightweight nylon cord. Heavier stuff on the bottom,
then sturdy metal cages. Guinea pigs and guinea hens
and rabbits expressed anxiety in their diverse fashions.

"Make sure you don't cover up the front of the cage,"
Bob said. "They need air."

"Teach your grandmother to suck eggs. . . ."

A net would cover everything once it was all in place.
The paper in the cages would come out just before they
closed up the *Phoenix*. Or maybe not. The cages stank,
but after all, organics were organics. . . .

Another load in place. Back out, and down to ground

level. Harry lit a cigarette. He was just about the only one on Thunder Ridge who smoked. He took two puffs and pinched off the end, put the butt back in the package. "OK, do we want to glue the mat in now? Or wait?"

Bob didn't answer.

"Lighten *up*, Pins. Nobody thinks—" Harry looked up. "Hi, Sherry, C.C. Alex, they brought you an exercise mat."

"Hi, Harry." C.C. rubbed his hands together briskly. "Okay. What can we give up? Alex, those mice are gengineered to produce juvenile growth hormones. That'd let the Angels grow their bones back, right?"

"That's what I'm told," Alex said.

"You need the seeds a lot, the guinea pigs and guinea hens and rabbits not as much. The diet supplements, of course. No bull semen, to bowdlerize a phrase. Sausage packed in dry ice?"

"Sausage, no. Eat it before we take off, if it's that good and won't keep. Dry ice, *hell* no. Carbon we want, but oxygen comes almost free from lunar rock. Did anyone think of sending lamp black?"

C.C. ran his eyes down the list. "I don't think so. I'll see what we can get when. How badly do you want these metals? And the honeycomb blocks? They're heavy."

"It's not really my department, C.C."

"Alex, you and Gordon are the only ones who can make these choices. And five passengers . . . Where the hell is Gordon?"

Alex waved toward the shadows where he had seen Gordon with Jenny Trout. "I told him we needed him, but—"

Bob Needleton said, "I confess I do not see why the fifth wheel has to be me." His ears and nose were noticeably pink.

Alex said, "Gordon. Sherrine. Hudson. Me. You. Shall *I* take the exercise mat?"

Bob was having trouble pulling the words out. "*We* pulled you off the Ice. The rest are gone. There's only me and Sherrine left—"

Alex said, "Hold it."

"Hold it, my foot. *You* and Sherrine have been—"

"You wanted to *know*, Bob. Sherrine had the *right* to know. Sherrine has to go into space because I slept with the Commander's wife."

Needleton gaped, then grinned. "We-ell. That's a better story than I expected."

"Well, it's true. Sherrine doesn't go, the Station Commander says he won't pick me up. Maybe you can live with that, but *I* won't volunteer to stay. I won't."

Bob looked at Sherrine. "All right—"

"He already told me."

"I didn't ask, Sherry. But why not six? Gordon's got a woman, too. What are we going to give up for Barbara? Dammit, where the *hell* is Gordon?"

Two voices echoed oddly, as if the entire hangar space had answered—

> *"Wanted fan on Chthon and Sparta and the Hub's
> ten million stars,
> Wanted fan for singing silly in a thousand space-
> port bars.
> If it's what we really want, we'll build a starship
> when we can;
> If I could just make orbit then I'd be a wanted fan."*

"Enough of this," Alex said. "Excuse me." He walked toward where Jenny and Gordon were leafing through notes, nodding, singing:

> *"Wanted fan for building spacecraft, wanted fan for
> dipping air,
> Sending microwave transmissions, building habitats
> up there.
> Oh the glacier caught us last time; next time we'll
> try to land!
> And when Ice is conquered, it will be by wanted
> fans!"*

Jenny said, "Gordon, that's nice. A little premature, maybe, hi, Alex, even a little overoptimistic—"

"Hi, Jenny. Gordon, we're deciding your fate while

you play. This is how you came here in the first place, remember?"

"And this is why I stay," Gordon said. "That verse I wrote for you, Alex. *And when the stars are conquered, it will be by wanted fans!*"

Alex became aware that the others had followed him. He said, "Gordon?"

"I am stilyagin, Alex. Nothing has changed. But there is room for poets here, and novelists, and I can always catch the next flight with Hudson's wife. My voice is needed here. I stay. Four seats, four passengers. Tell my family I kiss them from below. No, let me word that again," he said, while Sherrine and Bob and Gary Hudson looked at each other. "Wait, now—"

Sherrine took Alex's arm and led him into the shadows. She said, "Do you see what I see?"

"Oh, sure. If the *Phoenix* went up missing me *and* Gordon, it'd be a disaster. Lonny couldn't be voted dog catcher. So you don't have to come, but why don't you come anyway? Please?"

Sherrine smiled. "Okay."

"Stop toying with my affections and give me a straight answer."

"I'll come if I have to sit in your lap. Now we need to finish loading. Alex, didn't you say you didn't want the plastic corn?"

"Yeah. I appreciate the work that went into getting it, but we don't need plastic that much and we've got better use for the soil, and it doesn't even breed!"

"Well, it was here. Some dedicated fan sneaked it aboard."

"Damn. We'd better find it before it gets buried."

They climbed the scaffold. Sherrine asked, "How do you make love in free fall?"

Alex laughed. "Superbly. It takes a tether."

They eeled into the cabin. "Look inside things," Sherrine said.

"Yeah. Sherrine, this could be your last chance to make love in a gravity field."

"Mmm."

"We could even find a, what did we call those things, they were soft and you spread a sheet over them—"

"You're kidding, right? Bed."

"Bed."

★ ★ ★

Hudson laid out a map of the Dryden Research Center portion of Edwards Air Force Base and pointed to a building. "In there. Room G-44. There are three security containers in the room, and the IMU is in the lowest drawer of the middle one."

"And you're sure?" Bob Needleton asked.

"Yes, of course I'm sure. Actually, there are five of the damned things, but that's where they keep one of them, the one that's been tested most recently."

"And when was that?" Sherrine asked.

"About a year—no, more like two years. Twenty months ago. Major Beeson brought it over and we ran tests on the whole *Phoenix* electronics system. Worked like a charm, too. Then they took the IMU back, packed it in foam, and put it in the safe."

"And it hasn't been moved since?" C.C. Miller asked.

"Not that I know of," Hudson said. "And why would it? It's where it stayed between tests last time."

"When's the next test?" Needleton asked.

"Maybe never. Beeson was transferred. There's a civilian named Feeley in charge of technology studies at Dryden now."

"Feeley?"

"Yeah, the troops call him Touchy Feeley, of course. He's a Green."

"And brain dead, I suppose," Miller said.

"He's not brain dead, he's soul dead. Everything's kept in order, though, all the lab tools put away every day, all the reports filed on time."

"Hell of a way to run a lab," Needleton said. "But I suppose it's as well. Makes it likely your IMU will be right where it belongs." He studied the map. "Harry, it looks like we can go in from the hydrogen valve compound. Get inside there, and then open a new hole into

the main base. Fang, you've been watching the base, did
you ever see patrols at night?"

"Nothing," Fang said. "Guards at the gates, some
people in the operations building, some night crew at the
flight line. Nothing else."

"Not much to guard anymore," Hudson said. "One
time, they had the hottest airplanes and pilots in the
world here. Spaceships, too. Now—"

"Yeah," Needleton said. "OK, Harry, I guess we're set.
Let's do it."

They laid the bike on its side next to a mesquite bush
and walked the rest of the way to the fence. The twisties
holding the fence together hadn't been disturbed in the
three days since they'd broken in to start the flow of
hydrogen. Thunder Ridge was fifteen miles away, and
the sounds of the compressor and turbo expander were
lost in the howl of the desert wind.

"Damn moon," Harry muttered. "I like moonlight, but
there's too damn much of it."

Nearly full, Bob Needleton thought.

*By God! Ten hours! Dawn tomorrow, and I'm up and
out of here, off this Earth. If my heart doesn't pound so
damn hard it wakes up the guards ...* Sherrine would
be going, too, but not the way he'd thought. *Oh, well. I
get the best consolation prize there is. Free trip, too.
Four seats, and one's mine!*

The Hydrogen Valve building had its own fence, but
there was a gate from that area into the main Dryden
compound. Harry inspected the gate and its lock, then
whispered, "Damn good lock. It might be easier to cut a
hole in the fence, but that'll be more noticeable when
there's light. What should I do?"

"Whatever's quickest. By the time there's light everyone in the country will know." Bob took out his wire
cutters and started in.

Room G-44 was in a temporary building constructed
in the glory days of the 1950s. Like the engineering room
on Thunder Ridge, it had space for far more desks and

drawing boards than it held. Even so, many of the desks seemed unused.

A bank of three security cabinets stood against one wall. Harry went over and rubbed his hands in anticipation. "The middle one," he said. He ostentatiously took out a nail file and began to rub it over his fingertips. "No sandpaper—"

"Harry, damn it, get on with it," Needleton whispered.

"Right." Harry opened the tool kit and took out a drill, pliers, crowbar. "Well—here goes—but you know, just in case—"

"*What?*"

Harry pulled on the drawer. It opened.

"Like I said, just in case. And there's your gizmo, I think." He lifted out a plastic box and set it on the desk. "Let's see—"

"Harry, be careful, don't drop it—"

"Not me. Yep." He took out a smaller box that had been nested in foam packing. "And here we are. One IMU—"

The room lights came on.

"Harry, damn you—" Needleton shouted.

"Me?"

"Hello-o!"

They turned. An Air Force captain in combat fatigues stood at the door. The captain's submachine gun didn't quite point at either Harry or Needleton.

"Oh, shit," Harry said.

"Now what?" Needleton said. He eyed the distance to the gun. There were two desks in the way. He glanced at Harry, who nodded slightly.

"Death will not release you," the captain intoned. The submachine gun was pointing straight at Harry's navel.

CHAPTER TWENTY

A Fire in the Sky

Jenny Trout stared down the road. "Where the hell are they?"

"Maybe the lock was tougher than Harry thought," Sherrine said.

"It wouldn't be the lock," Jenny said. "Harry's good with locks. I'm sure glad Bob went along. Where the hell *are* they?"

"There's something coming." A light, a long way away. Fantastic, how far you could see out here.

"Two lights! It's a car!" Jenny shouted. "Get Hudson."

"Jenny, for God's sake put that gun away!" Sherrine said. "Gary!"

C.C. Miller came running out of the office. "Jenny, for God's sake, shooting people isn't the answer to everything!"

"Cissy, sometimes it is!"

"Not this time," Gary Hudson said. "Look, if you start a firefight there'll be a hundred Air Police up here long before any possible launch window." He stared moodily at the approaching headlights. "Whatever we do, it has to be done *quietly*."

"Oh. Okay." Jenny put the gun back in her boot.

Miller edged closer to Fang and spoke in a low urgent voice. "Stay with her, just in case."

"We can't just give up now!"

"No, and we won't," Miller said. "But there're more ways to futter a cat than just to stuff its head in a sea boot."

"Eh?"

"Ted Sturgeon's other law. Just go wait with Jenny."

The car was a small gray sedan, totally inconspicuous if you didn't notice that it had six antennas. It pulled up in the pool of light in front of the office, and Bob Needleton got out on the driver's side. He was moving slowly, carefully. Harry got out of the passenger's side, moving the same way, as if they were underwater.

"What the hell is going on?" Gary Hudson demanded. Somebody slid out of the back seat, lithe and quick like a striking shark.

Bob Needleton said, carefully, "Gary Hudson, this is Captain Lee Arteria, U.S.A.F. Office of Special Investigations."

"Oh, shit—"

"Death will not release you." Captain Arteria's voice carried even over the roar of the jet engine. Headlights glowed on the intruder's blue uniform and compact machine gun and sharp white smile. The Air Police captain moved like a man in free fall, Alex thought. Like Steve Mews. Strong and dangerous.

Harry Czescu and Bob Needleton had stopped moving. The night seemed to wait. C.C. cleared his throat and said, "Even if you die."

"Pay your dues! Pay your dues!" Was that a man's voice or a woman's?

"Lee Arteria?"

"Right. You're . . . Miller? C.C. Miller. Director of the LASFS."

"Chairman now," Miller said.

Gary Hudson demanded, "Will someone *please* tell me—"

"She's a LASFS member," Miller said.

"Or was," Bob Needleton said.

Lee Arteria said, "Nobody leaves the LASFS. Death did not release me, nor fafiation. It took me a while to figure that out."

"Which is all very well, but where is the IMU?" Hudson said.

"I have it here." Arteria handed across a box. She held her weapon like a prosthetic attachment. Hudson took the box while trying to evade the machine gun's snout.

"And you better get it installed fast." Arteria glanced at her watch. "It's twenty-three forty-two now. By oh-eight-hundred, oh-eight-thirty tops, this place will be crawling with police. OSI, blues, Greens, Army, Immigration agents, Post Office inspectors for all I know."

"Yes. OK." Gary Hudson held the box gingerly, like a hot potato. Small wonder, Alex thought, considering what—who—had come attached to it. "Okay. And, Alex, you'd better tell Jenny to stand down."

Alex went.

The hangar was larger from inside than it had looked from across the ridge. *Phoenix* stood proudly, enshrouded by scaffolds now. They turned on all the lights. That was safer than using flashlights. Furtive lights might be investigated immediately. Working lights could wait until morning.

"God, it's beautiful," Lee said.

"Not as beautiful as when she flies," Hudson said.

"It really will work, then."

Hudson gave her a sour look. "I don't want to seem ungrateful, but you're about the hundredth person to ask that. Yes, *Phoenix* is ready. More precisely, I'm enough convinced that it will work that I'm going up with it."

Hudson took the IMU and climbed up into the well above one of the landing legs. The opening was barely large enough to admit him. A few moments later he came out far enough to take a wrench out of his pocket, then climbed back in. Finally he emerged with a big grin.

"All's well?" Lee Arteria asked.

Hudson grinned wider. "Yeah. Now let's check things out—" He led the way up the ladder.

The cabin was crowded. The only empty spaces were the four seats, which could just be reached from above. Chickens protested the disturbance when Hudson turned on the lights. Lee watched from the hatchway as Hudson wormed into the command chair and pulled the panel toward him. He threw switches. Lights blinked yellow, then green, and the readout screen came alive. Hudson typed furiously at the keyboard.

"Hot damn," he announced.

"All's well?" Lee asked.

"Like a charm." He typed more commands. "There. I've got it in a test loop, but I don't expect any problems."

"And you can launch when?" Lee asked.

"In about ten minutes, or at oh-six-forty. We won't be ready in ten minutes."

"Six and a half hours," Lee said.

⋆   ⋆   ⋆

Jheri Moorkith was trying to be polite. After all, this was an Air Force Base, and he was talking to Air Force officers. It wasn't easy, though.

"Dammit, she lied to me," Moorkith said.

"How?" Lieutenant Billings asked.

"She said that message on the sermon board, 'Sermon by Nehemiah Scudder,' would lure them in."

"And it didn't. What makes you think they went anywhere near your church?" Colonel Murphy demanded.

"We know they went through Denver, and they crossed the California border at Needles four days ago. *Four days!* And you've known it all this time, and didn't tell me!"

"I sent you a memo," Billings said.

"Through channels," Moorkith said through his teeth. "Yeah, and we all know how that game is played. All right, but it's played out now. I have a directive here from the National Security Council putting me in charge of finding these enemies. Do you acknowledge my authority?"

Murphy braced. "Yes, sir." He didn't pretend to like it.

"Good. Where is Captain Arteria?"

"We don't know exactly," Billings said. "She's communicating through the Mount Emma relay station. That serves the entire Mojave Desert. She could be anywhere out there, but for all I know she's here in Victorville. This is where she told me to wait for orders."

Moorkith grimaced. "Colonel, I am ordering you: find her. I want to know where Captain Lee Arteria is."

"Why?" Murphy demanded.

"Because I think she has gone over. Find Arteria, and we'll know exactly where those astronauts and their fannish friends are. I'm sure of it. So find her!"

☆ ☆ ☆

Wheep! Wheep!

Lee tore off the fax sheet, read it and handed it to C.C. Miller.

BOSS IT'S GETTING STICKY. MOORKITH IS HERE WITH FULL AUTHORITY FROM THE NATIONAL SECURITY COUNCIL TO TAKE CHARGE. THE CALIFORNIA HIGHWAY PATROL TOLD HIM TWO MILKHEIM TRUCKS CROSSED THE BORDER AT NEEDLES FOUR DAYS AGO. MOORKITH IS UPSET. MOORKITH IS VERY UPSET. MOORKITH IS FURIOUS. HE'S SCREAMING AT COLONEL MURPHY. THE COLONEL IS SCREAMING AT ME.

DIRECT ORDER FROM COLONEL MURPHY: CAPTAIN ARTERIA, YOU WILL REPORT YOUR LOCATION AND CIRCUMSTANCES IMMEDIATELY. MURPHY.

COLONEL MURPHY SAYS I HAVE ONE HOUR TO FIND OUT WHERE YOU ARE AND GET A FULL REPORT AND THEN HE'S SENDING THE AP'S LOOKING FOR YOU.

HE SAYS THAT BUT I THINK HE SENT THEM OUT ALREADY.

I HOPE YOU KNOW WHAT YOU'RE DOING BECAUSE IT'S GETTING HOTTER THAN HELL AROUND HERE.

BILLINGS

Miller read it, then handed it to Bob Needleton. They

all stood in a group around Lee's car, reading in the light from the office windows behind them.

"That does look sticky," Bob Needleton said.

"It is sticky," Lee said. "Up to now I might just get away with saying you overpowered me. I'd look like an idiot letting you and Harry get my piece away from me after the way you telegraphed your moves, but I could talk my way out of a court martial. Now I have direct orders to tell my colonel where I am and what I'm doing. That's not a game anymore. That's Leavenworth."

"So what will you do?" Miller asked.

She looked around at their faces as they stood in a circle around her car. At the desert beyond. Then at the open door to the hangar. She could just see the base of *Phoenix*.

She still held the submachine gun. She stood for another moment, then got into the car, laid down the machine pistol, and began to type furiously at her fax machine.

Harry looked at Miller. They both looked at Hudson. Hudson shrugged.

Arteria got out again and retrieved her weapon. "There. Take the big tank trucks to the oil fields at Taft and abandon them. Have somebody follow in a car to take the drivers, then call this number and tell the duty sergeant where you left the trucks. Get away from there fast. Keep going on north to wherever you want to hide. Meanwhile, I've got the Air Police watching Cajon Pass to San Bernardino. About the time they get that covered, they'll get the tip about the trucks in Taft. Go on, move! This ought to buy us a few hours."

Hudson nodded warily.

C.C. said, "Sarge, Mark, a truck each. Bjo, you've got a hydrogen car? Fuel up and follow them and keep moving. Sarge, you're in charge."

"Right."

Lee Arteria stood up briskly. The gun had never left her side. "Now as to my price."

"So what's your price?" There was something in Bob Needleton's voice that said he already knew. What had passed between them in the car on the way here?

"I'm going up," Lee Arteria said.

Hudson shook his head emphatically. "We don't have time to repack. It's packed for four and we're only six hours from liftoff—"

"*Your* seat, Pins."

Needleton said, "Captain, I never said I wasn't going."

"I heard what you told me, coming here. You're staying to teach, you're staying to fight, you're giving up and leaving, you're not sure what you'll do up there, you'll be locked in a can with the woman who kicked you out and the man who took her. You're in a quantum state, Pins. Well, I'm flipping you over."

Arteria was moving forward; Bob Needleton was backing up. He didn't seem to be aware of it. His jaw thrust out mutinously. "If I give up my seat it'll be to something that's needed up there. What are you doing?"

Arteria was opening zippers. She was wearing lots of zippers. She said, "I've done too much to cover for you. I go up, or I go to Leavenworth. I caught you people! Fair and square, and then I covered for you."

"So you have to go underground. So do most of us. You can hide as easy as me. Easier. You know more about how to do it."

"Not good enough," she said. "You can't stop me."

"I can try. Maybe I can kill you before you summon help, maybe I can't."

"I don't have to summon anyone. If I don't report in, they'll know where to look."

"I don't believe you—"

Arteria laughed softly. She was moving toward him while dropping things: the submachine gun. Her leather jacket. A holdout gun from one boot, a knife from the other, then the boots. Handcuffs, the fancy pin in her hat. Bob Needleton watched in horror, retreating, and nobody else moved.

"Maybe it's a bluff. Maybe you couldn't alert your squad because you waited too long." Bob's threat might have been more effective if he weren't backing up toward the Operations Planning Room.

"Every cop on Earth knows my face." Handcuffs, a mace

delivery system, a horrifying armory. And her pants. Blouse. "They're all going to think . . . *know* I betrayed them."

She looked quite dangerous, Alex thought. She had muscles . . . smoother than Steve's, but powerfully differentiated. She looked to Alex like an alien life form, and more female every second.

Arteria was almost nose to nose with Bob Needleton. He'd backed up against a flat surface. She wasn't wearing anything at all now. She said, "What about a woman of childbearing age?"

"Okay," Bob said, "you're a woman."

"Open the door," she said.

"Door?" Needleton became aware of the flat surface behind him. He found a doorknob and turned it and backed through.

Lee Arteria said, "I'll be taking your seed with me."

"I don't, uh—"

"I didn't ask."

Slam.

Gordon was smiling broadly. "Wonderful! Just like 'God's Little Acre.'"

"Shouldn't we be trying to rescue him?" Sherrine looked at the stunned faces around her.

*   *   *

Hudson climbed out of *Phoenix* and gathered the others around him at the ship's base.

"All right," he said. "It's set. We launch at oh-six-forty-four on the dot. Commander Hopkins has the rendezvous set. He'll go when we report success."

"Who do you need here for the launch?" Miller asked.

"Once we get the roof opened, no one. We'll open that in half an hour, then you people scatter, and I mean scatter. Get off the base and take off in all directions. Can anybody go straight north across the desert?"

"We can," Harry said. "But maybe Jenny and I ought to stay. Stand guard."

"And do what? Not that I need to ask," Hudson said, as Jenny reached toward her boot. "Look: just now I won't be wanted for anything but stealing my own spaceship. I can land in a foreign country and the lawyers can take care of it. Kill somebody and they'll have extradition warrants out everywhere we can land! Not to mention that a bunch of Air Force johnnies who right now sympathize will be gunning for me. I have to come back to Earth to get Annie! No, thanks, Harry."

"No last stand?" Jenny said.

"No."

"Imagine my relief," Harry said. "Look, we'll be going out last, right? I'll take a coil of that stainless steel wire and close off the gates. We can drop broken glass on the road up, too."

"Well, that's all right," Hudson said. "But nobody gets hurt!"

"Except maybe us," Jenny said.

"If that's what it takes to get this ship up—"

"Yeah, Harry," Jenny said. She put the pistol back in her boot. "Where's that wire?"

"Now. One more thing," Hudson asked. "Where's Arteria?"

Everyone looked at each other. "She's still—" "She's with Needleton—"

"It would help to know her weight," Hudson said. "Harry, go ask."

"Well, all right—" Harry walked across the square from the hangar to the engineering building, and stood on the porch outside the closed door to the Operations Planning Room.

He stood there a while, then came back. "Actually, you won't be *very* far off if you say a hundred and fifty pounds."

Gary Hudson activated the speaker system. It wouldn't matter now, voices wouldn't add to the noise of the turbo expander. "MINUS EIGHTY MINUTES AND COUNTING," the computer said. *Damn, it feels good to hear that again!*

The door to the Operations Planning Room opened, and Lee Arteria came out wearing the silk kimono that Hudson kept in the shower in his office suite. "Yours,

Hudson? I like your taste," she said. "But someone seems to have moved my clothes."

"Next room. You won't need all the weapons, you know."

"I don't need any, do I?"

Hudson frowned. "Not by me. But I haven't told them upstairs about the change in the passenger list. Not too late to rethink it."

"Nothing to rethink. This career's over."

"So you run away. What do you think you'll do up there?"

She shook her head. "I'm not useless, you know. I have an engineering degree. Air Force ROTC. I wanted to work in the space program. I got my commission, but they didn't need engineers, and they did need police investigators. I was good at that, but I can learn anything." She smiled slightly, a thin, wistful smile. "I can make babies. My biological clock is going tick, tick, *brrinnggg*!"

"OK, you convinced me. I gather you already convinced Dr. Needleton."

"Let's say he's no longer objecting."

☆ ☆ ☆

"All right, the hour's up. Where is she?" Moorkith demanded.

Colonel Murphy looked embarrassed. "She ordered the helicopter to meet her at an area above Cajon Pass, but the place was empty when they got there. We're searching the area."

"Searching the area."

"Yes, Mr. Moorkith. She may be hurt, or taken prisoner."

"I don't believe one word of that," Moorkith said. "And neither do you. She's gone over. Helping them! That's what's happened. Now, Colonel, unless you want to explain all this to the Secretary of Defense, you will cooperate with me."

"What do you want me to do?"

"I want you to think! What could have persuaded her to help the Angels? She must know they'd be caught."

Lieutenant Billings had been listening quietly. Now he drew in his breath sharply.

Moorkith looked at him. "Well, Lieutenant?"

"Nothing, sir. Just a thought."

"Out with it," Moorkith said.

Billings shook his head. "Sir, it was nothing—"

"Tell us," Colonel Murphy said.

"Maybe they won't get caught, sir."

Murphy frowned. "Billings, there's no way! There's no place in this country, *on this continent*—oh."

"What in hell are you talking about, Colonel?" Moorkith demanded.

"Nothing, sir."

"God damn you people! You know something, you know something—" He stopped and looked thoughtful. "So. Not on this continent. Not on this planet, right? They have a way to get back to orbit, don't they? What is it? Where?"

"No place," Murphy said. "It's silly."

"Silly or not, Colonel, this is a direct order from me acting with the authority of the National Security Council: how might they get those Angels back into orbit?"

Murphy and Billings looked at each other helplessly. Finally Murphy said, slowly, *"Phoenix."*

"There's a *rocket ship* in Phoenix?"

☆   ☆   ☆

"MINUS FIFTY MINUTES AND COUNTING. TAKE YOUR LAUNCH STATIONS. CLEAR THE BASE AREA. CLEAR THE BASE AREA."

Bob Needleton was buttoning his shirt as he came out of the Ops Planning Room. Everyone carefully looked away as he came out onto the porch. "Where is she?" he asked.

"Getting aboard," Harry said. "Uh—you're not going to make trouble?"

"Huh? No. She goes. I'll be staying here to fight the danelaw."

He went down to the *Phoenix* hangar. The roof was open now, open to the stars burning brightly in the high desert. The moon was just going down, and there was the faintest tinge of dawn to the east, but straight above was cold and dark and clear.

Sherrine and Arteria were climbing up the scaffolding. Hudson and Alex stood at the top, sixty feet above.

"Go with God," Gordon shouted.

"Yo!"

Bob Needleton waved. "Good-bye, Sherrine. Captain Arteria . . . Lee. Name them after the kids in Doc Smith's *Children of the Lens*. Guys, I'm *hungry*."

"There's food left over," Harry said. "Look, we've all got our escape assignments. You're to go in Lee's car. They thought that would be appropriate. If you're—Sandy here will drive, he knows the area."

Hudson got into the ship.

"CLEAR THE BASE AREA."

"Guess that's it, then," Bob Needleton said. "Seems like an—I guess it's over. From the Ice to the Desert." He stood at the door to the hangar, reluctant to leave, until Harry pulled him away.

They reached the car. Sandy Sanders was already in the driver's seat.

Wheep! Wheep!

The fax machine startled them.

CAPTAIN LEE ARTERIA THIS IS COLONEL ANTHONY MURPHY. OFFICIAL. MISTER JHERI MOORKITH WITH AUTHORITY OF THE NATIONAL SECURITY COUNCIL HAS ASSUMED COMMAND OF OPERATION FALLEN ANGEL. HE HAS DECIDED THAT THERE WILL BE AN ATTEMPT TO ESCAPE OUR JURISDICTION BY ILLEGAL LAUNCH OF A USAF EXPERIMENTAL SHIP CALLED PHOENIX AT PRESENT HELD IN A USAF MUSEUM AT EDWARDS AIR FORCE BASE. YOU ARE HEREBY ORDERED TO DO ALL IN YOUR POWER TO PREVENT THE LAUNCH OF THE PHOENIX ROCKET. FYI MOORKITH LEFT HERE TEN MINUTES AGO WITH LIEUTENANT BILLINGS IN YOUR HELICOPTER, DESTINATION EDWARDS AIR FORCE BASE, REPEAT, DESTINATION EDWARDS AIR FORCE BASE.

"Holy shit," Needleton said. "How do we tell Hudson?"

"Cissy and Gordon are still in the blockhouse," Harry said. He looked at his watch. "I think they are."

"Harry, run this over," Bob said. "Have him read it to Hudson."

"Then what?" Sandy asked.

"Then nothing," Harry said. "Hudson ordered us not to fight, and it don't matter anyway. We can't fight a chopper. Can't even mess up the landing areas, there are too many up here. Get Bob out of here, Sandy."

Sandy looked to Needleton. Bob nodded. "Let's go," he said. "Who knows, if enough of us run away, maybe they'll chase *us*. Let's go."

Miller read the fax and shook his head. "I've got a bad feeling about this—" He punched the intercom button. "*Phoenix*, we have a problem." He read the fax.

There was a long pause.

"Okay, we got it," Hudson said. "Not that there's much we can do. We wait. Know any prayers?"

"Edwards," Lee Arteria said. "Moorkith said Edwards, so that's where they're taking him! I know Murphy, if they were coming to Thunder Ridge he'd have said Thunder Ridge. I think we're going to make it!"

"Cutting it damned close," Hudson said. "Miller, get your people out of here. We may be able to shave a few minutes off the launch time. I'll talk to Commander Hopkins. You people, get out. Now! Go!"

"MINUS TWENTY MINUTES AND COUNTING," the computer said.

"And who do you think it's talking to?" Sherrine asked.

"No one, I hope," Gary said. "But you never know about fans. And Harry."

"We're blind in here," Arteria said. "If I'd been thinking we could have rigged up a way to communicate with whoever's in my car—"

"Bob Needleton," Hudson said.

"Alex, is it always like this?" Arteria asked. "Waiting? I'm beginning to know what criminals must feel like—"

"*Phoenix*, this is *Freedom*," a woman's voice said.

"Roger, *Freedom*."

"I am patching in a relay. Stand by."

"Alex, this is Gordon. We relay to you."

"Roger, Gordo. Good to hear from you. What's up?"

"Not you, but Air Police helicopter has landed at Edwards main base."

"Eighteen miles from here," Hudson muttered. "Ten minutes flight—"

"Five," Arteria said.

"And they'll hear the compressor," Hudson said.

"I don't think so," Arteria said. "We drove a good halfway here before we heard it—but you can see the lights up here with no trouble at all."

"Oh, shit," Hudson said.

"MINUS FIFTEEN MINUTES AND COUNTING."

☆   ☆   ☆

"All right, now where is this *Phoenix*?" Moorkith demanded.

"*Phoenix*, sir?" the operations sergeant asked. The name tag on his coverall said "MacDaniel." "It's in a museum up on Thunder Ridge."

"Thunder Ridge? Where's that?"

The sergeant pointed. "You see them lights up there across the lake? That's Thunder Ridge."

Moorkith turned to Billings. "What in the hell are you up to?"

"Sir? You asked to be taken to Edwards. We're at Edwards."

"God damn you, you knew I wanted to get to the *Phoenix*!"

Billings kept a straight face. "Sir, you told Colonel Murphy I was to take you to Edwards. I took you to Edwards. I assume you want to clear this activity on U.S. Air Force property with the base commander. Sir."

"And where is he?" Moorkith demanded.

The operations sergeant looked at Billings, then back at Moorkith. "Sir, he's in Rosamond. He doesn't live on base."

"Then who the hell is in charge here?"

"Sir, that would be the Officer of the Day, Major Cobb."

"And where is he?"

"In the Operations Office, sir."

"You bastards are going to give me a runaround all night, aren't you?" Moorkith demanded. "You're all in this together. You're finished, Billings, you and Murphy and Arteria, you're all finished!"

"Yes, sir. Did you want to see Major Cobb, sir?"

"No, I want you to take me up to Thunder Ridge."

"Yes, sir. Sergeant, see that this chopper is fueled up and—"

"Damn it, NOW!"

"But, sir, we're low on fuel. And, Sergeant, I thought I heard a funny noise in the main bearing. Probably nothing, but you better check it out."

Sergeant MacDaniel fought with a grin and almost won. "Yes, sir."

"Space cadets," Moorkith said. "Sergeant, get me a car. That car. Right there. Are the keys in it? Good. You two, you guys with the guns, come with me. Now. Lieutenant, when you get your helicopter working, you can use it to get up on that ridge and stop that launch or you can stuff it up your ass. Either way, Billings, either way, you are finished. Done. Do you understand me?"

"Well, not quite, sir. Now I suppose it's pretty astonishing that a bunch of Air Force people would have an interest in space—"

"And you can quit stalling, too," Moorkith said. "All right, you men. Get in the car. I'll drive. Sergeant, open the fucking gate, and don't give me any problems about that."

Sergeant MacDaniel shrugged. "Yes, sir. Give me a moment to get the keys."

☆　　☆　　☆

Inspector Glen Bailey drove the Green Police car through Mojave and east on Highway 58, keeping his eyes on Thunder Ridge more than on the road. Any moment now, he thought. Any moment.

As he drove he sang softly to himself.

> *"And the Earth is clean as a springtime dream,*
> *No factory smokes appear,*
> *For they've left the land to the gardener's hand,*
> *And they all are orbiting here . . ."*

☆   ☆   ☆

Bob Needleton looked at his watch. "Stop," he said. Sandy pulled over to the edge of the road. Needleton got out and leaned on the car. He looked south, to Thunder Ridge, and waited. It was just before dawn, a few stars left in the west, none in the east, but it was still dark on the ground. Not quite dawn, Needleton thought. Not by Mohammed's definition, can't tell a black thread from a white one—

There was a flash on Thunder Ridge. Then another, even brighter.

☆   ☆   ☆

Jheri Moorkith could see the big hangar through the fence. The base area of Thunder Ridge was deserted, but there were lights everywhere, and the roof of the big building two hundred yards away had been swung open. The Air Police car stopped, and Airman Joey Murasaki got out. "Gate's locked," he shouted. "No keys."

The hangar was just ahead, but there was no way through the locked gate. Jheri Moorkith was tempted to scream, but managed to be calm. "Shoot the lock off," he ordered.

Sergeant Malcolm Lincoln sniffed. "Sir, that works better in movies than the real world. Maybe I should get a hammer out of the trunk and open it with that?"

"I don't care how you do it, open that gate!"

Two blows of the hammer smashed the lock, but the gate still wouldn't open. "It's wired shut," Sergeant Lincoln said. "Joey, get me the bolt cutters out of the trunk."

There was a bright flash from the hangar. The corrugated aluminum walls shook, and there was thunder.

"Hurry!" Moorkith screamed.

The hangar walls fell outward. *Phoenix* began to rise, slowly, majestically.

Moorkith turned to face the Air Policemen, who were staring at the slowly rising rocket. "Shoot it!" Moorkith ordered.

"Shoot it?" Sergeant Lincoln asked.

"Yes! Shoot! Shoot! Damn you, I order you, shoot it!"

"Sir—"

"Give me that damn gun!"

Malcolm Lincoln never took his eyes off the ship as he unslung the submachine gun. Then, exactly as he'd been taught, he slipped the clip loose and opened the bolt. He handed the empty weapon to Moorkith.

Jheri Moorkith fumbled with the cartridge clip. He saw nothing as *Phoenix* rose.

Sergeant Malcolm Lincoln watched with a faraway look as *Phoenix* flew upward, faster now. Thunder washed across him, and his ears hurt but Lincoln was grinning like a thief. As the rocket climbed she caught the growing light of dawn, but the jets were brighter than the dawn as *Phoenix* rode a fire into the sky.

CHAPTER TWENTY-ONE
Cruisecon

The big sailing ship had been designed for cargo, a high tech windjammer with four tall masts and sails that looked like airplane wings standing on end. They shifted constantly as *Gullwhale* raced at 18 knots through the Caribbean toward the Windward Islands. She could make 20 knots in decent winds.

Chuck had his videocamera bolted to the deck. The view tilted with the ship, heeled over by fifteen degrees. "February 31st, 23,309. This is *Gullwhale Crossing*, a videofanzine published by Chuck Umber. Rick Foss, what are we doing here?"

Foss was a lean, bearded man with a mad smile and an absurd hat. "We are here to hold Cruisecon, the first World Science Fiction Convention ever to be held at sea."

"And how did this come about?"

"Nice timing. I notice we're coming about. Well, *Gullwhale* was a Green research project, expensive even by NASA standards, but clean as clean can be. What she couldn't do," Rick Foss said, "was make money. Between the U.S. environmental regulations and the unsteadiness of the wind, nobody wanted to risk sending cargo that way."

"So we got her cheap," Chuck said.

Rick grinned. "I got her damn near free. This is her shakedown as a passenger resort cruise ship."

"Hotel bill and food all in the convention registration fee. Quite a coup, Rick."

"I didn't tell them it was a science fiction convention, of course. I just guaranteed to fill the ship up with people who don't mind being a week late so long as it doesn't cost them any more. But we're not in U.S. waters now—"

From the rail Poul Dickson shouted, "Ach, ja, now ve can sing ze old songs!"

A heavy-set black man stuck his head out of a doorway. "Land ho!"

Chuck swung the camera around to catch him. "Ken, shouldn't you be up in a crow's nest?"

Ken patted his ample bulk. "It'd never hold me. We've got Grenada on radar. We're still two hours away, but you should think about wrapping it up."

Rick grinned mysteriously. "I may have another surprise for you, Chuck."

"I'm talking to Bruce Hyde and Mike Glider. Bruce, you left the rescue party to spring any traps at Sherrine's apartment. I take it that was for misdirection?"

Bruce said, "Sure. At best we'd get the law looking in the wrong direction. At worst, we had the owner's written permission to be there, and a key. We went in through a window anyway, picked up a few of Sherrine's things—still nothing—walked *out* the front door and boarded Mike's van and drove north."

"Nobody stopped you?"

"No, but they were following us. I guess we could have stopped, but—"

"I wanted to cross the glacier again," Glider said. He held newsprint from the *National Enquirer* under his chin, for the camera, under a wide toothy smile. The headline said:

ICE NUDES ORGY ON GLACIER!

Bruce said, "We took the same track as before, with the Angels' death beam toned down a little—"

"How many of you?"

"—So we could—Huh?" Bruce laughed. "No, no, just me and Mike, fully dressed. We crossed to Fargo and went straight to the local TV station—"

"Hide in plain sight," Mike said.

"—and told them about joining the mating rituals of a tribe of naked semi-humans with pale blue skin. Don't look so disappointed, Chuck."

"We all got away clean after the launch. Maybe everyone got an extra day or two because of Moorkith," Glen Bailey said. "You remember how it looked when *Phoenix* went up?"

Harry Czescu nodded briskly. "I kept thinking, 'Ours always blow up. Ours always blow up.' But it was going smooth as silk—"

"Remember the vapor trail, sprawled all over the sky? They used to call that 'frozen lightning,' the Germans did, I mean. It's in Willy Ley's books," Bailey said. "In the thirties they thought their rockets were going wild—"

"It's just stratospheric winds blowing the vapor trail around," Mike Glider said, sticking his head into camera view. Umber scowled.

"Yeah, but it *looks* like something spun by a spider on LSD. The Green bigshot cop, Moorkith, he saw the frozen lightning and thought the *Phoenix* must have crashed. He was searching the desert for *Phoenix* while the whole gang drove away."

"I missed it all," Ann Hudson said. "I was in New York. I tried to follow it on the news, but how much could I trust? Gary didn't try to call me till he was already in orbit."

"But you're going up this time."

"You bet. God help Gary if he already knows how to

mate in free fall. Chuck, I want a copy of this tape to take with me."

"That's why I'm hurrying. I want it finished and copied before the ship takes off again."

"No trouble," C.C. Miller said. "We just drove off. We even got the clubhouse cleared out before the Greens came sniffing. But there are *tons* of it. If the Angels don't want it, I think we'll just leave it in Grenada."

"You mean it's aboard?"

"Oh, yeah. We sold the bull semen, but we've still got the plastic corn and acorns and honeycomb and powdered chlorine and five cartons of earthworms, and there's a package I don't know what's in it but it wants out BAD . . ."

"Gordon, nobody spotted you?"

"I could walk, even then," Gordon said. He got out of his deck chair and spread his arms and bowed. His head nearly brushed the floor.

C.C. Miller said, "Today I could hide him on a basketball team."

"What have you been doing since, Gordon?"

"Your viewers, they know. I publish *Wind Chill* in sections. Now Baen Books, they want it. I can publish because I won't be on Earth."

"You're going up?"

"Sure. Alex say my family ready to skin him if he can't produce me, so I go with Annie. Bring a copy of *Wind Chill*, tell everyone—"

There was a sharp sound, loud above the wind, and a sharp *crack!* "Hold it," Chuck said, and he swung the camera around. "It was—got it."

High in the sky over Grenada, a dot, descending.

"Comes down just like a falling safe, only faster," Chuck said rapidly. "Those rockets should be lighting any . . . any minute now . . . it's broad daylight so they won't be too conspicuous . . . shit fire, will you *light*?"

"*Phoenix* is slowing," Gordon said. "Rockets must be lit. See? Slowing."

"Yeah. Sorry. Ni . . . ice."

The cone had settled behind trees.

Umber laughed. "Your faces! The rocket was too far away to show much, but you watching it land, that's something. Okay, Gordon, you published autobiographical material, but there's a novel, too, isn't there?"

"I am working on it. Should finish, how do you say it, Real Soon Now."

"He did a verse for the song, too," Harry said.

"Song?"

"Jenny's song," Harry said. He took out his guitar.

The others gathered around, fifty fans on the deck of a sailing ship, staring across to an island where a spaceship had landed.

"The Angels fell. And rose again," someone said. "And by God we did it!"

Chuck was still filming. Harry began to play. Jenny sang, and the others joined in.

> *"Wanted fan in Luna City, wanted fan on Dune and Down,*
> *Wanted fan at Ophiuchus, wanted fan in Dydee-town.*
> *All across the sky they want me, am I flattered? Yes I am!*
> *If I could just reach orbit, then I'd be a wanted fan.*
>
> *"Wanted fan for mining coal and wanted fan for drilling oil,*
> *I went very fast through Portland, hunted hard like Gully Foyle.*
> *Built reactors in Seattle against every man's advice,*
> *Couldn't do that in Alaska, Fonda says it isn't nice.*
>
> *"Wanted fan for plain sedition, like the singing of this tune.*
> *If NASA hadn't failed us we'd have cities on the moon.*
> *If it weren't for fucking NASA we'd at least have walked on Mars.*
> *And if I can't make orbit, then I'll never reach the stars.*

"Nader's Raiders want my freedom, OSHA wants my scalp and hair,
If I'm wanted in Wisconsin, be damned sure I won't be there!
If the E-P-A still wants me, I'll avoid them if I can.
They're tearing down the cities, so I'll be a wanted fan!

"Wanted fan on Chthon and Sparta and the Hub's ten million stars,
Wanted fan for singing silly in a thousand spaceport bars.
If it's what we really want, we'll build a starship when we can;
If I could just make orbit then I'd be a wanted fan.

"Wanted fan for building spacecraft, wanted fan for dipping air,
Sending microwave transmissions, building habitats up there.
Oh the glacier got us last time, next time we'll try to land!
And when the Ice is conquered, it'll be by wanted fans.
And when the stars are conquered, it'll be by wanted fans!"

The End

Acknowledgments and Other Thuktunthp

Fallen Angels is sold as science fiction, but one could quibble with that: while the book is clearly fiction, the science is quite real.

Item: Although the *Phoenix* spaceship doesn't exist yet, it or something like it could be built today for between $50 and $200 million dollars.

Once built, *Phoenix* would operate the way airplanes do. It takes about the same amount of fuel to fly a pound from the United States to Australia as it does to put that pound in orbit. Airlines operate at about three times fuel costs, including depreciation on the aircraft. *Phoenix* wouldn't run much more. The operational costs of any system depend on how much you use it, but given the low-cost regime *Phoenix* works in, it should be used a lot.

Of course airlines have about one hundred fifteen employees per airplane; but most airlines need to sell tickets. The SR-71 program (which didn't) ran with about forty employees per airplane. NASA, with four spacecraft, has over twenty thousand people employed to support shuttle operations. This may explain why *Phoenix*, which wouldn't need more than fifty people to operate, would charge less than one percent of what NASA charges to put cargo in orbit.

Item: Despite all the talk of global warming, there is just as much scientific evidence for the coming Ice Age. Experiments have failed to detect solar neutrinos in the quantities expected, and astronomers tell us that we are going into a new period of minimum solar activity. The last such prolonged period was known as the "Maunder Minimum," and coincided with what has come to be known as "The Little Ice Age." Moreover, archeologic evidence shows that in the last Ice Age, Britain went from a climate a bit warmer than it enjoys now to being under sheet glaciers in considerably less than a century.

*   *   *

Of course our story is fiction. Many of the characters are fictional, too. But some are based on composites of real people; some are real people with their names changed; and some appear here under their own names. A few have even paid to be in the book! We allowed certain fan charities to auction off the right to play themselves in *Fallen Angels*. Because the book takes place in an indefinite future we have made free use of an author's right to change details of age, or occupation, or city of residence.

Readers who find the action of the book surprising must consider that we have, if anything, tamed down the reactions of organized science fiction fandom had there really been a downed spaceship in a society that hates science and technology.

As to the society protrayed here, of course much of it is satirical. Alas, many of the incidents—such as the Steve Jackson case in which a business was searched by Secret Service Agents displaying an unsigned search warrant—are quite real. So are many of the anti-technological arguments given in the book. There really is an intellectual on-campus movement to denounce "materialist science" in favor of something considerably less "cold and unforgiving." So watch it.

References

There are many literary references in *Fallen Angels*. A few are explained in the text; others are left for the delight of readers familiar with science fiction and fan publications.

One is worth explaining here. In Robert A. Heinlein's early work "Requiem," the hero dies in a successful voyage to the moon. He is buried on the lunar surface by companions who have no grave marker other than a shipping tag for a compressed air cylinder. When Mr. Heinlein died, he was, according to his instructions, cremated and his ashes scattered at sea from a U.S. Navy warship. Some of us feel it would be appropriate to honor him by placing a pint of seawater and a suitably inscribed shipping tag on Mare Imbrium. The poem to be inscribed is R. L. Stevenson's "Requiem."

Acknowledgments

Acknowledgment of everyone who has, either directly by commenting on the manuscript, or indirectly through his or her life and example, contributed to this book would require a volume a great deal longer than the book itself. We therefore apologize now for taking the easy way out: as you might suspect, this section is being written the night before the final manuscript is due.

The song "The Phoenix" is copyright 1983, by Julia Ecklar, and is used by permission of Julia Ecklar. The song "Starfire" is copyright 1983, by Cynthia McQuillan, and used with her permission. Both songs and many others much worth listening to are performed on tapes sometimes available at science fiction conventions. Excerpts from the songs "Black Powder and Alcohol" and "Bring It Down" are used with permission of Leslie Fish, and are available on her tape *Firestorm*.

We do want to acknowledge the special help of Gary Hudson, President of Pacific American Launch Systems, Inc., who generously helped us get *Phoenix* right. We only wish that we had the money to let him build the rocket. Any one of us would be glad to ride it with him. Ann Roebke Hudson deserves equal thanks. Clearly, any mistakes in the science and technology are ours, not theirs.

We also thank Jim Baen, our editor and publisher, and Toni Weisskopf, Executive Editor at Baen Books; we suspect that few books have ever been delivered this close to a previously scheduled publication date.

As to everyone else, you mostly know who you are. Thanks!

Larry Niven
Jerry Pournelle
Michael Flynn
*Hollywood, California,
and Edison, New Jersey, 1991*